BEFORE WE WERE WOMEN

A NOVEL

SUNITA REDDY

Publishing assistance provided by Ember & Vine Press.

Cover design by Hannah Linder

Interior design by Janyre Tromp

ISBN 979-8-9950432-1-8 (paperback)

ISBN 979-8-9950432-0-1 (ebook)

Published by CPR Books

Printed in the United States of America

Girls don't owe anyone their beauty—
They owe themselves their strength.

— AUTHOR UNKNOWN

A dark-blue Mercedes-Benz S-Class turns onto a tree-lined winding road off State Route NC 7. It slows to enter a circular driveway that encloses a pond with a beautiful Greco-Roman style fountain. Water spews from four open-mouthed fish carved in marble, static and suspended in air.

Thirty-six-year-old Ashley Spady, riding shotgun, looks out the open window. Her wavy auburn hair flutters in the breeze. She tucks it behind her right ear as the main building, perched on a small hill and nestled among tall pines, comes into view. Eight massive granite columns support a large, covered entrance. Fixed to the middle two columns is a painted metal sign that reads "St. Bonaventure."

The car stops, and the chauffeur retrieves a wheelchair and locks it in place by the passenger door. He helps Ashley into it, while she cradles in her arms a potted plant, a small picture frame, and a long box. She secures them in her lap, and he adjusts her legs and covers them in a silk shawl.

Her parents, Ryan and Kelly, slide out next. Ryan's assistant walks over and stands by his side.

St. Bona is an assisted living facility, and Ashley will now call it home.

Ashley directs her motorized wheelchair onto a ramp and enters the lobby. The others follow.

"Right on time." Ashley eyes her watch, which reads 10:00 a.m., the faint tremor in her voice betraying her attempt to make light of the moment.

"Welcome to our facility, Ms. Spady," the facility's director says. He greets Ashley's family as they enter the lobby of what was once a luxury hotel. "Please don't hesitate to call me if you need anything at all. You must already have my direct phone number."

He proceeds to introduce his staff. "This is Anita, supervisor of housekeeping. She'll coordinate your move-in."

Dressed in a pressed gray uniform, Anita stands at attention, admiring the stunningly beautiful, and elegantly dressed Ashley.

"Hello, Ms. Spady." Anita steps forward with a warm smile, her eye level only a tad higher than Ashley sitting.

"Call me Ashley," Ashley says.

"Beautiful plant." Anita offers to hold one of the belongings in Ashley's lap.

"Oh, thanks." Ashley lets Anita carry the box.

"I personally supervised the cleaning of your apartment. I'll show you the way to your room. Please follow me."

Ashley and her parents follow Anita, as does her father's assistant, carrying Ashley's handbag and water bottle. Anita leads them through the massive three-storied lobby that displays remnants of luxury of yesteryears. The polished old marble floor shines a dull gleam, with a lemon scent. An intricately designed but worn gold balustrade curves along the stairs, which encircle a large chandelier that needs dusting.

Anita takes note.

"I can see why this place used to be a hotel at one time," Kelly says.

"This complex was quite luxurious at one time, I hear," Anita says. "As the suburbs turned into new metros and business faded, the property was divided and sold."

At the registration desk, Ashley signs papers. On a board behind the desk, she notices colorful flyers, one announcing "Karaoke Nights Coming Soon!" They pass the director's office and turn left at the end of the hallway. Anita opens the door to unit 108, a two-bedroom apartment, one of the largest in the facility. Then with a smile, she hands Ashley the key. "It's all yours."

Once inside, Ashley looks around the living room while her father sighs. Ashley takes a deep breath and maneuvers her wheelchair to survey the remaining space. She inspects the two bedrooms and tests the wheelchair accessibility of doors and bathrooms. Thankfully, they are built to code. She slides the patio door open and guides her wheelchair outside. The rectangular cement patio is surrounded by a privacy hedge, and a round metal table and four chairs lay bare in the sun.

The patio is tiny in comparison to their large backyard at home, which boasts two giant oak trees and a swimming pool.

"I'm sorry, sweetheart," Ryan says.

She forces a smile and turns her wheelchair. "Why? It's perfect!" From a clearing in the hedge, she has a partial view of the quadrangle and a line of hydrangeas, their large pink bouquets blooming against their green serrated leaves.

As if a sign from the heavens, the clouds break free, letting bright rays of sun pass through the blooms. Surely the garden will become Ashley's haven.

"Arrangements have already been made for trips to your doctor's appointments, and I've confirmed your meal and cleaning services," Kelly says softly, as if such plans will make this easier.

Ashley gazes at her beautiful parents. They are separating. Ashley masks her stress with a fake curve up of her lips.

Ryan's misery and Kelly's meditative state are on display.

Guilt shades some of Ryan's misery. "I take the blame." His voice breaks. "Sorry, Ash," he says in the singular, but he looks at Kelly too, like he is addressing both. He apologizes intermittently and persistently, without clarifying what he's taking the blame for.

Ashley doesn't expect an explanation, and Kelly shrugs helplessly.

Ryan may still love his family, but it's far too late for an explanation. All three of them are lost and are moving toward a three-pronged split, and no one is around to stop the inevitable end.

Ashley wheels into the larger bedroom and carefully places her potted orchid on the windowsill. She lovingly strokes the broad, flat leaves with her thumb. The extra room can be used when her parents visit, which they promised to do. Each will soon move into a smaller, disability-inaccessible new abode, and Ashley isn't sure how feasible her visits to them will be.

"The apartment looks clean," Ashley says to Anita, focusing on the positive.

"Thank you." Anita stands taller. "I supervise the cleaning staff, and we take great pride in caring for every detail on the property." She sets the long box on the kitchen counter. "Please reach out to me for any of your needs." She pauses. "You look familiar, and I finally placed you. You were a model, for shoes? I remember seeing your picture in shoe stores and magazines."

Ashley's smile deepens her one-sided dimple. She nods. "You are a keen observer, aren't you? It feels like decades ago now."

"It is your auburn hair and your dimple that stood out in the posters, and of course your perfect running posture. I had a fetish for hair in those days." Anita bites her tongue, aware she is revealing unnecessary personal details. Suddenly cautious of her own unruly dark hair, she runs her hand to pat it down. She takes leave and hurries to direct the next new resident. "I'll see you tomorrow."

Thanks to a well-coordinated team of movers, and Ryan's assistant, Ashley's apartment is put together in less than three hours. Clothes, shoes, and toiletries are streamlined in drawers and closets. Exercise and therapy equipment is assembled. The refrigerator is stocked and the kitchen organized. As the movers work, Ashley unwraps the box that Anita had placed on the counter.

She eyes one of the taller men. "Can you please mount it on this wall for me?"

She places the framed picture on her nightstand. Flanked by her parents, with a tiara on, she'd celebrated her sixteenth birthday. How happy they all were that day!

As the final crewmember takes his leave, Ashley turns away from her parents. "All right then. We can say our goodbyes now."

"I'll visit soon" is all Kelly can muster.

A sob leaves Ryan. He wipes his tears and hurries past Ashley's wheelchair without making eye contact.

Now alone, Ashley addresses her plant, perched in the windowsill by her bed. "Prickly Peter, it's just you and me, buddy. Let's make this apartment our own."

It is to be the sole occupant of the windowsill by her bed, but it is not. A long, hairy insect scurries past it into a crevice in the window frame. Ashley holds out hope that it is not a cockroach. She has never seen one. "You are an uninvited guest . . . no, a pest."

She has no appetite. Lying back in her bed on an empty stomach, she stares at the three blades of the ceiling fan, working together, joined at an axle in the center, unlike her family now. Their family trio of over three decades is fanning out like the three spokes, each spinning apart from one another.

A chill goes up her spine. How will she accept this new life of solitude? No Harry, no children either. It is meant to be that way. She feels discarded. Or had she discarded Harry? She is not sure. Depressed despite being on an antidepressant, she makes a mental note to discuss increasing her dose with her physician at her next appointment. She turns on her side, finding solace in Prickly Peter, who bears witness to her sorrow.

A new chapter has begun in her life and a new location for her Peter. "Both of us are pretty hardy," she says, hoping to reassure the plant. And herself. "After all, that philosopher Sartre says that life begins on the other side of despair. Let's hope he knew what he was talking about."

R obin Zymanski, a tall, pale, broad-shouldered woman, stands in the lobby of St. Bona, a dog's leash in one hand. A white cane in the other contrasts her black flared pants. Her shoulder-length straight hair looks bleached. Her button-like nose crinkles as the smell of ammonia overwhelms her.

Standing close to her is James, her father, an affable middle-aged man of medium height. Muscular, he balances a heavy duffel bag on his right shoulder with a suitcase in his left hand. "Welcome to St. Bonaventure," the director says.

"Hello there." James steps up. "This is our darling daughter Robin. And Lily, my wife." He gestures toward a slender woman in a short bob, who stands nervously behind them. "And this pretty one here is Lucy." He ruffles the shiny brown fur as the golden retriever wags its tail.

Anita, after leaving Ashley's apartment, on her way to the lobby, short on time, cuts across the quadrangle that is bordered by three new buildings, which were added when the old hotel was converted into a nursing home. She enters the lobby in time to welcome Robin, the second new resident checking in that day.

After introductions, Anita steps forward and shakes Robin's hand, which is large and envelops hers. Robin sniffs. Anita looks down at Lucy, unsure who sniffed.

Just as she did with Ashley, she invites the family to follow her. "Come on, baby," Robin says to Lucy. The rhythmic clicking of her cane against the marble floor sets their pace.

Slowly the group veers left in the lobby, where open spaces were converted into work centers and business offices. "And here you'll find the medical clinic, recreation room, TV room, library, and an exercise room," Anita says as they pass each location in the hallway. "The annex houses a spa and a hair salon.

"As you know, we have skilled nursing, assisted living, and independent living in different buildings on the campus. We offer one- and two-bedroom apartments in addition to studio apartments like yours," she continues.

Farther down they walk past a covered sitting area, and proceed to room 118, a fully furnished medium-sized studio that will belong to Robin.

"I'll park our moving van in the loading dock and carry stuff in." James places the duffel bag and the suitcase in one corner.

Anita and Lily step in, and Robin follows, moving past the gray outline of a couch. In the breakfast nook sits a round table and four chairs. Sleeping area is to the right side and a small kitchen to the left.

"It is a fully furnished unit, but we removed the bed as you requested." Anita eyes the empty space where a bed had been.

"Thank you," Lily says, a little peppy for the moment.

"Robin wants to furnish her studio sparsely, you know, like in Japanese-style, to have enough space for her and Lucy to move around," James adds, carrying in a futon. He rolls it out.

"Good idea. Do you need anything else?" Anita asks.

Robin stands up.

"Could you guide me to the nightstand please? I can still see outlines of things, blurred, but it helps that I can see that much at least. Once I commit to the layout and distances to memory, I'll manage. And with my Lucy by my side, I'm never lost—at least so far. And my cane helps too." She retrieves two books from her handbag—dog-eared and yellow paged—and lays them on her nightstand. She gently taps them with the palm of her hand, like reassuring them of the safety of their new location.

While her parents read them to her, how innocently she had asked questions and how patiently they had answered. Those moments with her parents were her fondest.

"If there is anything else I can do to help with the move, please let me know. If not, I'll take leave," Anita says, noticing tactile buttons on Robin's toaster oven, microwave, and juicer as James lines them up on the kitchen counter.

"We live in Winston-Salem, only forty minutes away, and we're staying in town for another day, to make sure my darling daughter is settled in. We'll see you around." James moves toward Robin, and kisses her forehead.

As Anita leaves, two computer technicians enter, wearing Geek Squad caps.

"Robin's electronic communication system has to be set up correctly," James explains to the crew. "She has already contacted the Center for Disability so the service is uninterrupted."

He directs them to the long wall, against which the vision-assistance systems are lined up. Within minutes large monitors and their connections blink back to life, and Robin exhales in relief.

As the tech crew works, James continues his run, carrying in boxes and suitcases. He lays Lucy's fleece bed by the futon. A stationary bike is assembled.

Finally, Robin is settling down. It took months of preparation to be here, as multiple forms had to be submitted regarding medical history, vaccinations, disability status, special requirements, and medical insurance for Robin, not to mention papers for Lucy. Resubmission requests were numerous, the most challenging hurdle of all being the maneuvering of the Medicare and Medicaid bureaucracies.

"What about dinner?" James asks after a couple of hours, his voice hoarse from fatigue. "Can I warm the shrimp pasta we brought from home before we head out, darling?"

"I'm not hungry, Pops. Rest at the hotel. I'll see you both tomorrow," she answers, already dreading the next day's goodbyes. Her father will be heartbroken without a doubt, but he will be loud and gregarious, an act put on. He's likely rehearsed masking his agony so that she will not hear a hint of it in his voice, despite her hyperacuity to sound.

She does not have an appetite. Her fingers brush the face of her tactile watch. "Eight p.m." She yawns.

Robin pulls Lucy close and lays on her futon as the others depart. Soon her father settles in her subconscious. She looks nothing like him, nor does she look like her mother. He is a sturdy, clean-shaven man, with brown eyes, wavy hair, and a heavy paunch. His French onion soup and Thai chicken in red curry are her favorites. Her mouth waters as the memory of burnt cheese dances on her tongue. She smacks her lips, wanting to taste the smooth texture of red curry, her umami taste buds stimulated by the thought of glutamates, which give the red curry its flavor.

When she wakes in the middle of the night, she finds herself curled around Lucy, her pillow wet, and her eyelashes crusted from dried tears.

Anita
Greensboro
July 2009

nita wakes up unusually early that day, a rarity. Her body cramps as she clenches her hands into fists and loosens them. The unpredictability of life is looming heavy on her. Her own life is an example of that, but she can't stop thinking about Ashley, one of the new residents at St. Bona.

A model for running shoes now trapped in a wheelchair—the image torments Anita. She does not know if Ashley was in fact a runner or just a beautiful model. Her thick auburn hair in a high ponytail, her dimple, and her long legs were a vision when she'd seen her picture in a magazine and again at a shoe store. By then Anita was past her childhood obsession with hair and looks. She'd seen many a desperate resident in need over the years, but something in Ashley's face captivated her then, as it still does now.

She paces in her condominium, where she's lived by herself for fifteen years. Her only companion, a cat, perched on the couch, purrs, turning its face away from her.

Anita rolls her shoulders back and stretches her arms. A blank canvas on an easel beckons. A note covered in transparent plastic is pinned to its frame. She opens the blinds a smidgen to let natural light shine onto the acrylics, oils, and watercolors, each organized in rows and carefully labeled. Brushes, a porcelain palette, and a few lint-free rags lie close. There is order in the room, but not in her soul.

She begins earnestly, but her strokes are broken. The oils do not flow. She blames the tightness on her mood. Minutes pass. She closes her eyes. Slowly, dimensions and orientation solidify. She starts with eyebrows, and that is all she manages before the clock reminds her that she has to report to work.

Sauntering into the living room, she stands in front of the only painting of hers that she framed and displayed. A thirty-by-forty-five-inch canvas hangs on sturdy nails. In black paint her hair is drawn out like tentacles. She was a misfit in school, family, and life. Her cat's face looks back at her from the painting, a face that took the place of her daughter. She yearns for her daughter. Sighing, she heads to the shower.

Known for her punctuality, she clocks in on time at St. Bona in her crisp white uniform, the color for a Friday. She goes to her second-floor locker and leaves her lunch bag, purse, and a wrapped sandwich. She gathers her puffy hair into a scrunchy.

In the hallway, she comes across a mother and daughter, a visitor sticker on the mother's lapel. In a summer dress with a matching bow clipped to her hair, the girl—not more than seven years old—looks shyly at Anita. Her heart lurches. How much she wants to take her in her arms and kiss her, but knows she can't. She is barely able to greet them. The pain of losing her daughter is not going to leave her today.

She greets her staff of twelve with a forced smile—"Good morning, all"—and studies the daily roster. Satisfied that no one has called in sick, she assesses the facility's needs and makes assignments. Checking messages from residents and noting their individual requests, she unlocks the supply room, takes inventory, and passes out supplies, marking each one off her list—Windex, mops, dusters, air fresheners.

She acknowledges the two new high school summer interns assigned to her team for four weeks. "Dan, you follow me, and Elena, you shadow Mary."

Yet to get his growth spurt, Dan's reddish hair haloes his childlike face. He stands a step behind Elena, a whole head's length shorter than her.

Waist-length silky hair, small breasts, a straight nose, and lips turned down at the corners give Elena's pretty face the slightly detached look of a model walking the ramp. She turns quite a few heads.

Elena is making an entry in her journal. Anita longs for children of her own, but Dan's hesitancy and Elena's misplaced interest irk her. She had met many interns like them, who cared more about résumé building for college applications than learning the work.

"Let's make it a good day for everyone," she says, locking away the remaining supplies.

Around noon, she heads to the dining area to supervise, Dan trailing her.

"Which way is the dining room?" a frazzled-looking seventy-five-year-old asks. "Looks like I'm going around in circles."

"Let me take you there—I'm heading there anyway." Anita falls in step with her. "Once you come to the water cooler, take a right, and at this marble statue, take a left. The dining room will be on your right side."

"Okay, dear." The resident blows a kiss Anita's way.

"In fact, let's backtrack our steps and make sure you have it down pat," Anita says. They retrace their steps, all the while Anita pointing at the landmarks and turns.

In the dining room, Anita finds Ashley at the head of a table—fresh and radiant, every strand of hair in place. An aide stands by her side. Seeing Ashley actively engaged in conversation diminishes Anita's melancholy, so she scans the hall for Robin, who is nowhere to be seen.

Anita grabs the sandwich from her locker and knocks on Robin's door. "Hi, Robin. It's Anita." She waits for Robin to open the door.

"I do recognize that voice," Robin answers, opening the door.

"I didn't see you downstairs, so I thought I would check on you. And I have a summer intern, Dan Miller, with me."

Robin's facial muscles relax into a pleased expression. "New place, new room. I didn't have an appetite, so I stayed in my room. And my pops left food in the refrigerator for me. By the way, hi, Dan."

"You have a kind family," Anita says.

"Yes, I do," Robin answers. "And besides, my pops kept me busy helping me memorize the details of the room you see. We counted steps and marked corners and curves. I practiced so I can maneuver the space without a problem. Memory is the one thing God gave me in good measure. I'm putting that to fine use."

"I brought a sandwich for you from my favorite café, just in case." Anita hands her the sandwich. "I can toast it for you if you'd like."

"Really? You got me a sandwich?" Robin's eyebrows rise. "I never expected this personal attention here. I hope I can return that favor one day."

"No sweat, Robin. Call me any time you need me."

"An aide has been assigned to me for one whole week, to help me chart the rest of the facility. I can't wait to do that," Robin says loudly as Anita is leaving. "You'll see me around next week for sure."

ROBIN WALKS TO THE breakfast table, her cane preceding. There she opens the foil wrapping and inhales. "Flavor and fragrance test," the game she played with her father at every meal, helped her become familiar with the array of spices and herbs he used in his cooking—fennel, sage, cilantro, cardamom, and ginger were common accompaniments. He used saffron, berbere, sumac, and pimentón, gathering these rare ones at distant markets just to throw her off.

She bites into an egg sandwich, rye bread with raisins, with tomatoes and cheese. She discerns dill and chives too. Relishing the flavors of pepper and a touch of tabasco sauce, she enjoys every bite. In the tomatoes she tastes the sweetness of Anita's gesture. Relief spreads. She has a good feeling about St. Bona.

Her pillow stays dry that night.

ON MONDAY MORNING, like a woman possessed, she marches along halls and hallways, pathways and places, rooms, and recreation areas, counting steps, memorizing distances and turns, corners and crevices, with Sarah, her aide for the week, guiding her, and with Lucy by her side. Dan walks behind her, to catch her for a misstep and show her the way if lost.

Distinguishing light from dark, vague shapes from empty spaces, her comfort in all aspects of life solidifies when she commits details to memory, a steadfast habit that has anchored her since childhood. Her pediatrician called her memory "mnemonic," a rare ability that has proven to be a lifesaver now that her vision is fading.

Thirty-five steps to her left off the front door of her apartment and then 140 steps to her right, past the ice machine on her right gets her to the rec room. Two doors down, twenty steps from the rec room, is the dining hall. Along with counting steps and gauging distances with associations, orientation and intuition also come in handy. After the first week, comfortable with her memory of the place, she bids Sarah goodbye and ventures out on her own with her cane and her trusted Lucy by her side.

Apart from scouting spaces, her favorite activity is to lounge in the rec room and surround herself with chatter, a buzz, a hum, male and female, high and low, continuous and halting. Kind of like music of all genres being played at once, asynchronous with interludes of synchrony. Sometimes a participant, sometimes an eavesdropper, voices, when recognized, give her a sense of kinship.

It is Anita who introduces Robin to Ashley.

On first impression, Ashley's lavender-laden perfume, offering a hint of jasmine, smells of money. While Robin tries to dismiss her irrelevant thought, she sees the hazy outline of someone sitting in a chair. Electric whirring follows.

"Hi," Ashley greets cheerfully, explaining that she has just moved into St. Bona. "Who is this furry little fellow?" She leans toward Lucy.

Lucy snuggles deeper on Robin's feet. "I'm new too. This is Lucy, my little baby."

Lucy stands and wags her tail when her name is mentioned.

In the casual conversation that follows, they figure they are about the same age, having graduated high school only a year apart, and are the only children for their parents. They laugh at how quickly they share personal information.

"It seems I'm interrupting your conversation. I'll take my leave," Anita says lightheartedly bowing to them.

Later Robin and Ashley reminisce about their high school and college days, including their careers that followed. "Books were my world," Robin says. "Thank goodness for braille and audiobooks, or I'd lose my mind."

"Running was my thing," Ashley says. "In my previous life!" Her forehead wrinkles.

"Oh, nostalgia, the grinder!" Robin replies. "Talk about role reversal. I can run now, and you have the time to read!"

They share comfort and connection in their disabilities.

"Have you seen the garden yet?" Ashley asks. "It's one of the best, a sanctuary really."

Robin nods. "Well, seeing is believing, and I'll never know."

Ashley recovers quickly. "Well, we'll have to fix that. Come with me."

Within minutes Robin and Lucy trail Ashley's wheelchair into the courtyard, a routine that will soon become a habit. As Ashley parks her wheelchair in her favorite sunny spot, Robin takes a seat beside her on a nearby bench, shielding her photosensitivity with sunshades.

"The flowers smell so lovely," Robin admits.

"And the fresh air and sunshine add to that," Ashley chimes in.

While they share the quiet peace of nature, a friendship is blossoming.

I n the four months since Robin and Ashley moved in, they have spent countless hours together. Waiting for each other, engaging in facility-orchestrated activities together, even joining a knitting club.

A pang of jealousy has not escaped Anita at their connection. "How're you both doing?" Anita leans close to them in the rec room so they can hear her above the music.

On a small stage, a microphone is set to a tuned sound system, with disco lights flashing in red, green, and blues. Karaoke nights, a recent addition, draw residents as much as the bingo nights did.

After Anita's childhood music lessons ended, not once had she attempted to sing again. But music still excited her—the energy it generated and the people it gathered.

"Doing well, having a great time," Robin replies. "Thank you for insisting that I attend. Music brings me close to my mom, her favorite pastime. It has become mine too."

Ashley gives two thumbs up.

"Welcome to Freddie Mercury night," the emcee announces to loud cheers.

Anita fights a prickle behind her eyes.

The first singer croons "Love of My Life," and goose bumps sprout. Anita tries to tap her feet to the rhythm, but her past is coming alive. Suddenly she is nine years old and celebrating her birthday. Dressed in a pink lace dress, she frets over the clash with Live Aid 1985. Her parents' attempts to wrap her party early so they could watch Freddie Mercury perform on TV are fresh in her mind.

"Don't Stop Me Now" follows, an adrenaline-charged anthem celebrating life's joys. The St. Bona residents cheer, and those who are able to, dance along happily.

Anita presses her lips together. How proud her parents were of Freddie Mercury's ethnicity. How obsessively she practiced this song as a child. She reminisces about her music lessons, those that she quit in less than a year. She looks around.

"Bohemian Rhapsody" follows, and the entire crowd joins in.

Robin's neck and face flush, and sweating follows. She fans herself with her hand. "As a child I didn't care about music. I found joy in it only after I became legally blind. It accompanies me everywhere now, like Lucy does."

Ashley cocks her head to one side, her eyes closed. When "Bohemian Rhapsody" comes on, tears roll out. The lyrics questioning the reality of life echo in the room. Ashley cups her face and rubs her eyes, like she's tired. A gesture to mask tears that does not escape Anita.

At the closing, Ashley blows her nose. Robin and Anita remain stoic and silent in their seats as nostalgia tightens its noose on all of them.

Anita has the feeling she's not the only one who is being transported back to their childhoods and Live Aid 1985, when Freddie Mercury and his band, Queen, united the entire world through the power of music.

PART I

LIVE AID

July 13, 1985

1

Anita
Greensboro
July 13, 1985

On her ninth birthday, Anita felt like a princess in her new pink lace dress. The Saturday afternoon summer heat made her back itch, and her matching shoes, one size too small, pinched her feet. Sweat-dampened socks added to her discomfort, and her dark curls were getting progressively unruly. Yet she didn't care. She was happy in her dress and shoes as she'd desperately longed for them.

Tiny beads of sweat sprouted on her upper lip. She was permitted soft drinks that day, as it was a birthday party. She gulped down two cans of ice-cold Pepsi in rapid succession. Satisfied, she looked around. As her body cooled, she smacked her now numb lips and tasted the remnants of the sweet drink.

She joined her parents, Deepak and Rumi, and her sister, Ami, in the living room of their home and stood behind a table covered with a colorful Mickey and Minnie Mouse tablecloth. Ami, at ten, considerably taller than Anita, stood near the cake, which sat atop a stand in the center of the table. Surrounded by a few other families from the neighborhood, Anita beamed as she blew out all nine candles in one triumphant puff.

As the final notes of the birthday song echoed, her hand lingered on the cake knife, unwilling to cut into the perfect sugar-crafted image of Barbie on its surface. No part of Barbie—face, golden curls, or her gorgeous gown—seemed fair game to disturb. She contemplated this difficult choice a moment before bringing down the knife reluctantly to one corner of Barbie's gown.

They lived in a middle-class neighborhood where streets were lined with modest homes. Their Indian neighbors, like her parents, were part of the immigrant wave of the seventies and eighties that supported the demand for skilled workers in the rapidly growing high-tech industries in and around Raleigh and Durham. Greensboro, not too far away from these two cities, with its small-town vibe and affordability, was an attraction for immigrant families, who were under pressure to save and bolster their economic standing on foreign land.

Unable to forgo their conservative Indian lifestyle, Deepak and Rumi were dressed in polyester slacks and button-down shirts despite the subtropical heat and humidity of Greensboro. To Anita's chagrin, Ami was wearing a new lemon-yellow lace dress like hers. The color reflected beautifully against her light skin, setting off a perfect golden glow. When Anita heard a neighbor say, "You look like a princess in that dress, Ami," it stung.

Her parents were in celebratory mode that day on two accounts—Anita's birthday and the soon-to-be telecast Live Aid concert.

As they passed around slices of pizza, their subtle glances at the clock betrayed their eagerness to wrap up the party.

"Anita, would you like to open presents?" Rumi asked.

Anita wasted no time tearing into them. Out of the wrapped boxes came books, markers, and coloring pencils. A floral T-shirt and matching headband were to her taste, but they didn't quite spark the joy she had hoped for. One present she truly hoped for, a Barbie, wasn't there.

She sighed and glanced around the room. She was not too thrilled about the music show's clash with her birthday party either. Anita passed evenly cut wedges of cake to everyone before she settled down on the carpet in front of the television, her plate piled with remnants of the dessert. She didn't mind the irregular chunks. Just as she found comfort in the sweetness of the rich frosting, Ami snapped, "Don't ruin the carpet, Anita. Go sit at the table."

While the honorary aunties and uncles from the neighborhood settled on white faux-leather couches in the family room, children spread across the navy Berber carpet, all eyes on the television. The adults' chatter centered on the upcoming performance of Freddie Mercury and his band, Queen, which promised to be a moment of honor for the Indian community. "Please welcome Queen," announced the host, to a countdown from the crowd. The crowd size in the stadium made an impression on Anita, but it turned to confusion when the adults in the living room cheered as a man walked on stage.

"His name is Queen, Papa?" she asked innocently.

"That is the band's name, bitiya," Deepak clarified, calling her the endearing term for a darling daughter in Hindi, their native language. "And he is the band's front man. His real name is Farouk Bulsara, but that was before he adopted the stage name Freddie Mercury."

"He's of Indian origin, just like we are," her mother added with pride. In their admiration, Anita saw her parents' hope that the performance would validate the Indian community on foreign land.

Dressed in tight jeans and a white tank top that revealed his unshaven armpits, the purported star defied conventional norms for a public performance. No rhinestone-studded jacket paired with leather pants, and no long hair. The only telltale sign of anything that stood out in his ensemble was his black leather armband with pyramid-shaped chrome studs that encircled his right upper arm. He neither looked like a star nor like the other Indian men she had seen. To her, he looked odd, with striking teeth that resembled miniature fangs. However, she felt the energy of his performance reach every corner of the stadium and then spill into her family's living room. As his voice soared, she connected with the title, "We Are the Champions," which he sang flawlessly at the end.

Anita wondered who the champions were.

The TV commentators hailed Queen's performance as iconic, and with a grin, her father predicted, "The whole world will agree."

By association, she felt her parents' satisfaction in seeing a singer of her own ethnicity shine on stage.

"Prioritize education and do not dress like that, children!" cautioned one honorary uncle, and the other adults in the room nodded in unanimous agreement.

On Monday at summer camp, Anita walked tall, feeling special, but her excitement fizzled when the biggest music show wasn't referenced at all. Instead, the girls in her sewing class congregated in a corner and buzzed about the Disney movie *Return of Oz*, which they all seemed to have watched. Feeling left out, she settled in her assigned seat and stared out of the window.

Although disappointed with the lack of acknowledgment, she imagined herself as a singer. She practiced singing Queen's songs for hours, until she gave up on that dream with the realization of her inability to copy Freddie Mercury's four-octave voice range.

Picking up on her interest in singing, her parents enrolled her in Carnatic music classes, a classical Indian music form of vocals. She was excited, as the notion of a career in singing appealed to her.

"Learn it as a hobby, not as a career," they told her, making their intention for enrolling her clear at the outset.

On Saturdays at two in the afternoon, sitting on the floor, legs folded, Anita huddled with six other girls in the basement of their teacher's home and sang to the tala, the rhythmic framework of musical time. As they maintained the beat through clapping and waving, she sang with the others, their voices reverberating and echoing in unsynchronized frequencies. The beats were slow and the lyrics unintelligent, primarily in Sanskrit. She was unable to memorize them, the sounds and vowels different from English. She could not see how this music related to the music she was interested in. Freddie Mercury gave his music the energy of a party, and the music she was learning was too soft and slow. It was far removed from the rock and pop tunes that attracted her.

A few months into the lessons, her enthusiasm waned, and by year's end, she refused to continue, so ending her dream of a career in music.

But music was only the starting point of a deeper disconnect between her parents' expectations and her own. Her community's cultural insulation exacerbated the chasm, affecting multiple aspects of her life. Her societal relevance was also mushrooming into a larger issue. She questioned it but could not get an answer. Her appearance, sense of belonging, and identity became sources of uncertainty and conflict. Television shows amplified the divide, prompting her introspection about America, her family, and herself.

What form her internal conflict and the imbalance between her parents' expectations and her own would take, no one could yet know.

2

———

Ashley
Charlotte, North Carolina
July 13, 1985

A gleaming six-seater Cessna 414A sat on the runway, its engine revving to life. Twelve-year-old Ashley stepped onto her father's company plane in Charlotte, accompanied by her parents, Kelly and Ryan. As it soared into the clear summer sky, she sat in her seat by the window and adjusted her short linen skirt, which matched the color of her auburn hair, the hem a tad too short for her rapidly growing legs. She ignored her mother's disapproving look.

As usual, Kelly looked impeccable. She'd opted for a lilac sheath dress that reached her knees, its casual style masking the price. A soft shawl draped her shoulders, shielding her from the air conditioning.

Ryan smiled adoringly at his daughter, his navy sports jacket highlighting the deep blue of his eyes. He called Ashley's one-sided dimple her "beauty spot."

Ashley looked down and admired Charlotte, its lush green expanses a testament to its title as the greenest city in America. The Catawba River snaked along the western end, its surface glittering like stars in the bright sun, as if giving the city a five-star rating.

She nibbled on cucumber and cream cheese sandwiches and sipped fresh orange juice, excitement coursing through her veins. They were bound for Philadelphia, where they'd attend the Live Aid concert at JFK Stadium. Four days earlier, on July 9, Ashley had turned twelve. This trip was her birthday present. The global benefit concert was to raise money for the humanitarian crisis unfolding in Ethiopia, and her father's company had pledged a substantial amount.

Kelly didn't mind the concert or the trip, but Ashley's fascination with Madonna and her music frustrated her. It was not as much about the music as it was about Madonna's provocative stage presence and revealing outfits.

As their family of three entered the arena through a VIP entrance, they were surrounded by a deafening roar from more than ninety thousand music fans. Waves of infectious excitement ebbed and flowed in the arena. Ashley joined the energetic crowd, singing and chanting at the top of her lungs. She hollered the loudest as Madonna entered the stadium, singing Ashley's favorite tune, "Love Makes the World Go Round." The Beach Boys, Neil Young, Eric Clapton, Led Zeppelin, and Mick Jagger were scheduled to perform in the biggest concert event in history. But the highlight was Freddie Mercury's electrifying performance of "Bohemian Rhapsody," displayed on giant screens, his show being telecast for the transatlantic audience from Wembley Stadium in London.

"That's a lot of money, Dad!" Ashley exclaimed when it was announced that the dual concerts in London and Philadelphia raised $127 million.

"Yes, it is, darling. Enough to feed roughly a million people in Ethiopia for a year," Ryan explained, after doing quick mental math.

"I'm glad your company helped," she said, beaming with pride. "Like you, Dad, I'd like to help others someday."

"Of course you should, my sweetheart." His answer was drowned by the roar of cheers as Mick Jagger stepped onstage.

As their plane flew back to Charlotte later that night, Ashley's happy mood was further buoyed by soft chocolate from a dozen or so eclairs she guiltily devoured. It was a good day.

Against the backdrop of the night's sky, she admired her city's vast, lit downtown and its suburbs. She was not surprised that Charlotte was North Carolina's largest city and was home to some of the largest banks and financial institutions in the country. Her father was the CEO of a private wealth-management firm based in Charlotte, as his father had been before him. To her affable and able father, her mother played the role of a CEO's wife perfectly.

"Wonderful show," Ryan said to Ashley and Kelly as the trio walked off the tarmac. He wrapped his arms around them, kissing each of them tenderly on their foreheads.

As they drove south of downtown from the airport to the prestigious Myers Park neighborhood, home to large mansions and tree-lined streets, they were happy. Travel relaxed them, especially Ryan.

However, under the facade of a happy family, her parents' arguments and her father's verbal assaults erupted at home, like a volcano's unpredictable mood. When they did, they subverted Ashley's reality.

At the next outburst, to escape her father's voice, which sounded like the massive grinding of the tectonic plates, Ashley ran onto their street, flanked by beautifully manicured lawns. She ran with tears streaming down her face, the beauty of the majestic homes and their yards meaningless to her.

Such moments of escape took on a haunting melody. The opening lines of "Bohemian Rhapsody" rang true to her. She was caught up in her own reality and hoped for it to be a fantasy, but to no avail. The echoes of her parents' voices fueled her frantic pace. The lyrics resonated deeply with her pain, just as they resonated with Freddie Mercury's pain, she assumed. She wondered how one could deliver a powerful physical performance, like he did, singing such sad lyrics. From him she learned to transform her pain into physical activity.

Running freed her. Her tears kept pace with the rhythm of her running and established a heartbreaking harmony. But no one could yet know what other heartbreaks were scripted in her future.

3

————

Robin
Winston-Salem, North Carolina
July 13, 1985

A red Ford station wagon hurtled down Interstate 40 West, leaving Carolina Beach behind. Robin lay sprawled across the back seat, her head resting on her backpack and the seat belt loosely draping her torso. Her new book, *Sarah, Plain and Tall*, a birthday gift from her parents, rested on her chest.

The Zymanski family of three was heading home to Winston-Salem after wrapping up their annual weeklong birthday getaway to Carolina Beach, marking Robin's thirteenth and her father's fifty-first birthdays.

It was 10:00 a.m., and the summer sun was already blazing down. They took exit 220 and drove past Robin's middle school. The empty playground, dried and brown, reminded her of the winding-down summer break and her soon-to-start eighth grade. They were nearing the Krispy Kreme store right past the school, its sweet allure irresistible, like it always was. Her craving for a doughnut roused.

On the final page of her book, she clutched her stomach.

"I'm starved, Pops," she moaned.

Her parents, James and Lily, looked at each other and smiled.

"Now will you get down, Robin Blue?" James asked, once parked.

"Wait—I'm almost done," she pleaded.

A minute later, she closed the book. "Loved it. Happy endings are the best." She mimed a thank-you to her parents for the book.

As they headed in for Robin's favorite, original glazed doughnut, and coffee for the adults, they could not escape the large R. J. Reynolds's billboard, erected across the store, advertising Salem Lights cigarettes. The billboard stood testament to the city's long history with tobacco and the company. The city's alternate moniker, Camel City, in reference to the Camel cigarettes manufactured by the company, and the city's reliance on tobacco for decades, rankled James. He bristled at the poster displayed so close to the school, outraged that it misled young kids by touting low-tar cigarettes as safe, let alone advertising cigarettes to children at all.

They left the store with three doughnuts and two cups of coffee.

"One doughnut each," Robin announced.

They drove past the poster and turned left at "Camel Corner," Robin's nickname for the intersection. Their ranch home was twelve miles farther down a winding country road. The turn was her cue to gather her belongings for arrival at home.

Robin's pale skin burned an orange red, a stark contrast to her parents' deep tans. She knew she looked different from them. Her freckles, which normally scattered across her nose and cheeks, had darkened and merged.

Her inflamed face and freckles mirrored the orange-red wings and dark streaks of a Monarch butterfly. As her burn peeled, her face resembled a molting pupa, shedding its old skin. Her burns stung, and she'd complained during the four-hour drive. Her parents had offered ice packs and burn cream, seizing every opportunity to lecture on the benefits of sunscreen.

James had much to do that evening because their family was hosting a get-together to watch the three-hour Live Aid special on ABC, presented by Dick Clark. The event was set to be broadcast live at the same time via satellite from both Wembley Stadium in London and JFK Stadium in Philadelphia.

Lily was unsure of hosting, given there were only a few hours before guests arrived, but James was confident in his culinary skills and his ability to pull it off.

James fired up the grill on their covered deck, ready to cook burgers and hot dogs for the four guest families. Their old country home needed upgrades. The deck was due for a pressure wash and some new stain. A vegetable garden, positioned in the ideal southeast sun, was thriving and offset any upgrade the backyard needed. String beans cascaded from a canopy, while plump watermelons rested on the ground, indenting the fertile ground beneath them. Ripened tomatoes hung on the vines, like red ornaments on a Christmas tree. Peppers and eggplants were ready to be picked. Potted herbs and salad greens looked enticing.

A segmented platter held neatly arranged lettuce, tomato slices, and onions in circles. Nearby, bottles of mayo, mustard, and ketchup stood as tall sentries, like they could ward off flies. A bowl of creamy potato salad and golden corn on the cob sat on a tray on the east end of a side table, while strawberry shortcake, watermelon wedges, and orange soda cans were arranged on the west end, as if segregated by color. There were ten adults and three teenagers in all, including Robin and her parents.

In the family room, separated from the deck by a sliding door, Lily sat with guests on plaid couches, glued to the television while waiting for the program to begin. Music held a special place for her, despite her inability to carry a tune. It was therapy, alleviating her bouts of melancholy.

The ceiling fan spun at top speed to compensate for the lack of air conditioning in their home. Robin, dressed in shorts and a T-shirt, settled in her favorite place on the old love seat, a spot that perfectly molded to her body. She faced the television, applying a heavy layer of burn cream to soothe her skin. A nearby table fan directed at her made her sparse light hair dance to the tune of its blowing air.

She heard her mother's excitement as the time for the broadcast approached. But at the appointed hour, static lines and erratic voices filled the screen. The world's superstars in music were to perform, and her mother and their guests were going to miss it. Disappointment in the Zymanski family room was palpable.

Lily worried if it was their television. James rallied a few guests to tweak the antenna and adjust the dials. Just as they were about to give up and disperse, newscasters announced technical issues with the transatlantic satellite link-up, and their hopes returned.

Soon the satellite feed flickered back to life, delivering crisp images and clear sound. The room erupted in cheers.

Lily sat entranced, tapping her feet and singing off-key, while James focused on feeding his guests. She watched the show all the way to the final rendition of "We Are the World," though Robin was barely interested.

Done with the lathering, she preferred to reread her book that explored themes of loneliness and abandonment, topics close to her heart. She engaged with the other two girls only occasionally, while they whispered to each other about boys in their class.

She devoured all three doughnuts before the guests arrived and was not interested in the picnic-style food being served, as she craved her father's gourmet creations.

Robin did not grasp the fuss about a weird-looking man named Freddie Mercury and his band, despite being part of the 1.5-billion global audience. With no care for the stars or their music, she did not commit the artists' names or their songs to memory. That the show aimed at rallying support and raising crucial funds for the relief of a devastating famine in Ethiopia did not register with her.

Robin's disinterest stemmed from finding solace only in her world of words. Lost in that world for hours, her inner turmoil about where and to whom she belonged burgeoned into detachment from everything else. She was comfortable with her looks but was troubled by their origins, casting a shadow on everything she did.

She had exceptional cognition, and her teachers called her memory mnemonic. She recalled intricate details, yet there remained a vast chasm that her mind could not traverse—an inability to reach back to the very moment of her birth.

As she grappled with the question of her identity, the question "Who am I?" haunted her.

This inner turmoil would shape her tumultuous future, and the trajectory of her remarkable memory and cognitive capabilities remained to be seen.

PART II

———

THE PAST

4

ASSIMILATION

Anita

1976–1986

In 1972 Deepak and Rumi Kumar moved as graduate students from India to Durham, North Carolina, in pursuit of the American dream. After two years, Deepak held a postgraduate degree in material science, and Rumi in electrical engineering.

The following year, they welcomed their daughter Ami. Just as they were celebrating Ami's first birthday, Rumi missed her period. Anita was born on July 13, on one of the hottest days of summer of 1976, twenty months and a day after Ami.

Back-to-back pregnancies in quick succession added additional stress to their already pervasive subliminal pressure to acclimatize to a foreign culture.

Both held steady professional jobs in technology firms that collaborated with Duke University.

Their offices were in the Research Triangle Park, a sought-after and expensive geographic triangle—often referred to as RTP—formed by the three nearby research universities of North Carolina State University in Raleigh, University of North Carolina at Chapel Hill, and Duke University in Durham.

The growing Kumar family needed space. A long commute to work was not a deterrent for staking their own piece of affordable land and calling it home. They built a three-bedroom split-level house on a half-acre lot in a middle-class suburb with clean, narrow streets in Greensboro, forty miles north of Durham. The newly built suburb of cookie-cutter homes provided the greenery, space, and privacy that Deepak and Rumi, like most immigrants, had lacked in their native countries. They opted for charming but discounted new furniture, with little concern for ergonomic comfort, prioritizing style over comfort. Where one family appeared to be living comfortably, many others were attracted to the area. Soon house after house on their street was inhabited by Indian immigrants.

To Anita, her small community was a pool of brown people, with an occasional white speck interspersed, like the whitecaps in an ocean, as her family mostly interacted with other Indian families. But for the cold and for living in bigger homes and cleaner neighborhoods, Deepak and Rumi felt like they lived in India. Anita often heard them say to their friends, "Arre yaar, we are living better than most Americans in America!" Their grins highlighted their urgent need for orthodontic work.

On weekends, the aroma of curry wafted from seemingly endless stretches of kitchens, filling the air from daybreak to suppertime. Anita liked Indian food but dreaded the lingering aroma. Her worry that the distinct smell of spices would cling to her hair, clothes, and even sweat came true when her classmates sniffed her and asked her what it was that they were smelling on her, which made her uncomfortable. She feared that the scent would become her identity and categorize her community, and she wished her circumstances did not lead to this predicament.

There existed sibling rivalry in the Kumar home, and Anita knew it had nothing to do with Ami's lighter skin and long legs versus Anita's percolated coffee-like complexion and shorter stature, but it was about the perception of their parents treating them differently. "But we don't do that at all," they protested. Anita's rebellious behavior did not help her cause either. Though meek in outside social interactions, her questioning of rules and customs was witnessed in the confines of the Kumar home.

In elementary school, Anita had a handful of her Indian friends in her class, but she yearned for other friendships too. Around ten, she challenged her parents' demands that she exclusively associate with her Indian friends and adhere to Indian cultural norms.

"Why can't I wear shoes in the house, like they all do in America?" she debated.

"What's wrong with eating food with your hands? Food tastes better that way," they countered, when Anita challenged that custom.

"Indian culture is fantastic," they said, suggesting in an obtuse way that America needed moral uplifting.

"Your rules and expectations belong in India," Anita proclaimed, banging her bedroom door shut against the order to keep it always open.

"Why do you have to be so difficult, bitiya? Everything bothers you. Look at Ami. She doesn't seem to have a problem with who her friends are and how we live. Why can't you be like her?" her father asked.

"But why should our rules be so different?" she complained, although her deeper discomfort stemmed from her looks and from feeling unseen in class. She wanted to wear short dresses that fit well, but her long, shapeless outfits only marked her as different from her classmates. "I hate my hair" was all she was able to tell them.

"Why hate your hair? All you need is coconut oil to keep it down. Simple," her mother suggested, further agitating Anita with the idea of the oil's smell on her hair, while the other girls' hair in her class smelled of fresh shampoo.

It was not that her parents did not crave an American identity too, but they were never sure about what they wanted. Their ambiguity spilled over to what and how they wanted Anita to be, and that fueled Anita's ire.

Kumar family vacations prioritized educational enrichment and historical experiences over comfort and relaxation. By the time Anita was ten, her family had covered most of America's landmarks along the East Coast. The World Trade Center, Empire State Building, and the Statue of Liberty were the first to be scaled. One spring break, Anita and Ami were herded through the Smithsonian, White House, and Capitol Hill. Once it was a grueling twenty-four-hour car ride to Niagara Falls, only a day there, and another twenty-four hours in the car back. She'd been nauseous during the entire car ride to Pennsylvania and barely recalled anything from that trip.

During a visit to the Museum of Science in Boston, a discourse on the Indus Valley Civilization, tracing it back to 3300 BC and showcasing advanced urban planning and architecture, snagged her attention. A thrill went through her when she realized that her lineage could be traced to so long ago.

"Maybe I will become a history teacher, Papa," she said on the ride back home.

"Teacher, ha? How about a doctor or even an engineer? Did you see exhibits about the human body? I thought they were very interesting." He did not acknowledge Anita's interest.

Requests for a trip to Disney were met with excuses, and her dream of seeing Disney princesses with lovely hair and fair skin never materialized.

Obsessed with the idea of looking like Barbie and Anita's Caucasian classmates, she yearned for light skin and soft, straight hair. Unaware of the unyielding nature of her black, wire-like, thick curls, she spent hours brushing, determined to straighten them. Disappointed by the futility, she'd hurled her new hairbrush into the trash.

5

———

FITTING IN

Anita

1987–1988

nita touched the limestone wall in the living room with her open palms. She leaned forward and held her cheek against it. "Ooh! I like how cold it feels." She breathed in the warm air around her. "The house is so different from our house in America."

The main structure of Rumi's parents' ancestral home was supported by twenty-inch-thick limestone walls, interspersed and held up by carved wooden pillars. Its inner courtyard, surrounded by verandahs, circulated fresh air pulled in from the windows, while the rising hot air escaped from the central opening. The walls that held the ceiling high, the geometrically styled orange tiles that covered the roof, served to cool the interiors in the mercilessly hot Indian summers. Tall walls along the perimeter of the compound encircled the property, secluding the house from the neighbors.

For spring break, the Kumars were visiting India.

Rumi's two brothers, their wives, and children descended on the family home too. "Let's party every day for the next nine days." Deepak hugged his brothers-in-law. "Anita and Ami, learn to cook from your Dadi. Please teach them, mother-in-law." He touched her feet.

"I will. But right now, I'm very busy," she said, heading to the kitchen where she planned to spend the better part of the day despite having kitchen and house help. Pav bhaji, pani puri, lamb biryani, and other specialties adorned the dining table in generous portions throughout the day.

The highlight of the trip was the Hindu festival of colors, Holi, where even adults became kids for a day. Through squeals of laughter and screams of protest, they chased one another, smearing colored powders and squirting colored water with their water guns. As was custom, everyone donned white clothes to entice others to douse them in every bright color under the sun. Anita had the best time of her life until it was time to scrub herself multiple times to rid her body and hair of the colors that had left her, and everyone else, looking like colorful clowns. In the evening, at an outdoor cookout, loud music and dance unfolded as the adults downed bhang, a milk-colored toddy that got them mildly intoxicated and playful.

At eleven, Anita was at an in-between age, with the innocence of a child and keenness of an adult. Somewhere between gullible and shrewd, she oscillated from being respectful to disrespectful, disciplined to rebellious.

As much as Anita hated her Indianness in the USA, she felt at home in India. She blended in with the vast expanse of dry brown soil and of brown people. A muddy sea with no whitecaps. She had no issues with curry or otherwise. Seven thousand miles away in America, she felt the burden of an outcast. Yet she missed her home and life there.

After two weeks, the novelty of vacation fading, they ran out of things to do. As their cousins headed back to classrooms, Anita's family prepared to return to their own bedrooms and routines on foreign land.

Dadi, curious about life in America, enquired about Anita's school and friends. Anita hesitated, unsure how to express her unease and struggles. While Anita was reluctant, Dadi did not need prodding to share her story.

She gifted Anita a chain with a dangling pendant made in twenty-two carats of yellow gold, a family heirloom. As she secured the clasp around Anita's neck, she said, "Your grandfather and I are most proud of how all three of our children understood the value of education. We made sure they graduated college and became professionals. Knowledge is power, Anita. You should also have a good education and a career." She centered the pendant and admired it for a second in reverence.

"I was married when I was only fourteen, and by fifteen I had your mother. I didn't have much of a childhood or education. My in-laws were kind. Your grandfather, five years my senior, was understanding. But I was happy. I had a good life," she said, like she somehow managed to find her happiness.

Anita wondered how difficult it must have been for Dadi to find her happiness. Was Dadi really happy, or did she make herself believe that she was? This question was to remain unanswered for decades.

ONCE ANITA ENTERED MIDDLE SCHOOL, her discomfort with her looks turned into detesting them. Her much-anticipated growth spurt never materialized, and her small dark face continued to be eclipsed by thick curls that refused to behave. To her dismay, a new boy in her seventh-grade class called her "Birdie Bear." That was only the beginning.

6

PLUS SIGN

Anita
1988–1991

"Small like a bird, hair like a bear," Anita heard the chant everywhere she went. Raucous laughter followed. The heckling spread and clung to students across grades, like spilled crude oil that refused to be scrubbed away. Ashamed of her looks, she prayed to evaporate into oblivion. To Anita, she looked like the other Indian girls around her, maybe a shade darker than others. For no reason, she was singled out, and her misery only magnified when other Indian kids distanced from her, like they were escaping the fire that charred her. She felt the betrayal.

"I hate how I look. Nobody wants to be friends with me." She was finally able to share her concern with her parents, only to be brushed away.

"You're so beautiful. Look at the shine on your skin. No American has that shine," her father said.

"Beauty is only skin deep, bitiya. It is the character that matters. You be nice to them, and they will want to be friends with you," her mother chimed.

Oblivious to her dilemma at school, her parents continued to pressure her to observe Indian etiquette. Their expectation to dress conservatively, excel at school, and not to party, date, or smoke was in line with their idea of proper behavior. Digging her heels in resistance, with each repeated demand, her "no" became her declaration of autonomy. Reveling in this power was becoming a habit.

To her credit, Anita did not let the heckling crush her confidence. Trying to fit in differently, she gravitated toward kids who dressed and looked the opposite of Barbie. Goth was her new style. Deepak's and Ami's dark shirts, large and loose, were paired with chunky shoes. Kohl, borrowed from Rumi's dresser, landed as black smears on her eyelids, with side extensions from the corners of her eyes.

She ignored rules, initially the ones laid out by her parents, later by her teachers too. What started as a power struggle in middle school became full-on rebellion when she entered high school. Her rejection of demands and even simple requests was nothing short of mutiny.

Testing her parents' and teachers' patience gave her a thrill. She schemed and loved it. She woke up with plans. It started with small things, like sneaking a cigarette into the girls' bathroom at school. Being summoned to the principal's office many times did not deter her. Having fully embraced this behavior, threats of punishment at home and at school made her more defiant.

Her defiance was a mystery to her parents. Her teachers labeled her attitude as false bravado. She hoped at least her school counselor understood her, but instead she was branded as an attention seeker.

"We give her enough attention," Deepak lamented.

"Maybe too much," Anita retorted.

Therapy sessions were recommended.

"What is therapy?" Rumi asked.

"Have never heard of such a thing in India," Deepak remarked.

Only her high school adviser, Mrs. Detris, gave her a rare understanding ear. "Anita, whoever or whatever it is you're fighting, you can win through education. Education is everyone's strength. It'll be yours too. Remember that." Her words echoed Anita's grandmother's wisdom.

"You aced the aptitude test with eighty-five percent. Keep it up," she continued. "Everyone faces high school drama. We all doubt ourselves. I did too."

The adviser's guidance was a balm on her insecurities. In the moment, Anita believed her. But outside the adviser's room, harsh reality loomed. The taunting and alienation were relentless. Black dominated her ensembles. A beaded choker and black nail polish became her everyday companions.

"So this is Goth? The dressing? Or does it mean something else too?" Deepak and Rumi asked.

Anita had gravitated toward a group of five outcasts. While among them, her alienation from others became tolerable. Their conversations were vague, esoteric. They projected superficial coolness, while the trajectory of their lives was anything but cool. Their immature actions and empty words of bravado masked their desperate pleas for help.

They were knocking for assistance, but no one was at the door.

The tumult in their lives was hidden, but not its physical manifestations, like Annie's bruises on her wrists and face. Their existence went unacknowledged, like the forgotten stepchild in a family. Their circumstances were unfinished sentences, and their lives hazy skies that refused to clear.

Then there was the handsome senior Sebastian—tall, loud, and opinionated, with bold and boastful talk, the talk of a man in a child's body and mind. He rarely spoke of his family and was consistently reluctant to go home. In a rare unguarded moment, he joked that his alcoholic parents subsisted on welfare checks that ran out in the first ten days of the month.

His lighthearted humor was his appeal, and his knack for storytelling, his attraction. Anita's reflection in his stunningly deep-amber eyes made her look fairy-like, shiny and glistening. How he bent to listen to her, like there was no one else around them that mattered, was magnetic. As he looked down, his soft blond hair fell across his forehead, like a silky veil. She longed to run her fingers through his locks, but shyness held her back.

She craved his attention and got it. He flirted with her often, adding to the excitement. Soon they were a couple. Ignoring everyone else in school became easy after that. The bullying faded, the bullies on a hunt for a new thrill, a fresh, innocent prey. With her parents at work, they spent afternoons after school at her place and experimented.

"I know how pretty and erotic Indian women are in this book *Kama Sutra*, which I once glimpsed in the library." He clicked his nails nervously. "I heard Indians are experts in the art of making love."

He was eager and gentle, and she, desperate to forge a connection and belong to him. Human instincts, controlled by hormones, seized them, and for both it was a first. The desire for inclusion and acceptance paralyzed rationale. Their afternoons together became an expected ritual, much like the comforting tradition of afternoon tea.

As Thanksgiving approached, reports of AIDS and homosexuality dominated the news, following Freddie Mercury's passing. Anita still could not fathom how her parents admired the singer's success and accepted his controversial behavior and appearance, yet failed to understand her need to forge her own path.

HIV, promiscuity, and contraception were discussed in health class as curriculum, but it was too late for her.

At Christmas, her confusion heightened. Her breasts got tender, face turned fuller. So as it happened, Anita missed four periods before she realized it. When her midsection ballooned, she understood the full implication of her state. The nausea made sense. Panic rose, along with the food in her stomach. She contemplated her next move. Walking around in loose-fitting Goth outfits, she bought time.

Upon hearing the news, Sebastian turned pale, matching the color of his eyeballs' white, though still able to maintain his erect posture. For all the tall tales he told, he had nothing to say and only stared blankly. Anita did not see deception in his stare, just plain immaturity and fear. With no hope of help from him, she prayed, never having prayed in her life before. She begged the invisible God for the situation not to be real. But when she finally approached her mother with the predicament the day after the new year, it became really real.

She was fifteen.

7

—————

CONFLICT

Anita

1992

"What are you saying?" Rumi asked. When she did not get a response, she raised her voice. "Say it again." She stopped wiping the breakfast table and frowned.

"I missed my period," Anita mumbled. "I am sorry." She gazed down at her stomach.

Rumi dropped the kitchen towel on the floor and grabbed the hem of Anita's loose shirt and flipped it. "Hey, Bhagwan, yeh kya ho gaya?" she screamed, asking God what the heck happened.

Anita's rounded midsection protruded like a cantaloupe, its striations resembling the stretch marks on her skin.

Deepak stepped in from the living room and fell to his knees when he saw Anita covering her stomach in haste. "Did we do something terrible in our previous lives to be punished like this?" he wailed.

"Who did this to you? Did he force himself on you? Someone we know in the neighborhood or at school?" Rumi blurted, shaking Anita's shoulders. "We must call the principal or even the police then." Rumi was sweating profusely, despite the winter weather.

"Shh. Lower your voice, and don't call anyone yet. I don't want anyone to know." Deepak held his forehead in his palm.

"Okay, but you quiet it down. You're the one wailing," Rumi retorted. "We must get to the bottom of this first. Do you even know what you did, Anita? Who was it?" She ran to draw the curtains on the main floor.

"Mm, Sebastian," Anita said hesitantly.

Rumi's mouth stayed open.

"Who in the world is Sebastian?" Deepak was running out of patience. "I'll—"

"Shh," Rumi interrupted. "You stay quiet. Let her talk first."

"A senior in my high school," Anita replied meekly, standing in the doorway, clicking her fingernails. Like an innocent child, she spilled the tale of her trysts with him, as if she were telling them a story she'd read.

"You don't get it, do you?" Deepak snapped.

"Go to your room and wait for me," Rumi directed. "And, Deepak, let's go to our bedroom." She pulled the curtains closed there too and sat next to him.

"What do we do now?" Deepak rose and paced, his hands clasped behind his back. "Did we make a mistake coming to America?"

"Too late for that discussion, Deepak. I'll call Dr. Patel tomorrow," Rumi said in a hushed tone. Now she was crying too. "I can't believe this is happening to us. I feel sick. What about her future?" She wiped her tears. "She's still a child."

"I know. I'm terrified about that, but I'm also concerned about family honor. Let's keep it on the low until she sees the doctor. And no one in India should know about this, understood? Maybe Dr. Patel will give us a solution." He sounded hopeful.

"Maybe." Rumi doubted it, as Anita's stomach certainly looked six months in size.

"You brought disgrace to our family, little sister," Ami said the next day, shaking her head. "And you ruined your life too."

Anita stopped eating her cereal and looked at her parents.

Deepak developed dark circles around his eyes and had barely slept, while Rumi remained stoic. She was the only one who did not make Anita feel doomed.

"Sorry, Maa. I'm scared." Anita leaned her head on her mother's shoulder.

"We'll take care of you, baby." Rumi drew her close and caressed her.

Curtains drawn, in the confines of the darkened house, they all stayed indoors for a week.

The winter's short days did not help the gloom inside. To hide indefinitely or leave town to guard their family's secret was not an option, as they had neither the know-how nor the means. With no kin in America, where would they go? To go to India, certainly not—where the shame of having a child out of wedlock would forever mark their lineage.

The family avoided the local grocery store. They let the telephone ring unanswered and later kept it off the hook. The doorbell was ignored. Mail was collected after dark. They drove straight into the garage and lowered the door immediately.

But the parents' thinning bodies and Anita's growing belly could not stay hidden for too long, for their sustenance depended on their jobs and the income. They returned to work, subdued and confused about their lives in a foreign land.

For her last semester before high school graduation, Ami returned to school.

Anita barely ventured outside, but once after dark, at the mailbox, one hairy, triple-chinned Indian auntie perused her from head to toe, her eyes narrow, pausing her gaze on Anita's stomach. After a moment of staged contemplation, she said, "We didn't come all the way to America for this!"

"For what?" Anita mumbled. "Do you have night vision?" she asked, going off on a tangent. Her grandmother was a mother at fifteen and grandmother at forty. "I should've been born fifty years ago then." Her rising pitch reflected concealed vulnerability.

The lady huffed. "You're shameless!" her husband said, his vitriol volcanic. With that, the whiff of scandal that was Anita's pregnancy spread in the close-knit community like quicksilver on a slick surface.

It was the same auntie who had asked questions like, "What did you score on your math test?" and "What did your maa cook for you today?" Cars, furniture, clothes, anything new at all was discussed and compared. "How much did you pay for it? We were lucky that it was on sale when we bought it" were comments that were borne from the need for exclusivity. Discounts and deals roused unusual amounts of interest.

At the first chance they got, some of the so-called aunties and uncles imparted ample advice. Many extended fake sympathies, secretly relieved it was not their child and their family in this quagmire. Anita hadn't liked the nosy ones anyway; now she despised them.

After multiple inquiries from her school were ignored, under a threat of investigation from social services, Anita returned for the spring semester of her sophomore year.

"Bitiya, we'll take care of you. But don't talk to Sebastian anymore, understood?" Deepak set the stage for his expectation on her first day back at school. She simply nodded, torn between her longing to see him and her disapproval of his reaction to the pregnancy. The first person who'd made her feel desirable, showering her with the attention she so starved for, she could not forget so easily.

When she heard "Pregnant and pitiful, tsk, tsk, tsk" on the school bus, she asked her parents to drive her to school. Fortunately, this time the bullying did not gain traction.

In between classes, she walked around, checking out Sebastian's usual hangouts. But he was not there, and neither were the other Goth members, as if they'd dispersed, unable to withstand the storm that was Anita's reality. A new hangout, if there was one, wasn't shared with her.

"Rumor has it that Sebastian dropped out. Isn't that sad that he's not going to graduate?" asked Renee, a girl from the Goth group, when they crossed pathways in the hallway the following week. Her jet-black hair, combed back, stood in contrast with the silver nose ring that sparkled when she switched glances from Anita's face to her expanded belly and unbalanced form.

"Do you have his phone number?" Anita looked around nervously for Ami, not wanting the news of this inquiry to reach home.

"I don't." Renee shrugged. "But the office should have it."

Withstanding her longing for Sebastian, not seeing a way forward, and for fear of betraying her parents' trust once more, she did not pursue the number. For all her previous rebellions, vulnerable in her current state, a different kind of sadness enveloped her, a sadness that was for her family.

As the American dream for her daughter shattered, Rumi planned the next move. In this, Anita felt a newfound respect for her mother.

Dr. Patel, an Asian-Indian physician in her late fifties, showed a great degree of sympathy for Rumi and constrained disapproval for Anita, who felt its underlying sharpness. She accepted it as an expected reaction to her teenage pregnancy, especially from all Indian people, including a physician.

When Dr. Patel addressed Anita, she neither answered nor made eye contact. Rumi answered for her. Anita stared at the exam room walls adorned with framed pictures of pretty, pregnant moms happily posing in their stylish maternity clothes. Anita presumed that they were likely beautiful Caucasian models who were not even pregnant. Their faces were not puffy like Anita's, nor did they have the mask of pregnancy. Anita's already dark cheeks and forehead were deepening in discoloration. There also was a chart of birth control options in a table form, with pros and cons listed in detail.

An ultrasound was done next. As the black-and-white images of multiple fast-moving body parts, full of life, rolled on screen, like in an underwater silent movie, Anita's life, in contrast, was coming to a standstill, so it felt.

"Look at the cute little fingers, and there, clenched in a fist now!" the ultrasound technician cooed. She pointed at the long umbilical cord drifting through the amniotic fluid, like the thick, sinuous underwater reed swaying gently in the ocean's current, its lifeline pulsing softly.

Dr. Patel confirmed what they feared. "You have entered the sixth month of your pregnancy. You must have felt movements for at least six weeks now?" She looked at Anita with part question, part statement.

"There are not many options now, other than placing the baby for adoption, if that is what your family is looking for," she said to Rumi when Anita stepped out of the exam room to get her blood tests drawn.

Anita was referred to a social worker for direction and was enrolled in childbirth classes for teen mothers. The only instruction she remembered from the classes was the rhythmic *ha ha hee hee* of pushing, which to her eerily sounded like monks chanting in prayer. When the social worker discussed the option of placing the baby up for adoption, Anita's parents embraced the idea. Soon decisions were made, as if Anita had no say in it.

Feeling trapped, she tried to distance herself from her state, cut herself off from that part of her body that carried the baby. But every kick that woke her up from sleep and every new stretch mark she noticed in the shower pulled her in more. But did she have a choice? Despite holding hope for weeks, she did not see how her family could raise the baby.

Dr. Patel, an obstetrician, was regarded highly in the community as a role model for her Indian patients who aspired for their children to become doctors. Like busy physicians, especially obstetricians, she spoke fast and moved fast. She didn't spend much time with Anita in earlier months but did more so with Rumi, consoling and reassuring her.

But as Anita approached term, Dr. Patel spent considerable time discussing what was expected in labor, keeping the conversations cheerful and reassuring.

Once in a philosophical mood, Dr. Patel said, "As someone said, difficulties may seem insurmountable and happiness fleeting, but by thinking that, we propagate our grief and lose our happiness. You, too, will learn to move on from this difficult experience one day."

Anita made eye contact with her for the first time and gave her a blank stare. "Go fuck yourself, lady" came to her mind, but she instantly felt remorse, cursing her reprehensible teenage impulse. To think that of someone who would be on duty for many hours, readily available at a moment's notice for Anita's and her baby's safety . . . she felt ashamed.

Dr. Patel counseled her regarding options for pain control in labor. From childbirth classes, Anita remembered it had something to do with the spine. When Dr. Patel said "epidural," it did not sound familiar.

"Breathe deep and relax your pelvic muscles," Dr. Patel instructed while gently and patiently introducing her gloved fingers into Anita.

At one of her last appointments in the office, Dr. Patel had said, "The cervix is two centimeters, fifty percent effaced, and ripe." As the nurse charted the details, the doctor added, "The head is engaged."

She now looked at Anita. "Your body is getting ready. It could be any day now."

Anita felt relief that the day was near, ready for her nightmare to end. Little did she know that the end of one would mark the beginning of another.

8

———

AGONY

Anita

1992

The first contraction came at 5:00 a.m. Half-awake, Anita arched her back and found relief. But when the next wave hit ten minutes later, arching didn't help. Pressure descended into her lower back and radiated to the groin, making her want to urinate. She tossed and turned, not wanting to rouse, but the urgency escalated.

Unable to ignore further, she stood and barely made it to the bathroom, when warm wetness ran down her legs unabated. The blood-tinged mucus that followed was hint enough to head to the hospital.

When Anita was admitted in labor three weeks before her due date, she masked her terror with indifference. As a young intern wheeled her into the labor unit, she noticed a sign above the entrance that read, "Your Health Is Our Sacred Calling." She hoped for it to be true. When the three nurses who took care of her for the duration of her stay were kind and without judgment, she was thankful that they embraced the motto of the hospital.

Once she trusted them, labor did not bother her. She followed their instructions, accepted ice chips in between contractions, and bore the pain in silence. They wiped the sweat off her brow and rubbed her back when she was in the throes of labor. She breathed deeply when she was told to and pushed when asked to.

They held her hand when the pain was unbearable. Sometimes she pitied the nurses for their crushed fingers. Other times she gripped the side bars of the sturdy labor bed, with its rigid, uncomfortable surface, and bit her lips until they turned blue.

When asked whom she wanted as her support person in labor, she looked at the nurse and whispered, "You." She'd decided long before that the process was going to be purely between her and her baby, the baby whom nobody wanted. So it was only her nurses for all the hours of labor, and her doctor in the last hour, who guided her through the process.

She chose not to have family in the room. If her parents wondered why, they did not press for an answer. They waited patiently in the waiting room, praying for the nightmare to end.

An epidural or even simple analgesics were not chosen to bear the pain, the agony, her punishment for the choices she had made.

As she writhed in pain with unrelenting waves of contractions, she did not shed a single tear. She wanted no one's pity. She had felt more than her share of that, fake and real, for some time now. Furtive glances at her growing belly and subverted smirks were fresh in her mind.

After fifteen hours of labor, Dr. Patel was summoned to her bedside. "Fill your lungs, hold your breath, and push as hard as you can."

Anita clenched her teeth and pushed to a count of ten each time. She heaved until her veins popped and hemorrhoids sprouted. With measured restraint, she suppressed her primal instinct to scream.

At exactly 7:00 p.m., her body felt like it cracked in half as a baby slid out, shrieking as if protesting from being evacuated from its cozy nesting ground. On its heels, Amniotic fluid tinged in blood gushed. Other body fluids spilled too, their distinct pungent smell wafting mercilessly in the room.

"A baby girl. Ten fingers and ten toes!" Dr. Patel announced, protected by her mask and gown from the ravages of the ensuing smells and spills. The meaty placenta and its membranes stained in green meconium followed. In a swift motion, she emptied the uterus of blood clots by plunging her upper arm into Anita's body as the torn vulva shrieked in agony.

Following that, Dr. Patel transformed into a deft seamstress as she effortlessly worked the semicircular needle and suture, approximating and darning the ragged edges of the split vaginal orifice. The needle plunged deep into Anita's tissues and managed to travel all the way to her heart, stinging and piercing it mercilessly.

Dr. Patel thanked the nurses and other personnel assisting for their services. "April twelve seems to be a popular day to have a baby. Looks like all the expecting mothers in town decided to deliver today. Anita, your baby is number ten for the day shift. A record."

Anita's nurses had stayed past their scheduled shift of twelve long hours to see Anita through her ordeal. She appreciated the teamwork and their dedication toward her.

Her body was shaking uncontrollably now.

Dr. Patel approached her, looked at her kindly, and stroked her disheveled hair. "The chills are normal and temporary. They reflect the expected hormone surges. I've ordered sufficient pain medicines for you. Let the nurses know if you need them." She turned to leave, hesitated, and turned back. "All will be well. You're not alone. Another mother is also placing her baby for adoption today." Dr. Patel then nodded, her head tilting in ways that were ambiguous and confusing.

With time, relief from physical pain, Anita expected. Resolution from the stigma, she hoped. But detachment was crucial for her. While pregnant, she'd deliberately suppressed thoughts of the baby's health, sex, and appearance. She'd gone through the motions with stoic silence and hoped for no attachment and entanglement with the baby. To leave her memories behind unencumbered was the plan.

But once the baby came, she had an overwhelming wish for her to be healthy. It was an instinct she never knew existed. Upon delivery, Dr. Patel's cheerful tone had reassured her. But the pull and pressure of her instinct to cuddle her baby, to shower her with love, this dilemma tore her inside and out. To touch, to hold, to smile, to smell her baby—each a quandary. Emptiness everywhere, but in her breasts, filling up with colostrum she could not feed the baby.

She had been in control when she had let the pregnancy and the delivery pass without emotion. She'd had no idea that her concern for the immediate well-being of her baby and her future, which totally encompassed her now, were maternal instincts. Even if she did, she would not have guessed that this force of nature, this instinct that was bestowed on all mothers, was so dominant that no one had the power to control or mitigate it. It was a change at the cellular level that was impervious to manipulation. Only time could temper its intensity, but in that moment, it could not be willed away. Anita understood that now.

Anita's nurse approached her and asked if she wanted to hold the baby, reassuring her that it was okay not to. "She weighs six pounds and one ounce."

Without hesitation, Anita stretched her arms. The nurse slid the warm bundle into Anita's arms, and she saw wetness along her baby's eyelashes. She tried to wipe it away.

"They are not tears, only drops of antibiotics," the nurse said.

Anita nodded. "No tears for you in your life, baby."

In the short time she held her, she noticed dark, soggy hair under the cap and beautiful light skin that shone under the bright overhead lights of the hospital. The color she had craved! Her baby's tiny, symmetrical face was Sebastian's. Anita hadn't thought of him in weeks. She longed to see her baby's eyes, but they remained shut. If they opened, it was no more than a sliver. She wondered if it was the bright lights or that her baby did not want to see her. She hoped it was the former.

As she admired her baby, she mumbled, "Rani," queen in Hindi. The name that had confused her a few years ago regarding its gender alignment seemed befitting for her daughter now.

"I wish you to live like a queen," she whispered softly into her baby's ear.

Her family had chosen a closed adoption. That said, no personal information regarding the adoptive parents would be given to Anita, and vice versa. The adoption records were to be sealed until the child turned eighteen, at which point the child could access them if she chose to.

The only information shared with Anita and her parents was that the well-educated couple, married for six years, was financially established and unable to have a child of their own. On inquiry, it had been revealed that the couple was Caucasian. "They are an ideal couple for your daughter," the adoption agency representative had said.

Ideal for whom? Anita had thought. *Will my daughter fit in this family? Will she ever feel like she belongs to them? How much will she stand out? Will her looks alienate her in the community like they did me?* She only had questions and no answers.

The legalities of the adoption process were expedited by an agency representing the adopting parents.

Being sent home without a baby, Anita was discharged the very next day, as if the hospital was washing its hands of her. She was given medicine to suppress her breast milk. As she was wheeled out into the frigid cold, she sat askew, leaning on her right hip, with a large sanitary pad wedged between her legs and with searing pain from sutures that held her bottom together. Her swollen genitals and her engorged breasts were the only telltale signs of birthing a baby. Empty-handed and emotionally confused, she did not feel the blast of cold air as she left the hospital. She hoped that she would never return here again.

9

A SIGN

Ashley
1972

Kelly Marlin and Ryan Spady were college sweethearts and married a year after graduation, unusual for 1958, as marrying while in college was the expected thing to do. He'd pursued her passionately, and she'd responded sensibly, with no urgency. They settled into comfortable lives, but after being married for three years, Kelly was disappointed that she did not conceive. Expensive medical tests followed, which included repetitive ovulation tests, sperm counts, and hormone levels. Unlike other couples, this was no financial burden, as they were financially secure through Ryan's well-paying position. They went through three cycles of intrauterine insemination without success.

An emotional roller coaster churned its way through Kelly as the cyclic hope of pregnancy was dashed with a cramp, followed by monthly bleeding. The cycle repeated every four weeks, their hopes slimmer each time, disappointment deeper every time. After three years, one day in the middle of a treatment cycle, Kelly abruptly decided she wanted no part in the struggle anymore. Ryan agreed, and all the scheduled exams and treatments were abandoned.

Ryan was a partner at a successful wealth-management firm. He went about his job with the ease of a seasoned grandmaster, but when Kelly took up a part-time position at his firm at his insistence, she sensed occasional hints of stress, as in a clenched jaw or in the inflection of his voice. With time, she encountered minor outbursts at home, his anger directed toward his partners and clients. A good night's sleep was all it took to calm him, and life was as usual in the morning.

With no financial burdens, they found happiness in traveling. Travel relaxed Ryan. They scoured books on travel at the local library and made their plans. They bonded over charting their itineraries in historic and exotic lands. Together they loved to discover the magic different landscapes had to offer. Such trips helped them get in tune with each other, and along the way, they discovered more about themselves too.

Traveling became Kelly's passion. Planning kept her busy. The high of traveling freed her from the burden she carried within, and the stress-free time on a trip excited Ryan. He knew her inability to conceive gnawed at her, though she rarely talked about it.

In the autumn of 1972, they traveled to Milan, the land of Leonardo's *The Last Supper*. At the time Milan was also gaining a reputation in fashion. With their already mapped-out itinerary, they traveled north by train from Milan and spent four days enjoying the beautiful vistas of Lake Como.

Kelly had planned the destination with two things in mind. She had seen a beautiful painting of the lake, by artist Clarkson Fredrick Stanfield, at the Tate Museum in London and fallen in love with it, and ever since she'd wanted to see the lake in person. She'd planned the trip for September, hoping to see the early morning mist rise from the lake as sunlight streaked through, just like it did in the painting that so enchanted her.

The other pull was the ancient Roman legend that if a woman urinated in water and it turned cloudy, it signaled fertility. Even through her own denial in believing such a tale, this tidbit still attracted her to the lake. Once at the lake though, she did not have the heart to desecrate the waters, and later she laughed at her own foolishness for considering such an antiquated test.

When they returned to Milan from Lake Como, they fell in line with standard tourist destinations and visited the Duomo di Milano and the opera house Teatro alla Scala. Short on time, they rushed to the church of the Dominican convent of Santa Maria delle Grazie, on their way to the airport, to see *The Last Supper.*

As instructed, Kelly turned off the flash on her camera while she waited for their timed entry. From the audio guide, Kelly learned that the work on the painting commenced in 1495 and was completed in three years. She had seen pictures of the five-hundred-year-old master-piece but did not know what to expect of its current condition, given that restoration work was done some thirty years earlier. Paint was reat-tached to the wall using clear shellac, making the mural darker and more colorful, while the overpainting of earlier restoration work was removed.

Upon entering, the climate-controlled, dimly lit, medium-sized, brick-walled room looked unremarkable. But once she saw the painting on the far wall, the aura transformed. Areas of bare wall and chipped paint interrupted the bright colors, but they failed to diminish the essence of the image. An odd sense of serenity enveloped her. Trans-ported half a millennium in time to the era of the painting, and then two millennia to the history depicted on the wall, she sat perfectly still.

Ryan and Kelly were Catholic. They'd attended Mass every Sunday as children, but as a married couple, they chose not to join any local church.

In the heart of the mural, at its core, she saw how a regular evening meal for Jesus had unexpectedly turned with a shocking revelation of an impending betrayal. Jesus's death was a pivotal moment in the history of humanity. The world had lost its Savior, but life went on. Good and bad things continued to happen. Loving people and evil people carried on. So much had changed in the world, and yet it had not. Human emotions of love and deceit continued to exist in the same proportion and with similar intensity from ancient times. Each event and all people had a role to play in this world. The world was balanced by this.

At the crossroads of her life, in her vulnerability, she was perhaps looking for a sign, a clue, in history and in its precedence. The world's story must be already scripted, and hers was too.

It dawned on her that, as childless as she would be, she too had a part to play. She was a part of this balance, and her existence was essential to humanity. She wasn't yet sure how though. Without her and everyone else, nothing would exist exactly as it was supposed to exist. Kelly felt the years of burden lift. The black dark that enveloped her was dissipating.

Is this how it feels to be spiritually reborn? she wondered.

A few weeks after returning from Milan, despite the cold outside, she felt warm. Kelly suspected early menopause for her symptoms, as she had not had a period in over three months. She joked about it with Ryan, but he worried about her only when she was plagued by incessant nausea that progressed to emesis. A quick trip to the doctor followed. Kelly would remember the chain of events of the day, always with a smile, for years to come.

"When couples going through fertility issues abandon all hopes of conceiving," Dr. Rogers said, "and are resigned to their situation, freeing their minds, that is when the miracle happens. And it has come true once again. Lack of stress is a wonderful thing."

Kelly was fourteen weeks pregnant. Excited and guarded at the same time, a flurry of celebratory phone calls went out to their parents and friends. Anxious of her high-risk pregnancy, she reluctantly quit her job. They bought a heavily updated sprawling residence that had just come on the market, close to Kelly's parents in the prestigious Myers Park neighborhood, and not too far away from the Myers Park Country Club, where they played tennis as members. It nestled on an acre lot with two stately live oaks occupying the far side, creating a natural screen that shielded neighbors. The house was once featured in a local architectural magazine for its unique design, the main floor being labeled "Frank Lloyd Wright" inspired.

They both fell in love with how inconspicuous the main entrance was, but it unsuspectingly opened into a huge foyer with one of the largest chandeliers in the Charlotte area, leading into an even larger space that was the great room. That unique feature of a low, nondescript entrance gave the space a larger-than-it-really-was sense upon entering. The opposing wall was entirely replaced by large rectangular windows overlooking an oval swimming pool outside.

They had barely moved in when Kelly's scream launched their next phase of life.

10

A GIFT

Ashley

1973

"**T**he baby is coming." Kelly grabbed her stomach with both hands.

Ryan sat bolt upright. The bedside clock read *July 9, 1973: 01:11 a.m.*

"Let me grab your bag," he said, his voice high-pitched.

He helped Kelly into his yellow Plymouth Hemi 'Cuda convertible on that warm July day. But their baby was not due for five weeks.

"I feel something coming out," Kelly moaned.

As he drove to the hospital in panic, at a speed that many cars couldn't handle, he was glad he owned that particular muscle car. "We are almost there, Kelly. Remember the breathing. Slow and steady, deep and deliberate."

He intermittently scanned the passenger side of the car for signs of a baby. He had no time to inform Kelly's doctor about these developments.

He stopped the car at the entrance to the emergency room and, leaving the key in the ignition, rushed inside. "I need help with my wife. Our baby is coming," he blurted at the reception.

A sleepy attendant snapped to action. He grabbed a wheelchair and summoned a team. Kelly was then transferred to the maternity ward in what appeared to be a highly orchestrated drill.

Ryan parked his car and arrived panting at the check-in desk on the maternity ward, to distant beeping sounds and faint screams of laboring mothers.

A tired, portly, middle-aged nurse in a white knee-length uniform greeted him. "Let me direct you to the waiting room, sir. We are trying to reach Dr. Rogers urgently, as your baby is turned the wrong way," she announced without further explanation. She mumbled about a full moon and hurried away.

Ryan, sweaty and lightheaded, slumped onto the closest wooden chair with a thud. He sat alone in the large waiting room lined with multiple rows of chairs, wondering where the other fathers were. He did not understand what it meant for the baby to be turned the wrong way, and the nurse did not have time to explain.

It was an agonizing forty minutes before the same nurse arrived and congratulated him on the birth of his daughter. "I knew it—I always knew it was going to be a girl!" he said to her, thrilled, as she looked on casually, like a veteran nurse who had seen this display many times. He followed her, bursting into Kelly's room ahead of her.

Dr. Rogers, an elderly physician with a stooped posture and a pair of reading glasses perpetually balanced on the tip of his nose, entered Kelly's room soon after. He peered over his glasses at Kelly. "Your daughter would not stop kicking her feet as she came out feet first. It was as though she was in a hurry to run out of you. She might just become a runner one day." He chuckled.

He explained that Kelly had, surprisingly, a quick labor for a first-time mom and that delivering five weeks early ensured that the baby was not too large. That made delivering her baby vaginally in breech position easy and possible.

"Delivering a baby in breech position, butt or feet first, is fraught with complications. You and your daughter are lucky." He pulled up his oversized green scrub pants stained with spots of darkened blood.

Kelly and Ryan were thankful for Dr. Rogers and all the years of expertise he carried with him.

They named her Ashley, after their favorite actress, Elizabeth Ashley, who'd played the role of Corie in the original Broadway romantic comedy production of *Barefoot in the Park*. Ryan and Kelly's inaugural date had been to see that show.

The new parents could not contain their happiness as they brought their precious bundle of joy home. Little did they know that the joys of parenthood would be tempered by many challenges scripted in their family's future.

11

———————

SPEEDY

Ashley
1973–1983

"**S**top kicking your legs so much, sweetie," Kelly gushed, struggling to change Ashley's diaper. Afterward when Kelly laid Ashley back in her crib, her legs shot up to kick the mobile dangling above her. She squealed when her large toe brushed against one of the tropical birds that rotated slowly. As her legs descended, the rhythmic, coordinated up-and-down movement resembled both a biker's pedaling and a runner's stride. Ashley's perpetual movement strengthened her leg muscles, as they never failed to put up a fight during diaper changes.

Her continuous activity exhausted her enough that, as early as eight weeks old, she was sleeping through the night, giving Kelly and Ryan much-needed respite.

Ashley's first steps mimicked a run, like she was born to run. There was no stopping her, as she liked a good chase. The only means to contain her was by placing barricades across hallways and strapping her down in the high chair. What Dr. Rogers had said about her was coming true.

Ryan had a commanding voice that held attention. He often nudged Kelly and said, "The only traits she inherited from me are my athleticism and voice. Thank God she mirrors you in looks." Ryan loved Kelly, and she complemented him.

At the first kindergarten parent-teacher conference, Mrs. Lloyd, Ashley's teacher, remarked, "Ashley is a delight in my class, and her consideration of other children is special." Toward the end of the meeting, she added, "She's always the first one to reach the swing set during recess, and she's a riot on the playground, as no one is ever able to catch her in a game of tag."

Ryan's eyes gleamed with pride, and Kelly smiled softly. Ashley was their precious child, their prized possession. Kelly considered her a gift from God.

In the spring of first grade, Ashley joined the YMCA coed soccer team. Direction and goalpost meant nothing to the teams as they chased the ball en masse, congregating around the ball and moving like a horde of animals that followed their leader. Ashley was one of them, but she was the fastest runner in the horde.

While most parents sat on the sidelines and took pictures of their children in their colorful YMCA team uniforms, her parents admired their daughter's agility.

When Ashley tried basketball in the fall of second grade, her dribbling skills were passable, but she stood out as the best rebounder. Her speed showed on the tennis court too. Whether Ashley had the footwork needed to maneuver a soccer ball, or had the ability to expertly dribble the basketball, or had the hand-eye coordination for a good game of tennis, she was the first to get to any ball.

Her parents were athletic, and they played tennis at an impressive level, making them competitive partners. Ashley's physical ability didn't surprise them, but her speed did. Yet to Ryan, his daughter's speed and movements appeared restless. Often he intercepted her whirlwind pace and gently held her hand in his and said, "Slow and steady wins the race. Slow down, Ash."

Kelly was soft and methodical; motherhood brought that side out even more. The awareness she'd gained in Milan, that everyone had a role to play, reverberated in everything she did. She talked in terms of role and responsibility, duty and destiny, reveling in the role of a mother and spending an inordinate amount of time with Ashley.

She treaded between dreams and visions that guided her and was hesitant to share them with Ryan, as he dismissed her intuition as nonsensical. She'd once insisted Ashley change her dress just before her birthday party. "That color will not go well with today," she'd said, without explaining her dream from the night before. Seeking clarity between superstition and reality, she sought a church. Was she searching for meaning in her dreams or seeking validation of her faith? Whatever the reason, church brought her peace.

She spent time in church committees, planning and helping women in need, giving back to other women what the church in Milan had given her—a sense of purpose and belonging.

Ashley accompanied Kelly to church when Ashley was young, but Ryan never did. He did not like the divided attention and questioned Kelly's need to spend time in church.

"I don't know why you need to go to church at all. For almost fifteen years of our married life, you never did. Why now? You know we donate money, don't you?" he complained.

"Money doesn't solve all problems, Ryan," Kelly said calmly. "I'm trying to offer people hope, sharing my experience in Milan with them. And my work at the church helps me make sense of my thoughts and connects me with God . . ." She trailed off, unable to explain how it helped her, while he refused to understand her need.

Kelly's life was a delicate balancing act. On the surface, she played the role of corporate wife with ease, planning trips and playing tennis. But her true passions were taking hold—motherhood and guiding other women through her prophetic visions.

Ryan was spending more time in meetings at work, his regular promotions piling more responsibility on him. He was on a short fuse, losing his temper more often. This quiet shift drove a wedge between Kelly and Ryan, transforming their ideological differences into an emotional chasm. There was love in their partnership, but layers of friction were solidifying.

His volcanic personality and anger issues were pushing Kelly further toward church and spirituality, seeking tolerability.

But Ashley saw her mother as loving, kind, and dignified, a woman who was revered at church, and her father as a larger-than-life personality, a wonderful dad in a position of authority and wealth. She saw her family as a loving unit that created many joyful memories through their travels.

But when Ashley, just ten years old, heard her father's rant reverberate across every corner of their large house for the first time, she was lost.

It was past her bedtime. The ruckus was so loud that even from her parents' secluded first-floor master bedroom, it reached her. Scared, she tiptoed down the stairs and eavesdropped on their heated shouting match, mostly driven by her father. Her mother stood her ground with measured responses but gradually sounded meeker.

The argument was about a forgotten pickup from the dry cleaners. "Do you even know that I have an important meeting tomorrow?" her father bellowed.

Ashley retreated to her room, scared, confused, and shocked all at once. But there was no hint of discord in the morning, with the love and respect her father normally showed her mother still intact.

Ashley was home early from school when, a year later, she witnessed another outburst. Ryan's face turned red, and his distinct voice shook and echoed. This time, she ran into the backyard not to embarrass them.

She kneeled in the pew the following Sunday. "Please, God, let them not divorce."

This cycle, although on a slow loop, shattered her idea of her family as perfect. How her sweet father could turn into a terror was confusing. He was a loved CEO of his company, and their family was well respected in the community. But once his face hinted red, Ashley knew what was coming. She either ran to hide in her room or escaped to the backyard, taking whichever door was closer and path nearer. Once outside, she jumped into her hammock, tied to the two oak trees, and cupped her ears, blocking the commotion.

The hammock used to be her favorite spot. On hot summer days, she had lain in it for hours, cooling herself, thinking what more in life could be better. But now the hammock was a contraption that engulfed her, swallowing her from all sides, creating an escape so she could shed tears for her family in solitude.

12

───────

MIDDLE SCHOOL YEARS

Ashley
1985–1987

shley was humming a Madonna song. They had just returned from Philadelphia, the trip her present for her twelfth birthday.

"Let's plan another trip," Kelly said after dinner, as she pored over travel guides from the library, especially the Lonely Planet's Netherlands guide.

"It's still summer break for Ash, so why not," Ryan replied, looking up from his office files.

"I haven't even unpacked my bag yet," Ashley moaned.

Kelly's planning was already underway, the tour of the house and the secret annex where Anne Frank and her family had hidden during World War II added to the itinerary. "Aren't we all so lucky to live in freedom?" she said, studying a map of Amsterdam.

Five weeks later, Ashley didn't feel so lucky. It was a Sunday, and Ryan's irritation started with a phone call from his assistant. When changes to terms of acquisition of a company his firm was acquiring were discussed, it triggered an explosive temper. He slammed the phone, displacing his anger. "Where's my folder?" he raged, tearing the house apart.

Ashley convinced herself that work stress was to blame for her father's outbursts, but deep down she knew better.

Unable to tolerate the commotion, she sprinted off their property and ran along their tree-lined street to get as far away from the conflict as possible. Her feet moved and her tears flowed. The echoes of her parents' voices fueled her frantic pace. She ran faster than she ever imagined she could, as images of her father's fury crept into her mind, like she was racing toward a finish line of peace.

"Bohemian Rhapsody" was fresh in her mind. It was as if the lyrics were written for her. She hoped the situation at home was fantasy, not the reality.

Her burden lifted with every stride. Sweat evaporated, taking the latent heat of her body along with it, cooling and soothing her heart and mind. The stress at home was released on the road. Often, by the time she returned, her father's anger was tempered, and the emotional embers cooled. Running was becoming a habit, a release, a high, and she was no longer running just as an escape.

For months, the lyrics played repeatedly in her mind as she ran. To break free of the sad lyrics, she counted her steps. With each right-foot stride, she counted from one to one hundred, then restarted the cycle. She covered six feet between numbers, and soon she knew exactly how many miles her feet had covered.

For all that transpired between her parents, for what it was worth, Ryan was ever so patient with Ashley, never losing his temper in public.

Apart from occasional outbursts at Kelly, there was a generous dose of love and pampering in the Spady home. Ashley, a playful prankster, loved hiding her father's glasses, moving her mother's car keys around, and suddenly screaming "boo" when a friend turned a corner.

On April Fools' Day, Ashley couldn't wait to unleash pranks on the unsuspecting around her. Her parents knew to be prepared, but they managed to forget every time. One early morning, she groaned and moaned loud enough to get their attention. As Kelly approached, Ashley screamed, "Appendicitis. I am dying." By the time James was summoned to her side, she sat up in her bed, grinning. "April fool's, you two."

Kelly couldn't admonish her, and James shook his head.

Running that had started as a desperate escape now gave her joy. Soon she was running with the ease of a seasoned expert. Joining the middle school track team was a natural fit. She attended a private school with her friends, who were children from other wealthy, influential families—old money, Ashley assumed.

Amid her growth spurt, with her ever-growing legs, she was a star at track meets. She ran the one- and two-mile events and did well. The strategy of counting from one to one hundred kept her from distractions.

With encouragement from her coaches, she paid attention to personal fitness, working with trainers on muscle strengthening and stretching regimens. Thanks to her mother, their dining table was adorned with lean meats, baked fish, salads, and fruit for most meals. Ashley learned to count calories from her mother. A banana had one hundred calories, toast stood at one hundred too, a whole egg at seventy, and a slice of pizza was four hundred. A large cookie added three hundred calories, and stir-fried noodles had six hundred calories a serving. How many calories seemingly small portions of food contained was an eye-opener and thus started her obsession with calorie counting, which would last all her life. She memorized numerous other details about calories, to her friends' chagrin, and rattled the numbers off to caution them when they ate fast food.

Entry into teenage years heralded a new age of consciousness about appearance. Taking great interest in wearing clothes that fit well and colors that coordinated, she owned numerous pairs of running shoes of different brands.

Kelly characterized Ashley's behavior as a fetish. "And I refuse to indulge it."

But her father smiled at the mother-daughter squabble and permitted the spending.

"I'm sorry, Mom," Ashley said guiltily after shopping sprees. "But I promise I will donate more from my allowance at my school's next charity fundraiser."

Along with consciousness of appearance came awareness of the fluidity of strides, air flow in her lungs, and motion mechanics. Conscious of changing textures under her feet, cognizant of the temperature and humidity of the air she breathed, she ran to the finish line body and mind in sync, form and function intact.

At fourteen, Ashley had long, slender legs. "I pray I don't grow too tall like you, Dad," she complained, aware that five feet to five feet, seven inches was the ideal height range for runners.

"Height gives authority, darling." Ryan's voice hinted pride.

She celebrated when her growth stalled at five foot, seven inches. In training, she learned to direct muscular force into forward propulsion for long, graceful strides, her narrow hips and slight frame ideally suited for long-distance runs.

"Finish line is not your goal. How you let your body feel the run is important," her coach said.

She finally understood this as she clocked a record run at a high school track-and-field event.

The Spadys still relished travel, as it served a purpose beyond exploration. For Ryan, traveling was a stress reliever, calming his temper, and Kelly and Ashley relaxed too. Their trips also helped mend the fractures that developed in their family unit during the year.

Ashley's planned runs on foreign lands and the varied landscapes added further joy to her travels.

Stories of kings and queens and their trysts with destiny interested her; wars and their ravages, triumphs, and defeats captivated her. During private guided tours, she listened with rapt attention, imagining lives from generations ago. At the Tower of London, she pondered if King Henry VIII's treatment of his six wives amounted to abuse. At the Van Gogh Museum in Amsterdam, she heard how the painter physically and emotionally mistreated his second wife.

"Men doing foolish things," she said to her mother, and didn't get a response.

In Athens, Greece, she was taken by the story of the first marathoner in the world, Pheidippides, who in 459 BC ran nonstop from a battlefield in Marathon to the Citadel in Greece to deliver the news of the

Athenian army's victory over the Persians, before dramatically dropping dead.

"Oh no!" she said when the tour guide ended the narration, saddened by the tragedy and grasping the importance of proper preparation and training.

In Paris, at midnight, they took a family picture, with the twinkling Eiffel Tower in the background, their white teeth glowing in the flash as they said, "Cheese."

"We're a perfect family." Kelly admired the picture.

"Far from it, Mom," Ashley replied, shaking her head.

13

THE EARLY YEARS

Robin

1972–1979

Sitting in her father's lap in his favorite rocking chair, Robin watched the television screen zoom in on a noisy litter of six adorable puppies, almost all white, with barely there black spots, as their mother licked them tenderly.

Her father pointed toward their newer-model 1974 nineteen-inch Sony Trinitron color television, encased in a heavy wooden cabinet, and said "dalmatian" at the same time as her mother said "adoption."

As the television glared, with its two antennae sticking out like rabbit ears, shining brightly on her pale face, highlighting her light hair and freckles, she gazed at her parents' faces alternately and then at the screen.

For Robin Blue Zymanski, her earliest memory was of two words: *dalmatian* and *adoption*. It was no surprise that words would be her world.

She was eighteen months old.

Robin had an attentive father and a gentle mother. They read to her at all times of the day, cuddling her as Robin's blue eyes precisely followed every word on the page in front of her.

James worked as a production manager at Rockwell International, a major employer in Winston-Salem, and Lily as an assistant librarian at the local library.

James worked with engineers involved in developing and manufacturing sophisticated machine parts needed for Rockwell's aviation division.

Lily assisted in reviewing newly released books for possible purchase by the library and enjoyed reading books to children at story time. In her singsong voice, she knew exactly when to pause, alter her tone, and stage an expression. It was like she was playing a part in a production. It was no surprise that the children listened to her with full attention.

And her role at the library could not have worked better for the Zymanski family. By the time they'd brought Robin home, Lily had known exactly what books to read to their child and how to read them.

Her job at the library placed her among people, and her interaction with young children brought her joy. It was an important means to curb the occasional melancholy that consumed her, episodes of which reared their heads without notice.

"My Robin." Lily planted a warm kiss on Robin's cheek, while James playfully protested, "No, she is my darling daughter." They competed for time with her. As they playfully tugged her toward themselves, claiming more rights to her attention, her big-boned body swayed, her cute button nose flared, and her blue-green eyes, reminiscent of a robin's egg, squinted as she squealed in laughter.

She was named Robin Blue for those very eyes.

Her eyes held mystique beyond the color, evoking the captivating image of Planet Earth in space—blue-green and round. In her world of words, she would one day seek to learn everything about the world.

She called them Moms and Pops.

"She is Mom, not Moms." James's attempts to correct were futile.

At eighteen months, she talked in clearly composed language. By her second birthday, she could recite entire pages from books read to her. She memorized nursery rhymes at the first go. When enrolled in preschool, her teachers recognized her gift for remarkable memory. They called it photographic. When her parents asked her what she did in school, she repeated conversations she'd had in their entirety and described every event from start to end of her school day.

At three, she remembered her dreams too, an unusually young age to do so. "Last night I rode my pet eagle high into the sky, only to scoop down to lift off her lost baby eagle from an apple tree and return the baby back to its nest."

She told it to her preschool teacher with such clarity and conviction that her teacher said, "Good story, Robin. Did your mom read that story to you at bedtime last night?"

"No. I saw it in my sleep." Robin looked perplexed.

"Yes, of course. Brilliant indeed" was all the teacher could say. Robin's parents read her stories of how animals carried and birthed babies. When Robin was five, it dawned on her that "adoption" was being used in reference to her, but she was unaware of its significance. With each passing year, her comprehension of the word deepened. As such, she never could zero in on the time, place, or context when she sensed the full meaning of the word and its relevance to her.

When she did, a vague sense of unease and mild turmoil rooted in her, in an unfathomable place. It lay dormant, surfacing rarely and momentarily. That it had the potential to tether deeper, take hold, magnify, and erupt, leading to a total breakdown, was not lost on her. Concealing this took effort, but she did.

Her unease about being adopted burgeoned into her sleep too, changing her usual pleasant dreams into convoluted piles of images that hung on the verge of nightmare and confabulation. They traversed between scenarios that did not connect—unwed moms, teenage pregnancies, drugged-up women, pitifully poor families with dozens of children. Memories of the disconnected portrayals sprouted randomly. She remembered them all. Her body shuddered sporadically as a reflex, a telltale sign of their random recollection.

WHEN ROBIN WAS SEVEN, Lily read *Anne of Green Gables* to her, a recent Christmas present. In the heartwarming tale of the young orphan girl Anne, Robin saw her own life, as much as a seven-year-old could. She was reassured, albeit in the moment, by how Anne was loved and eventually adopted by good people.

"Moms, am I your Anne then?" she would ask whenever Lily would read the story, pointing toward the book, looking for reassurance.

Lily would nod vigorously every time, quelling her urge to correct how she was addressed.

Time and again, Robin would be drawn to the book to find strength in Anne's story.

"I HAVE ABIBLIOPHOBIA," Robin announced one Sunday morning. All it took was "phobia" for Lily's ears to perk up.

James looked over his newspaper. "What is that, Robin?"

Robin tapped her forehead and held her finger there. "I'm worried that I'll run out of books to read."

James shook his head. "My darling daughter, let me and your mom worry about that." He signaled to Lily that all was under control. "Your mom's library can get you as many books as you want." James did not worry about anything yet, but it was to come.

So began a new phase in Robin's world of words, of using obscure phrases and words. Whether she did this unbeknownst to their obscurity, James did not know. But he let her.

"Pops, commonly used words are about five thousand, and a well-read person knows, say, twenty thousand words, but I'm going to memorize all one hundred seventy-one thousand words and some forty-seven thousand archaic ones listed in the *Oxford English Dictionary*," she proclaimed proudly.

James hoped she wouldn't.

Robin managed well at school despite her insatiable appetite for reading. Between classes, she sneaked in a few pages, but at home, she moved quickly from one book to the next. Reading was her sanctuary, calming her anxiety and immersing her in an alternate world.

Her ability to remember and recollect obscure facts with eerie accuracy was unparalleled. When she was nine, her pediatrician called her a mnemonist, saying that was someone "with an ability to memorize vast quantities of information across various cognitive domains, not just through photographic memorization." Occasionally she approached her parents, more so James, for clarification of concepts. Once she understood an idea, followed a theme, or mastered a concept, she retained it permanently. And building on such understanding became easier.

Her brain retained an enormous amount of information. But her ability to remember every detail was not all good for her, according to her pediatrician, because forgetting "makes our brains more efficient." Her extraordinary gift of memory and learning put her at risk of getting lost in the details.

To channel his exceptionally talented daughter's functioning, and to streamline her recall with strategy was James's challenge. While he worried that her restlessness was from information overload and focused on channeling that, Robin was anxious and curious about the unknown weave of her story. When she tried to grasp this complex array of self-discovery, feelings of abandonment, and restlessness returned.

"Robin is like a black hole. Black holes absorb everything that comes their way, and scientists haven't figured out what they do with that energy. I hope she will figure out what to do with the information she absorbs." He shared his concern with Lily.

Challenging her with puzzles and LEGOs, James tried to sharpen her focus, hoping that in time she would figure out the art of filtering the infinite bytes of information her brain gathered through a sieve, so she could prioritize information to save and information to discard.

James wanted Robin to have hobbies, to expand her horizons, and to take her away from books. In line with his passion for cooking, his interest in his vegetable garden paramount, he shepherded her outdoors to help him, enticing her with the promise of her favorite dishes later that day.

Robin ventured out reluctantly. Between rows of cauliflower and lettuce heads on one side and asparagus on the other, she strolled distractedly, without really noticing them. Upon prodding, she snapped a handful of spinach leaves off the vine.

Hesitant to touch anything without gardening gloves, she peered through the wire mesh around the beds and managed to pull a few weeds and dig for a rare potato. She sat on inverted wooden crates, under a canopy of tangled vines of string beans, nibbling spinach leaves, with a book, her dirty gloves still on. Evenly placed pots of herbs —oregano, basil, rosemary, and parsley—encircled the canopy, giving it a feel of a secluded gazebo.

She also perched on watermelons and pumpkins and listened to her father's stories as he tended the nearby beds. He once told her a funny story about his trip to McDonald's when he was six, with his brother, who was two years older. "We had enough money only for one burger. Like good brothers, we shared, but to satisfy our ever-growing appetite, we added three packets of ketchup and one packet of hot sauce to a cup of hot water and drank it like soup."

Robin laughed. "How ingenious, Pops. I bet it was your idea."

Often preoccupied, she fell behind in her chores. Caught up in one and lost in it, she failed to maintain schedules.

In her cluttered room, she tripped over tangled heaps of discarded clothes, empty Sunshine Hydrox cookies boxes, and Space Candy wrappers. Robin called her messiness her "huck muck."

James hoped it would resolve by the time she was a teenager, not knowing those years would be the worst.

14

ELEMENTARY SCHOOL YEARS

Robin
1980–1985

"Make sure you pack everything you need," James said. "We leave early tomorrow."

"I'm all packed up, Pops," Robin answered, eager for their annual trip to Carolina Beach.

Although she needed new swimwear and clothes, as she'd grown inches and was fast surpassing Lily in height, she made Lily shop for them, not particular about style. However, her prized possessions, her books, were carefully selected and stacked in a large tote bag. Hidden among them was a present for her father, as there was no chance of misplacing it if it was stored there.

Planning her father's birthday every summer gave her the most rush. Handmade and carefully wrapped for him over the years were bracelets, cards, painted aprons, and embroidered hand towels, her gifts for him becoming increasingly elaborate as she grew older.

Her favorite presents from her parents were books. She borrowed her choicest books from the library, yet she loved the surprise of carefully picked and freshly released titles that the library didn't carry.

After the kitchen, the beach was James's allure and the ocean his love. He had not seen the ocean well into his college years, and it drew him in deeply, like a magician's trick.

The beach was a place where Lily was happy too, her happiness magnified by James's enthusiasm for it.

As a family, they spent days relaxing and building sandcastles and blowing iridescent bubbles that danced in rainbow hues. At five, Robin had chased those bubbles. Later, she'd graduated to crafting them and cheekily admiring her distorted reflection—a stretched face and ear-to-ear grin that rivaled a whale's smile—on their convex surface.

Through the passage of summers, they stayed at the same two-bedroom condominium facing the beach. It had undergone multiple renovation cycles to modernize, and it was a game to run through the list of changes.

"Fresh paint in the bedrooms. Wooden counters are now marble slabs. The appliances are brand new." Robin rattled them off with solid accuracy. She dashed out of the double doors of the family room, down the boardwalk, and onto the beach, the warm grains of sand shifting and sliding under her steps. She jumped in the water with her floatation devices on, with James right on her heels, guarding her and keeping her afloat like a long-laboring mother whale did, by pushing its baby to the surface immediately after giving birth.

July 3, James's birthday, was conveniently close to the Fourth of July holiday, adding an extra day to their beach vacation. The year James turned fifty, Robin baked a large cake and placed fifty candles in the shape of the number fifty. She bestowed fifty kisses upon him and remarked, "A half century, is that correct?" I wish for you to live to celebrate an additional semicentennial, golden jubilee, and quinquagenary birthday!"

James laughed, only partially grasping the meaning.

Their partying continued for another week, until Robin celebrated her twelfth birthday on July 12. Her cake read, *Twelve on Twelve.*

"Best summer yet," Robin summarized, as she shoved her bag of dirty clothes into the cargo area of their station wagon.

Lily neither agreed nor disagreed. She turned quiet and stared blankly at nothing.

"Mom's still in hurkle-durkle state?" Robin asked a week later.

James rolled his eyes.

She went on. "That is a Scottish term for lingering in bed when one should be up and about."

It was Monday morning, and James hurried to drop Robin off at camp. Lily was mired in an unshakeable fog of melancholy, without reason, and had not left her bedroom since their return.

After dinner, as Robin lay stretched on a couch in their sunroom, reading her new book, the sun's last rays trickling in through open slats, James approached her and placed a hand on her outstretched leg. "I know you're curious about your mother. What's affecting her is not a physical issue but a psychological one. I don't know how much you can understand, but she suffers from depression, a mood disorder." He massaged her leg gently.

To her young brain, there was now a medical term to explain her mother's sullen mood.

"Such episodes started shortly after we lost baby Kristen," James explained further.

"Baby who?" Robin asked, narrowing her eyes.

"Your mother's depression started after a series of miscarriages she had many years ago. It worsened when one pregnancy seemed to proceed well, until it didn't. She went into early labor after her water broke at seven months. Doctors' attempts to stop the labor didn't work. We named her Kristen, tiny and delicate, weighing only two pounds. The best doctors in town couldn't save her for more than a day."

Robin listened intently, hoping her relaxed posture gave the impression of casual interest. She fidgeted. Her father's eyes turned misty. Not knowing how to respond, she lowered her gaze to her open page.

"After delivery, the doctor examined your mother and said that her womb was only half-developed. There was a small chance surgery could fix it, but a higher risk of losing it to excess bleeding. He told us that unless it was surgically corrected, she could never carry a baby to term." He sighed.

"You mean her uterus is only half-developed?" Robin asked after a period of uncomfortable silence. In her world, such words came naturally to her.

James nodded, ending with, "Your mother improved a great deal after we brought you home."

In the early morning hours the next day, Robin saw an image of a dalmatian with half a face, a missing front paw, reading a book that was half-torn, and she woke up with a start. She wondered how a uterus could only half develop. She wondered if any of her parts were short on development, and if they were, how she would know?

Robin, at twelve years, had found the answer to why her parents had adopted her. However, the reason she was placed for adoption remained unanswered. She imagined a darker side to her life and how, if revealed, it would affect her now.

Overall she was happy where she was. Her allegiance was with her parents. If she had a chance to ask her father about her story, she let the moment pass.

She leaned on books for balance, and they placed her in alternate worlds, where she fell deeply into their stories, inserting herself into characters and their dilemmas, forgetting her own.

Robin had playmates in her two cousins. The Zymanskis hosted Thanksgiving, while Christmas festivities were at her grandmother's. Robin's innate concern was that she looked different: large-boned, blue-green-eyed, pale-skinned, with light hair that looked bleached. She never failed to notice the surprise on one's face when she was introduced as Lily and James's daughter. To her growing agony, no one attempted to mask their expression either.

"Scandinavian look," her aunt commented once.

James had a large network of acquaintances and friends. He engaged people with sincere interest, talking and listening to them. He was the first one to welcome new neighbors with a homemade pie. His affinity for life and people was clear when he laughed and entertained. No one ever declined his invitation. A connector, people named him as the person who introduced them to most others in a group. But for occasionally being borderline boisterous, he was well-liked.

His genuineness showed, and along the way, his cooking and his penchant for hosting helped manage Lily's melancholy and assemble playmates for Robin.

For Robin, her parents, extended family, a few playmates, and her books made her world. She was thankful for being a Zymanski and for having a family she belonged to. She leaned on books and the memories she made from them for balance. But her quiet, internal struggle for equilibrium lingered.

15

HIGH SCHOOL YEARS

Robin
1989–1990

Ms. Merriwether, Robin's eleventh-grade language arts teacher, summoned her at the end of class.

"What did I do now?" Robin exclaimed.

Ms. Merriweather was an engaging teacher, but she and Robin did not see eye-to-eye, as Robin was often caught in class reading unassigned books.

However, in Robin, Ms. Merriwether saw a well-read role model. "Nothing. I need a favor. Could I pair you with Sachiko, our new student, for projects? You'll be doing her a huge favor."

Robin wrinkled her nose. "If you insist, Ms. Merriweather."

Sachiko Katzu's father had been relocated from Japan to head his company's North American subsidiary. Her ability to read in English and comprehend was on par with other juniors, but her conversational skills needed practice.

"Don't be afraid to talk. Your English is good," Robin encouraged Sachiko, mistaking Sachiko's mellowness as shyness.

"I'm not scared. It is just a habit. Being soft spoken is a sign of respect in Japan," Sachiko clarified.

"*Sachiko* means 'a child of joy and happiness,'" Sachiko's mother told Robin, halting, searching for the right words. "She not want to leave her friends in Japan and come here.

"Because of you, Sachi is happy again. Thank you."

"I'll make sure she finds more of it in America, Mrs. Katzu," Robin reassured.

On a Sunday morning, Robin drove Sachiko to Krispy Kreme in her father's old Ford station wagon, which was hers now. The R. J. Reynolds billboard was long gone, unable to withstand America's national campaign against tobacco, and in its place was a Krispy Kreme board with its blinking blue sign that read "Fresh hot doughnuts," indicating a new batch being made.

They stood in line for twenty-five minutes, surrounded by the sweet aroma of the sugary glaze. "My favorite dessert. If I'm not careful, I could eat a dozen at a time. You know, Winston-Salem is the home of Krispy Kreme and its famous original glazed doughnut," she told Sachiko, proud to share her hometown's history.

"It is now my favorite dessert too," Sachiko said after only one bite.

They strolled down the mall, admiring the window displays at Victoria's Secret, their teenage fancies arising. Charlotte Russe and The Gap were visited and explored. They tried matching sweatshirts at The Limited.

After a movie and extra-buttery popcorn, Sachiko commented, "A perfect finale."

Her parents called her Sachi for short, but Robin called her Sylph. In her world of words, that name had come to Robin when she'd first met the slender, graceful Sachiko.

Sachiko had smiled, trusting Robin's choice. It was only later that she'd understood the meaning and thanked Robin for it. "You made me feel like a flower, slender and graceful. How special."

Sachiko left her shoes at the door as she entered Robin's house. Robin did the same at Sachiko's, whose house was impeccably clean, furnished with sofas in clean lines and made of natural wood, in contrast to the bulky, overstuffed look of American designs.

Sachiko's room was no different. It had a desk by the window, bare except for a lamp and a pencil holder. A six-foot-wide dresser sat along the opposite wall. Robin wondered why someone would want their room so clean. There was no bed, only a futon on the floor, folded to one side.

"That will be my bed at night. A tidy bed calms the head," Sachiko said, proud of how she ably translated a Japanese saying into English.

Robin deduced the futon to be a permanent arrangement by choice.

"We wash them periodically and aerate them in the sun. To keep them clean," Sachiko explained. "In Zen Buddhism, keeping one's surroundings clean is a form of meditation and purification."

Before eating, Sachiko and her parents put their hands together and said, "Itadakimasu."

"It is how we thank the person who prepared the meal for us," Sachiko explained. "Also, we meditate daily to get self-control." She paused. "And develop onsight." Her forehead crinkled. "I mean insight," she corrected herself.

As only children in their families, they found joy in each other.

Robin found peace among Sachiko's family. Her body felt lighter, more focused when she returned home. She wasn't sure if it was the people or their streamlined surroundings that brought her such calm.

In her dream that night, Robin was a Buddhist monk, sitting in an immaculate Japanese garden, on a futon strewn with white flowers. Slowly she chanted, "Me and myself," her voice echoing within her and around her.

She had not seen the Katzu family meditating or chanting, but in her understanding, chanting was what meditation was.

Robin was trying to incorporate abilities that were missing in her life, while Sachiko worked on integrating into American culture. At the start of the spring semester, Ms. Merriwether, who was also the director of the drama club, summoned both to her room. By then, Ms. Merriwether and Robin had developed a respectable affiliation and subtle adoration for each other.

"You both seem to be doing well with each other," Ms. Merriweather commented.

Robin shrugged. Sachiko nodded.

The teacher handed them each a brochure. "This year, our drama club chose *Julius Caesar* as their season finale. And I'm short on actors," she began.

Robin instinctively shook her head. "No, Ms. Merriweather. You know I can't act."

"Robin, you just have to say the dialogue like a parrot. With your memory, I know you can carry lengthy monologues. We'll plant you in one place for the entire scene, and you just have to imagine that you are reciting poetry in class. I have the perfect role in mind for you. Sachiko, I have a role for you too."

"Let's do it," Sachiko nudged.

Ms. Merriweather raised her eyebrows, peering over her reading glasses. "It's settled then, isn't it?"

"Hmmm," Robin agreed reluctantly.

Like good partners, they practiced, Robin helping Sachiko with diction and Sachiko offering acting tips. They read Shakespeare out of curiosity.

"Nobody marks you," one said.

"Yes, my Lady Disdain," the other responded. "What the heck does that even mean?"

They laughed while reading from *Much Ado About Nothing*.

On the stage, Ms. Merriwether positioned Robin in a sideways stance, occasionally even with her back to the audience. "Just say the words so the play can move on," she instructed.

"But for the dialogue, she is just a prop. We can't have a play without her though," the assistant director, a parent volunteer, said.

Sachiko, short on dialogue but deft at acting, balanced Robin on the stage.

Robin wore large hats, often with oversized, baggy robes, so her facial expressions and body language were obscured. She stood in the most dimly lit corner of the stage. *Even better*, Robin thought. She played Portia, Brutus's wife, in Act 2, Scene 1, when Portia tried to get Brutus to open up about what it was that was bothering him.

Before an audience of parents and students, she started the 225-word-long monologue. "Is Brutus sick and is it physical . . ." In her flowing robe, when Robin tripped and flailed her arms to position herself, it appeared that she had lunged toward Brutus with the purpose of pleading with him. The audience applauded, assuming it to be a planned act.

So started Robin's phase of reading Shakespeare's plays and sonnets. For how fast she read books, only Shakespeare slowed her. For the first time in her life, she reread paragraphs. She asked her parents for clarification but could not get any. This led to many discussions and a certain bonding with Ms. Merriwether.

For a while, she spoke to her parents with words like *thy, thou, thine,* and *canst,* to which they merely shook their heads and shrugged. When her father talked to her about keeping her schedules and chores in line, she responded, "All the world's a stage, All the men and women merely players," from the comedy *As You Like It,* contending that she, in life, like others, was merely a player being whom she was destined to be.

"THE BARD HAS TAKEN OVER YOU." James clapped.

Complementing each other's strengths and weaknesses, Robin's and Sachiko's differences became the foundation of their bond. Their passions and interests intersected, their empathy for each other evident. But Robin's vulnerability remained wrapped and buried. Her inability to share the one most intimate detail of her life that troubled her, her adoption, left their friendship incomplete, like one loose nail in a frame, one broken egg in a carton. The circle did not close. The bolt never fastened.

To Robin, Sachiko's return to Japan after graduation was a loss akin to that of the ten-year-old boy Jessie in the book *Bridge to Terabithia*—he struggled to recover and build a bridge to his future life in the aftermath of losing a dear friend to an accident.

"Thank you for opening my eyes to a different way of living. You and your family came into my life when I most needed it. What I learned from you and your parents will be my life's work to master, if I can at all." Robin bowed to Sachiko. Sachiko bowed too.

"This was just a preview. You need to visit Japan for the full experience," Sachiko said, eager to see her friend in the future. "The importance given to one's freedom for independent thinking and creativity in

American society is the way forward in the world. That's my takeaway from America, and that hopefully won't take me a lifetime to master."

The teenagers promised, and in their innocence, they believed in the prospect of lifelong friendships.

"I just have to build that bridge," Robin said to her father once she bid Sachiko goodbye.

THROUGHOUT MIDDLE AND HIGH SCHOOL, Robin had envisioned herself as many things. But one that stuck was that of a writer. She enrolled in writing courses. She followed her teachers' instructions to trust her instincts. "Robin, first thought is your best thought. Develop on that," several had said.

She attempted writing in fits and starts, like an engine spurting to life for short periods and stalling inordinately. Writing needed discipline, which she had, but when she attempted to write, she unraveled. Retrieving ideas and visions from her mind's eye and delving deep into her dreams and experiences to write, rattled her. Keeping herself contained took effort, more effort than she was able to garner. The process never materialized.

When in college, Robin joined the theater group. "Just out of curiosity," she told her father. By that time, she had grown more confident on the stage. Still, with so many talented students taking theater as a course and competing for parts, her presence was hardly required.

Only rarely, when they needed her on short notice, did they give her parts heavy on the dialogue, with little need for acting, like in high school. Some plays were both written and directed by students, while professors acted as their advisers. When she sat in the audience during rehearsals, she developed ideas for better character structure by reimagining the narrative. Initially she let these ideas fall by the wayside, unsure of her role and place.

When she did receive a role, she quietly offered ideas to adjust the dialogue and hesitantly proposed small modifications to her own performance. On a good day, she was heard. That was how it began.

Over time, her voice became increasingly recognized. Emboldened, she offered suggestions for better flow of scenes.

"Yes. For the flow," they all said.

"The flow is the most important part of a play. It can make or break the production," the theater adviser agreed.

At first, her editing skills attracted occasional requests for suggestions, but over time, she was consistently sought for her opinion. It was no surprise she became a new addition to the team. This role worked for her beautifully. This experience with editing would become a springboard for her future career choice.

When asked what her plans were after college, Robin told her father that if she could not be a writer, being an editor was the next best thing. "That way I can help someone else become a better writer, polish their language and ideas. I'll still be involved in the craft of writing, only I won't be the writer."

James nodded in appreciation, relieved that his daughter was finding her way in the world.

Robin's connection with the drama club would prove crucial for her career, and her friendship with Sachiko, critical for her survival.

16

NUMB

Anita
1992–1994

Deepak lingered in his study in the dark. The family seemed to have lost their appetite, as their kitchen, once the family's busiest core, was cold and dead. Ami left for school early, came home late, consumed what little she ate while glued to the television, and locked herself in her room to finish homework. Rumi was the only one who made normal conversation, but no one was interested.

Sadness, on the verge of mourning, lurked in every corner of their home.

Ami, a senior in high school, could not wait to graduate and distance herself from the family's circumstance. Anita's behavior embarrassed her. She'd barely talked to Anita when she returned home from the hospital. She'd looked at her with pity and reached out to her only once, in a rare moment of kindness. Under all the previous subtle and overt layers of sibling rivalry, there had been a tender connection between them. Still, forgiveness was not in the cards yet.

Anita understood.

At her six-week postpartum visit, Dr. Patel addressed Anita's contraceptive needs.

"There is no need for it." Anita was clear, surprising Dr. Patel with her first-ever conversation.

When Dr. Patel insisted that she consider options, Anita said emphatically, "There will be no sex in my future, ever."

In July, Anita's sixteenth birthday slipped by, eerily silent and unnoticed.

Five months after Anita's delivery, Ami moved into her dormitory at Northwestern University. Attending this university was Ami's dream, and her parents' too. Having one daughter in college was a relief. They hoped for college for Anita also. They reassured each other with, "Maybe at our local community college."

As for Anita, she started her junior year without fanfare. Maintaining a low profile, she kept to herself. When she passed the usual hangout of the old Goth group, agitation surfaced. If Sebastian had graduated, she did not know. She did not have a phone number or address for him. They'd never taken pictures together. He'd disappeared from her life just like that. At times, she wondered if he was even real.

She ate lunch alone, and she sat in the library during other breaks and doodled for hours. It became an unconscious activity while her mind was preoccupied by subconscious dread. With either a pencil, pen, or marker, whichever was available, her hand moved freely, first along the margins of her science book and then on whole pages, with no formal design or intent. The lead gray of the pencil, blue ink from the pen, and black liquid of the marker were her colors. They blended easily, like good cousins, their dark tones glad to have found company with one another. Straight lines and squiggles merged with swirls, hundreds of them and never-ending ones. Geometrical patterns and intangible whimsical figures, layered and overlapped, were created without constraint.

What started as a distraction, an escape, became an outlet. Later, she would experiment with watercolors, gravitating toward dull colors to reflect her somber mood. To create depth and texture, she added sand for grit, dried petals for softness, and shards of glass for glimmer.

Many years later, she discovered that people often doodled to handle stress and frustration. As an expression of guilt and a way for the subconscious mind to communicate in symbolic expressions, drawing strengthened one's recall by 29 percent. When she read this detail, she was convinced that doodling came to her to keep her daughter's distant existence alive.

Uncharacteristically for her, she started wearing the gold chain her grandmother had gifted her. The chain had a pendant of Lord Ganesha, the revered elephant god, believed to grant strength, remove obstacles, and usher in auspicious beginnings.

"I'll make sure I have a happy life, like my grandmother did, and if I believe in this idea, I can make any situation a happy one," she wrote on the same page on which she was doodling. "Drawing strength from the pure gold the chain is made of, and the faith it symbolizes, I'll make this chain my connection to my dadi and to that belief," she added. She tore the page and saved it under the schoolbooks stacked on her desk. She later placed it in a transparent plastic cover and pinned it to her easel.

In the summer after her junior year, she landed a job as an aide at St. Bonaventure. Ami's old Chevy was hers now. The heavy rusting on the passenger-side door and the quarter panels blended with the maroon color of the car. Nonetheless it wouldn't have bothered her. She worked part-time hours helping residents with showers, making beds, cleaning bathrooms, and vacuuming floors. Diapers, bedpans, wipes, and walkers were her newly discovered sights, some of which she'd used herself after her delivery.

No one knew her story. There was no judging, and the job paid decently. Away from home and school, she shed the accumulated, ugly layers of guilt and shame, lightening herself. She molted from a pupa to a butterfly. She wasn't ready to fly yet, but her new circumstance of no judgment and of financial independence freed her.

This freshly discovered perception of release at work intensified the misery and agony at school. Already an outcast, she'd found herself even more ostracized after her pregnancy, which led her to question the point of it all.

Two weeks after starting her senior year, she informed her parents she was dropping out. They weren't surprised. It was as if they were expecting this, though they'd prayed for better. Having no fight left in them, they simply nodded. Nothing she did disappointed them or shocked them anymore.

She worked with keen interest. Her manager thought it was unusual for a teenager to work with her intensity. He wondered what her story was, but all he did was compliment her. Her work was physical, but to her it was more than that. It set her free from school and judgment. In this freedom, she saw a role for herself, a role to help others. A role that did not need a degree.

In the residents' fragility, she saw echoes of her own turbulent past. Displaced and dependent, yearning for acceptance, for love, and for tender care, the inhabitants often felt that they were abruptly removed from their familiar dwellings prematurely. They believed that they did not belong there, like Anita had felt in school.

In their old age, childlike again, stubborn, and temperamental, they demanded attention. She watched with amusement, looking for parallels in her own behavior from not too long ago.

One middle-aged Mexican resident reminded Anita of her grandmother. Not understanding English, unable to comprehend what was said to her, she nodded, her nod ambiguous, reminiscent of Dr. Patel's gesture after Anita's delivery.

Anita remembered how kind her nurses were to her while in labor. She tried to pass that forward when residents needed extra help. "To help them all is my sacred calling" was her new mantra. She wholeheartedly believed she'd made one good decision after an unending streak of poor choices.

17

FOR FREEDOM

Anita

1994

Rumi stepped into their living room to find books and newspapers neatly stacked. Shoes were in their designated spots. "When did you learn to clear things so well, Deepak?" she asked, walking into the kitchen.

Anita, wearing yellow rubber gloves and mopping the floor, turned, not expecting to see her mom back early.

Deepak entered behind Rumi and eyed the straight vacuum lines on the carpet in the breakfast nook. The kitchen floor shone as brightly as the countertop.

"Thank you, bitiya," he said, with two thumbs-up.

Following this Sunday ritual, Anita surveyed the pantry and the refrigerator, taking notes and making lists. Later, she restocked them both. While she was courteous, respectful even, her parents refrained from giving her advice.

In her rebellious phase, she'd failed to understand when her mother said, "You will never know how much we love you until you have a child of your own." She hadn't cared to acknowledge the sentiment then, but now she was beginning to. The missing piece in her relationship with her parents was their understanding of her and her respect for them. She hoped they'd see her disrespect as a symptom of her pain, not a measure of her love.

She desperately longed for her pregnancy and daughter to be acknowledged, but they were not. Lacking courage, for fear that her parents would find that insulting, she squashed her urge to reference her daughter.

Around this time, her parents downsized, as their social circle had shrunk considerably—they were ostracized, to be precise. Deeming Anita a bad influence, other parents controlled their kids' association with the Kumar children, leading the Kumar family to withdraw from all community activities.

Insulted and ignored, they decided to move into a condominium thirty miles southeast, to a suburb of Durham, closer to their workplaces. Their careers were shaping better than their original expectation of the American dream. Innovation was in high gear and times were exciting, as Rumi worked for Intel on chip design, while Deepak served as a material science engineer at Cree Inc., a leading semiconductor company. Their jobs placed them among researchers who won prestigious Nobel Prizes and US presidential awards for their work.

Deepak and Rumi tried to coax Anita to move with them. "To start fresh," they said. "Restart school, maybe," they added hesitantly.

"But I want to figure out my life on my own," she told them. *Maybe I don't want to leave the place where my daughter might still be.* This thought she could not share with them.

She doubted her ability to fit in a new school elsewhere, given her past struggles. She liked St. Bona, as nobody engaged with a lowly teenager working in the housekeeping department. Anonymity helped, and she was reluctant to switch jobs. Her parents knew better than to pressure her, despite their worry for her safety and ability to live independently.

Anita rented a studio apartment and had the choice of owning some of her parents' old furniture. She moved her bed, an old couch, a scratched-up breakfast table, which she paired with four white plastic chairs from a thrift store, and set off to start her new life, away from the prying eyes of her community.

The first day she spent alone was liberating—freed from her parents' worried looks that were a constant reminder of her life's miserable history.

Anita's needs were few. Her work was physically tiring, and the fatigue helped her emotionally. She did not have friends. The few she knew as colleagues were from work. Doodling remained her go-to activity. It fed her soul for the moment.

The black, gray, and dark-blue colors of her doodling balanced the dull colors of St. Bona. She was in a steady state. On her own, in her solitude, no turbulence, no storms, no disruptions. No associations, no laughs, no tears. For a time, this stillness was good for her.

18

HIGH SCHOOL YEARS

Ashley
1988–1991

"I hate Dad for how he treats you," Ashley said timidly, gathering enough courage to engage her mother about her mistreatment.

Kelly had returned from church, and Ashley had targeted her mother then, as she was at her most peaceful self.

Kelly stopped unbuttoning her jacket and turned around. "Hate is a strong word, Ash. Yes, we're allowed to dislike the ones we love, but if those times are short-lived and rare, and the long stretches in between are filled with love, don't you think we should continue loving them?" The answer spilled out of her like she had rehearsed it. Without waiting for an answer, she continued, "And that is why I haven't stopped loving your dad."

"Well, yes, we should," Ashley replied, believing it to be true.

To a fifteen-year-old, the explanation was simple and straightforward. No divorce! That too was a relief. Hormones, acne, boys, and clothes, in addition to assignments and training, needed her attention. She brought home good grades and many medals from track events.

After a year, as a high school sophomore and having witnessed enough incidents, once again, she could no longer ignore them.

. . .

"HE HAS a lot of pressure at work. We must be patient, Ash," Kelly explained this time.

At other times, she justified her mistreatment as "He loves me, so he vents his frustrations on me, that's all." She had a way with words, responding smoothly and succinctly, like a philosopher.

"It's never physical, you know" was yet another rationalization.

"Everyone has a role to play, Ash. This is mine—to be a good mother to you, to be bound by my duty and my destiny," she explained her tolerance.

Her answers pacified Ashley, albeit only temporarily, as her frustration surfaced later. Aware that the circumstances were fundamentally wrong, Ashley was ashamed of her father's temper and her mother's tolerance of it.

IN HER SENIOR YEAR, Ryan stayed home for a week, uncharacteristically subdued, and her usually authoritative father conversed in hushed tones.

"What's wrong? Why are you and Dad acting weird?" Ashley asked Kelly.

"Dad is taking a short break from work. The stress is getting to him. You see, he has been advised to enroll in anger-management classes, something to do with his interaction with a colleague. This will help all of us. I heard his father had similar issues. Love is important, but patience with whom we love is even more important. Ash, it is a virtue. Our duty toward him should always come first. That is what life and family are about." Kelly busied herself fixing Ashley's bed and wasn't really waiting for a response.

"Understood, Mom." Ashley sighed with a blend of relief and concern.

Time passed. Her calendar was full.

The highlight of her senior year was winning the state two-hundred-meter dash and the five-thousand-meter track events. She qualified for and competed at the national meet but fell short of the top-three finish.

As her high school years ended, she applied for and was accepted, with a sports scholarship, to the University of North Carolina at Chapel Hill. Its academic emphasis and strong track team were instant attractions for her. With her family's surplus income and an established college fund in addition to a trust fund, she acknowledged the scholarship as a badge of honor but declined financial support.

Ashley worried about leaving her parents, her mother especially, and wondered if her presence was ever a buffer in her mom's relationship with Ashley's father, knowing that her dad's outbursts had returned, despite anger-management sessions.

Ashley did not know how to confront her father. She loved him and he loved her dearly. Her unwillingness to add discomfort to their loving bond might have been it. Lack of confidence might have been too. Her mother's varied explanations provided an escape from facing the ugly truth of their family dynamic. She eased her guilt by thinking that confronting him would not make a difference.

Kelly reassured Ashley of her resilience and labeled what she was going through as her "burden of love." "You tolerate hardships for those you love. There are many types of burdens you must invariably assume when you love someone, Ash. I am willing to accept those burdens for you and Dad."

On the last day at home before her move, she gave them tender hugs and lingered, surprising them, as she labeled such hugs *overreaching* and *uncomfortable*. She had called them "an unnecessary infringement of personal space."

For Ashley, the UNC-Chapel Hill campus being only three hours away from Charlotte was appealing. The institution, surrounded by seven hundred acres of verdant land, with a charming mix of modern and historic buildings, many inviting outdoor trails, cool restaurants, and fun activities, was love at first sight to Ashley.

Emily and Rose were her roommates. Their schedules and chemistry with one another worked well, as they were runners too. Rose, a quiet force with medium height and stocky legs, managed to generate enough power to propel herself at a fair speed, with enough endurance to make a good long-distance runner. Emily had a loud, infectious laugh that got her attention. Tall and with a high torso-to-leg ratio that lowered her center of gravity, stability was her strength. With a higher cadence, she had a perfect running style. When irritated, she unknowingly rattled off in her native Korean.

Between the quiet and the loud, Ashley was a balancing medium. If being on the same track team helped their friendship, their professed love for crepes only deepened it. They called themselves crepe girls but liked dressing as Bond girls.

They even once attended their campus Halloween party in hipster shorts and body-hugging T-shirts, with flat hats that sat like crepes.

The three traveled with their college team, guided by their coach's Navy SEAL mantra: "All in, all the time."

Despite Ashley's calorie counting, maintaining a healthy, lean body mass was a challenge in the first semester.

"Every extra pound gained will slow you down by zero point two seconds a mile," the assistant coach cautioned.

Back on track with weight and fitness by the end of her freshman year, she was competing in tight races.

"Life is not a race. Everyone has a place in the world and has a role to play. You will find yours too. Duty and destiny will guide you" was her mother's advice before races.

It would be many years before Ashley understood the full meaning of it.

19

———

COLLEGE YEARS

Ashley
1991–1995

A poster in the women's restroom on the college campus read, "Do you feel safe in a relationship? If not, you may be experiencing domestic violence. Please contact us if you are in crisis and you need help." The contact number and location of the shelter were provided.

Only a week away from Thanksgiving break, Ashley gazed at her reflection in the bathroom mirror. Her one-sided dimple was deep and distinct. She resembled her mother.

Her thoughts drifted home to her parents' troubled relationship, which they denied. Initially even she had denied the truth, selfishly not wanting them to divorce. And later she'd conveniently dismissed it, blinded by her love for her father and her belief that he could not be an abuser—and that her mother was not meek enough to be a victim. It was not until high school that she'd gained the maturity to extricate herself from the denial, and yet she'd continued to accept her mother's explanations as valid.

As her parents drove her home for Thanksgiving, the car radio played a tribute to Freddie Mercury, who had died three days earlier.

"A young death, what a loss!" Ryan turned to look at her. "You remember the trip we took, Ash?"

Ashley nodded. "One of the best trips ever, Dad."

"One of the greatest rock stars of all time," ran the commentary, "with an incredible vocal range and flamboyant stage presence. Tormented soul, but with unapologetic individuality."

Ashley's mind drifted to "Bohemian Rhapsody" and how its haunting lyrics had accompanied her troubled runs. When misappropriation of the raised funds was mentioned on the radio, she tuned out. "Why don't they focus on the organizers' best efforts—you know they tried," she said, irritated.

After break, hesitant at first to relive the reality at home, she only signed up for one day of volunteering at the shelter. For orientation, she watched the mandatory slide show. The first slide defined *domestic violence* from the *Merriam-Webster* dictionary in its most basic form— "the inflicting of physical injury by one family or household member on another; also: a repeated or habitual pattern of such behavior."

A more elaborate definition from *Oxford* flashed next—"any incidence of violence, threatening behavior, or abuse (psychological, physical, sexual, financial, or emotional) between adults who are or have been intimate partners or family members, regardless of gender and sexuality."

The third slide read, "In the United States alone, more than ten million people experience domestic violence every year."

The next slide listed the reasons why DV continued—financial dependence, social stigma, fear of retribution, lack of confidence in the ability to fend for themselves, threat of harm to them or their children, desperate to maintain a family for their children, and love for their partner were listed as reasons why men or women continued to suffer relationships or returned to the same situation repeatedly.

Overwhelmed, she didn't pay attention to the slides that followed.

On her first day of volunteering, when she saw black eyes, broken noses, and bruised faces, in their vulnerability, she saw her resolve to help them strengthen. Many tangible roles for herself came into alignment—of a counselor, a helper, a donor.

Her sadness deepened when young children were pulled into the vicious cycle of hell and uncertainty. Many accompanied their mothers on repeat visits. She thanked her mother for keeping their family intact and her father for not being physically abusive. It could easily have been her tailing her mother into a shelter one day. She thanked her lucky stars for that.

When shelter employees wore purple ribbons in support of DV survivors, Ashley did too. At school, she hesitated to wear one, not wanting to discuss her interest in such work. She was looking for purpose and was slowly finding one. In the years that followed, embracing the spirit of giving, she bought Christmas presents for everyone at the shelter. Unable to gauge the number and diverse needs for various age groups, she gathered gifts over time, seizing sales. In addition, she sponsored the shelter's special holiday meal.

Working at the shelter gave Ashley access to terms she had never used with her mother. Ashley, older and mature, was ready to use the new terms in conversations with her. During winter break, she told her mother that verbal abuse was domestic violence.

"*Violence* is a strong word, Ash. We are in couple's therapy. With God's grace, we are making progress. You stop worrying" came the quick reply as she headed toward the door, projecting her intention to conclude the conversation.

Three months in, Ashley's eyes widened as she recognized Jamila. Jamila's attempts to conceal her split lips and bandaged jaw couldn't hide her familiar face. Ashley had seen her before—not here, but serving meals in her college cafeteria. Her two-year-old tagged along.

Ashley greeted her, and Jamila responded hesitantly. "I'm taking courses in medical assisting so I can find a better-paying job. I don't have another choice. I've had to take refuge here a few times. Once I have better income, I'll move out. But I'm having a hard time keeping up with classes and passing the exam."

Then she hesitantly asked, "You're a college student. Can you tutor me a bit so I can pass?"

Running had been Ashley's escape; education had to be Jamila's. Ashley understood this.

For five months, she worked with Jamila, sitting in a coffee shop in the late afternoons so Jamila's son could nap in the stroller while they worked and sipped on lattes and shared large chocolate chip cookies, which Ashley bought, mainly for Jamila.

"Don't forget to register for the exam, and I can help you pay for it," Ashley reminded Jamila during one session.

"I don't know when I will be able to pay you back," Jamila said.

"Don't worry about that now," Ashley responded.

Ashley was packing to vacate her dorm room for the summer when Jamila entered with a copy of her medical assistant's certification and a box of chocolates. "Congratulations, girl." Ashley drew her into a warm hug. "Very proud of you."

"I'm looking for a job and a better life for me and my son. Thank you for your help." Jamila wiped away tears. "And may God keep you from any type of harm in your life."

IN HER SOPHOMORE YEAR, Ashley moved into an off-campus apartment with Emily and Rose, cementing their bond. Ashley kept her friendships small and selective, like in high school, as if too many would risk exposing her family's secret. Her carefully constructed friendships led to assumptions on campus.

"Chip on her shoulder," one commented.

"Queen-bee attitude," another sneered.

"Looks, money, and privilege do that to you," a third said.

Emily and Rose did not harbor the same sentiments. However, they did notice that apart from good looks, money, and talent, Ashley had a vulnerability. They observed how her eyes shifted, reluctant to talk about her family. She even hesitated to share details about her work at the DV shelter. But Ashley ignored the comments and accepted her sensitivity. She successfully guarded her secret, and for this she was thankful.

ON SELF-ASSESSMENT OF her standing on her track team, she understood that as a runner, she did not have a professional future in track. She met runners who were clocking new records. In 1993, the loudest buzz in the track-and-field and basketball departments at UNC was the recruiting of Marion Jones, one of the country's fastest high school runners and standout basketball players at the time.

Ashley graduated in May of 1995 with a double major in marketing and sports physiology.

Unable to commit and trust, her tendency to overanalyze personality traits, especially that of men, paralyzed her. Fearful of volatile behavior, she scrutinized every detail of their demeanor, leaving her with only brief romantic interludes. Her vulnerability prevailed.

20

—————

ENDLESS PURSUIT

Robin
1990

"Do you want to know your birth parents' identities?" James asked, just after Robin's college application frenzy eased.

"You mean my fake parents, Pops?" she asked, her spoonful of spinach soup suspended in midair.

"Good with words, as always. Yes, that's who I'm talking about. I can help the process, maybe even hire a lawyer in their pursuit."

It was not the first time Robin had considered investigating her parentage. After she'd turned eighteen, she'd visited the local library and scoured hundreds of articles about adoption in the United States, especially the late 1960s and early 1970s, focusing on 1972, her birth year. Prior to 1973, in the so-called "Baby Scoop Era," when abortion was not legal in America, thousands of young girls were sent away to maternity homes to surrender their children in secret. No one was even aware that an adoption took place. Given the procedural hurdles and complex circumstances, after much introspection and agony, she'd decided not to pursue her adoption history—until James alluded to it.

"Are you sure, Pops? Given the statistics I reviewed, the chance of tracing them is slim. In the sixties and seventies, courts sealed original birth certificates and replaced them with amended documents with the adoptive parents' information, making it difficult to trace back. What could the courts do though? One hundred seventy-five thousand babies were given up for adoption every year at that time. That accounted for one baby out of every twenty to twenty-five births. A huge number!"

"Anyway, we don't have such big numbers since 1973, when abortion became legal. Access to birth control and decreasing social stigma was all a good thing," James pitched in, like he had been reviewing these numbers just like Robin had.

"You read my mind about my pretend parents. This is not the first time I thought you had a psychic moment about me, Pops," she said of their deep connection, an uncanny understanding of each other's moods, likes, and dislikes.

He smiled as a tiny droplet of a tear settled on his bottom right eyelid. It balanced on an eyelash, hesitated for a moment, and dropped just before Robin drew close to him and hugged him.

Robin adored her gentle father, who took great care of her mother. He was the glue that kept their family together. She tightened the embrace and quoted Shakespeare from *Othello*. "We know what we are, but know not what we may be." Then she added her own twist. "Do we even need to know what we were?" she questioned.

Then, without waiting for his reply, she continued, "If you insist on tracking them, I'm not going to say no."

"Let me share a few details I know about your birth," he said later that evening. "We were told that you were born at Davis Regional Medical Center, formerly Davis Community Hospital, in the city of Statesville, North Carolina, to a healthy teenager from a middle-income family. We adopted you as a five-day-old baby, which was arranged through our friends at a local church. A judge sealed the process quickly, with very few details exchanged between the families."

She nodded.

James sought legal counsel, and the attorney advised patience. "The cogs of the wheels turn slowly in such cases, especially when churches were involved in adoption processes before 1973. They were caught in the middle. They had good intentions and were trying to help families in the best way they knew how."

The impending search and its details did not help Robin. They dug further into her turmoil.

21

COLLEGE YEARS

Robin

1990–1994

"Pops, there is nothing more depressing than good advice. Don't worry. I will be scatheless," Robin reassured her father, as a freshman at the University of North Carolina at Charlotte. "I am looking for a home-away-from-home experience."

Pursuing a double major in literature and journalism, she'd made it her priority to join a sorority.

"Darling daughter, I've heard too many stories about partying and excess drinking at such places."

"The sorority gives me multiple instant sisters. I always wanted a sister, remember?" she reminded him.

She shrugged off his advice and joined one anyway. She needed to belong, to be anchored, to be connected. Sachiko was her closest sibling-like bond. She hoped to find a similar equation with her sorority sisters.

More books surrounded her. Her classes engaged her. The sisterhood treated her well, but restlessness had its way of rearing its head and manifesting in different ways. She made numerous plans that needed constant modification, as she was unable to keep them.

Robin hoped for an update from the lawyer each time she was summoned to her dorm's phone. There occasionally was, but often it was about how slow the process was, as access to records was limited. Davis Community Hospital closed in 1984 and moved to the new Davis Regional Medical Center. Between the courthouse, the hospital, and the church, records were unavailable, proof that the paper trail was sealed with the actual purpose of limiting access.

She tried to move on, but the desperation to discover versus the anxiety of a potential hit, and concern of its aftermath, clashed and resurfaced repeatedly, like weeds that refused to perish.

After many dead ends and mounting lawyer fees, months of searching ended with a story of a flooded church basement where the records were stored. Her roots would lie buried, submerged in the confines of a church basement, the story of her origin elusive. Sleepless nights followed muffled sobs, punctuated by gasps, so as not to disturb her roommate. She cherished her parents—all three belonged to one another, but her sense of abandonment deepened. At such times, her mind wandered toward Sachiko, wondering what she would do in this predicament.

Reading, her go-to activity, rooted her in the present. It reined in restlessness, while writing was troublesome, the hope of which was long gone. Meanwhile, drama club and editing drew her in deeper.

She buried herself in books in between parties and meetings. At any point, she was reading three books—she called three her magic number. "We can't keep up with one plot at a time. How do you keep track of three?" her roommates asked.

"I function better in chaos, don't you see?" she replied.

Strewn with clothes, shoes, empty boxes of food, and books perched on every possible surface, her dorm room was an example of it. When friends came over, she crammed them under her bed.

"My internal and external chaos are balanced—nothing wrong with that," she commented flippantly, knowing very well that everything was wrong with that.

When her unrest escalated, she called Sachiko, chatting with her for only a precious few minutes, as international calls were expensive.

Sachiko's soothing voice calmed her, transporting her back to her high school years.

"How I wish you were in college with me. We would have had a blast," Robin bemoaned.

Sachiko pacified her. "People think by living in worry, it will lessen the impact when a problem befalls them. And if it didn't happen, they were then just lucky. Mistakenly some assume that happy people are naive and gullible—don't be misled by that. Learn to live with happiness as a choice, Robin."

"As you say, Saint Sachiko," Robin joked, as most of the advice eluded her, except the last part about happiness. "Happiness, here I come," she announced into the receiver.

Then Robin devoted entire weekends to cleaning her clutter. She briefly considered replacing her bed with a foldable futon, which she couldn't hide her strewn things under. Cleaning put her into her own version of Zen. For a time, she slowed down and prioritized her chores. She completed her assignments, met her advisers, and took directions from them regarding future classes.

She even called her parents, patiently inquiring about them, sharing select details about her life on campus. If her parents wanted to know more, they knew better than to ask, as any interest shown immediately elicited exasperation. So they just listened.

In Robin and Sachiko's friendship, their teenage promise held. Sachiko wrote to Robin periodically, but Robin replied only rarely. Placing more value on verbal conversation than the written word, Robin sent rare postcards with scribbled messages.

Sachiko joked about it once in her letter. "But you are the writer!"

"Yep, a wannabe writer," Robin wrote back. "I read a lot, remember almost everything, but reading and writing are two different things. Writing has not come to me, and maybe never will. I have grappled with that uncertainty all my life. It's like my own shadow telling me I am a fake." Her longest reply to date.

Robin envied the simplicity of thought Sachiko's letters conveyed. Robin imagined Sachiko's life to be simple and uncomplicated.

After a few weeks of calm, uncertainty, restlessness, and chaos seeped back into her life like water through a crack.

Apart from books, Robin found solace in people and their company. They milled around her like flies to honey, streaming in and out of her room. Her talent for storytelling and entertaining was natural but was also a trait learned from her father. She had numerous connections with no depth, and she labeled them *friendships*, though they didn't as much qualify as acquaintances. A few exploited this weakness, some mistaking it for flirting. Such friendships were becoming her weakness.

When a sorority party extended late into the night, Robin felt her control slipping after two drinks. A handsome senior she had been friends with had downed many more drinks than two. Chatting, giggling, and kissing were entertaining until certain movements and positions were assumed. She winced at the look of a serious pursuit on his attractive face. But only when she felt his weight, pelvis on pelvis, and all four of their extremities were bared and entangled, did she sense the gravity. When cues to stop went unacknowledged, she attempted to extricate herself from under him. As she tussled with him, she reached for an empty beer bottle and brought it down to get his attention. Unfortunately, it shattered on impact with his bony elbow, cutting a substantial gash on his upper arm. Blood gushed. She shrieked and he screamed. Then all hell broke loose.

Alarm spread. Her sorority sisters congregated around her. "What should we do now?" they asked.

"This doesn't help my detachment from attachment" was all she said, tugging her clothes into place, the chaos not lost on her.

"Apply pressure," said a premed student.

"Should we call 911?" another asked.

"I can drive him to a hospital faster. I am sober," a third said.

At registration in the emergency department, the cut was explained as a slip and fall injury.

A victim, and feeling violated, Robin blamed herself. "Was it my fault? Should I have resisted earlier or spoken up sooner?" None of her sorority sisters had an answer. It was, unfortunately, her introduction to physical intimacy with the opposite sex, and with that, what little hope she had for a future romantic relationship disintegrated.

She shuddered at the thought that her reckless behavior could have led to a pregnancy. Quite unexpectedly, she wondered if she was a discarded baby of rape or even incest. This dark possibility haunted her more than the violation.

22

FOR SHOES

Ashley
1995–1997

Ashley clicked through sales figures when her manager stepped into her cubicle.

"Got a minute?" he asked, grinning. "You like shoes, right? You walk like you know them."

She knew her shoes and had worn over two hundred pairs of running shoes. She turned. "Why do you ask?"

He laughed. "Marketing wants a real athlete to represent our new line. You ran track at a collegiate level, didn't you?"

Ashley blinked. "I did. Why?"

"We need someone who can wear them like she means it. You've got the looks—and the résumé."

She folded her arms. "So I'm a walking ad?"

"More like a running one," he said. "Think photo shoots, interviews, travel. Are you in?"

She smiled. "I could be."

Ashley had been hired as an assistant sales associate at a national sports marketing company. Her job required travel with her manager to attend sporting events and trade shows with a goal of increasing sales of sports equipment to high school and college gymnasiums. Now her manager was asking her to step into an additional role, a glamorous one, and she was game.

During the photo shoot, orchestrated by a consulting advertising agency, she followed their instructions. "Pull your hair into a ponytail, then turn and look into the camera." She did as told. Click went the camera, and the snap was approved.

"Let's get your hair braided, and then you run into the sunset."

She ran on outdoor tracks and along picturesque, rugged trails, in athletic shorts, skirts, and leggings, all highlighting the shoes as much as her legs.

It helped that Ashley liked the shoe brand, so it translated to her becoming an effective spokesperson for them.

"I told you she got your looks," Ryan said to Kelly, both proud to see their daughter in sports magazines, on banners at sports meets, and in local television ads.

When students met Ashley, they were enamored by her minor celebrity status. To engage prospective buyers, she wove stories around her high school and college running days, as storytelling was her mastered personal style to promote the product successfully. In addition, her full-bodied voice, like her father's, resonated with listeners.

She loved her work. And the travel and modeling were a bonus. Work felt like one big holiday. Life felt like it was where it should be, but she could not say the same for her mother.

Emily called to share that the men's marathon Olympic trials for the upcoming 1996 Summer Olympics were being held in Charlotte on February 17. The three friends planned to meet.

Emily, now married, lived in New York City. An athletic director at a private school for girls, her favorite part of the job was walking into the school gymnasium when it was filled with giggling teenagers, reminding her of her own youth. Her loud personality came in handy for controlling distracted teens.

Rose, a self-employed graphic designer and still single, fiercely guarded her privacy and independence.

No one had ever been an overnight guest at the Spadys', for a reason, their well-constructed plan was a success for many years. She prayed that her father would be on his best behavior when her friends were hosted, and luckily, he was.

Watching a new generation of marathoners compete, Ashley and her friends happily relived their college running days.

Later that summer, they celebrated when Michael Johnson broke world records in two-hundred-meter and four-hundred-meter track events at the Atlanta Olympics, in his golden Nike shoes and in his signature upright posture.

"How I wish I had my own pair of such golden shoes," Ashley lamented.

For work, at a high school running meet, she casually mentioned to the participants that she had run on six of the seven continents.

One runner, playfully jostling another runner while listening, asked, "I bet that leaves Antarctica for you. So when is that run planned for?"

"You must have run like Forrest Gump!" another runner quipped with a grin.

The kids erupted into laughter. "Did it give you hope?" the runner added, playfully referencing the iconic film.

The group's hearty chuckles filled the air.

The question caught her off guard. She forced a smile. "I don't know about channeling Forrest Gump, but I liked it, so I kept running."

Later, that question threw her into a contemplative silence. Her mind drifted to the turmoil that had sparked her journey, an escape from a demonly form of her father. The pain in her had carried her to distances she had never known she could cover, at speeds she had never known she could muster.

She remembered the opening lines of "Bohemian Rhapsody." She understood the singer's pain even better as an adult.

She also remembered running lockstep with her father—a loving father always and a devoted husband mostly—5Ks with him on six different continents. Vacations were not planned for runs—they just happened to run for fun while they were there.

James did not allow her to run on her own. "For your safety on a foreign land, I have to run with you" was his stance.

He struggled to keep pace.

"Tennis-court sprinting isn't the same as real running, Dad," she teased.

Panting, he pulled her close. "Father of a daughter is a lucky man," a sentiment he loved sharing.

Running gave her a release, and more. It was her savior. The pain that once weighed her down later fueled her forward. It brought her rhythm and happiness. The rush of endorphins was undeniable: unadulterated joy from her body in flight, lighter with each stride, and mind untethered, more liberated with every step.

23

———————

A CAT AND A FRIEND

Anita

At work, it was only when Anita scrubbed the same floor a million times, until it sparkled and her arms and back ached, that she could suppress ruminations about her painful past. The physical pain superseded her emotional ache. Creating physical pain became a habit, firmly ingrained. So, in all the years, always on the move, she refused to sit idle.

She was perceptive to residents' stories and sorrows. Her dedication was noticed as true concern, as she often stayed past her scheduled work time to listen to them. Some she pampered, while some she cajoled, treating them like children, forgetting that she herself was still a child. Residents were drawn to her, giving her excellent reviews and, from a handful of them, generous Christmas presents.

She refrained from disclosing her own pain to anyone, as talking about it made it freshly real. Throughout her pregnancy, words of sympathy had burned her more than advice did. Sympathy scalded her. Advice would maybe have supported her.

Initially, not used to living alone, the familiarity of her parents' old furniture gave her a sense of security, and she saw no reason to lose it. Except for a new mattress to replace her sagging old childhood mattress, nothing else was replaced. The mismatched table and chairs reflected her situation and reminded her of the contrast between her life and the lives of others.

She liked the quiet inside the studio, but the noise outside engaged her. The gentle hum of the cars, the rare honking, and dogs barking reassured her that the world outside her studio was not a lonely place.

AFTER A BUSY DAY AT WORK, she came home exhausted, her muscles protesting the abuse. It was as if the contractile apparatus of her muscle fibers, the myofibrils, went on strike, refusing to relax, throwing her muscles into a spasm, her back and calf muscles protesting the most.

The aching lulled her into sleep. Her soft childhood comforter wrapped her stiff muscles, like bandages on wounds. She cuddled it, healing, and as the clock struck midnight, her muscles recovered and relaxed, dragging her into deeper slumber. She woke up ready to repeat this physical cycle. No dreams, no introspection—a blank mind was what she had.

Anita's condominium was where comfort was, where pajamas hung, a toothbrush lay, and bedside slippers waited. Her place of work, St. Bona, was also such a place for her, without those things. There was comfort in the physical work and in her calling to help others.

She shuttled between the comfort of her condominium and her place of work with an unacknowledged abyss in between but managed her balance successfully, relying on the comfort of familiarity.

Anita lived alone for years, but later had a companion in a cat, a stray cat that she adopted. Its body was peculiarly divided in color, snowy white on one side and metallic gray on the other. She cleverly positioned herself, signaling her needs, like a skilled signer, facing Anita with her snowy side as a signal for food, and her gray side camouflaged with shadows and dark corners when she did not want to be bothered. The cat suited Anita perfectly because they were both conveniently detached from each other.

A soft meow greeted Anita when she entered her apartment, as a reminder that Anita was not alone. Anita appreciated that welcome.

Other than that interaction, they both selfishly protected their privacy and quiet, knowing the other was there but making no attempts at bonding. The only difference between them was that Anita was emotionally guarded, but the cat was absolutely emotionally honest, like Ernest Hemingway said all cats were.

Leary of attachment, Anita did not name her feline companion. A stray cat could always stray again.

At work, anonymity was comforting. Anita's initial instinct to avoid residents' visiting grandchildren stemmed from deep-seated discomfort with that interaction. It plunged her into a chasm of worthlessness. Likewise, taking refuge behind a pillar to hide from her high school adviser, Mrs. Detris, had stemmed from shame.

It took years for the weight of those feelings to lift. As her pain eased, she eagerly scanned for her daughter among the adorable little girls who visited the facility, her heart skipping a beat at the hope of spotting her. She longed for one of them to be hers. Her daughter would have turned four. One glance at a child's face and she'd imagine her with Sebastian's handsome features. Though she had no picture of him, her memory of him remained vivid yet.

When a child smiled at her, a rare tingling spread in her, and in a special way, it tickled her from within. She wanted to feel their soft skin and hold their tender bodies, but couldn't.

Later at night, she'd imagine herself among them. Maybe as a teacher, whose suggestion for a career was not received well by her papa a decade ago. She still remembered. As a nanny now? A nurse at a children's clinic? What would Papa think? She was trying to rediscover purpose among children, without success. But in the morning, she conveniently discarded these imagined roles and followed the status quo.

No one ever visited her studio, but she kept all surfaces shining and every corner dusted. On Saturdays, she did not rest until her chores were complete, including her meal prep for the week.

On Sundays, her body intuitively refused to follow the routine. Waking up late, already famished, she stopped at her favorite café, as if for an appointment, just before families trickled in for Sunday brunch. She was surprised at her own enormous appetite, which surfaced regularly, like a weekly date. Ordering three entrees from the menu, she ate them all, wondering what the waiter thought of her.

"I am storing fuel for the week," she joked with one waiter as she paid.

The July she turned twenty-one, she ordered her first beer but did not care for the taste, making it her last. She recognized the new café manager as someone from her grade in high school. Medium build with prominent scoliosis, his torso had a permanent right-sided tilt. With cropped hair, bright eyes, and light skin with an unusual shine, he shuffled rather than walked. Anita recognized his shuffle more than his face. She thought their recognition to be mutual, but still both failed to acknowledge their familiarity. Only after her third visit to the café did a faint knowing smile surface on his lips, and she reciprocated.

"Paul Andrati," he said.

"Anita Kumar," she said.

Perfunctory hellos followed.

The following Sunday, they chatted casually. Shy, he needed gentle prodding to begin, but once he started, he did not know how or when to stop. Anita guessed him to be a loner too. After a few conversations at the café, they decided to meet for an early dinner at a nearby Italian diner.

He had unexpressed thoughts and no audience to share with, and Anita did not mind being his audience. His harmless talk was a distraction, and she realized that under his shy, quiet shell, he was well-informed and opinionated. Two misfits who never quite found their place in high school and beyond finally fit in with each other.

They met for dinner a few more times, and soon it became a ritual that occurred with the regularity of an ardent Christian attending church. He reported on the day's news, but their high school days were never referenced. He talked about the Monica Lewinsky scandal without the sleazy details. Matthew Shepard's murder pained him. "I am against discrimination of any sort," he announced.

They enjoyed their weekly dinners and conversations and went home to be by themselves. This arrangement suited them both well. If they knew where the other lived, they did not discuss it. Neither did they talk about their living arrangements. If he was surprised at how much she ate for brunch, he was not surprised at how little she consumed for dinner.

Anita wondered if her history was a mystery to him. If he knew anything about her story from high school, he did not divulge. "This strategic ambiguity suits me," she told herself, using a new term that had caught her attention when watching television.

"I am enrolled in management classes at the community college," he told her once. "My plan is to own a chain of cafés one day. Providing employment for people, that is what drives me. My back hurts and my one foot lags, but I don't pay much attention to these things. I don't see them as setbacks. Just God's way of reminding me that I am human and am supposed to have obstacles."

Once, as she sat at their usual table waiting for him, she saw him shuffling across the street in a hurry. She gasped as a rushing car sped by him. She jumped to her feet, ready to sprint to his aid, when he emerged from behind the passing car unscathed. What she felt that day was a new feeling—fear of losing him. He was becoming a habit, in a good way. Inspiring even.

Their body language spelled a disinterest in romantic hookups. No flirtatious smiles or looks. No suggestive comments. Dressing plain and simple, avoiding salacious gossip, they became confidants, albeit sharing with discretion. They solicited each other for opinions and counsel when needed, sharing only their minor challenges, disappointments, and successes, minimizing them. They sympathized with each other when needed but never shared too many personal details. And that was all it was. Only friendship.

24

FOR EDITING

Robin

1995–2000

"Pops, my dream job is to become an editor-in-chief one day," she told him on the eve of her new journey.

James's response was encouraging and understated. "Not a bad goal to have, but make sure you do what you're expected to do as an editorial assistant, if not more. Make yourself heard. Make yourself known."

She was hired by Algonquin Books in Chapel Hill. Established in 1983, a young nine-year-old business, they focused on publishing literary fiction, short story collections, essays, memoirs, and nonfiction works. A time of significant change for publishing, emerging nontraditional publishers' and authors' reach of the internet was creating stiff competition for traditional publishers. Self-publishing, being explored as a novel model, was also disturbing the status quo.

"Pops, I never got to read the oldest extant printed book, the Buddhist text *The Diamond Sutra*. It dates to 868 CE from time of the Tang dynasty. Nor have I read *The Whole Book of Psalms*, the first book printed in the USA in 1638. I should have at least read that one. How come I didn't?" she whined.

"You can do that now and tell us what you think of it," James suggested.

Mass media communications through the World Wide Web expanded people's access to information and reading materials. Publishing processes were transitioning from traditional manual methods to digital production. A sudden rise in popularity of nonfiction and young adult literature was transformative too.

Digital technology worked in Robin's favor. Her transition from editing school plays to editing as an editorial assistant felt like an extension of what she'd done in college for fun. Part of a team that reviewed submissions, assessed content, verified sources, and fact-checked, she also copyedited, proofread, and helped review final drafts for errors and consistency.

"My goal seems daunting, Pops," she complained once. "I have no graduate degree and no Ivy League education."

"Your mnemonic memory and your confidence, darling daughter, are your biggest assets," James reassured.

With that encouragement, her goal set with confidence, paired with humility, she set out to work.

Her editor, also her mentor, analyzed plot, structure, and language of submitted works, while she studied his style. She took a manuscript's lengthy journey as her own personal journey and followed its formatting, illustrating, sales, publicity, and marketing, the process taking many months.

A lifetime steeped in books, her keen sense of language, and her understanding of genres made her an able assistant. Turning over her work at a phenomenal pace, she astonished the team by recalling entire paragraphs and quoting them verbatim. This facilitated cross-referencing works the entire team was reviewing. Student interns were in awe of her ability, and when her colleagues heaped praises, she brushed them off.

Widespread use of computers and their reach were still in their infancy, and plagiarism often slipped through. One of the elements of editing was validating an author's work as authentic, and twice Robin alerted her editor to her concern for complete authenticity of a reviewed work.

Her abilities did not go unnoticed. Within a year of starting at the press, she was promoted to assistant editor, and in her new role, she worked to build relationships with authors, agents, and industry professionals by attending literary events and conferences.

During a visit home, Robin found her mother in a mild cycle of depression. Lily was in the early days of the newly introduced category of antidepressant medicine Zoloft, which was touted to work in a novel way, with fewer side effects. It was yet to be calibrated to the right dose for her. Robin, at thirteen, had seen her mother further subdued and somnolent for days after electroshock therapy. It did not produce the desired benefit, and Robin was thankful that her mother never had to endure it again.

When her parents visited her in Raleigh for Sunday brunches, it gave Lily a chance to venture out for sun and scenery on the forty-minute drive. In time, she was thriving, as her new medicine was finally titrated to the right dose.

"Now don't look under the couch—you might find a dead bat!" Robin cautioned her parents as they stepped into her apartment.

Robin was captivated by her father's gentle demeanor. He was very much comfortable in his skin, but she was still not in hers. "You are my halcyon," she told him.

"What does that mean? That I'm your light?" he asked.

"Not halogen, Pops. It means you bring me peace."

Having seen her mother suffer multiple episodes of depression, Robin knew exactly what she did not want to endure in her own life. Emotional conflict was one reason for depression. And the only way Robin knew how to stop her own internal conflict was by staying busy, and that she did successfully.

Her imaginary world in books was her rescuer, and work kept her occupied, but she was also fueled by a desire for companionship and emotional intimacy. To shake away the feeling of abandonment that plagued her, she maintained an infectious party spirit.

Like in college, she organized events and gatherings meticulously, she presumed. However, she managed to miss a few details, like inviting key people to certain events and planning another event to appease them. The cycle repeated. There were movie nights and themed parties that morphed into wild dance bashes. Her apartment was always hosting.

Her bright clothes added to her energy and magnetic personality, but she struggled with commitment and often found herself in a cycle of starting and ending relationships.

She interacted with writers whose work her publishing company represented. On business trips she mingled with talented aspiring writers and publishing executives, fishing for new talent to reel in the next bestseller. She found the prospect of meeting and dating new and unknown men exciting.

Numerous dates and casual encounters followed, but her thrill was dominated by the emotion of lust, of being sought, of being wanted. She dictated the terms and controlled the narrative. Her date's marital status was of no bearing. They were mostly middle-aged men. She did not feel responsible for the direction of their moral compass. However, her guilt and self-loathing came the next morning. They were but fleeting, until the cycle repeated.

The flirting and the early courtship were most exciting. Many were hookups that lasted only as long as the conference was in session. Rarely did she continue long-distance relationships, and when she did, she found erotic the longing for a planned reunion.

A few of her dating experiences were lavish. One publishing executive showered her with expensive gifts, while another arranged sleek limousines for her to travel in. The flavor of dating young, aspiring writers was sweet and short-lived, as she found their belief in pure intentions and magic of everlasting love burdensome.

When she sensed a relationship getting too personal, it became an entanglement she did not desire. With that, the end of the relationship neared.

25

FOR LOVE

Ashley
1995–2000

Ashley wiped her brow with Kleenex. She'd run the distance from her apartment to her favorite bakery, a narrow storefront on a busy street. Fresh Ezekiel bread was stacked among many other enticing baked goods. She picked up half a loaf, felt the warmth against her sweaty palms. Behind her in the checkout line was Joseph, Rose's boyfriend.

"Hello, Ashley. Early morning run?" He stepped closer to her. "Meet Harry, my colleague." He pointed toward a tall, athletic figure dressed in weekend casuals. "He lives within walking distance from here."

"Hi there." Harry joined the line, holding a box of oatmeal cookies and a smaller box with a single chocolate cupcake with glittery yellow icing.

"Beautiful cupcake." She eyed the contents of the boxes. "I am sure it tastes way better than my Ezekiel bread."

Her auburn hair was stuck to her wet top. Dried salt lines were forming around her underarms.

"It matters that the owner of the bread is beautiful, doesn't it?" His brown eyes sparkled, and his full head of blond hair shone.

Ashley blushed. It was attraction at first sight for both. Ashley crossed paths with Harry again, their casual meetings blurring between chance and intention.

During one encounter, she discovered that athleticism was not the reason for his athletic look.

"I don't exercise," he said.

She found it to be true.

He was enchanted by her voice. "Evenly paced and expressive."

"Like a gentle breeze on a sunny day," he said another time, exaggerating, cozying up with her as she shoved him away.

Ashley was drawn by the promise of love but was leery of trusting. "How do you know how they will turn out to be?" she exclaimed to Rose. "Who knows if they are who they appear to be? They may have anger issues lurking!"

Rose looked at her skeptically. "Is this about Harry? Did you see any signs? I can inquire with Joseph if you'd like," she said, not too enthused about getting involved.

Despite reservations, Ashley made plans to meet Harry periodically and then often.

Harry worked on a computer mostly, whereas Ashley was about traveling, meeting people.

"I ease into a place and make it my home. I don't see the need to travel," he told her, comfortable with his stance.

After days of travel, Ashley loved spending time with him. For Harry, life was less about drama, more about living. He wasn't rushed or flustered. He often repeated the Silicon Valley mantra, "To be done is better than perfect."

His style was effortlessly casual, with clothes thrown together without much thought. His way of life relaxed her. Yet one thing stood out: his impeccably groomed hair. Not a strand out of place. He fussed, checking his reflection before leaving home, ensuring his locks were perfectly coiffed. Ashley found this detail amusing.

Ashley loved calling out "Hairy Harry, are you ready?" before they went out. Once, she hid his hairbrushes and watched him go berserk.

Enamored by her playfulness, he feigned exasperation. "How childish!" He pinched her cheeks until they turned red.

Following the principle that opposites attract, her speed to his calmness, her travel to his work from home, and his casual dressing to her diligence made it difficult to avoid the magnetism.

Ashley worried that this seemingly nice, easygoing gentleman had hidden flaws—hidden from the world were flaws in otherwise perfect men, like her father.

They cooked together. In Harry, Ashley found someone who partnered well with her schedule and regimented diet. The only outlier was desserts. Harry couldn't resist anything sweet—their first encounter with oatmeal cookies and the cupcake in his hands was proof enough. While he grazed on regular food, salad and dessert were the dishes he devoured.

"My way of balancing good with the bad," he explained. Knowing that she seldom ordered dessert, he made sure to leave the last bites of his dessert for her.

That gesture was romantic, but for Ashley, it was a declaration of a deeper connection.

As the new millennium dawned, Ashley was experiencing something new. It was love, while Harry had already fallen for her. She called him "My Old Handsome Hunk Harry." The first time she called him that, he broke out into a wide, sideways grin. And then she said, "How about H3O for short, in reverse?" And she split into laughter at her own ingenuity. "H3O, you are my elixir!"

He shrugged. "Whatever you wish, Ash, my angel."

Harry owned a loft, which Ashley ran up, thumping her feet every step, every time. Hearing the thumping, Harry would step out to give her a big hug at the top of the stairs as he said, "Ash, I have been waiting for you all day," even if he hadn't. She loved the welcome.

Through casual walks in the streets of Raleigh in summer, they functioned as a couple. Misty mornings of fall deepened their passion. On chilly wintry days, they held hands and nuzzled under throws and blankets.

They scouted for obscure cafés and hidden restaurants as they discovered downtown Raleigh together. He grew up not too far from downtown and called himself a proud local. His parents had recently found comfort in the bright sun and hot summers of Florida. Harry was connected to the downtown vibe, and Ashley was on her way to embracing it.

He drove her to the same battered women's center she had volunteered at in college; his commitment to her steady, her work ethic solid. Their schedules, habits, and comforts were falling into place.

"If this is how it feels to have a soul mate, then I must have found mine. Our romance is straight out of a movie," Ashley told Rose. "Two bodies, one heart, actually."

"What is the problem then?" Rose asked.

Ashley desperately wanted a life with Harry—if only someone could reassure her that his consistent, temperate attitude and behavior were real and permanent. After two years, she still hesitated to call him her boyfriend, twenty-four long months not enough for personality and character authentication. Her parents loved him, and Rose and Joseph were reassuring of him.

"My baby sister died at five from leukemia, Ash. Living simply and loving wholly is the only way I know to live," Harry said, trying to ease her anxiety.

"I need outside counsel and a guarantee, but who and how?" Ashley lamented to her mother.

"There is burden in love, Ash. To love is to accept that burden. Don't be afraid." Kelly reassured her of the power of trust and love.

Ashley was uncertain of the burden in love but was certain of one thing—her commitment required more time, but if only she knew that time was running out.

26

PROPOSAL THAT WASN'T

Ashley
July 2001

"Just the two of us," Harry said.

When he picked her up in a navy jacket and smart dress shoes, Ashley's eyes widened. "You look like a GQ model, or even Brad Pitt!" she gushed, her eyes flirtatious. "My H3O! Let me make myself look cute too."

She changed into her favorite black velvet pantsuit, pairing it with three-inch black stilettos. With her hair in a low knot, she complemented him.

As the maître d' seated them at their reserved table, an arrangement of roses caught her attention. In the flickering pale-yellow light of an ornate candle, they glowed deep red, matching the wine in a bottle resting tilted in a bucket of ice. An elaborately decorated cake topped with the numbers 2 and 9 sat on a cake stand in the middle of the table.

Over a meal of buttered lobster and grilled vegetables, Ashley wondered if all the arrangements were a bit too fanciful for Harry's taste. When he reached into his jacket, she broke into a sweat, imagining a proposal in motion. Excited and nervous at the same time, she patted the beads of sweat sprouting on her upper lip, wondering if it was too soon. She wasn't sure what her response would be. For over two years, she had searched for signs of volatility in his behavior and had found none. She had studied his face for clues of rage and expressions of anger and analyzed every gaze and move, but she'd only come across his permanent state of calm. If it was a facade, it was a solid one.

But he only retrieved his phone. To her dismay, instead of relief, she felt disappointment, which lingered all evening, like the bitter aftertaste of a sugar substitute that refused to wash away.

As if the phone reminded him, he said, "Ash, why don't you move in with me? I love having you around, and it would be easier for both of us. I checked with your landlord, and your lease is up in six months."

"Aww, you sure did your legwork," she responded, with forced cheerfulness, desperate not to wear her true feelings on her face.

"I know your apartment is overflowing with succulents," Harry remarked. "Guess we'll have our work cut out for us, relocating your little green friends."

"Well, those are the only kind of plants that survive while I travel. Moreover, I like how succulents take their time to grow. Slow and steady —that is what my dad used to say—wins the race. And I think they are a great reminder of that. Simple, resilient, and beautiful, kind of like how you are, is it?" she questioned coyly.

He raised his eyebrows. "Are you sure?"

She cut the cake, and he fed her a spoonful. The candlelight deepened the brown of his eyes. In that moment, she felt securely moored in the same boat with him and felt the beginnings of their beautiful life together taking shape.

"August eight is Happiness Happening Day. Make happiness happen," Harry wished her on the phone, three weeks later.

She was packing for a business trip to Sedona. "I'm planning to. What more happiness can there be than running the Gateway Trail and the Granite Mountain Trail? They're lined with giant saguaro and barrel cacti. I never fail to marvel at them. Don't worry—I'll be thinking of you when I see them." She blew a kiss into the receiver.

"I hope you do," he said. "Stay safe."

When her alarm went off at 4:30 a.m. the next day, she rolled around in the hotel bed, unable to slide out. Sluggish and tired, she blamed jet lag and constant travel. The air in the hotel room felt dry. Lying in bed, staring at the ceiling as the air-conditioner unit rumbled on, she blamed the higher altitude and the rarified oxygen. The feeling persisted, and she missed her morning run two days in a row, a rarity.

The next day, she managed a light jog to one of the four zones of vortices, areas purported to give positive energy. Centuries-old junipers, their trunks twisted, their long roots burrowing deep, seeking water and resisting infection, stood strong, believed to be proof of the energy. Interspersed were the mesquite and the saguaros, existing symbiotically.

Finding a flat surface of sandstone to sit on, she watched the sunset beyond the hundreds of junipers that lay ahead. The red rocks brightened in the setting sun, while the gentle hum of the ancient earth passed through her. She returned to her room energized, hoping to bring Harry with her the next time she visited.

Traveling to Asheville with Emily and Rose in early fall, celebrating all three of them turning thirty, remained on the cards, despite Ashley's weariness. She labored to get to Mount Mitchell, the highest point in the Blue Ridge Mountains, and Mount Pisgah, in the Pisgah National Park, taking breaks and stretching.

They celebrated at a noisy corner restaurant on Main Street that served their favorite kind of crepes. They raised their glasses, singing their personal song loudly, to the amazement of the other guests.

"Emily, Ashley, and Rose
Look at them pose
Crepe girls they are
Happy and loud as always they are."

They burst into girlish laughter.

"On this happy occasion, I want to make an announcement," Ashley said. "I've decided to move in with Harry. And that calls for another drink."

They posed for pictures, making faces and teasing one another about whose face looked the weirdest. On other days, they ate take-out food in their hotel room. Through incessant teenage-like giggles, they caught up with one another.

But Ashley's exhaustion lingered.

That night as she analyzed her situation, she wondered if she'd skipped her period. She was fastidious with contraception and was surprised that the thought even came to her. An elite athlete with minimum body fat, her menstrual cycles were random at best. For that reason, she was not in the habit of tracking them. Now she worried that she'd missed a few pills. Distressed, she could not sleep. She stared into the dark as Emily lay by her side, snoring. Frozen in place from foreboding, she didn't move all night.

She wanted to go home.

27

PANIC

Robin

2000

"Let me help you, ma'am." The driver, in a crisp white uniform, took Robin's bag and loaded it in the sleek black limousine waiting for her at the arrival terminal.

She slid onto the soft leather seat. The windows were tinted, and a bottle of champagne rested in the ice bucket. On her way for a rendezvous with a publishing executive, she stretched her legs and looked around.

She reclined her head and let the ambience soak in. Soothing music played, but she was anything but soothed. Her face flushed. Soon her heart raced. Her fingers turned cold, and she began hyperventilating.

A familiar cramp took hold deep in her pelvis, one associated with the passing of a clot. There was wetness. Menses out of sync, she wasn't prepared. Anxious and claustrophobic, when just a minute before she'd thought the interior was too expansive, she forced her thoughts toward Sachiko. Memories of her happy times and conversations with Sachiko calmed her, but it wasn't working. Perhaps the trick's influence was abating. She needed to ignore the reasons that held her back from traveling to Japan, and she urgently needed to reconnect with Sachiko in person.

In the moment, she needed fresh air but could not operate the windows. Helpless, she rapped sharply on the partition to get the driver's attention. She requested that the windows be rolled down, hoping the fresh air would magically blow away her anxiety.

"Take me to the nearest restaurant or hotel," she blurted.

Her panic subsided as she entered the restroom. She inserted a quarter in the slot and retrieved a tampon, and for another quarter picked up a sanitary pad.

She cleaned up, inserted, and padded herself. "Whew! That much for women and their periods."

Four weeks later, she prepared for another panic attack, but it never came.

Her second panic attack had no connection to a limo ride or her menses. What unnerved her was that it happened on a seemingly normal day. Unfortunately, her panic episodes sprouted like pimples, at the most inopportune time, unexpectedly, their presence irrelevant and painful.

She talked to Sachiko, a voice of sanity in Robin's insane life.

"You owe me a visit. You promised," Sachiko said, taking Robin back to her promise from many years ago.

"Finally, that time has come, my Sylph!" Robin replied.

While making plans for her first overseas trip, on the eve of the millennium's first Thanksgiving, Robin was eager to get home.

To beat the traffic was her intention, but with many deadlines looming at work, it was not to be. Throughout the stop-and-go drive, her thoughts mulled over a manuscript submitted by a young writer who was just out of his teens. Her team's consensus was that the work was different, alluring, and she thought the same as well. She wondered about the potential of his young voice in the literary landscape.

As she came out of the consideration, she missed her exit, as she could not read the signs clearly. She took the next exit and made it home in time for supper. She remembered her occasional difficulty with visual clarity and dryness. Chalking this up to extended screen time, she wasn't concerned.

The next morning, Lily was unusually energetic, her usual modus operandi for Thanksgiving. Cooling temperatures and festive atmospheres buoyed her moods. Thanksgiving was a rare time when she cooked up a feast and invited her extended family. She playfully pushed James out of the kitchen, claiming her stake of the area. Recipes and ingredients for buttery mashed potatoes, green bean casserole, cranberry sauce, and stuffing were laid out. The turkey was prepped and ready to be loaded into the oven.

"I need people and I have them. Aren't I lucky?" she hummed unevenly.

"Perfect song for the day, Moms," Robin said.

Most dishes were ready but needed final touches, which James blessed them with. While everyone sat down, grateful for the food and family, their hands joined in a circle, Robin knew how lucky she was for being placed in the Zymanski family. But in the next second, her heart fluttered, and the eggnog backed up in her mouth. Her breath shallowed. Avoiding eye contact, she locked herself in the bathroom. Cold water on her face eased the discomfort.

The following week, she saw Dr. Jones, her gynecologist since Robin's dreaded first pelvic exam. The doctor cautioned about sexually transmitted infections with professionalism, aware of new boyfriends in Robin's dating life.

"Any questions?" Dr. Jones asked, handing Robin a prescription for contraceptive pills.

Robin mentioned her dry eyes and vision issues, but not her panic attacks. She blindly believed only Sachiko could help her in that realm.

"See an ophthalmologist. If you can't get in with one, see an optometrist," Dr. Jones suggested.

Three months later, Robin saw an elderly, balding optometrist in his small office, which had the vibe of someone's private home, not a place of business, as it was once a residential building that was converted into commercial space. "You are near-sighted." He scribbled numbers on a script pad and handed it to her. Out of the seventy or so frames displayed, she chose dark, wide-rimmed frames that sat well on her button-like nose. She turned right and then left in front of a mirror, studying her profile. One week later, her glasses were ready to accompany her.

"Japan, hither I come," she said, trying them on.

28

ONE UNSEEN ROCK

Robin
March–April 2001

"Can't wait to see the cherry blossoms" was the recurrent chatter on Robin's flight. She hoped her trip was for something more profound than that. Filled with mostly first-time visitors to Japan, her flight landed at Narita International Airport in Tokyo on a Friday morning in late March, after flying for more than twenty-four hours on multiple Japan Airlines flight connections from New York through San Francisco and Honolulu.

The trip was Robin's first real international sojourn, if traveling to Mexico and the Caribbean were not included. While the prospect of traveling had stirred genuine excitement, she didn't let the looming threat of panic attacks while in transit interfere with her plans. Determined to keep her promise to Sachiko, she had calibrated her emotions well, and her finances too, as the strong American dollar gave her spending strength against the Japanese yen.

The ten-day trip had been planned high on hopes to contain her panic attacks, find peace, and learn the basics of Zen meditation. She hoped to find the calm that she had found in her earlier association with the Katzu family. Zen meditation, she had read, was a Buddhist practice that involved thinking about not thinking. It advocated sitting upright and focusing on breathing, especially the movement within the belly, and finding inner peace through mental and spiritual practices. She understood the words and the physical posturing but not the essence.

"You look the same," Sachiko said, hugging her.

"Ten years is a long time not to change." Robin laughed, feeling awkward. There had been a connection over the phone despite the distance, but in person, there was inhibition, a disconnect. Something about meeting in person after a decade.

"Yet my Sylph still looks distinctly sylph!" Robin complimented Sachiko's slender figure.

They walked through the modern airport to take the Shinkansen to Sachiko's house. Robin couldn't see the city, only an occasional train station, as the bullet train whipped past the terrain.

Sachiko's husband, Taro, invited Robin in, with Nobu, their two-year-old son, in his arms. "Robin-san, welcome to our house." Taro bowed, trying to put her at ease.

Their nineteenth-floor apartment was small and clean, as Robin expected it to be. She was shown to a child's room, now hers. A folded stroller stood by a basketful of toys. The walls were thin, and voices in Japanese surrounded her. With Taro, a stranger to her, at close quarters right outside her door, she felt caged, restricted. Like foreigners often do.

Nobu was not yet walking. "Developmental delays," Sachiko explained.

Robin's breath caught in her throat. On a quest for peace and discovery, she returned to her room feeling uncertain that there was any hope of finding what she came for.

Yet like they say, a connection once steadfast can be revived to its original strength in a short time, like a bear woken from hibernation is alert at once. And that was what happened between the friends, through their touring of temples, skyscrapers, and cherry blossoms. A familiar word and a knowing look made them teenagers again, and their bond came tumbling back.

They strolled under the cherry blossoms and bowed in temples.

Robin admired the clean streets and realized that her imagined idea of tai chi and meditation being practiced in parks wasn't true. From the highest point of the Tokyo Tower, she found Tokyo to be a concrete jungle, just like New York.

They found their way through crowded markets, merchants and customers equally polite. To Robin, the gelatinous sticky rice of hanami dango was insipid, and the smell of seafood overpowering.

"The crowds in the streets and stores are mostly tourists," Sachiko explained. "Naturally, most Japanese adults are busy at work, and children with schoolwork."

Just like in America, people seemed to be in a hurry, preoccupied with their quest for upward mobility, and students were burdened by the pressure of performance. Robin wondered if she would find the peace she came for.

After Robin used a public restroom, which had all the fittings of an ultramodern bidet fitted with deodorant spray and a seat warmer, she said, "Thy bathroom doth shine with radiant cleanliness."

"I haven't heard Shakespearean in a decade," Sachiko squealed. "How I miss it! We have Krispy Kreme here now, but no Shakespearean theater."

On their last day in Tokyo, they visited Sachiko's parents in Yokohama, an industrial port city. Mr. Katzu had suffered a stroke and was still recovering. This too disturbed Robin.

"Mr. and Mrs. Katzu." She bowed to them, noticing their aged faces reflecting worry.

Mr. Katzu's smile spread across the left side of his face, even as the right half stayed immobile. At lunch they put their hands together and said, "Itadakimasu," like they had a decade ago.

Robin passed around the buckeyes from a box she'd gifted them but hesitated before offering it to Mr. Katzu. He slowly reached for one with his left hand and tucked it under his left cheek.

After spending five days in Tokyo, Robin traveled to Kyoto, the ancient royal capital city. On her own she explored the golden pavilion and its manicured gardens, taking pictures for others as they posed. Even in the early morning hours, the Arashiyama bamboo forest was crowded. She walked five hundred meters, as one among hundreds of tourists, between the sixty-feet-tall bamboo stalks as they swayed, but was unable to hear their rustle. The pale-faced geishas in traditional attire looked out of place and lonely, like she herself did. She sat through the long tea ceremony, noticing the rustic architecture of Japanese teahouses. Through it all she felt like just another tourist making the rounds. She was nearing the end of her trip. Back in Tokyo the next day, she would be catching a late flight back to the States.

On her last day there, short on time, she visited the rock garden of Ryōan-ji temple as an afterthought. She walked into the small courtyard and sat on the steps, with scores of others, in silence. Fifteen stones of various sizes were divided into five groups and placed on a sea of white gravel. A placard there explained that the gravel signified water and waves; rocks, islands, and mountains in a Zen Buddhist way of projecting simplicity, absolute minimalism. Only able to see fourteen stones at a time from any one angle, the unseen fifteenth stone projected the unknown mystery of life.

As she settled in contemplation, the morning sunrays fell on her, as if blessing her. In its simplest form, the world was represented in front of her, mountains and oceans miniaturized. In that moment she realized that the art of living was in simplifying daily living and its issues. Simplifying thoughts, and to look for a simple solution for challenges. If an answer didn't come, wait for another day, another moment, but not undermine the current instant for it.

Mindful of the moment, her surroundings, and the meaning they held for her, for the first time in her life, she understood what simplicity and mindfulness meant and how they came together. The thought consumed her, and her breathing became effortless. She was at peace and felt more alive than ever before. The moment too important for her, she let time pass. More time than she planned for the visit, yet she did not panic. She would find a simple alternate solution for this delay in her tour.

Sachiko was a medium that the world had introduced to Robin as a means to her need. She sent a thank-you along the universe's way. She recognized the Katzu family as unique. It was not in being Japanese or in their religion or having unburdened lives. But it was about how they reacted to life and living.

It was not Japan, but it was in the belief. She believed she would find herself and her peace on this trip, and she did. This magic she was expecting to find was within her, waiting to be discovered.

She thanked destiny for simplifying her life by placing her in the Zymanski and the Katzu families. She thought of her parents in reverence and prayed for peace for them too.

When she returned from Kyoto, the apartment wasn't a cage anymore. "I liked the sushi and ramen, and the temples were great, but the best part is your family," she told Taro.

She'd come prepared to share her deepest secret, which she hadn't shared with anyone yet—that one loose nail that remained in her relationship with Sachiko. But she didn't see the need to anymore. That fact seemed irrelevant to her now. Who she was going to be mattered, not who she was. She gave Sachiko a tight squeeze, securing the loose nail and fastening the framework of her friendship.

Her parting gifts from Sachiko were a Japanese silk scarf and a book about Zen Buddhism. "I didn't give you the book earlier because you weren't ready for it," she said. "I know what you came for." She helped Robin pack. "One finds it when they are ready for it, and you are ready. It is easier to take small steps in how you want to live. So take one step toward that goal today and let the momentum build."

In less than eight weeks, Robin would be the associate editor of her division, another turning point in her life. Little did she know that in her destiny, this watershed moment was going to shift to another dramatic event representing the unknown mystery of the fifteenth stone.

29

———

HOMEWARD

Ashley
2001

Ashley called home.

"How are you doing dear?" Kelly asked.

"I am coming home this weekend. No reason. Just want to see you guys," she said about her visit. Embroiled in fear of a skipped period and fatigue, she still tuned in to her mother's voice and conversation, searching for hints of distress, resignation, or despair.

"What's new, Ash?" Ryan inquired.

To her surprise, she talked to them at length that day, not referencing her physical ails. Her conversations with them in her teenage years had been perfunctory. With the passage of time, aided by the understanding of an adult, her impatience had dissipated. In her newfound dilemma, in the long chat, she was looking for comfort.

When she drove into their neighborhood, besides her predicament, her old unresolved tension returned. Her mother sounded relaxed, but Ashley's instinct told her that her father's verbal abuse was on the rise. She hoped it to be her imagined instinct, not reality.

As she approached home, she noticed three small pumpkins sitting on a large, weathered haystack by their mailbox, a significantly scaled-down version from her childhood years of fall. She liked the fall chill. Walking through the garage on that Saturday morning, she was greeted by brand-new, his and hers 2002 model Callaway golf bags and spiked shoes, soon to be retired for the season.

The aroma of cinnamon tea was spouting from a latte machine, her dad's new contraption, was welcoming. "Can I have some too?" she pleaded.

Ryan was sipping his. "Of course. I have one ready for you, darling, sweet and milky, how you like it." He handed her a ceramic mug.

"What are you up to, Mom?" She hugged her.

"Guess what I am baking for you?" Kelly asked.

"Hmmm. Ham and spinach frittata?"

"How could you have known? Your dad must have leaked the surprise, am I right?" Kelly pursed her lips dramatically, worsening her wrinkles.

The Spadys were well-maintained in an athletic way. Avid tennis players, they made a good mixed-doubles team in their league play, but golf was their new obsession. They owned the best paraphernalia for the game, Ashley had no doubt.

"A gentler game of finesse and focus" was how Ryan described it.

Ashley studied Kelly's face. She noticed new wrinkles around her eyes and that her hair was a lot grayer in her temples. She appeared shrunken, Ashley having to look down at her.

Ryan walked with a stiff back. "Too much golf," he explained.

They were sixty-five, and Ryan had been forced to retire a year earlier. Office politics had pushed him out, though he still held a seat on the company board.

Kelly had hinted that his days there were limited too.

Like them, Ashley's once impeccably decorated and maintained childhood home was also showing signs of aging. Their house used to be painted every three years. "To maintain the sheen," her mother used to say. The sheen was missing now.

Italian leather couches in burnt orange and firm backs set in chrome metal frames were still in vogue, but the cushions were showing signs of wear. The carpets were crisscrossed with traffic patterns. Numerous expensive pieces of art, collected over the years during their many overseas trips and displayed in lighted curio cabinets throughout the main floor, lay in a fine layer of dust. Objects once seen as prized possessions of art and wealth, and bought in the name of future value, sat unassumingly on shelves. The place looked sterile, no life.

Harry's loft, its high ceiling hosted by traditional beams above hardwood floors smoothed by wear, stood in contrast. It was cozy, with a happily lived-in comfort. She was excited about her move but terrified about the prospect of a pregnancy. She was not ready. The hurdle weighed heavily, insurmountable.

"Mom, you look tired. Do you need to hire extra help for the house?" she asked, disheartened with Mom's rapidly aging look.

Ashley stepped outside. The landscape by the large patio in the backyard was overgrown. Rusting irrigation pipes showed in the flower beds. Rows of pines, three stories tall, marked their property line. The two oak trees were overgrown—so long were their gnarled branches that a few extended to the edge of the swimming pool. Three cracked tiles along the pool's edge showed, like chipped teeth.

She looked at the empty hammock, still bright in southwestern colors, stretched between the oaks. On good days it used to be her favorite spot. But the memory of it as a place of escape was more potent, a reminder of heartbreak.

Back then, when in autumn squirrels ran up and down the cracked grayish trunks of the oak trees, which stretched like bodies of alligators, she had wondered if baby squirrels also had parental discord in their lives.

The next morning, deviating from years of waking up at dawn, she rolled out of bed late to the aroma of vanilla and rosemary wafting into her bedroom. Vanilla bread casserole and egg souffles sprinkled with rosemary were rising to the perfect temperature set in the oven, and ready to be devoured.

"I love vanilla—no wonder it was voted as the most favorite smell in the world." She inhaled. She was hungry and had no nausea, which was good. But still, her concern mounted.

On Sunday she dragged her parents to her favorite crepe place. "One savory and one sweet, that is what I would like," she said to the waitress. She cleaned a roasted vegetable-scallion crepe topped with sour cream and followed it with a large Belgian chocolate crepe loaded with strawberries, through oohs and aahs.

"Crepe calories don't count!" she declared. Still no nausea.

And on Monday morning, just like that, her flow started, red and steady. As relief washed away her pain from cramps, she whisper-screamed, "I never thought I would say this, but I love you, my cramps."

Relieved, later that morning, she hugged her dad, who supported her always, and held her mom's loving gaze for a long time.

Her mom gave her a reassuring smile and a nod to signal that she was managing. "Take care, Ash." She waved as Ashley walked backward down the driveway, emotionally and physically refreshed—until her Mom's sweater sleeve slid back and exposed an unmistakable remnant of a healing bruise encircling her wrist.

Ashley drove off for a work trip, not feeling so refreshed anymore. Her mom's assertion that there was no physical trauma in her marriage, and that nullified the definition of domestic violence, came tumbling down. Her dread of a possible pregnancy was now replaced by a different fear.

Kelly's vision in that pivotal moment in Milan, which she shared often, was of purpose and belonging. Now, Ashley wondered if destiny had been misinterpreted by her mom. To be a mother, yes, but at what cost was she willing to remain a wife in the name of duty and destiny? And for how much longer could she sustain this fragile existence?

30

THE FALL

Ashley

2002

A left-side parting and a short bob with an undercut replaced Ashley's ponytail and bangs, a professional makeover her hairdresser recommended. She was now the manager of her division, a position she had been vying for since the time her manager had retired. Her colleague's seniority had been skipped over, a coup of sorts for Ashley's regional director, whose favor she was in.

She managed her staff of eight delicately, balancing respect and authority. With her new position came more traveling, which she did not mind, as movement and motion were innate to her since the time she'd arrived in the world nearly three decades ago.

The idea of personal fitness was gaining traction in America, with private fitness centers and home gyms becoming the new fad. Her company was paving the way for such new concepts, and recruitment was active, which meant a larger office was leased.

She was planning her move-in with Harry, but first, she was decorating her new first-floor corner office. On the wall across from the window, she prominently displayed a large poster of herself from her stint in advertising: on an outdoor trail, near dusk, her high ponytail bounced to one side, form-fitting running shorts highlighting her narrow waist, the setting sun shining on the shoes, blazing them into focus. She couldn't help but wonder how seven years at the current job had flown by so quickly.

"Let me fetch the new sales graph from my office." She stepped out of the conference room. She raced up two steps at a time, like she always did. Suddenly she lurched forward, slamming her face into the edge of a step at an awkward angle and twisting her left foot. Blood dripped onto her beige silk blouse, soaking through to her bra. Dazed, she sat up, helped by a colleague. The unexpectedness of the pain left her numb. As she limped off to the bathroom, she saw how grotesque her nose looked under a large developing bruise, and how uneven that made her face look. She stuck a Band-Aid across her nose, put on a jacket to conceal the stain that had darkened to resemble the shape of the Great Lakes, and managed to complete her presentation, carefully breathing and speaking through her mouth.

Once past the numbness of the shock, her swollen nose a focal point of pain, the throbbing flowed across all segments of her face, like ripples from a pebble thrown in a still pond. Her foot was manageable, but her mental capacity was dull.

"Can you drive me to my apartment?" she asked Harry when she called him.

Harry drove to her office building and helped her limp to his car. "Do you want me to spend the night?"

"That is sweet, but I can manage. And you have work to catch up on."

At her apartment, he laid out a few Advils, a bottle of cold water, grapes, and cookies on her nightstand and left.

The next day, when her nose was nothing short of a bright and battered Rudolph's, she saw her family physician, Dr. Desai, a kind old Indian. She barely tolerated the exam, so he ordered an X-ray of her face and foot to make sure there were no fractures.

In addition to recommending icing, he prescribed anti-inflammatory medicine to slow the edema and Vicodin for pain. He advised that she return for a follow-up examination the following week.

She used Vicodin that night and fell into a deep slumber. In the early morning hours, as the throbbing returned, now equally intense in her foot as well, she took two more Vicodin. Her body relaxed as lightness descended from her face all the way down. She was enticed by the magic. She timed them at eight-hour intervals the following day. Mild anxiety set in when she reached to find only three tablets remaining at the bottom of the prescription bottle. She was astonished at how easy it was to fall prey to the seduction of a narcotic.

Refusing to get entangled in the lure of medicine, she flushed the three remaining tablets down the toilet.

She was familiar with prescription drugs like muscle relaxants, steroids, and narcotics being overused. Athletes, after years of training only to be sidelined with a sprain or spasm, often found the bait to use and abuse medicine irresistible.

"Take good care of your feet," her high school running coach had cautioned repeatedly, disapproving of girls wearing stilettos at parties. "Feet," he'd lectured, "are two remarkable body parts, with fifty-two of the body's two hundred six bones—twenty-five percent, that is—with scores of ligaments, muscles, and joints that act as screws, axles, and levers. Complex structures, so respect them, as they carry the weight of your body."

Now her nose felt as important as her feet had.

By week's end, her body was well on its way to healing. Her x-rays, thankfully, did not show fractures.

She told Dr. Desai about her fatigue though. "There were no other falls, but I held my grocery cart for support once when my legs gave in."

"Are your periods heavy?"

"No," she replied.

"Anemia and thyroid issues are the most common reasons for fatigue in women. I'll be checking those levels."

That night a nagging premonition woke her up from sleep.

31

BEFORE THE CHRISTMAS CHEER

Ashley
2002

Timing was everything to the runner in Ashley. The waving of the flag, the gunshot, the whistle, and the leap that followed were precision-bound. Even a second behind at the starting line predetermined the result of a race. This obsession with time was unknowingly built into her everyday life.

Uncharacteristic for Ashley, her balance with time faltered on that Tuesday after work. Ashley and Harry had made plans to meet friends for dinner, before Christmas chaos set in. Rushing to grab coffee, her hand stiffened. The mug wobbled before it slid out of her grip and shattered. She yelped in agony as the hot coffee seared her feet.

Harry resisted using his favorite line to slow Ashley. "Most misery is caused by rushing."

As the heat singed her skin, she whimpered. Harry doused her feet in cold water and dug out an ice pack hidden under tubs of ice cream. Clear, viscous fluid was collecting under raised domes of epidermis, like taut balloons. They stood in contrast to the scarlet all around. He covered the burns in a white lotion and laid the ice pack on top.

The storm began with sleet and freezing rain at noon the next day, and by midnight, they lost power. Huddled around their small battery-operated space heater in Harry's loft, they waited for dawn. At daybreak, what appeared to be a winter wonderland at first glance was a catastrophe, with downed electric wires and tree limbs scattered haphazardly across roads and yards, entangled with telephone lines. A three-quarters-inch sheet of ice paralyzed Raleigh's streets and most of the Piedmont region of North Carolina.

The ice storm raged for twenty-four hours, and they weren't among the two hundred or so people who went to ERs with carbon monoxide poisoning from the use of kerosene and gas-powered heaters. Power returned after three days.

"At least I've got free ice for my burns," Ashley joked.

By the time life returned to normal, her burns had healed, and she barely missed work, thanks to the ice storm.

Muscle stiffness remained though. So the next time Ashley consulted with Dr. Desai, it was not for the burns.

He tested her reflexes by gently tapping a knee hammer just under her kneecap. He moved to flexing and extending her extremities against resistance. His voice, though kind and gentle, reflected concern. "I'll make a referral to a neurologist, a nerve specialist. I do not want you to worry about it. He'll order a few tests, and we may have a simple answer and an easy solution to the problem."

The neurologist took a detailed family medical history, in particular genetic history.

"My parents and extended family are healthy," she told him.

The number of tests ordered unnerved her, but he explained the details in as many simple terms as he could.

"There is always Google to understand them better," she said, and immediately regretted it.

Blood tests, muscle biopsy, an electromyogram, and genetic tests followed. For the EMG, needles were placed at forty-five-degree angles through her skin into her muscles, and the reaction to nerve impulses was tested. She bore the mildly painful process in hopes of normal results.

But the enzyme creatine kinase was abnormally high in her bloodstream. The muscle biopsy showed degeneration. The EMG recorded a low amplitude of muscle activity. They all pointed to one condition.

32

DURHAM

Anita

1994–2000

Since their move back to Durham in 1994, having no prying neighbors and inquisitions helped Deepak and Rumi transition into their new lives. Living in a modern space and active in the local Hindu temple, they found peace in spirituality and service. The stigma of their daughter's teenage pregnancy was fading and soon to be forgotten, easing the sharp claws of circumstance.

Durham in the 1990s, as a city, placed them in the center of the technological revolution that was taking place in the country and the world. They continued to work in RTP, which was host to hundreds of new technology and biotech companies and thousands of well-paying jobs. Innovation was in high gear, and that in turn led to rapid urbanization and population growth, adding billions to North Carolina's economy.

Along with the advances in technology, the stock market was amid an unprecedented boom. Both Rumi and Deepak were in fields where their technical skills were in great demand. They were managers on high-profile projects, where stock options paid big dividends. Making more money than they'd ever imagined, they were also getting paid significant bonuses, without ever expecting them.

They were affluent professionals in their fifties, regarded at work, respected in the community, and revered for their service and donations at the temple. They were part of a thriving community of successful Asian-Indian professionals in Durham. The city's population had doubled in the prior decade. The area was booming. Large office complexes rose up regularly. New businesses, small and large, sprouted on street corners and in neighborhoods. Elaborate apartment complexes were built to accommodate the growth.

Anita made the thirty-mile drive from Greensboro to visit them, especially when Ami visited, the sisters' comfort with each other reestablishing. Anita craved dal chawal, a simple home-cooked meal of lentils and rice, infused with Indian spices, the same spices she'd detested as a teenager. Over the decade, the thirty-minute drive from Greensboro to Durham turned into a sluggish hour-long commute. Anita preferred the slower pace of Greensboro and was relieved she'd not moved with her parents.

In her parents' neighborhood, young professionals were moving in, including Indian immigrants, driving into their expensive homes in luxury cars. Immigrants were acclimatizing faster than before, their buying power and confidence in full display. They had broken free from traditional enclaves and career stereotypes.

As the new millennium dawned, beyond the Y2K scare of impending chaos and technological failures that never materialized, the younger generation of Indian and South Asian diaspora resisted parental pressure, breaking free from traditional expectations of careers in medicine and engineering. Instead, they were working in industries of their choice. They became store managers, artists, interior decorators, entrepreneurs, and small business owners, taking pride as teachers, nurses, and service professionals, without the stigma their parents' generation had imposed.

The beautiful fall foliage of the Piedmont region made the drive to Durham in fall one of the most enjoyable. Since the spring of 1992, when her daughter was born, spring as a season of rebirth had ceased to exist for her. So she let springs pass without note. Summers were too hot. Winter and the holidays reminded her of lost opportunities. By default, fall became her preferred time of the year.

In fall came Diwali, the festival of lights, commemorating Lord Rama's victory over the evil demon king Ravana—when good triumphed over evil. Following the legend that people lit lamps to welcome Lord Rama back to his kingdom Ayodhya, the Kumars poured oil in terra-cotta lamps and placed them on their stoop and in the foyer. They draped their boxwoods in Christmas lights.

One Diwali day, at her parents' insistence, she attended the Hindu Society of North Carolina in Morrisville, near Raleigh. Two priests from India performed elaborate rituals, followed by a cultural gathering of a thousand families in the social hall, a number that was beyond Anita's imagination, when a mere fifteen years earlier, there were no more than fifty families in the area. The American and the Indian flags were mounted on either side of the stage, and an Indian girl of eight belted "The Star-Spangled Banner," followed by the Indian national anthem in perfect dialect.

Dressed in ethnic attire, children and adults sang in their native language and danced to popular movie songs. It must be the strength in numbers, as children were proud to celebrate their culture, unlike she was at their age. Never having imagined the assimilation and acceptance of the Indian community of such magnitude in her lifetime, when plans for Holi were discussed, Anita fondly remembered her grandmother, who'd passed on.

Through the expanding Indian diaspora and her more ethnic interactions, she found comfort in meeting people who looked like her. She met scores of immigrants and their offspring, confident and comfortable with their looks and careers. Now, she was too, though certain aspects of life were incomplete and unsettling.

She didn't miss the luxury cars and big homes; a simple life suited her. Being a high school dropout in a family of high achievers irked her, shamed her even. Paul was currently enrolled in college, and that gave her hope. She wanted to be a college graduate too, but what she needed to tackle first was getting her GED. The GED was comprised of four core subjects: language arts, math, science, and social studies, and once passed, earned a high school equivalency credential.

Nervously she approached the local librarian for guidance. When she perused the recommended math workbook, a handful of the geometry problems looked familiar but none of the algebraic equations made sense. Disheartened, she opened the science book, and the first page carried the equation $2KMnO_4 + 5H_2C_2O_2 + 3H_2SO_4$ and was labeled "OXIDATION-REDUCTION" in uppercase letters. In the language arts section, the written word made sense, but the content hung heavy.

Overwhelmed with this introduction, she caught herself drifting off too often.

33

DISCOVERY

Anita

2001

"Welcome," the smartly dressed new manager said at the reception desk, her high cheekbones and angled jaw adding to her beauty. Her pink lips matched her jacket, as did her dangling earrings. She smiled and looked in the direction of Anita and Paul's regular table at the diner.

Paul hadn't arrived yet, and Anita was captivated by a pretty face encircled by dark curls. A girl, around nine or so, sat at a table past theirs, her lips curled in a tight circle around a yellow straw, sipping cola. Her circular mouth reminded Anita of someone she'd kissed a decade ago. When the girl looked up, her eyes sparkled. Anita knew those eyes, having seen the amber in them only on one other person in her life before.

Transfixed in time and space, she heard muffled voices for a time and then radio silence. Everyone and everything around her froze in place. Even a tap on her shoulder didn't register. When Paul shook her arm, she blinked in rapid succession before his face cleared.

"Come, let's sit down," Paul said, shuffling to the table.

Anita looked around to see who the girl was with, when the

manager approached the girl with a slice of apple pie. With her left hand, she stroked the child's hair.

"Don't mess my hair, Mother," the girl complained.

"Sorry, baby. I'll be off my shift in ten minutes. You'll be a good girl in the meantime, won't you, Maizie?" She blew her daughter a kiss.

Maizie nodded. By the time Anita recovered, Maizie walked by, following her mother out of the café.

Anita was thrust into a whole new world, a world where her daughter not only existed but lived in her own town. She closed her eyes. She, who had scanned every girl's face for her daughter and had lost hope, found her daughter in the diner where she came on most Sundays. Was it real? Would she see the face again? What next? These questions she didn't have an answer to played on repeat.

"I am a big brother now," Paul was saying. His words sounded drugged and distant, like a zombie's.

She opened her eyes.

"They have assigned me a ten-year-old boy, Devin, who doesn't have a father. He needs a male role model, you see. I'm meeting him tomorrow. Exciting, isn't it?"

No response from Anita. She looked straight ahead, expressionless.

Paul turned back and saw no one.

They split the bill as a rule, but that day Anita didn't volunteer to pay. Paul paid, and she didn't protest.

"Are you alright? I'll see you next Sunday, won't I?" he asked.

In her apartment she stared at the blank canvas resting on her easel. To reproduce the newly revealed eyes, she mixed burnt sienna with cadmium yellow in equal proportions, then added a tinge of raw umber. She assessed the dimensions and proportions and started with the dark pupil and surrounded it with the warm yellow glow of sunrise for the iris. She added striations that mimicked sunrays, like she'd noticed when Maizie had walked by. The amber wasn't the exact tint, but she proceeded with shading to add depth. Dark eyelashes and eyebrows followed. A single stroke for a nose, and a few for hair, gave the desired look. The focus was on the eyes, the rest of the face basic.

She stepped back. "Sebastian-like," she blurted, saying his name for the first time in nine years.

The next day she worked robotically and headed directly to the diner, never having done that on a weekday in all the years. There was no girl, nor the same manager. She didn't know how to inquire about them, so she waited while drinking two cups of coffee.

Back in her apartment, for the first time, she didn't find security in her comforter. After tossing and turning, she rose and paced. She doodled, and by the time she came to her senses, she had filled pages with a new three-dimensional geometric design. When at dawn caffeine and adrenaline levels dropped, she fell asleep with her head on the breakfast table.

At the diner the next day, she avoided coffee and ordered a full meal. She waited for the shift change, and when Maizie and her mother did not show, she went home disappointed, though not losing hope.

The following Sunday she kissed the Ganesha pendant. No luck. That table was empty. With shoulders slouched and head bent, she headed toward her table when she spotted Maizie sitting at a table farther away from theirs, close to the kitchen. Anita sat at her usual spot, turned strategically to face Maizie. Light skin, manageable hair in a ponytail. Soccer shorts and cleats on, she was not short for her age. The more Anita stared at the face, the more she imagined it to be Sebastian's.

She followed their car. Their two-level family home had a white picket fence. Zinnias bloomed in window boxes. Knowing where Maizie lived made her existence concrete. Twice Anita drove around the neighborhood, palpitations ringing in her ears. She was treading new ground. *Stalker* was the last thing she wanted to be. School premises were out of the question, for fear of being identified as loitering. She did not know what else to do, as it was too premature to talk to her parents and too personal to share with Paul.

"Why are you getting into the mess again? Leave it be," Ami would reprimand.

Unable to suppress her desire to share, she told the Mexican resident. "Oleo, I think I found my daughter. In our town! Never did I ever imagine it like it happened. Comprendo?" She asked in the little Spanish she knew. "But there is not much I can do about it. My hands are tied. She seems well taken care of and happy. That is good enough for now, don't you think?" She cleared the lunch tray. "Take care. I will see you tomorrow." She knew Oleo did not understand much of what she had told her.

As a fifteen-year-old who'd feigned indifference, Anita had paid attention to the legalities of the closed-adoption process. Under the agreement, biological parents lost their right to information about their child. Only the child, at eighteen, could seek the identity of their biological parents. But Anita still carried hope for an earlier reunion with her daughter.

After two weeks of nervous anxiety and sleepless nights, she slept better than before. She worked with the same commitment but with an unusually hearty laugh.

34

CLOSED EYES

Anita

Ami was an intern in the emergency room.

An old spark of joy shone brightly in their parents' eyes when Ami was around. Away from home and the notoriety surrounding Anita's pregnancy, Ami had blossomed in college and fulfilled her parents' dreams by becoming a physician, a matter of great pride for them. Occasional laughter also returned to their home in carefully calibrated measures.

Anita and Ami's sisterly love was returning. They bonded over watching new seasons and reruns of ER on NBC. George Clooney as Dr. Doug Ross and Noah Wyle as Dr. John Carter were America's heartthrobs and were Ami's too. Anita maintained a neutral emotion toward them. Deepak and Rumi joined to watch, too, but could not refrain from clicking their laptops to meet work deadlines.

Ami snickered at the histrionics of the show, commenting on how exaggerated some scenes were. "In real life, it's not like that. It's not glorious, just challenging. We deal with noncompliance and some who are downright irresponsible. We take care of alcoholics and drug addicts. Many don't have insurance."

Anita heard discontent in Ami's voice, frustration even. "Do you like your job?"

"Of course, I do," Ami answered defensively.

Anita had doubts. How disappointing if, after years of advanced training, Ami was already disenchanted with work and patients. Did she simply become a physician as a badge of honor, especially for her parents? If true, to what end? Anita sighed, hoping for it not to be true.

Anita was training too, for her GED, in a way. Living in a bubble, her experiences were limited. Hence analysis, deduction, and comprehension suffered. Paul's discourse on current events brought needed perspective, its reach limited though. Her initial unfamiliarity with equations was giving way to recognition. Learning basic computer use at their local library at Paul's insistence was also aiding her GED prep.

Irrespective of Ami's attitude, the television show captivated Anita. The blood and gore didn't bother her—how lives were saved caught her attention. When a patient was rolled in with CPR in progress, she got goose bumps, even more so when they were saved.

"Your health is our sacred calling" came back to her. Working in a facility that housed the elderly and the sick, she wanted to save lives too, if the need arose. She needed to train in basic life support. She was going to ask Paul to enroll at the American Red Cross too.

Anita was curious if her parents ever wondered how their two girls, brought up under the same roof, under similar circumstances, had turned out to be so different. One, a physician, another, a high school dropout. She hoped they were not blaming themselves for her missteps.

During one visit, their parents declared that they were proud of both their daughters, but to Anita's surprise, they said they were more so of Anita, for whom she had become.

Her father said, "Your maa and I've now lived equal numbers of years in India and the US. After all these years and fears, I feel I equally belong to both worlds. I don't have to choose anymore. I thought the two countries were a world apart, but I understand that people, families, and values are the same everywhere." He paused and cleared his throat. "They are colored differently, that is all. This land of opportunity has offered us opportunities no other country would have."

He looked around for a response, but finding none, he continued.

"Adapting and embracing what is good in other cultures is key. The value placed in America for good work ethic, respecting the law, being rewarded for hard work, and donating to charitable foundations is admirable." He breathed in deeply. "No other society encourages individualism and ingenuity as this one. We were wrong to enforce our opinions on you. When in Rome, do as the Romans do hasn't been said in frivolity." His nostrils flared.

Concluding his uncharacteristically long monologue, he had shown more emotion in that moment than at any other time Anita could remember. It was her usually quiet father's way of accepting his changed ideology.

"Doing an honest day's work with commitment. That is what life is about. Against all adversity, our bitiya has prevailed," Anita's usually talkative mother succinctly summarized, looking adoringly at Anita.

Anita could only force a laugh, that moment truly special for her. There was a genuineness in their praise, and she believed them. Overpowered by their love, she wanted to share the news of spotting her daughter. But common sense prevailed. She had no proof, just a mother's instinct. Not wanting to ruin a good moment, she let it be.

Deepak and Rumi gifted Anita things she could not afford, without making her feel inadequate. They respected her need to be self-sufficient.

When Anita's old car broke down, they surprised her with a new one. "A new car is for its reliability," they insisted. "A cell phone is for your safety," they explained. In the guise of a real estate investment, they bought a two-bedroom condo for Anita in the same building she was renting one in. "Even you get a bedroom of your own," Anita told her cat.

ANITA'S TRANSITION FROM random doodling to doodling with the intention of painting had happened by chance, having used leftover paint from an art assignment in school.

In the early part of the shift, she'd pored over books in the school library and instructional material on painting. She'd explored linear scale, proportions, life drawing, composition, creating depth, shading, grid drawing, and elements of design. A few made sense, but most didn't, so she ignored them and followed her own instincts.

Diverse places infused distinct energy to her art. Not to be restricted by location, she traveled with her easel and required supplies from one space to another. Within her condo she sometimes squeezed herself into tight corners on purpose, to surround herself with a restricted vibe. One time she'd settled into her dimly lit closet for a closed-in one.

Her art evolved and landed in a comfortable mix of doodling and painting, their distinction blurring on her canvas. Her paint strokes blended with squiggles and swirls. Lines mingled with forms and faces.

A face caught most emotion, and two of them together even more. And in her life, she saw people in twos—her parents, Ami and herself, Paul and her—and always just under the surface, her daughter and herself. She depicted faces in round shapes surrounded by mostly circles and stars—representing friendliness and hope in the world of doodling, she'd learned after the fact.

She was relieved about this representation, as that was what she would have exactly intended anyway. Slowly the dull colors she chose were replaced by bright ones as needed, and she added textures too. The bright colors and textures were like condiments that enhanced the flavor of her art and her life too.

The only painting she'd ever framed and hung up—which she'd painted a year before she'd seen Maizie—was of herself and her cat. It adorned the wide, empty wall of the living area of her condo, which had an open floor plan. It was initiated as a mother-daughter image. As she tried to paint her daughter's imagined face, no face seemed perfect. "Let it be in my pure imagined state," she'd decided, and painted her cat in her daughter's place.

The hung painting, with a balanced mix of doodling, had her cat sitting on her lap, with a burdened look on its round face, like she was uncomfortable with human proximity. Not wanting to choose an eye color, Anita had painted her cat with closed eyes, her white half of the body in contrast with the black couch. A gold chain around the cat's neck and body extended to encircle Anita's wrist. It hung like a heavy metal-link chain, binding them. Anita had drawn herself round faced also, with exaggerated eyebrows to balance her hair, spread out like tentacles. She'd painted her own eyes plain and bland. "Like my life," she'd thought at the time. Numerous circles and stars were scattered and interspersed.

That she'd been unable to look into her daughter's eyes at birth had given her an extra sense of loss. She had worried that she'd never connect with her daughter's soul. After seeing Maizie's eyes, the windows to the soul, received her special attention when painting. She compared shades of honey, maple syrup, and the one beer she'd drunk on her twenty-first birthday for their color.

In the nearest grocery store, she gazed at various brands of honey and maple syrup. She zeroed in on Manuka honey, which came the closest to the amber she wanted, like the mild amber of lightly caramelized crème brûlée. Equal portions of yellow ochre, brown, and golden yellow did it. That became a recurrent color in her palette.

There were numerous other paintings born from private struggles and unspoken emotions, never to be gifted, nor to be displayed. Tucked away, they were never to see the light of day, like a mouse storing food crumbs for a later day but hidden in a place too hard to find, that they might as well be lost forever.

Her unique art was for herself.

35

___

THE AMERICAN DREAM

Anita
2002–2003

Anita had driven the same route to St. Bona for ten years. That Monday, a fall day in 2002, was no different. The day before, she'd gotten a glimpse of Maizie, from a distance, getting into her father's car. Two other girls followed Maizie into the car.

Her daughter had friends. She was happy about that. Ever so careful not to be noticed as lurking in the neighborhood, she drove by the two-story house without pausing, even though her instinct was to slow down.

Anita was familiar with every house and tree in Maizie's neighborhood. She drove around the neighborhood like a police officer on his beat. She hardly saw Maizie, as at ten, Maizie was not of the age for impromptu outside play with children in the neighborhood. All Anita got was an occasional glimpse of her getting in and out of the car and an appearance on a rare occasion at the diner. Anita did not mind. Maizie was getting taller, prettier. Braces with red wire sprouted in her mouth.

An unexpected urge to hug her and kiss her, run a hand through her hair, peer into those amber eyes, sprang. An overreach might lead to a restraining order, she feared. Rules of adoption were still fresh in her mind. She was committed to avoiding a maelstrom, and anything done in haste would jeopardize her daughter psychologically—and that she would not allow.

As she drove to work, the colors of her favorite season were brewing an idea for a new painting.

"St. Bona feels like home, a place of comfort to me," she'd told Paul the evening before. "I started as a teenager, uncertain, with no direction, no goals." There was no answer for why then, but deviating from her inability to share personal matters with anyone, she'd said, "I'm a high school dropout, you know."

He nodded.

"You're an inspiration. I'm working toward my GED now." She placed her credit card on the bill.

"Did you register for the test yet?" He retrieved his card.

"I'm planning to take it in early spring. Need another six months for preparation." She split the leftovers into two boxes.

"Register now. Having a deadline helps," he'd said, reaching for his share of the leftovers.

She would register for the test at the end of her shift that day. She walked to her locker, mentally sketching the painting. But her creative momentum was interrupted by a summons to the director's office. Though the director respected and liked her, and the feeling was mutual, the early morning call unnerved her.

Nervous, she knocked on the door.

"Please enter," the director said, a man of moderate stature, with a perfect body except for his surprisingly spindly legs. They appeared too fragile to support his frame. But for this unbalanced physical trait, he was a man of balanced thought.

"Take a seat, please." He gestured toward one of the two chairs aligned with his desk. He handed her an envelope. "Relax. It's all good."

The letter read, "Congratulations on your appointment as the supervisor of housekeeping."

"I've never really supervised anything or anybody in my life, let alone managing my own life," she said nervously.

"Trust me. I've seen you in action. I admire your spotless attendance and your respect for others," he said with a smile, shaking her hand. "The administration is confident that we've made the right choice."

Later, at a small ceremony, she was presented with a plaque and a gift certificate in appreciation for her decade of service, where a formal announcement of her appointment as the new supervisor was made.

Her active engagement and leadership were on full display within two weeks, when on December 4, Greensboro saw one of the largest ice storms in its history. Anticipating staff shortages, she rallied staff volunteers to stay at the facility overnight. Her call proved to be right when, by the next morning, the city of Greensboro was paralyzed under nearly an inch-thick sheet of ice.

Organizing sleeping arrangements for staff in empty resident rooms, coordinating shifts, and ensuring rest for everyone, she sprang into action, activating generators, distributing extra blankets, and serving meals.

When power was restored two days later and the city thawed out of its icy grip, the director said, "You're already proving to be the best supervisor this facility has ever seen."

Staffing issues were a perpetual problem across the facility, with absenteeism propagated in all departments. Among her staff, the ones who complained the most were the most persistently irresponsible. She drafted schedules on an old computer that sat on her desk, relying on computer skills she'd learned at the library at Paul's insistence. Scheduling was a never-ending game of chess as she moved pawns for requests of emergencies, filling in the grid as pieces fell.

Anita enforced a strict dress code. Fastidious, she washed and ironed six sets of her uniform weekly, the sixth set stashed in her locker for backup. An occasional resident noticed her crisp, ironed lines and commented, "You are the only one on whom uniforms fit perfectly that they do not look like uniforms at all."

Most staff wore uniforms that resembled crumpled old paper bags, like they'd rolled out of bed and straight to work, as if St. Bona was the last place they would rather be. The uniforms covered their out-of-shape bodies. These were jobs when they were in the mood to work, temporary fillers to pad their pockets when they needed money.

Life was on an upswing for Anita, but a new concern brewed that was rekindling her anxiety. Ami was dating Cody, a kindhearted pediatrician in training, a Caucasian. There was even talk of an engagement, which her parents did not object to, confirming their cultural assimilation. Cody, a charming storyteller, often shared humorous anecdotes about his young patients, like the one with a pencil stuck in his nose, or the kid who faked illness to skip school. "I love children," he said often.

Anita forced laughs and correct responses to his narrations, but his association with children felt torturous, stirring jealousy. Her unease also centered on how much of her story he knew. Had Ami betrayed Anita's trust by sharing intimate details with this stranger? The prospect stung.

To avoid awkwardness, she sidestepped conversations about work and education with clever excuses and hasty exits. Her desire for a GED and further education had nothing to do with his perception of her. She was already on her way, but with him around, passing her GED took an urgent turn.

In spring fresh blooms brightened the landscape of St. Bona, and so were Anita's days—her parents' validation, her promotion, and her manager's trust strengthened her. Her teenage unease eroded, replaced by confidence. For a life that evolved with no plans at all, she was happy with where she was. No one cared about her hair or skin color, and neither did she. No taunts—only praise and respect from her peers.

On Paul's insistence, she registered for the test and mailed the fee. Encouraging her and educating her, Paul was a dependable, dear friend. Wanting to surprise her parents once she enrolled in college, she did not tell them about her plans for getting her GED. Financially and as a family, they were all doing well. Their stature repaired and restored, Anita no longer carried the guilt of tainting. She did not yet know how to manage her daughter's situation, but that could wait. Was she genuinely happy, or was she, like her grandmother, adjusting and accepting her situation as a happy one? This weighed on her mind. In the toss-up, she believed the first one. Good things were happening. Her American dream was falling into place.

36

OPEN EYES

Robin

2002–2003

"**K**eep your eyes open. This will take only a second," the young ophthalmologist said as she squeezed two yellow drops into Robin's eyes. "Dr. Ranke" was embroidered in bold green letters on her lab coat.

Given that glasses had offered no solution to Robin's issues, especially with nighttime driving, she was having further tests.

"Close your eyes now. They'll burn for a minute while your pupils dilate." The doctor adjusted the height of her stool and focused bright light into Robin's eyes. "I'm examining the outside and inside parts of your eyes," she explained. Making notations in the chart, she used terms like "retina," "optic disc," "aqueous," and "vitreous humor."

She reviewed tests that were done earlier. "Your results are okay, but I am recommending that you follow up with me in four weeks. We'll repeat some of these tests to confirm a few changes."

As Robin's anxiety and unease of earlier years had dissipated and her psyche had cleared, this request for repeated testing did not create havoc. She made the appointment and focused on her interview for the position of associate editor in her company, a position that would take her a step closer to her lifetime goal of becoming an editor-in-chief. She was short on experience but was considered for her talent and dedication to her craft.

In preparation for the interview, she stood in front of her dresser and practiced her responses, observing her body language in the mirror. To lighten the pressure, she occasionally remembered her theater days and answered self-imposed questions with a dramatic flair. "'Throw me to the wolves—I will return leading the pack.'" She quoted the Roman philosopher Seneca—whom the line was typically attributed to—acting it out like she was on a stage. The meaning of the message was not lost on her.

Robin's trip to Japan had marked a significant shift in her journey, a watershed moment, when her undisciplined life had found a path. Her unsettling had found proper ground. For what she was looking for, she had found the moment, the place, and the idea on her own accord, in her own quiet. Who she was did not matter; who she chose to be mattered. Where she originated did not matter; where she was going mattered. This awareness was critical to her functioning for the interview and her testing. She cautioned herself to keep her answers simple, like she was trying to do with her life and thoughts.

In two weeks, she was announced as the new associate editor.

Four weeks later her tests were repeated. "Rods are cells that help with light and night vision, and cones help with color vision," Dr. Ranke explained.

It was a Tuesday morning on Dec 3, 2002, when the expected was confirmed and finally given a name—retinitis pigmentosa, a chronic degenerative genetic condition of the eye. The expectation of this diagnosis had exhausted Robin in the preceding months, as she'd found enough information about her symptoms on Google.

"A mutation is a chemical change in the DNA, altering its sequence," the genetic counselor explained. "One either inherits the abnormal gene from their parents or develops it as a new mutation at conception. Although born with the mutation, symptoms do not develop until later years."

The ophthalmologist clarified further. "You'll have decent vision for a while. Over time your field of vision will get narrower, and colors will fade. Eventually you will lose functional vision—over how long we can't predict. Your ability to distinguish light from dark and shapes will remain for a long time." Dr. Ranke tried to give her hope.

Robin struggled to maintain her composure.

The world around her mirrored her mood. The dot-com bubble had imploded, leaving a trail of economic devastation. From an unprecedented high in March 2001, the stock market fell to record lows over eighteen months. In October, two months prior to Robin's diagnosis, the NASDAQ dropped 76 percent from its peak, and the Dow Jones by 25 percent. Her financial worries mounted, fearing for her parents' retirement funds also. But most of all, she dreaded telling Pops about her diagnosis, knowing how devastated he'd be.

A snowstorm predicted for the day after her diagnosis turned into an ice storm, encasing Chapel Hill in ice. It turned out to be the biggest ice storm the Piedmont region had seen in forty years. Tree branches and power lines snapped when the ice got to a quarter of an inch. Dagger-like icicles, three feet long, hung from eaves. Without power that night, she sat still, staring at the candlelight and trying to find her balance. Her future seemed as bleak as the struggling flame, her insides as frozen as the outdoors. When she closed her eyes, she saw waves of sand and gravel. The last thing she remembered before she froze to sleep was to call Sachiko when phone service resumed.

With every answer that she found, she had ten other questions that needed an answer. She was once more at the crossroads of her life, like when she was eighteen years old. Did she revisit her quest to trace her biological parents to know her prognosis, or wait to see what her future had to offer? She was told that even in families with the same mutation, progression varied.

If one of her biological parents had it, was theirs the slowly developing kind? Even if theirs was not, she prayed for hers to be.

Swept up in the tsunami of her degenerative illness, she struggled to stay afloat amid the gigantic tidal waves of shock and agony. Her days slowed. She called off work. Partying stopped. Dating stalled. Initially unable to share her agony with even Sachiko, she read the book Sachiko had gifted her innumerable times, but the help she hoped for didn't materialize.

At her grandmother's for Christmas, Robin was listless.

"You've lost weight, darling," James observed.

"Just a little, Pops," she replied.

When her cousins made conversation, she merely listened.

That she'd struggled to choose gifts for the family was obvious in her selections.

When her parents visited her in Raleigh after the holidays, the state of her apartment was the first giveaway.

Stepping over books and clothing to get to the couch, James stood in the middle of the room, hands in his pockets, looking perplexed. "You're becoming a teenager again, darling."

The next time they visited, James was certain that something was amiss. Robin looked pale and withdrawn. "Come sit with me, darling," he said, picking a time when Lily was napping. He wrapped his arm around her shoulders and noticed her fingers looking more slender than he remembered. "What's bothering you, darling daughter? Problem at work?"

She shook her head.

"A boyfriend problem?"

"Come on, Pops." She shrugged.

"This hurkle-durkle mode doesn't suit."

She couldn't stop smiling at the reference.

"You can tell Pops anything and everything, you know that, don't you?"

And that did it. From start to finish, she told him, like it was a story about someone she knew.

Stunned by the revelation, James sat still. "Why didn't you tell me sooner, Robin Blue?" was all he said, his tone subdued. "Come here." He took her in his arms. "I'm here to take care of you, so don't you worry about a thing, understand?" He stroked her hair.

Neither cried. She'd cried enough already, and he didn't want to then. Later, when he made dinner, he worried if his tears would make the food too salty.

"I'm taking you back with me, dear," he told her the next morning. "No discussion about that. A few weeks at home will do you good. I know how to take care of you. I know the signs."

"Signs? Signs of what?"

"Of needing help. Of melancholy. I'm an expert when it comes to that." He smiled half-heartedly, unaware that melancholy was settling in him too. He'd forgotten what it felt like, as he'd felt that only once before, when they had lost baby Kristen.

Without as much as a minor protest, Robin applied for medical leave and followed her father home, trusting him to show her the way.

"Visually impaired? Are you talking about blindness?" Lily stopped in her tracks when James broke the news to her.

"Yes, I am," James said.

"Is this really happening? My beautiful daughter, with a gift of photographic memory, will not be able to see anymore!" A sob left her.

Trying to reassure her as much as James was trying to reassure himself, he said, "Don't worry, Lily." He wiped both their tears. "She is a mnemonist, remember? Her memory and cognitive abilities are sharper than ours. She'll memorize by sound, touch, smell, and taste. All four senses will sharpen, and with that she'll compensate for her loss on a far higher level than regular people like you and me." He blew his nose. "And I'm there to take care of her, am I not? I need to retire, and I will."

"How's Lily doing?" the psychiatrist inquired, familiar with James and Robin from years of treating Lily.

"She could be better," James responded.

Robin answered a questionnaire and handed it over.

"I'm afraid that you're depressed," the doctor said, stating the obvious. "Just as much as you need medicine, you need to see a therapist too. When we started your mother on Zoloft, it was a new medicine. We now know it works very well."

Robin nodded. She took the medicine without protest, like a dutiful child.

In early spring, while James gardened, she sat outside, yet again not interested in gardening, like when she was a young child. While her father cooked and told her Aesop's fables and other stories of perseverance, she listened.

James made phone calls to friends and took advice. He read books about adaptive behaviors and technologies.

He suggested learning braille. "I'll learn it with you, dear," he said. "We'll see who learns it faster." Reluctantly she signed up, but was soon toying with her dad's capacity to memorize. "You're no match to me, Dad," she teased him.

"I give up." James raised his hands.

When she grew weary of braille cells, she called Sachiko.

"I'm really sorry to hear about your diagnosis," Sachiko said. A long pause followed. "I'll pray that yours doesn't progress at all. Is there anything I can do to help?"

"You'll be my counselor on this journey, won't you?" Robin's voice was even, steadfast in her attempt not to lose control.

"Of course! I hope that I can be one for you," Sachiko answered.

Sachiko talked to Robin for hours, without Robin responding much. Sachiko reminded her of her trip to Japan and the concept of the fifteen stones and the gravel that surrounded them. "Keep your thoughts simple. The problem is not now. Don't waste precious time in worry about the future," she suggested gently.

Spring was helping. Zoloft and therapy were doing what they were supposed to do. Her childhood home was comforting. She reread the book Sachiko had gifted her, able to follow better now.

"Sachiko coming to America, and my trip to Japan, were all meant to prepare me for this time. Simple thoughts and simple solutions should be my life rafts," she told her father. "And you, Pops, are my steersman," she said, referring to him as a navigator in old English.

"A what?" he asked, seeing her smile for the first time in a long time.

When a placement firm contacted her out of the blue regarding an editor position, her interest piqued at the prospect, and suddenly she missed work. It reminded her of her life's goal of becoming an editor-in-chief.

"I'm ready to move back to Raleigh and get back to work," she announced the next day, half-packed already.

The publishing company in need of an editor was small, specializing in educational materials, instructional manuals, flyers, and books written by emerging authors. She dove back into preparation, eager not to miss the opportunity. Diligently she prepared, drawing on her past experience. Updating herself on recent publications, political controversies, writing styles, and bestsellers, she reviewed business models for publishing companies. She rehearsed answers to potential questions regarding her management style, content controversies, and conflict resolution.

But when she was offered the job, she was not so sure.

37

THE DIAGNOSIS

Ashley
2002

"You have muscular dystrophy—MD," the neurologist said. It sounded like he was handing a premature death sentence to thirty-year-old Ashley. "There are many kinds of MD, from different mutations. Some cases present in childhood, and others, like yours, do not appear until adulthood. Progression is unpredictable."

Ashley blinked back tears. "What kind is mine?"

"Limb-girdle muscular dystrophy—LGMD," he replied. "There is weakness in your shoulder, upper arm, pelvis, and upper-leg muscles. Early on there is muscle pain and stiffness, which you have. Difficulty climbing, rising from a seated position, carrying heavy objects, reaching overhead, and holding arms outstretched will be gradually affected. Weaknesses in muscles like hands and feet, a weak voice, and difficulty swallowing may happen much later, if at all."

MD led to progressive degeneration and weakness of the muscles, he explained. Like retinitis pigmentosa, a genetic disorder one was born with, the mutation was either inherited from a parent or one that developed new at conception.

As a teenager, Ashley had memorized names of muscles, ligaments, and joints, like a medical student: Quads, hamstrings, Achilles tendon, tarsals, metatarsals, patella, gluteus maximus, and more—all involved in running. She even knew what plantar fasciitis, stress fractures, and bursitis were, common ailments plaguing runners. Now new names like pelvic girdle, latissimus dorsi, pectoralis major, trapezius, abductors, and adductors were thrown at her, but she had no interest in memorizing any more terms.

Eighteen months had passed since 9/11. The world was reeling under the specter of terrorism. The recently declared war in Iraq was ongoing. The global turmoil was mirrored in her internal strife. As the external battle raged, she fought a private battle. Though she acknowledged the cruel reality that soldiers and civilians caught in the crossfire faced mortality daily, the thought did not offer her solace.

It took Ashley two months to share her diagnosis with her parents. At home, sitting around their kitchen island, she saw her parents' aging faces reflecting off the polished granite top. Their wineglasses were filled.

Ashley emptied hers, licked to clear the lingering taste on her lips, and announced, "I've been diagnosed with muscular dystrophy."

Initially their faces did not register any emotion.

Then her father said, "There you go again, sweetheart. We're not falling for it. This is not one of your jokes again, is it? It's not funny."

She played along for a minute, then shook her head. "I've had muscle weakness for some time. I have a genetic condition called muscular dystrophy. It's been confirmed." She looked at her parents and hung her head low, mindlessly zipping and unzipping her jersey.

Her mother's shoulders slouched; her father fidgeted in his chair.

After a few seconds that felt like forever, she heard her father clear his voice. "Genetic condition? Now what's that? Are the doctors sure? No one in our family ever had such a thing!"

She'd not cried about her diagnosis until then, but hot tears were building up. Something about sharing with loved ones. As she fought them, the barely there hum of the kitchen exhaust magnified to a loud din. It was as if the tears were being sucked back in, flooding her eyes and ears, blurring her vision, and echoing the sounds. Then both her parents were talking at once, and she could not hear anything at all but the deafening echo in her ears.

Over the hours that followed, she explained to them what muscular dystrophy was. She felt like a doctor, answering their unending questions as best as she could. As midnight approached, their conversation ebbed, leaving only silence.

"The doctor wants to run genetic tests on both of you," she said softly, alerting them to what was to come.

They retreated to their rooms, hoping to wake up in the morning to the realization that it was all a bad dream. But sleep eluded them, as did dreams. The house was shrouded in silence.

In the morning, faces pale, they moved like malfunctioning robots. No talk of crepes. No activity in the kitchen.

She left Monday morning, not much having been said about the future.

It took two abnormal genes, one from each parent, to manifest Ashley's condition. "A rare coincidence that your parents, unrelated by birth, carry the same aberration," the doctor explained at the next visit. "Even when both parents carry the gene, there is only a twenty-five percent chance of a child being affected."

Unlucky for Ashley, she was one of them.

Her neurologist encouraged her to join a support group. Reluctantly she joined one that met in a church basement. At the first meeting, she felt her nausea rise, reaching her glottis, as she saw one member using a walker and two others sitting stiffly in wheelchairs. A few voices were muffled, their speech slow and halting. Blank stares surrounded her. She collected information, detailing available resources in the community, and never returned.

She ran still, albeit at a slower pace. Muscle relaxers eased her stiffness. Physical therapy helped, such exercises not new to her.

She was referred to a counselor too. Sermons and analysis followed, along with discussions of the five stages of grief. Beyond the initial shock, her therapist analyzed Ashley's shift to anger. Her anger simmered, and irritability crept in as an interloper at inconsequential situations—like during casual conversations and in long grocery lines. Conversations with her parents became tense, and even strangers weren't spared. She worried that she had anger-management issues like her father.

She remained cognizant at work, maintaining a cheerful attitude. And through multiple doctor appointments, she managed her responsibilities, never sharing her diagnosis with colleagues and superiors.

Ashley stalled the process of moving in with Harry while she was undergoing medical tests. She had hoped for a "simple answer with an easy solution," like Dr. Desai had suggested. But that was not meant to be.

She blamed travel assignments for delaying the move, having set in motion a plan she'd already made. Loving Harry too deeply and truly to burden his future with her condition, she had not told him yet

She was heartbroken on two counts: her failing health and its impact on her purported future with Harry. However, when she decided to part ways, the thought of breaking Harry's heart was a heavier burden than breaking her own. A clean separation would be simpler for her but shocking to him. So she moved ahead with a plan for a slow break, to soften the blow, hoping to make it believable and respectful.

In line with her plans, she signed up for multiple business trips, not returning home in between. Staying away helped her grief, which was settling in following her phase of anger.

As Ashley's planned distancing from Harry was set in motion, her distress reached a peak. She needed a distraction if her plan was not to falter. For this she needed to be on the move. Knowing that her days of travel, especially international, were numbered, a new level of urgency to travel took hold.

38

POSTER ON THE WALL

Ashley
2003

"Let's visit Spain again," Ashley suggested to Emily and Rose. "And feel like teenagers once more."

For their second visit to Spain, they planned to re-create the magic of their first trip in college. Right from their arrival at Madrid-Barajas Airport, they felt like everything had changed, yet not at all. When the three of them, among hordes of other visitors, stepped into a beautiful spring day dressed as tourists, it felt familiar.

But what changed was that their dreams had given way to the realities of responsibility and partners to report back to. No longer backpacking and staying in hostels, their itinerary was planned with comfort in mind.

While they could spend liberally, they chose to eat street food, like they did eleven years earlier. Not bound by schedules and reservations, they ate on the go, hung out where the locals did, and relaxed for hours in the local cafés that spilled onto sunny curbs.

They visited the iconic Basílica de la Sagrada Familia in Barcelona. Still under construction, which had started in 1882, the goal to complete the project had been pushed back every time. The scaffolding and barricades stood as reminders that the project had spanned generations, serving as a testament to the perseverance and dedication of the church.

Hundreds of completed spires rose skyward, each dedicated to a biblical figure. They took pictures by the stained-glass windows that sparkled in filtered light. In the apse, they stood at the altar and prayed.

For Ashley, an unusual comparison took hold. Her life felt like an unfinished project with obstacles and an uncertain future, like that of the church.

Sleep that night was fitful. She dreamed of her childhood home crumbling around her. Her four-poster bed buckled and caved in under the collapsing ceiling, trapping her. The once-carefree girl with a future full of promise was buried under the debris. But moments later she saw the Sagrada rising from where her home fell. Standing taller and stronger through decades of change, it stood the test of time and sustained. As she was waking up from her early morning dream, she saw herself walking out of the Sagrada as a middle-aged woman—strong, able, and independent. It was a sign.

She remembered her mother's long-ago story about her trip to Milan. Finding similarity in their mother-daughter experience, she wanted to believe in the dream. The vision of duty and destiny, and dreams her mother relied so heavily on . . . Whether it was good for her mother or not, Ashley was not sure, but she wanted to be completely invested in her own vision.

On the last day of the trip, they scoured the city for crepes. Like always, they sang their crepe-girls song, to the amusement of fellow diners, and requested the waiter to snap their pictures. They even captured their adventures on Rose's new Sony camcorder.

They recalled an April Fools' Day in college, when Emily and Rose successfully pranked Ashley. On a Friday night, when they returned to their apartment, they'd noticed flung-open closets and things scattered on the floor.

"Ssi-bal! We've been robbed!" Emily had exclaimed, using her Korean. "And where are Ashley's shoes?"

Missing were Ashley's twenty or so pairs of running shoes, some of them yet to be used. When Ashley dialed 911, they'd called out, "April fool. We finally tricked the trickster."

As laughter from the memory faded, enveloped in the poignancy of their camaraderie, clinging to her wineglass, Ashley's tone turned serious. "I've been diagnosed with muscular dystrophy. And not an April Fool's joke."

Emily's brows raised and Rose gasped as the moment stilled. Rose reached out and gathered their hands to show solidarity, perhaps. News of the intended breakup with Harry saddened them further.

After the trip, Ashley's parents and coworkers commented on how energized she seemed.

"You need to go on more trips like that," her regional manager quipped.

Ashley gave him a wry smile and moved away.

She later ordered a large sign that had "I Had a Dream" painted in rainbow colors, and she hung it on the wall across her bed. A representative from the company had called to reconfirm the wording. He'd asked if, in fact, she wasn't quoting Reverend Martin Luther King's "I Have a Dream" speech. She'd understood the confusion and clarified she wanted it exactly how she had ordered it.

In the months that followed, she was consumed by grief. Withdrawn, she tried antidepressants at the recommendation of her therapist. Harry's calls went unanswered. Her parents visited her more often. She sobbed when she saw them. They let her. If they shed tears, it was when Ashley wasn't around.

39

SEEING EYE

Robin
2003–2006

"There is some good news, Pops! I got the job. I wasn't sure if I should accept it, but my physician said that there was no reason to quit yet, if I was able to deliver the goods. So I've decided to take the offer," Robin announced over the phone.

"Congratulations, darling daughter. Only a step away from your goal. This calls for a celebration," her father responded.

In her new position as an editor, she had higher pay, better benefits, and more autonomy. Work was busy, but she also had an alternate mission, a personal agenda—preparing for a different life, one with muted colors and fading light.

Robin contacted the North Carolina State Center for Disability Services and sought direction for advocacy and assistance to meet her needs. She was referred to a myriad of companies that helped with assistance technologies. Through the National Federation for the Blind, she had resources offered at no cost.

She delved into 2003 federal and state disability guidelines with a fine-tooth comb. Soon her knowledge of Medicare, disability, and medical insurance coverage and laws exceeded that of her health-care providers. She compulsively researched braille, screen readers, and braille displays. Printed materials in large font and ZoomText, for screen enlargement for online images, also aided her.

She enrolled in the American Braille English version of braille classes. It would help that she learned AEB while she could still see. She analyzed and memorized the distribution of braille dots, arranged in two columns of three dots each.

A braille cell with one dot was an A; two dots in a vertical column were a B. Two dots lying side by side, a C, and so on. Numbers were preceded by a separate braille sign. While she learned a different way to read, her superior cognitive capacity and her photographic memory, in addition to her will to learn, were evident from day one.

By the time she completed grade 1 and moved to the more advanced grade 2 braille, James was in no competition for her. While he struggled to learn beyond the basic alphabet, she moved to mastering signs for grammar, punctuation, and mathematical notations.

She was leading two parallel lives, one of light, literacy, and public life, and the other of darkness, dots, and secluded apartment life. Over three years she had good days and bad ones. Through ups and downs, she relied on medicine, her father, meditating, leaning on the lesson learned on the steps of the rock garden on a sunny day many years earlier, trusting a childhood friend's wisdom. As her vision failed, she adjusted schedules and driving times, avoiding dusk and nighttime. Her colors were getting duller, and her peripheral vision was narrowing.

Once Dr. Ranke said she was nearing legally blind status and driving was not advisable, she applied for disability and planned to move home. It took four months for her disability and other required paperwork to be in place. She made sure her SSDI—her Social Security Disability Insurance—was approved too, for medical coverage. After twenty-four months, she would qualify for Medicare.

Once done with the legwork, her decision made, she met the executive editor and informed him of her condition.

An elderly gentleman, statesman-like, he looked small behind his large mahogany desk. Numerous pictures of his grandchildren adorned the walls. He himself was grappling with the idea of retirement. He had risen through the ranks, and he admired that about Robin, his affinity for her visible at every meeting.

He sighed. "Both of us are asking ourselves what is in the next chapter of our lives. I will support you in any way I can."

She shook his hand and thanked him for his support. Just as she was exiting, he said, "Please let me know if I can be of any help."

She turned back and smiled. "I just might."

On Robin's next ophthalmologist visit, Dr. Ranke said, "Robin, you should consider getting a guide dog."

"Hmmm. I must think about it, Doc. Unfortunately, I've not once longed for a pet." Having never taken care of anyone else but herself, she contemplated how a pet could be incorporated into her life.

All it took was one stumble and a large gash on her elbow to accept the idea.

"Pops, Seeing Eye is one of the largest guide-dog schools in the country, my doctor told me. It's been in business for seventy-five years," Robin told James.

"Then we should visit for sure and get you a guide dog," James said. Already retired, he had started remodeling projects in the house.

The Zymanskis drove to New Jersey for Robin to train with her assigned dog, Lucy, a beautiful golden retriever with a dense, lustrous coat.

"C'mon, Lucy. Let's meet your new companion." The trainer approached Robin. "You can pat her." Lucy's soft fur reminded Robin of the plush mink coat that she'd once tried on during an escapade with a wealthy publisher.

"WHAT'S UP WITH THIS curl at the tip of your tail?" Robin cuddled Lucy. "You're mine now, aren't you?" Lucy inched in closer.

Paired for their gentle personalities and Robin's requirements, the early days were a sensory overload for both, but they grew accustomed to their distinct scents, habits, and idiosyncrasies over a training period of twenty-five days.

At eight weeks Lucy had been trained by volunteers called "puppy raisers." As a baby she was taught simple commands and exposed to environments she might encounter with her future partner. When she was fifteen months, she returned to Seeing Eye for further formal guide-dog training. She was one of the 260 or so special dogs that were matched each year, each of them working for seven to eight years before they were retired as pets.

Lucy successfully minded curbs while walking with Robin. On trial runs she stalled, wary of traffic, and demonstrated uncanny spatial awareness. She responded to Robin's commands and ignored other dogs and distractions.

For the $50,000 it took to train Lucy, Robin only paid $100 for her. She was overwhelmed by the generosity of the donors for her cause. Meanwhile, Robin couldn't recall if she had ever been so generous to others. All her life she had been too busy finding herself, scaling hard-to-reach goals, fighting her demons, and trying not to sink.

On their drive back, Lucy sat in Robin's lap, keenly surveying the changing landscape on the way to her new home.

"We're at the Camel Corner, almost there," Robin whispered to Lucy, the spot still bearing the name despite the billboard being torn down many years ago.

Robin did not feel like an only child anymore. "You're the favorite kid in this house now." Robin rubbed Lucy's belly.

"Are you my soul mate?" Robin would ask her every morning, handing out a treat and nuzzling her nose.

James took care of both Robin and Lily with countless meaningful gestures every day. "Never underestimate the big importance of small things" were his oft-repeated wise words, and he lived by them.

Robin continued to put additional plans in motion. Through grants and assistance programs, she had the home version of Jobs Access with Speech system installed, a popular program that supported both screen readers and braille displays. Designed to work with the Microsoft Windows operating system, it allowed Robin to switch between screen-reading and braille-display modes seamlessly. The setup was no less than a mini computer lab.

"The screen reader will read the text on the screen to me in a synthesized voice, Pops," she said. "Any computer can be made accessible with the correct software, so don't you worry. There is a voice-to-text function, also called 'speech recognition.' So when I dictate, it'll convert it to written text on the screen."

She opened the function. "Let's test it," she said. "Hello, Pops" came up on the screen as Robin said those two words.

"Wow!" James reacted.

She asked the screen reader to read it back to her. "Hello, Pops," said the baritone voice.

"See, this is how I know if the message I want to send is correct. If not, I can edit it. That is called 'echoing," she said, eager to share her rapidly expanding tech vocabulary and developing skills. "I can customize the voice, but for now it reminds me of my math teacher's voice, and I like that."

Robin proceeded to demonstrate the braille display next. "Look, I'll read the text in braille now." As the text appeared on the screen, she placed her hands on the braille keyboard and read out loud, "'Today is a good day.' Did I read it correctly, Pops?"

"Yes, you did, darling. When were you ever wrong when it comes to language and reading?" He put his hand on her shoulder.

"Now let me type the response in braille," she said. "I agree," she typed in braille, and it appeared on the screen.

"You did it again, darling," he said, this time massaging her shoulders, knowing that hours on the computer strained her neck and shoulders.

She practiced reading PDF files and edited on Google Docs like a woman possessed, absorbing the functions like a sponge. Once a text was read to her by the synthesizer, she remembered paragraphs and pages on the first go and edited them without errors. There were frustrations and disappointments, many, along the way, misspelled words, malfunctioning software, slow internet speed, misunderstood cues—but through it all, she remained positive and patient so as not to worry Pops.

James stood sentinel, ever vigilant and supportive of his beloved daughter, assisting her in every way he could. Years earlier he had switched jobs to be the operations manager of a biomedical firm. Through his social connectivity, he knew engineers who were experts in such digital tools, and they came to Robin's help when systems malfunctioned or needed upgrading.

While the latest human-computer interface technology was being put to full use at the Zymanski home, it was to be seen if Robin's plan would fall into place.

40

———

UNRAVELING

Anita

2003

Anita arrived at the test center with her ID, calculator, two 2B pencils, and a water bottle. She left her cell phone in the car. Two years of planning and one year of preparation was at stake—not only for herself but to honor her parents' wishes and to make Paul proud.

At the center, she presented her ID and spotted her seat number. Her assigned seat was in the center of the room. Eighty students surrounded her. She kissed her pendant for an auspicious beginning. For ten minutes an instructor gave specific directions on timing, how to fill the bubble, and what to do and not to do. "If you are stuck on a problem, move on to the next so you don't lose time."

She wrote her assigned ID number and broke the seal of the first section.

A passage filled the top half of the opening page. "Birds in the Amazon forest," the passage began. That was when she broke into a sweat. Her throat dry, she took a sip from her water bottle. That didn't help. Her heart raced. The taunts came alive. "Small like a bird, hair like a bear" rang fresh and clear. She was the epicenter of an earthquake, and the room folded on her, desks and chairs inverted.

When she came to her senses, students were hunched over their papers in silence, their pencils in use.

"If you fail, you'll be back to being a loser," roared the cracking voice of the seventh-grade boy.

Anita shook her head to clear her ears of the voice as she skipped the first passage. She read the next passage twice. Run-on sentences and jumbled words were all she saw. *Irresistible, irreprehensible, irrelevant*—they all sounded the same. Geometry figures looked like doodling designs. When time was up, she was only halfway through.

"What's happened to me? Why am I not catching a break?" she screamed, while leaning on the hood of her car, retching. But her stomach was empty. Leaving the car in the parking lot, she walked 5.6 miles home. She didn't attend the afternoon session. Her phone was in the car. She didn't want to talk to anyone. Her life felt futile.

At work on Monday, even St. Bona, as a sanctuary, turned into a myth. It was announced that the current director was going on indefinite medical leave and an interim had been appointed, someone Anita had no regard for. Indecision was his folly, condescension his habit.

Sure enough, she was called to the new director's office. "I want a new report on staffing and budgeting for supplies. It has come to my attention that supplies are being misused. I need you to be more diligent," he said curtly.

"I will be," she said meekly, recent setbacks weighing heavy on her.

Anita contemplated abandoning her car again and walking the seven miles home—to lock herself in her condominium and never leave it again.

Instead, she drove home, surrendering to yet another day of disappointment. Back at work the next day, she prepared the new report.

"Leave it there—I'll look at it when I have time" was all the interim director said when she handed it to him, without as much as acknowledging her presence in his office.

"So how did it go?" Paul asked the following Sunday.

She did not want to talk about the aborted test, not yet. "It was okay.

Let's order—I'm starving." She signaled the waiter to divert the conversation.

While Anita was scanning for Maizie, the waitress arrived with the bill.

"I'm sure you did well," Paul said. He studied the bill and tucked his credit card into a slot on the folder. "I don't have good news. My neurologist says my scoliosis is worsening, and it is putting too much pressure on the nerve that goes to my right leg, weakening it. He is recommending surgery."

"Surgery?" Anita pinched her brows.

"He wants to put a bunch of rods in my spine to straighten it. I'll be bedridden for a few days, he says, and will need months of rehab."

"That sounds serious. How can I help?"

"I told him I wasn't ready for surgery."

"Why did you say that? I can see that your right leg is dragging more lately."

"I know my shuffling is worse and more painful, but understand that I spend four hours with Devin each week. You don't need a hundred friends to make you happy—all you need is one, and I'm that for Devin. I'll finish the school year with him and then decide what I want to do."

Anita slid her credit card into the same slot. "He's lucky to have you. If only every kid had one person who truly cared . . . imagine."

"Exactly. I simply want to help a child who has lost his father to cancer."

"But what about you? You need to take care of yourself too, Paul." Anita patted his hand. "I have so much to learn from your goodness. You're a perfect human being and my best friend. But where were you in high school when I needed you the most?" She smiled.

"I was invisible in school, remember?"

"Invisible? I don't remember that."

"Most people looked right through me, as if I wasn't there. My disability made them uncomfortable," he said, unbothered. "I learned to accept myself the way I was. I stood in my own truth, and then it all became easy."

"I couldn't accept myself. That was my problem. I was the picked-on one, if you remember," Anita said.

"People naturally fear anything different from what they know," Paul said. "Their bad behaviors just reveal their own ignorance. I've learned to wish them peace."

"I wish I could be as wise and steady as you are, Paul. I admit, their cruelty has had too much power in my life."

"But not anymore," Paul said. "Today is a new day. And you're getting your GED."

"Yeah, about that . . ."

"Listening . . ."

"I must confess . . . I didn't finish the test," she added hastily.

A serving platter slipped out of a waiter's grip and splattered onto the floor. Above the rattling and diners' sympathy for the waiter, Anita did not hear Paul's reply.

"Suzie, let's order. I'm starving." It was Maizie.

Anita turned to see a tall middle-aged man with salt-and-pepper hair, wearing a quarter zip. Two Maizies flanked him. Anita did a double-take.

"Suzie is lazy and crazy," one of them sang.

"Identical twins, are they? They are just so beautiful," a patron commented.

Anita turned toward Paul, mystified.

"Oh yes, my daughters are double trouble, you know," the twins' father answered cheerfully.

Anita's head swam with stars as she stood, disoriented. Paul steadied her as she wobbled along. How had she been so wrong? Was it that each of the girls had come to the diner at different times, never together? Had their parents been dividing their parental responsibilities by managing one child at a time?

Anita turned back for a second look, as if her mind needed to confirm what she'd just witnessed. Sure enough, there at the back table sat an attractive, well-dressed father enjoying dinner with his twins. "How can that be?" she said aloud.

"What can't be?" Paul asked.

She shook her head, as her words wouldn't surface. Instead, a roaring wave of grief rushed into the space where Maizie had been living in her heart, the space where she had connected with her long-

lost daughter, the space where her hope had rekindled. And now realizing that she'd been wrong about Maizie being her daughter, the wall
she'd built around herself as an unwed teenage mother . . . had been
breached. She was broken beyond repair.

41

P. DANBY

Anita
2003–2009

Night after night she woke up with a start, her heart pounding from a dream she did not remember, or rather did not want to remember. She felt parched but did not have the will to address it. Disjointed and displaced, she struggled to recover from her disappointment.

"Are you okay, Anita?" her colleagues asked her at work, without referencing her missing laughs.

"Yes, I'm fine. Thank you" was her polite reply. Punctual and professional as ever, she went through the motions. Despite her apathy, her work, an ingrained habit by now, did not suffer. When Oleo waved to her, Anita did not want to talk to her. The pain was overwhelming, as Oleo was the only person she had shared Maizie's story with. But the simple, toothless smile she could not ignore.

"You know, I fooled myself," Anita said, holding Oleo's hands.

Oleo admired Anita's pendant.

Anita simply tucked her pendant inside her shirt, temporarily doubting the significance of Lord Ganesha removing obstacles.

Her director, back to work after his medical leave of absence, saw her on hands and knees vigorously scrubbing old floors, shining spotless glass doors, dusting inaccessible crevices with a hint of violence, like she was fighting an invisible demon in them.

Although pleased with his return, Anita had not acknowledged him, and when she did, it was with a wry smile.

She resembled the sixteen-year-old he'd first met: fully diligent, punctual, and committed. And completely detached and aloof. He did not know her story then, nor did he know now.

After having rushed out of the diner, Anita dreaded going back there. The following Saturday, her day to clean came and went. She did not have an appetite. Lying in bed through mealtimes, skipping them, wrapped in her comforter, she did not find comfort. Sunday morning she still lingered in bed, reluctant to face reality.

By evening she did not want to worry Paul, her only trusted friend, having left him without a goodbye. She had to get her bearings back. That was the only way out of the chaos she'd created for herself.

Cheeks hollowed, eyes sunken, she arrived at the diner before Paul did so she could sit facing away from the table Maizie and Suzie sat at.

Paul would notice the shift, as she had recently been insisting on facing one way, saying, "I like looking into the restaurant and its patrons, not at the windows." Her ruse had worked.

When Paul arrived, she greeted him with overcompensated cheerfulness, unable to share the unvarnished truth, the reason too personal and the torment too real.

"In four months I'll be taking my semester finals," he said, in his usual style of imparting facts without flair.

She nodded. She did not respond to Paul's cues, and GED was not referenced anymore.

Her disappointment with herself would not abate. How could she so gullibly believe she could identify her daughter by the way of looks? Was she even sure how Sebastian looked anymore? It had been eleven long years! She remembered his eyes. They'd fooled her then, and they'd fooled her again now. Amber was not her favorite color anymore. She blamed nature and life itself for the deception.

She remained withdrawn, and her parents noticed too. "Are you okay?" they too asked.

How much she wanted to surprise them by starting college. But that wouldn't be. She would be a high school dropout for life.

Spending more time indoors doodling again, her sadness was reflected in the sorrow of the painted eyes. Grim expressions, moist and mournful, they did not have amber in them. In her most recent painting, she highlighted tears more than she did the eyes.

Six months later, at the American Red Cross, she stood among the mannequins and proudly held her BLS certificate, standing next to Paul and twenty-five others. "Thanks to you, at least one of my dreams came true." Paul nodded.

She'd agonized over practicing cardio-pulmonary resuscitation on the baby-size plastic models, but had persevered. That the course was mostly applied hands-on training, rather than a written curriculum, helped.

"These minor successes make larger goals manageable. Let's keep going," Paul said.

Out of necessity, she learned advanced computer skills at the local library—how to make charts, graphs, and spreadsheets for her presentations at managerial meetings. Once again the course was practical— interactive learning enabled her training significantly.

A big brother to two more boys besides Devin, all high schoolers, Paul was enrolled in an online MBA course. Busier but committed, he never missed a Sunday dinner with Anita.

The following year, Anita helped nurse her father back to health after prostate surgery, his recovery taking longer than expected. For the multiple doctor visits that followed, he required short-term disability. She sat with him in the doctor's office, helping him with his catheter. She helped Rumi in the kitchen and learned the Indian way of cooking. She followed recipes and perfected making cauliflower curry and samosas, deep fried potato fritters made in triangles. At Indian festivals and gatherings, she engaged in conversations, but at times she'd be alone, watching her parents' friends and their families flit around in brightly colored clothes, talking loudly, unable to maintain quiet even during religious ceremonies.

Still, she dined with Paul every week. His right leg was dragging more, his muscles and nerves tiring faster. "Nerve atrophy," his doctor explained. "The pressure on the nerve in your back must be relieved. Otherwise you won't be able to walk at all one day."

When delaying surgery was not an option anymore, Paul agreed to proceed. To his relief, Devin had graduated high school by then. The two other boys were settling down too.

"Only two days in the hospital, but weeks of physical therapy as an outpatient. And I won't be able to drive for four weeks," Paul told Anita once a date for surgery was fixed.

"My cousin said he'll visit me at the hospital," Paul said two weeks before his surgery.

"Paul, please let me help," Anita pleaded timidly, for fear of over-stepping her boundary. She was hoping her offer would not be rejected. They had not visited each other's homes, never needing to before. They'd guarded their spaces of sanity like they were the inner sanctum sanctorum of a temple.

Paul called Anita once his anesthetic wore off. "The surgeon said my surgery went well."

"Thank God," she said in relief.

He gave her his home address, and two days later, when he was discharged from the hospital, she drove to his brick-faced split-level home. "P. Danby" read the sign on the mailbox. She parked outside the one-car garage and sat there for some time, letting the weight of the moment settle in. Their deep friendship was getting deeper.

The yard was freshly cut. A few boxwoods stood on either side of the entrance. Carrying in the groceries she'd brought, she followed Paul's cousin into the living room. A copy of *The 7 Habits of Highly Effective People* lay on the coffee table. Books filled every shelf there was. Walls were bare, like hers. She was led to Paul's bedroom, where he lay under a thin blanket. He looked longer reclined than upright. A walker was by his bed. The latest copies of *The New York Times* and *USA Today* lay on his nightstand. She saw stubble on his face for the first time.

Paul introduced his cousin to Anita. "My only family in town."

Anita saw similarities in their prominent foreheads and strong, square jaws.

"How can I help?" she asked.

"Just talk to me," he said.

She did, for hours.

"I have all the time in the world," she told him the next day. "I took the whole week off to spend with you."

She handed him his pain pills on a schedule and ChapStick for dry lips. She helped him in and out of bed, prepared food, and cleared dishes. When his cousin couldn't be there one night to help, she stayed overnight, a first.

On Sunday they ate dinner together, Paul in his bed and Anita sitting on a chair by him. She drove him for physical therapy appointments, his right leg still weak. Their conversations flowed effortlessly. She held his hands, another first, when he moaned in pain. She rubbed his back, easing his stiff muscles.

They watched in horror at the images of windblown homes and flooded cities that flashed on television as breaking news when Hurricane Katrina made landfall.

"Cities and communities are for sure breaking apart," Paul said. "The poorest and the handicapped will suffer the most," he predicted.

Stories of missing children and pets and pictures of people on rooftops inundated their television screen.

Paul's meticulous plans were taking shape, one day at a time. He signed the lease for a space for his café and casually mentioned it to Anita without fanfare.

"Will you design a sign for my business?" He showed her the plans of the layout. Anita agreed.

On a rectangular metal sheet, she traced the letters to spell "PAUL'S CAFÉ" and painted them encircled with stars. She was there by his side on inauguration day, proud to be his friend. His cousin was there too, greeting and welcoming customers.

When Paul opened his second café, Anita was there again. Yet again, she made the sign.

His cafés were doing brisk business, crumpets and croquettes their bestsellers.

"Croquettes are like the samosas we make at home," Anita said to Paul after tasting one of them.

"Then make them, and we'll sell them here," he encouraged her.

The first batch she made sold in a day.

"This is your share of the money from their sale." He tried to pay her.

"Nah. Please use it when you're with Devin and the other boys." She felt honored to contribute to Paul's noble cause.

"Let me make a business proposition then. Make samosas every week if you can, and we can be business partners, if you'd like."

"I would love to." She welcomed the distraction.

She experimented with different shapes and fillings for the samosas, finally settling back on the standard triangles and the potato filling.

When Anita's parents downsized, she helped. Unopened boxes from their move in 1994 were opened, reviewed, and assessed for monetary and sentimental value. Ami was there too, both sisters to lay claim on memories they wished to carry with them.

The first box Anita opened had her high school books. Instinctively she closed the box, but one book with a purple cover caught her attention. Her junior-year science book, the book that had birthed her doodling. In black ink, every margin was filled with lines that curved, angled, slanted, and stretched, making meaningless connections. Picking up a pen, she doodled again on the empty preface page, connecting endless lines in random designs. She ended it with a large question mark, like she was questioning herself about her life. The book that had meaningless patterns had saved her and led her to painting. It was a memento. She placed it in her takeaway pile.

While going through the family albums, numerous black-and-white pictures of her childhood surfaced, followed by gradual transition to color. Her baby picture she studied with interest, focusing on her eyes. Long black eyelashes and big black pupils. Nothing fancy, only plain and ordinary, like her life. This saddened her.

She added her dadi's picture to her takeaway pile, of Holi with her cousins too. Also her parents' earliest picture in the USA, their family picture in front of the first house they owned. Anita, on her first day of high school, stood out for her awkwardness. She revisited, picking through the memories of her early life, of joy and pain, piecemeal.

The last page had two pictures: one official passport-size picture of Ami at her graduation, and another of her move into her dorm at Northwestern.

Then there were no more.

Years passed. She had all but forgotten and given up on her dream of a GED and college.

42

FINGERTIPS

Robin
2006–2009

"Pops, let me show you what I learned today." Robin dragged James to her desk. "I figured an easier way to memorize punctuation."

He watched her long fingers deftly sail along in the sea of braille dots, deciphering notations foreign to him.

"No more huck muck," she said, dragging him to her room, like a small child showing off newly learned tricks on the monkey bars.

"I've never seen your room this organized, my darling daughter," he said, having always worried about her ability to organize things and her life.

"I've walked Lucy and myself in the neighborhood and managed to bring us both back in one piece" was another declaration of her growing mobility, a fading bruise on a knee and a stubbed toe, signs of a missed step or a run-in not referenced.

Able to discern light from dark, to follow gray tones and blurry shapes, to count steps, and to use tactile clues and smells and sounds and her memory, she navigated, independent, within the confines of their home and in their neighborhood.

In the kitchen they regaled each other with their stories while cooking. Lucy snuggled on Robin's feet, warming her perpetually cold toes. Robin busied herself chopping vegetables, stirring pots, and sniffing out ingredients.

"I've learned a thing or two from Lucy, didn't I?" she joked about her sniffing.

After tasting, she guessed the ingredients some more. James called it the "flavor and fragrance test."

"Watch out for those precious fingertips," James cautioned when Robin followed the shapes of vegetables, exploring their curves and contours, slowly demonstrating her tactile skills as the knife's edge danced close to her fingertips.

"Is this the correct size?" she would ask, unfazed by the many cuts and scrapes that were later bandaged and soothed.

She peeled carrots and potatoes, starting at the top and swiping down swiftly, rotating them 360 degrees, gauging the transition from rough surfaces to smooth.

Robin brought stories to life, both imagined and read, as she modulated her voice like her mother used to. Occasionally she broke into a Shakespearean monologue, reverting to her teenage whims, while James, shaking his head, conceded yet again, not following any of it.

"Pops and Moms, I'm blessed to have you as parents. It's your love that holds me together. I think one good gene I have inherited from my fake parents is the courage to live. The other defective gene they might have passed on to me, I won't hold it against them," she joked once.

They laughed at the reference to her fake parents, a moment when they were finally able to find humor in an allusion to her biological parents.

The clanging of pots and pans and the chatter in the kitchen brought back a semblance of normality to their family. In college, missing her father's cooking, her mood had dictated her eating. Her inability to maintain schedules and plan her meals had compounded the problem, which had led to eating at odd and irregular intervals.

Waiting until starved and devouring greedily or simply skipping meals altogether, she'd only gained six pounds in her freshman year, which were fortunately distributed to the contours of her bony frame that needed filling.

But now in her third decade of life, such habits were not forgiving. Her waist and hips merged into one long cylinder—the curves her bony frame had developed in college were long obliterated and then some. Soft bands of blubber protruded from under her brassiere, over her pants, and in other obtrusive places. The onslaught of overstretched skin and the accompanying white streaks of stretch marks on her once-smooth breasts and pannus were accelerating.

Sedentary life in PJ's all day was of no help either, and when her favorite jeans refused to come off, she recruited her mother for assistance.

"Your too-good-to-pass-up food is responsible for my Rubenesque figure!" She blamed her father. "I shouldn't let my eyesight dictate how I live. Physical health and spiritual health are both important, aren't they? How come you haven't told me that yet?"

A stationary bike was dusted and moved from the basement. "The solution is simple, my darling daughter. While I cook, you ride the bike," James said, oiling the wheels.

Robin couldn't sustain more than twenty minutes at the start, but with a goal of losing fifteen pounds, she persisted spinning through muscle cramps and back aches, sweating through higher speeds and resistance.

Robin often approached her father to tell him something but ended up listening to him, sometimes for hours. Second born in his family, during the depths of The Great Depression, his stories were mostly biographical.

"While my carpenter father saw his work disappear, my mother took charge. You know, I trailed her everywhere. She was my first teacher, of course. She told me Aesop's fables as I watched her slice, dice, stir, and cook. You see, the morals and principles apply to cooking too—preparation, planning, and patience." He stopped kneading dough, in deep thought.

"Once my mother was chopping onions, and I thought she was crying." He sniffled. "But only in college did I learn that a gas released from onions reacts with water in our eyes, producing sulfuric acid that burns our eyes." He chopped red onions into perfect slivers. "So much for science lessons."

He never failed to narrate his oft-repeated story about his special concoction, a spinach soup. "When I was seven, my mother let me experiment with smoked asparagus, spinach, and fennel for a soup. My brother loved it despite his distaste of vegetables, and for that, my mother was thankful. This soup became a regular dish on our dinner table."

"It is still," Robin replied.

"After the Second World War, my father returned with only a foot drop, but he walked and lived like the burden of the world was on his shoulders. There was little money around. My mother used to say that good cooking came in handy only when there was money to buy the goods. So I worked multiple jobs, finally graduating from college at twenty-eight, to make my mother's dream come true," he said wistfully.

Robin managed her laundry and did dishes. Exercise, a daily commitment, took an hour. Music and audibles accompanied her, with Queen and "Bohemian Rhapsody" now a lesson in the unifying power of music. She walked Lucy when weather permitted.

Robin maintained an email commentary with Sachiko, about everything and nothing, giving Robin a practice partner to experiment with braille, voice recognition technology, and echoing. Like they were in the drama club, their roles reversed, with Sachiko encouraging and correcting as she finessed Robin's communication skills—just as Robin had done for Sachiko in high school.

Robin emailed short stories, jokes, and poems, and wrote about Lucy and everyday successes and failures. Sachiko analyzed the parallels of spirituality and her marital journey, of bliss and struggle, and the sorrow of losing her parents.

Still, Robin was unable to share her adoptive history.

The exercises were part practice, part therapy, with Sachiko fulfilling her role as a counselor, a position Robin had asked her to take. They conversed too, international phone calls more affordable.

"Like a good braille reader, I can read four hundred words in a minute now," Robin told Sachiko.

"So much faster than the two hundred fifty words that most readers read, isn't it?"

"Yes, that's true, because braillers use two hands simultaneously to read."

"You're good at this. Everyone will mark you," Sachiko said, evoking the dialogue from *Much Ado About Nothing.*

"Not true, Lady Disdain," Robin replied, roaring with laughter.

The final leg of Robin's plan was coming together. Once convinced of her skills, she contacted her previous employer and took him up on his offer. To her surprise, he had not yet retired.

"Being legally blind may seem contradictory to working as an editor, but not anymore. I've enough assistance with technology that I can work again. I can edit, proofread, and help with a manuscript if you'll give me a chance," she told him.

She explained the marvels of screen readers, braille displays, and editing. He was curious, if not amazed. Two of his assistants were promptly dispatched to assess the validity of the technology and her ability to use it. Her publisher had always liked her zeal, now even more.

She landed a job as a private contractor to work remotely at her own pace.

"Our borrowed daughter, more precious than one born out of us ever could be, setting an example for others. She can take care of herself. Now we can rest easy," James said to Lily, thrilled and relieved at the same time.

She had been well into her physical and spiritual journey, and with work in hand, she was even more so now.

Her cousins and friends from work called on her occasionally. Visits from colleagues were few, the two-hour distance a hurdle. When she mentioned reading books, the conversation went silent.

"You see, I do that with my braille display and screen reader," she explained.

"That makes sense," their tone relaxed.

After three years at home, as her outside interactions dwindled, she craved them. And wanting to live independently and relieve her aging parents' burden, she broached the subject hesitantly.

"Why would you want to leave the comfort of our home?" James asked perplexedly.

"Pops, try to understand. I'll have help, and Lucy will be by my side. Living independently is important to me," she explained.

It was not long before they found a place that met all their requirements.

43

ONE LAST TIME

Robin
July 2009

"Let's celebrate our birthdays on the beach, like always. One trip before I move to St. Bona," Robin suggested.

When in elementary school, Robin had drawn birthday cards for her father. As a preteen she'd baked his birthday cake. As a teenager she'd cooked a meal for him. In college and thereafter, she'd had elaborate meals delivered to the beach. They'd eaten at a table set close to the water's edge, sipping wine, water lapping at their feet, the sun lighting the sky orange.

Robin could no longer see the beautiful hues in the sky, but what little light she saw, she enjoyed as wind ruffled her hair and waves massaged her feet. She liked the tingling in her soles as sand rolled under her feet and the salt water left a sticky residue around her ankles. Lucy sat just outside the water's edge, watching a double-crested cormorant dive into the water and a sanderling peck at sand fleas.

"I can't believe Pops is turning seventy-five," Robin said.

Lily moved close to her. "And I can't believe you'll be thirty-seven this week. Seems like we brought you home just the other day. Where did the years go?"

All three held hands. Robin felt her father's bracelet, the one she had woven in robin's-egg blue yarn for his fiftieth birthday.

"See, Pops, I'll always be with you, right there on your wrist."

"My darling daughter, from the moment I saw you, I loved you like I've loved no one. I'll never be too far away from you either."

Robin heard a light tremble in her father's slowing speech.

She touched his face and felt his beard. "What's up with this pogonotrophy?" she said, to lighten the mood, referring to his act of growing a beard.

"There you go again." He laughed loudly until his eyes were wet.

Tears of sorrow they were. Darkness surrounded them, enveloping James and Lily and adding to Robin's already dark world, for their last time on a beach.

44

THE LETTER

Ashley

For Ashley, work continued, and so did medical exams and therapy sessions. As her symptoms progressed, she switched to a parallel role that did not involve travel.

Avoiding climbing stairs, she withdrew to the confines of her office, only interacting with others during meetings. Getting in and out of her chair was cumbersome, as she needed leverage, which was often her desk.

Other physical changes were emerging. Her walk slow and deliberate, like a patient recuperating from a stroke. Her gait, mobility, and behavior oozed change, unacknowledged by her colleagues, reflecting their professionalism. She wavered between the issue of medical privacy and workplace divulgence.

With her symptoms on a slow but relentless march, she struggled with her disability and others' perception of it. Helpless occasionally, hopeful most other times, oscillating between highs and lows, she adapted.

One day, expecting to see her parents, she opened the door only to find Harry in front of her, a potted succulent with tumescent serrated leaves in his hand.

Her Handsome Hunk Harry, dressed casually, with hair that appeared professionally set, looked as attractive as she remembered. In her vulnerability, flustered, she lowered her gaze. She studied the tiny flowers and leaves on her crumpled nightgown and bizarrely wondered if the leaves mimicked the serrated ones in Harry's hand. Lost in her thought, she wobbled and grasped her cane for support.

He caught her and stood there for a long time, hugging her with his free hand.

"My Harry," she murmured.

He led her to the couch, cradling her elbow, and helped her settle in. He found a spot for the plant on her kitchen table, then took her hands in his. He did not ask questions, and she didn't attempt to explain.

"I had to see you. You broke up with me, but our connection is not something that can be broken. It can be adjusted, mended, and redefined, if that is what you wish." He looked into her eyes, his eyelids blinking rapidly. "Ash, it is you and me. The Angel and The Elixir. All you had to do was tell me what you wanted me to be in your life, and I would've been that."

"For all the practical jokes I played on people, God played a real joke on me," she said. Tears flowed and her nose reddened. "I'm sorry. Please forgive me."

He accepted her apology, reassuring her that nothing about her disability mattered to him.

Leaning forward, he hesitated before he kissed her forehead. When she did not resist, he traveled lower, until he met her tremulous lips, letting the wetness of her tears conveniently merge with that of his kiss. Through the salty sweetness of the moment, he carried her into the bedroom. She was far too swept with emotion to resist. He proceeded gently, maneuvering her stiff shoulders and tired pelvic muscles. Her body cooperated just so, enough to show their physical longing for each other.

In that act of careful adjustments and acknowledgment of limitations, she understood why she loved him. And she knew that her love for him would outlast her.

In the ensuing months, Harry was a constant presence in Ashley's life. As a pair, they balanced their routines and movements, Harry excitedly and Ashley unsure.

Ashley felt alive and hopeful again. But her uncertainty was growing. After a few months of mulled contemplation, she handed him a letter and requested that it be read when he was back in his apartment.

He slid into his car. Unable to wait, he slipped his index finger into the glued edge of the envelope and bluntly dragged it sideways. He hadn't felt the paper cut on his index finger until he later saw the bloodstain on the envelope.

He felt dread in anticipation. His vision blurred for a minute before the evenly printed alphabet came into clear view.

Dear Harry,

My Hairy Harry. My Old Handsome Hunk Harry. My H3O.

As essential as water is for survival, you were and are more than that to me. You are my H3O—my life's special Elixir. That is what you will always be.

My life has taken an unimaginable twist. A future without you in it is unbearable. Although this fills me with despair, it would be even more painful for me if you were involved in my life. I don't want to give you a life of compromise. I couldn't live with guilt.

Love empowers us to rise above our challenges. I am not underestimating your ability to take care of me, but spending my life indebted to you, with no means to repay you, will add an inordinate amount of misery to my life. Every day with you will remind me how inadequate and dependent I will be on you.

Once my mother spoke about the burden of love. I understand it now. Renouncing my love for you will be a burden that I will bear for a lifetime.

I will be weak in my knees for you. Ha-ha—now that I have weakness everywhere, not just in my knees!

We will remain friends but not depend on each other. Please visit me occasionally, but please not unannounced. I need time to prepare my heart for the onslaught your looks will bring on!

I urge you to move on with your life. A broken heart does not equate to a broken life. Hopefully you will find someone just a little less compatible than me, so you will think of me occasionally in a special way.

People fall in and out of love all the time. Nothing is permanent, so is love. I will reach out to you when I need you. You don't owe me anything, but it will sadden me if I don't get to see you for a visit occasionally. The world cannot be that cruel. You will never be too far away in my thoughts. I wanted to be your everything. I accept my misfortune, my friend. Lots of hugs to you.

Ash

He was not surprised. He had seen it in Ashley's eyes, just before she'd given him the letter, like she was asking him to forgive her for her betrayal. But still his stomach knotted, his heart pained. He sat still for a long time, until a honk startled him to the present. His hands shook as he turned the key in the ignition and slowly eased out of the parking spot, wondering if circumstances would ever allow him to see her again.

45

BACK HOME

Ashley
2006

As Ashley's condition progressed, she soon needed a walker, for fear of falling. So at thirty-three, she applied for disability and moved back home.

Away from home, she had lived in the pretense that everything was all right on the home front. The idea of moving back added anxiety to her already stressed life. This time, mobility impaired, she would be trapped. No running away. No escape. Her slow gait a hindrance to even the backyard exit, making her hammock, her cocoon, inaccessible.

Ahead of her move home, a friend of her parents was contracted for changes and renovations to facilitate her wheelchair. An entrance ramp was added. A new main-floor bedroom with a bathroom was built with disability access. Wide doors, walk-in shower, sturdy handles, support bars, and other accessories were installed.

Her new bedroom, relocated near her parents', brought additional anxiety.

A prized pedestal bought in Rome years ago, from an antique dealer, was shifted into her parents' already cluttered bedroom. It once supported an ancient obelisk in a museum, the dealer had told them.

Extraneous pieces like curio cabinets and console tables were moved into the basement. "For safekeeping," her mother said. Pieces of art collected over the years and hoped to be of monetary value, not just sentimental value, were mere knick-knacks to Ashley, whereas for her mother, they were part of her connection to her past, to her travels that she remembered with adoration.

Ashley made sure to hang the "I Had a Dream" sign in her new bedroom, across from her bed. She hoped this to be the first thing she saw upon waking.

None of her childhood accessories in pink were to be moved into her new bedroom, for lack of space. Gone were her days of sleeping in her white-laced canopied bed with matching paisley sheets. A special hospital bed with handrails and emergency buttons took its place, surrounded by canes, walkers, and a wheelchair. *Too much metal* was her first thought. She drew comparisons with the side rails of her crib and sound monitor her parents had used to safeguard her as a baby to similar contraptions on her hospital bed. Life was coming full circle already.

Her only possession that had a semblance of life and hope in her new room was her plant. Prickly Peter, she named it. It sat on the far corner of her desk, where the combination of sunlight and temperature was ideal.

She was never one to read books for fun, but now they had become her occasional companions. She was even watching afternoon soaps in the company of house help, who doubled as her aide.

Her father drove her for therapy sessions and medical appointments. She used her walker mostly, but some days after physical therapy or multiple doctor appointments, she resorted to her wheelchair.

Her parents were sixty-seven. Slowly the long-standing fractures in their relationship were surfacing, like a submarine rising when in trouble. Cracks that her mother perceived as minor in her married life now morphed into major fault lines. Her behavior changed drastically, as if she blamed her husband for her daughter's plight. For all his transgressions she so easily forgave, she could not forgive him for her daughter's suffering, irrationally and illogically. She retreated into a shell.

Naturally, Ryan's response was an outburst. For the first time, he carried on even knowing Ashley was nearby. He finally resorted to pleading, another first, but Kelly's indifference persisted.

All her previous talk of duty dropped. She had to find blame for their destiny. She moved out of the master bedroom. There was talk of separation.

"Why now, Mom?" Ashley asked.

"It is time. It just is," she replied.

For Ashley, life had been about timing and speed. After her diagnosis, time and motion crawled like a sluggish, muddy river at a dead pace. Her parents' impending separation slowed it even more. Ashley had questioned her mother's tolerance of her father's abuse, but in her selfishness had never suggested a solution—the idea of separation and divorce had been too personal and too traumatic.

She was at an impasse, unable to imagine life split between her parents' separate homes. Confined to her bedroom, she stared at her favorite sign, looking for direction. She hoped for another dream, another vision. But none materialized. The only life in the room, her Prickly Peter seemed to sympathize with her, as if he too realized that she would need more help in the future and her parents wouldn't be able to provide it.

Worried that she was now the catalyst for the conflict in the family, she convinced her parents that she should move to an assisted living center, where she could get skilled help without being a burden. Money was not an issue, as her trust fund could cover many expenses.

PART III

PRESENT DAY

46

SYMBIOSIS

St. Bona

2009

"Have you seen the garden yet?" Ashley asks. "It's one of the best. My sanctuary really."

Robin nods. "Well, seeing is believing, and I'll never know."

Ashley recovers quickly. "Well, we'll have to fix that. Come with me."

Within minutes Robin and Lucy trail Ashley's wheelchair into the courtyard, a routine that will soon become a habit. As Ashley parks her wheelchair in her favorite sunny spot, Robin takes a seat beside her on a nearby bench, shielding her photosensitivity with sunshades.

"The flowers smell lovely," Robin admits.

"And the fresh air and sunshine add to that," Ashley chimes.

While they share the quiet peace of nature, a friendship is blossoming.

White cottonwood seeds float through the air, reminding Ashley of her childhood chases. One lands above Robin's right ear, like a planned hair accessory. Ashley moves to flick it, but on second thought leaves it in place, knowing that nature will carry it to another predetermined destination.

"It is past time for tulips, crocs, clematis, and daffodils. Daisies, peonies, and ranunculus are also done," Ashley explains, reminiscing about the well-manicured garden of her childhood home. "Hydrangeas are in full bloom now. Encircling them are the petunias waving their long, colorful arms. Red and yellow marigolds line the walkways. Zinnias and roses are grouped in separate pods on opposite sides. Pansies, asters, and mums will come when the weather turns."

"You forgot the lilies. Their fragrance is unmistakable," Robin adds, inhaling slowly.

"You're right. I missed them. There are many other plants and flowers used as fillers in the corners and crevices, which I don't recognize. And a few uninvited guests have also crept up, joining the party," she says, alluding to the weeds.

"White flowers are my favorite—lilies the most, like my mom's name," Robin says. She wonders whether her lifelong affinity for white flowers was a premonition for losing her color vision or simply because white stood as an aesthetically pleasing contrast to the colorful butterflies that landed on them. But at the root, she knew she liked them because of her mother's name.

Sometimes she is active in her "world of words." The term *zoanthropy* comes to her mind, a word that describes when one strongly identifies with an animal or magically imagines oneself to be one.

In second grade she'd become captivated by the perilous journey monarch butterflies chartered to survive. Sitting outside now, she imagines herself as a butterfly, free and beautiful, flitting around quietly from one pretty flower to the next, drinking sweet nourishing nectar, spreading pollen, dancing in the magic yellow dust of nature.

She hears a buzz. Unbothered, she remains still. She compares butterflies to bees. How the harmless, dainty butterflies glide quietly, while bees, capable of stinging, drone annoyingly. She thinks of it as God's way of alerting people like her when a bee comes along. *Nature's way of balancing, like we do with our disabilities and talents.*

The smell of freshly cut grass, the rustle of the leaves, the soft crunching of gravel, the chirping of sparrows, and the sound of the wind as it tousles her hair transports Robin into an imaginary wonderland. For a second she feels like the seven-year-old Alice in Wonderland, lost in the world of magic.

"For me, summer is when crows caw. Where are all the crows nowadays?" Ashley asks.

"Global warming maybe? Or is it the pesticides that are slowly killing them, like they did the bees?" Thereafter, Robin pays attention and hears distant cawing, but Ashley doesn't.

On Sundays, Robin also hears faint church bells that go unheard by others. Such sounds she keeps to herself selfishly, like she owns them.

"Oh, the rockery," Robin says when Ashley describes the rock garden.

"A what?" Ashley asks.

This takes Robin back to the Kare Sansui Temple. Fifteen rocks grouped in threes. No greenery, no water. Just gravel. A powerful idea of the complex world represented in the simplest of forms. "Don't overthink. Keep it simple," she reminds herself. Drawing strength from that reminder, she once again offers a silent prayer, thanking God for sending Sachiko into her life.

Sometimes Robin and Ashley observe silence to honor nature. While Ashley soaks in the colors, Robin lets the sounds and scents talk to her. As they say, the sense of smell is most closely linked with memory and emotion, more than any other sense. It has the longest memory and the strongest connectivity to the hippocampus, the brain center for emotion. So Robin's emotion, memory, and sense of smell are painfully and strongly intertwined.

Memories of their kitchen, of bottled spices and homemade sauces and stocks, leave her longing for home. She misses her parents terribly sometimes, the ache so strong that she doesn't eat all day. But she is one of the luckier residents of St. Bona, as her parents visit often, and she goes home too, especially for the holidays.

Lily's deepening depression overwhelms James, yet he persists with his upbeat talk. He cooks for Robin, even though the variety and quality are gradually diminishing, along with his apparent interest in cooking. The flavor and fragrance test is slowly fading away. Fennel, saffron, sage, cilantro, paprika, thyme, basil, cardamom, and ginger—her memory of their flavors is receding, like the light in her life.

Robin and Ashley joke about their disabilities self-deprecatingly. They acknowledge the ironic reversal of their lives. Robin, formerly sedentary, is transformed into a fitness enthusiast. She humorously attributes her exercise routine so she can indulge in eating. Meanwhile, Ashley, once too busy to crack open a book, now devours pages daily.

Bingo nights are loud and fun. The excitement for winning money, even inconsequential amounts, is palpable. Their schedules are planned around karaoke nights, so as not to miss them.

Nostalgia sneaks up on them circuitously, in a voice, a smell, a story, like an unannounced guest, making them quieter.

"Nostalgia! Our evil twin," Robin calls it.

"I don't know about pleasure—it sure does bring dread," Ashley explains. The first karaoke night, the Freddie Mercury night, was soaked in such experience for them.

"What's one thing you'd do if your disability were resolved today?" Ashley asks Robin.

With studied calm, Robin replies, "Go see my pops."

Ashley does not wait to be prompted for her answer. "I'd marry Harry, which can't be. So I guess I'll go for a run and let my mind roam free."

Some days they watch rain pelt windows until the emerging sun paints a rainbow. When the weather is uncooperative, they sit in the rec room and share their pasts. Philosophical observations and stories of travel, friendships, and hardships dominate. When conversations wane, Robin recounts her favorite tales, like she did to her father, drawing an audience.

In fall, in preparation for winter, they devote time to knitting. Robin collaborates with Ashley and others in the knitting group. As they work the yarn off the skeins, they fashion scarves, headbands, and throws for one another and donate some to charity. Of all the various stitches, the seed stitch and its nodular feel is Robin's favorite. For the stitch, she counts knit followed by purl, ending in knit always on an odd-number count, then restarting the next row with knit again, counting—her way of life.

Paying attention so as not to drop a loop, Ashley lets Robin in on a secret. "I use the same perfume every day so you can detect my presence even from afar."

Robin stalls her needles. "There's no need for that. I'll recognize your voice from anywhere."

Ashley finishes her count. "Your smile I'll recognize from a distance too."

As seasons progress, when warmth is replaced by coolness, the two friends sit meditatively wrapped in sweaters and throws. Ashley gives a scene-by-scene commentary as snow transforms the grass carpets outside to white blankets. Through the floating pollen of spring, hot air of summer, brown and gold of autumn, and Christmas lights of winter, they bond, developing interests and creating new lives.

Their relationship is becoming symbiotic. To Robin's butterfly, Ashley is the flower. To Ashley's cactus, Robin is the mesquite.

They share the philosophy that the best things in life are free and wild, believing that about the garden and their newfound friendship—their beauty undeniable, their sustenance uncertain.

47

———————

AIDES

Ashley

"**I** got you," Karen says, standing in a wide stance and steadying herself. "Hold the metal bar," she instructs as she helps lower Ashley into the bathtub. Ever so punctual, Karen arrives for her four-hour morning shift after dropping off her two high schoolers. A trained medical aide with a pleasant face, her stocky, muscular body mobilizes and supports Ashley when needed. Her presence is as much for Ashley's convenience as it is a necessity.

She lays Ashley's clothes on the bed and helps her out of the tub.

Soaking in hot water relaxes Ashley's stiffness, which helps with the stretching and strengthening exercises that follow.

In between, Karen runs the laundry and dishwasher. Together they make a list of errands, and while Ashley rests, Karen handles grocery shopping, schedules doctors' appointments, and fills prescriptions. This regimented cycle repeats every day like a perfectly timed and choreographed Broadway show, its actors delivering a well-planned script. Ashley favors the discipline, having been innately intertwined with her running and other schedules her whole life.

Once a week Karen gives Ashley's motorized wheelchair a thorough wipe down. It is a sleek, high-tech model, and Ashley frequently upgrades as new features are added. "It costs me money, but I'll not regret the enhanced experience" is Ashley's philosophy when she upgrades a wheelchair at her own cost.

Robin names Ashley's wheelchair the "Hawking" after the physicist and cosmologist Sir Stephen Hawking, who had ALS.

"The Hawking!" Ashley exclaims. "His was one of the most technologically advanced wheelchairs, I hear. It had a computer synthesizer mounted that converted his typed words to speech. Very advanced."

"Exactly," Robin replies. "Like my screen reader. But as his condition progressed, he had a computer chip attached to his glasses with an infrared sensor that was triggered by blinking and later by movement of only a single cheek muscle. Can you believe that? Words were created with these signals, I guess. The words were then sent as a text, and the synthesizer generated them in speech form. Such complex technology! I only understand some of it because of the gadgets I use now."

Reminded of future deterioration, Ashley does not care for the name initially. But she comes to admire Dr. Hawking's perseverance and welcomes the moniker as an honor. She hopes never to need such a customized wheelchair as his. Unwelcome thoughts of her end-of-life journey creep insidiously, and she knows no one, including her own doctors, has an answer.

Her new Quantum Power Chair has adjustable seating for repositioning and comfort. Ashley uses the elevator ability and adjusts it to countertop height. Warm oatmeal topped with crushed walnuts and strawberries await her for breakfast. She eats a spoonful with extra chews to help swallow.

The doorbell rings. "I'll get it," she tells Karen. Using minimal hand strength, a newly improved feature, she maneuvers the controls and reaches the door. She uses the seat elevation mode to get into a semi-standing height. Then she opens the door.

48

THE VISIT

Ashley

"Hi, Ash, my angel," says a strained voice. She hears him before she sees him.

Harry, still lean and handsome, steps from behind Rose.

Everything goes still.

It has been four long years since Ashley last saw Harry. In the aftermath of letting him go, unable to drag him into an abyss with her, she ached for him more than she would ever acknowledge, but her decision remained steadfast, with no regret. And after she moved home to Charlotte from Raleigh, the distance helped ease the pain of separation.

But now she is in St. Bona, in Greensboro, not too far away from Raleigh.

"Hello, my H3O," she manages after a long pause, staring, her voice barely audible.

Harry takes a step back. He doesn't hear her. She remains in her awkward posture, half-sitting, half-standing.

She notices his hair first, like she had the very first time she met him. He'd been so particular about his hair then, but he didn't seem to be anymore. Thinning and widow's peaks are obvious. Even her own hair growth has slowed, as she doesn't have to shave her legs as much. Her gaze moves to his face next, registering new lines on his forehead and a few age spots.

To him, she has not changed—the dimple is as deep and the auburn hair as full and wavy. Her once-toned arm and leg muscles are thinner, and her calf muscles swollen.

Karen steps out from the kitchen and welcomes them. Rose rushes to hug Ashley, while Harry stands in place, shifting his weight from one leg to the other, hands in his pants pockets. Their eyes lock, and they forget to blink.

Rose clears her throat. "We're only fifty minutes away now that you moved to Greensboro, Ash. An easy drive, wasn't it, Harry?"

"It was. Yes, it was" is all Harry can muster.

They are seated, Harry sitting straight up, cross-legged, hands on his knees, right hand on his left. Rose does the talking. Cookies are laid out, and coffee is offered. Weather and work are discussed. Neither Harry nor Ashley is able to look at the other without feeling awkward.

Phone numbers are exchanged. After an hour Rose and Harry take leave with a promise to revisit. "Take care. I'll call you before I visit," Harry says, and waves.

That is when she sees it.

A thin gold wedding band. Ashley's heart skips a beat and stalls. When it resumes, the ring's presence doesn't sting as much as she once imagined it would.

That night, flashes of his wedding band actually bring Ashley relief. Her guilt can ease now, and she is happy for him. "Did you call him and give him our relocation signals so he can visit? A married man now. And that is fantastic, isn't it, Mr. Peter?" she whispers to her companion. She runs her index finger across the turbid green leaves, massaging them lovingly. "Time to polish and rework my equation with him, you agree?"

Ashley likes the reconnection. She will be happy to be his friend, to have someone in her life who cares about her.

Once a month Ashley sits in her wheelchair in neatly pressed clothes, every strand of her freshly highlighted hair in place, waiting. With the scent of the air freshener in the hallway, her signature perfume of lavender and jasmine around her, she feels like a child on

Christmas Eve, unable to contain the excitement of what is to come as presents. Her muscles relax and her body feels light. No tightness, no spasms. Is it possible? In fact, the feeling starts three days earlier in anticipation. She doubts it to be real, but she knows it is.

On the said date, Harry appears in Ashley's doorway right at 10:00 a.m. Karen lets him in, as excited for Ashley as Ashley is for herself.

Ashley is at a loss for words, but he, it seems, comes prepared with topics of conversation. He starts with a commentary on his drives, timing them and announcing "One hour and six minutes" or "Fifty-four minutes, record time" as he steps in. This is followed by remarks on traffic patterns and then the weather.

With this opening both their nerves calm, awkwardness lessens, and then a magical feeling descends. This transports them both back a decade. Flirting and teasing, followed by laughter, replace the initial inhibition. They forget that anyone else is even there at all.

Karen hears their laughter from the adjacent room and is thankful for this interaction. She imagines them as how long-lost lovers would act, hesitant at the start, their comfort growing as minutes pass. She expects him to sit leaning forward with full attention, and her reclining back for support. Karen feels like she is infringing on a sibling's private love life. But to her, her infraction doesn't seem wrong.

Around this time a second aide, Xhinzou, is hired as evening help. Her shoulder-length black bob frames her round face, highlighting her golden yellow complexion. Her shortened American name is Zuzu. A few residents, including Robin, playfully call her Zazu, after the red-billed hornbill Zazu from *The Lion King*. Zuzu doesn't mind, and when Ashley summons her, she replies with a fixed smile. "I fly to you soon quickly."

Zuzu has a teenage daughter. "Nobody like work late, but I not like leaving daughter home after school. So I come when husband come from work." She loves to talk, telling Ashley and Robin tales of her earlier life in China and her journey to America. "I like America best."

She takes pride in her work, and it shows. "When children no good, life no good," Zuzu says, commitment to her family clear.

Ashley recalls her mother's sacrifice. How committed she had been to her sense of duty for Ashley and her family.

Harry has the aura of a happily married man. He looks well taken care of emotionally and physically. Ashley senses signs of prosperity in his confidence and feels pride.

"I've replaced you with a new romance in my life," Ashley says once.

Harry looks discomfited with this reference to romance.

After prolonged eye contact, she points to her books. "Those are my new love. I just read *Pride and Prejudice*, and now I know why it was voted as one of women's all-time fave books in the world!"

He talks about his infant son, brushing aside inquiries about his wife, minimizing her part in his life. Ashley understands that he does it on purpose, in consideration of her feelings.

After two hours of banter, he goes to his car and carries in an insulated bag. In his simple yet complete home-cooked meals, Ashley senses only love.

"This is chicken saltimbocca, a new recipe," he announces once. He eats a mouthful. "I hope you don't find it too salty." He chuckles.

Sometimes her muscles do not cooperate, so he eats just as slowly as she eats, so as not to hurry her. For her changing needs, he brings food that is soft, easy to chew and swallow. As lunch ends, he tells her his prepared joke. He delivers it animatedly and makes her laugh.

After lunch he announces, "Time for act two."

He proceeds to help Ashley with her gadgets and electronic needs, to keep up with updates, and to pair her cell and tablet. He works on her television setup and then the Hawking. All of them are dusted, adjusted, and serviced as needed. Reconnecting tangled cords takes him the longest.

He also makes sure Robin's computer, braille display, and screen reader are updated and that her cell phone stays compatible with them. Issues that take multiple phone calls and appointments with technicians, he sorts out in minutes.

After, he helps other residents with their needs, most often with their cell phones, though rarely with their e-readers.

"Ash, visiting you brings some meaning to my life. You know, what do I do with all the technology I mastered if not to help you and your friends?" he says softly.

Then he tells Ashley's friends the same joke he told her earlier and laughs the loudest at his own joke.

At 3:30 p.m. they have coffee, followed by his favorite desserts, which he brings along. He eats two full portions to his satisfaction, the second serving guiltily, while Ashley barely takes a bite. "That filled my stomach, and you filled my heart today," he says, clearing the table.

He ends his visit abruptly at 4:00 p.m. He doesn't like to say goodbye. "Got to go" is how he announces his departure. A quick kiss on her cheek, and he is gone just as Zuzu is coming in, whom he barely addresses.

She looks at him quizzically, comes in, and says, "What wrong? Always hurry, like he steal."

49

MANAGER

Anita

2010

For eighteen years Anita has treated her daughter's birthday as any regular day, a coping mechanism to mask her pain, except for one birthday, her daughter's ninth. On that day, nine years earlier, Anita woke up early and whispered, "Happy birthday to you, darling Maizie." Ruthlessly, that excitement and anticipation were cut short.

But today, April 12, 2010, her daughter's eighteenth birthday holds new significance. It rekindles hope for contact. The ball is in her daughter's court: Will she choose to reconnect? Will she come knocking on Anita's door? Which door? And when?

The uncertainty lingers.

On a whim, Anita signs up for 23andMe to participate in their DNA feature, a service to find and connect genetic relatives but not designed to find biological parents. After submitting her DNA saliva sample, she waits for a match. She is not surprised to find her parents, sister, and family in India absent from the registry. But the one person she is searching for is not registered either.

Steadily, Anita pacifies herself with her trusted mantra: "Everything will be okay in the end. If it is not okay, maybe it is not the end!"

That summer Anita is promoted to interim manager of both the housekeeping and dietary departments. She handles a staff of twenty-eight and three summer interns. "We would love for you to be our permanent manager, Anita. But for that you need a high school diploma. You have until Decemeber 31 of next year, some eighteen months to get that," the director says.

Something that has been buried for years is now awakened. The need is reborn. Renewed anxiety and fresh fear take hold. Implicitly envious of the high schoolers assigned to her, she squashes her initial temptation to ask them for assistance to lay the groundwork for her GED. To calm herself, she decides to stay interim manager for as long as it is allowed and then revert to her role as supervisor.

Elena, now a newly minted high school graduate, is reassigned to Anita, along with two new interns. Dan also returns for the summer but works in the kitchen. Taller than Elena now, a healthy stubble on his face, his eyes light up when food is discussed. Thin as he is, it is not about what he gets to eat but about what he cooks for others. In his new path, cutting boards, knives, and ladles excite him. He inhales sauces from boiling pots, like a perfumer, and lets out long-drawn *ahhhs* every time.

His special affinity to Robin, one of the first residents he met at St. Bona, is for her discerning taste. By the end of his shift, he works in one special dish for her, always approaching her later to discuss the recipe, impatient for her praise.

Elena, prettier than the summer before, her baby fat replaced by chiseled angles, and efficient as ever, finishes her assigned work faster than any other intern.

In her competency, Anita sees her own reflection but does not approve of Elena's distraction with writing and reading at work.

When Elena's dark eyes steal glances at Dan, Dan meets her gaze too, confident, unlike in the past. Anita likes them now, rooting for their romance to be nothing like hers. Set to be freshmen at the University of North Carolina at Chapel Hill in the fall, Elena's planned majors in writing and sociology, and Dan's in culinary and nutritional science, were par for the course.

As a manager, Anita has her own office, her first. It is a far cry from the communal break room she shares with forty-two other employees, where her sole personal space is a second-floor locker. Her assigned office is a narrow, odd-shaped room in the far corner of the administrative building, a space converted to an office as an afterthought. A small ventilator doubles as a window. The orientation of the room and the positioning of the ventilator allow the early morning sun to stream its slanting golden rays into the room, making it her special place.

The only personal touch in the office stands by her desk, a lovely croton with maroon and mint-green variegated leaves, a gift from a resident. The radiant beams reflect light off its leaves, swathing the small room in a red-green glow. She wonders if the door that her daughter will knock on will be her office door. She imagines her daughter standing in her office, her symmetrical face in contrast to the quirky asymmetry of the room, her presence enhancing the allure of the red and green.

Nailed to the walls are plaques she's received, commemorating her years of service, and her framed Employee of the Month certificates. On a narrow bookshelf sit never-lit candles, a few unread books, and an empty picture frame, all gifts from residents.

"No pictures of family?" asked a staff member once.

She likes interviewing new job applicants but finds the task of evaluating performance tricky. Not out to break their will, she approaches their annual reviews with kindness. She ensures no frivolous comment ever leaves her lips.

Day by day she develops and implements policies and procedures, ensuring state and federal regulations are followed, and manages mandatory inspections, which are most stressful. She's expected to maintain superior hygiene in all public places, follow food-handling protocols, and keep proper records of aerosols, fabric protectors, air fresheners, room deodorizers, and other supplies that have the potential to be abused, huffed, or snorted.

At one staff meeting, she is surprised to meet a young Indian recruit as the supervisor of security. She is no longer the only Asian at St. Bona.

Once considered far off from the stereotypical trajectory of the Asian immigrant expectation, her position is becoming more mainstream now.

She maintains active engagement with residents to see if their needs are being met. With keen sense, she registers changing needs. Respecting the residents' privacy, anything she does to assist them, she does discreetly. As a manager she attends multiple meetings, taking her away from her time with residents. In between, she notices confident glances and smiles between two teenagers. Their budding romance is very much unlike hers was. In the open, without hesitation they seek each other and hold hands. And everyone around is rooting for them.

50

THE READ

Anita

"Are you two arguing?" Anita approaches Robin and Ashley, her concern showing as a crinkle between her eyebrows and pinched eyes.

"Arguing? Not at all. Disagreeing? Yes," Robin clarifies.

"We're dissecting the central idea of the book Ashley is reading to me," Robin explains with playful lightness. "Are we not allowed to disagree?"

"No disputes allowed on my watch," Anita jokes, as she straightens brochures and magazines on an end table.

"We debate routinely at our book reading. Only you haven't heard us," Ashley says from her wheelchair, looking at Lucy napping at Robin's feet.

Anita adores their friendship. She knows her jealousy of their connection is unwarranted, yet she is. In her friendship with Paul, she carries the burden of her inability to share her deeper insecurities. In that, she now feels that their friendship is incomplete.

Ashley resumes reading in her usual voice, which commands attention. The language and text flow better when read aloud than when

Anita reads for herself. Anita is drawn in. Each sentence distinct, not run-ons, synonyms, antonyms, and iterations clear.

It reminds Anita of her eighth-grade English class, when the whole class read aloud, by turns, assigned passages from *Catcher in the Rye*. The protagonist Holden's angst related clearly to her then. Being bullied at the time, she recognized the parallel, making her bitter about her life.

Anita stands transfixed, listening.

"You're welcome to join us if you're free," Ashley invites.

"I'm free after three thirty in the afternoon on most days," Anita says, trying not to sound too eager.

The following week she joins a group of five in Ashley's apartment. Nicole Frist is one of them. Never hesitant to share her opinion, she endured breast cancer early in life. Diagnosed without delay, it was treated with simple surgery and chemotherapy. But eighteen years later, it returned. She went through multiple new rounds of chemotherapy in addition to radiation. She is living through a myriad of side effects and physical issues, leading to significant weight loss and weakness. Assistance is what she needs, and St. Bona is there to provide it.

For a little over an hour, Ashley and others take turns reading chapters from *A Tree Grows in Brooklyn*, an American classic written by Betty Smith. The coming-of-age story of Francie Nolan, while she navigates poverty, an alcoholic father, and her Irish-American heritage as she tries to escape poverty through education, strikes a chord with Anita. Drawing comparisons in Francie's struggles and her own, Anita can't wait to reach the book's conclusion, like a child eagerly waiting for a sweet treat at the end of a stellar school day. What resonates isn't the protagonist's struggle with poverty but her unwavering pursuit of education, exposing Anita's shame: no high school diploma, despite the opportunities she had. Now her promotion as manager depends on it. She wants it to be permanent, not interim, to make her parents proud, to stay relevant, to contribute more.

"As a teacher myself," Nicole says, "what struck me most, apart from Francie's desire for education, is how her teachers treated her differently because of her poverty. I made a concerted effort not to let my beliefs and ideas get in the way of understanding and treating all my students the same."

Anita remembers the only sympathetic ally she had in school, her adviser, Mrs. Detris. Nicole as an inspiration, Anita's interest in a career as a teacher rekindles.

When asked to read, her heart skips a beat. She has not read a book in years. Her failed attempt at passing the GED is seven years behind. Her palms get sweaty. Her voice cracks. While she tries to clear it, she feigns shyness. "I don't want to interfere in your activity." Her fear of misread words may lead to her complete unraveling, holding her back.

After fielding a repeat request, she feels compelled to share the reason for her reluctance.

She seizes on a private moment with Robin and Ashley. "I've never read anything substantial since high school. Anything of merit I've done on paper is doodle and experiment with paints, and even that I describe as mere random lines of color." She hesitates, unsure, looks around, and lowers her voice. "I did not graduate from high school. Other than my family, my friend Paul, and the director, no one knows this."

If they are surprised, they do not show it. She does not offer an explanation, and they never inquire. With a degree of chagrin, she adds, "It would be nice if I got my GED. I tried to once on my own but failed to complete the test."

"No harm in trying again," Ashley encourages.

"I need to build my confidence first, to contain my anxiety. You both can help?" The request pours out unrehearsed.

"Mmm. Ashley can be your tutor, maybe, but I can be your editor if you ever need one," Robin replies.

"I did tutor someone in college, a long time ago. Jamila," Ashley says, lost in thought. "She became a medical assistant, and I wonder what she is now. Maybe a nurse. That experience must qualify me as a tutor then." Ashley smiles, lightening the mood.

As much joy as it is listening to books and finding tutors in Ashley and Robin, belonging to the reading group is what takes hold for Anita. She never really belonged anywhere, other than the momentary inclusiveness in the Goth group. That temporary joy dissipated faster than it had taken hold and led her to a path of solitude and castration. She hopes that will not be the case now.

51

THE UNRAVELING

Anita

2011

"Robin and Ashley will be my tutors," Anita tells her director. "They're willing to help me prepare for the GED. Is that allowed?"

He deliberates, as such a request has never come across his desk, but he doesn't take long to decide. "Anita, you're our valued employee. You have our support if this is done in your own private time and in private quarters. And I'm sure it will not interfere with your work." He lays down his expectations.

Excited, Anita yet again gathers necessary information, this time on her computer. Once Ashley understands the curriculum, tailored test plans progress, and Anita's everyday routine starts with a purpose now.

"Rely on context clues and imagination—they help in understanding and memorizing" is Ashley's first advice to her pupil. They start with the basics. "Slow and steady, that is what our pace should be." Ashley echoes her dad's advice from her childhood.

On a drab wintry Sunday afternoon, after the holiday cheer is long past, deep in winter's monotony, Anita composes a practice essay on teenage social pressures on her laptop, a recent birthday present from her parents. She pauses and closes her eyes. The topic is rekindling anxiety from introspection.

After a long, deep breath, she opens her eyes, looks up, and addresses Ashley—and Robin, who happens to be there. "Something about this topic. You know, growing up I felt like an outsider. I didn't fit in with the mainstream kids." She hesitates. "I worried that I looked different in brown skin, dark curly hair, and an unappealingly small frame. So I hung out with kids who also felt the same. They were Goth. I turned Goth too."

Ashley nods.

"Brown skin" stands out for Robin, only now realizing that Anita is not Caucasian. Reflexively, Robin drifts into her own struggles with feelings of abandonment.

Anita returns to her assignment. She massages her temples and smacks her dry lips. Rubbing the back of her neck, she heads to the restroom. Ice-cold tap water on her face cools her. Her thoughts drift from the essay and enter the dark and lonely void of PTSD.

She returns but needs a release from her entrapment. Unable to sit still, she stands up and paces. In her audience are two individuals who reinvented themselves from their own struggles. Surely they will understand. On an impulse she shares her secret. "It's amazing how we want to belong, to be part of a group. Our Goth group was a group of misfits who rebelled. That was the only way we were noticed. My parents agonized over the choices I made. The more they restricted, the more I rebelled. And a tall, good-looking white boy of sixteen, from a broken home, didn't know any better either. And I was pregnant at fifteen. I gave up my baby girl for adoption and dropped out of school the following year."

Years of agony and guilt pour out like water rushing out of the opened gates of an overfilled dam. Her burden is washing away.

Relief surges. She cannot hold back. "I was the black sheep of the family. Both my parents have advanced degrees in engineering, and my sister is a physician, and I ended up being a high school dropout. I struggled with my identity, and I hope I am now on my path to self-discovery. Thank you both for being a part of this journey."

Robin reads Anita's emotions and wonders which pain is worse—

that is, if people's pain can be quantified and compared—giving up a baby for adoption or being someone who has been given up. She cannot decide.

Nevertheless, she attempts to pacify Anita. "I don't know if you know that I was an adopted child and have great parents. My pops is better than any other father. Take it from me—only good people who love babies adopt one. They are the chosen ones. Don't you worry."

Anita is still pacing. "I hope so. I named my daughter Rani, for 'queen' in Hindi, so she would live like a queen. I liked the name Queen after watching the band play at Live Aid."

Her pace slows. She remembers it from years ago. "It was my ninth birthday. Pizza and cake, and yes, we had Pepsi. Freddie Mercury in his skinny jeans and a tank top, flaunting his unshaved armpits. My father, or any other man that I knew of at the time, would never walk into public dressed like that. My parents connected with his Indian heritage and accepted his need to be different, but they couldn't understand my struggle with my looks and my issues at school. They pressured me further to be more Indian. How strange," she finishes, relieved she is able to share her long-suppressed dilemma.

Ashley's face lights up with the memory of Live Aid. "I was there at the concert in person. The show was great, but the idea behind the concert, of raising funds for famine victims in Ethiopia, was inspiring. I went to see Madonna but connected with "Bohemian Rhapsody" and its lyrics more," she says, without elaborating why.

Even after all these years, she is unable to share her scars from the past. They remain too sensitive.

Robin strokes Lucy. Anita's physical attributes as an Asian are coming together in her subconscious, and the new image makes no difference to her.

Robin is not eager to pitch in, but after some time, she does. "In my family, my mother was the only one interested in the show. I didn't understand the power of donating and sharing until I got my Lucy through the generosity of others. I was in my own world, fighting my own demons, about who I was and where I belonged," she says, in a reflective mood.

Anita logs out of her laptop and sets it aside. "I didn't want to associate with anyone after giving up my daughter for adoption. I did not have many friends. And with the one I thought I had a good bond with, my life took an unexpected turn. Losing my daughter left me with nothing. Being a loner was less complicated, so I became one."

"Being on this side of adoption did the same too. All my life I had difficulty keeping relationships, always afraid of losing people, of abandonment. If I sensed I was getting close with someone, I broke up with them before they did."

The weight of her own unspoken experiences settles on Ashley. Memories of her parents' marriage and her fragile dance between trust and relationships surfaces. The what-ifs of her lost love with Harry still linger.

"It took many years to heal, work at St. Bona being my savior. It took my family a decade to recover and two decades for me to find my way." Anita gathers her books.

"I agree. Most of my life, I wondered who I was, not knowing that it really didn't matter. It only mattered who I was going to be. My innocent friendship with Sachiko was my savior," Robin says.

Anita stands up to leave. "If we don't like the ending, maybe it is not the ending. I have always relied on that, and it seemed to have worked. Let's see where that belief takes us."

The wintry mix outside brings a dark chill into the room. Quietness surrounds them. Their birthdays are all within four days of each other's. None of them seems to be interested in that coincidence. Feelings of loss, uncertainty of relationships, sense of abandonment are what they are focused on. Their thoughts wander toward their childhoods and youths, ruefully pondering how vastly different their takeaways are from the same event in 1985, the Live Aid, and how their lives took unforeseen turns, leading them through places and experiences they never knew existed, placing them in intersecting paths, where they are slowly forging relationships and trust.

52

ROSETTA STONE

Robin
2011

"Why not start a book club?" Robin asks, the idea taking shape as an offshoot of their group book reading. As an assistant editor, she had reviewed books for book clubs and written suggested questions for discussions.

"Why not?" ask the others.

Pending approval, a format is planned. Their membership is capped at eleven, a nod to its founding year of 2011. The club is to meet on Saturday afternoons for an hour in the recreation room, with an optional mid-monthly session, the final Saturday of the month reserved for a comprehensive discussion of the book. A proposal is drafted to this effect and is presented to the director. It is approved with a few stipulations, like cleaning up after themselves and maintaining controlled noise levels.

The local library is to supply the books. One community resource the group taps is the Sunshine Book delivery system, which, through community volunteers, delivers library books to elderly citizens. Additional books are obtained through Amazon purchases and Kindle downloads.

They call it The Rosetta Stone Club.

Ashley explains that her suggestion is borne out of her memory of the stone she saw at the British Museum in London, back when she was free and able to travel the world. Behind a bulletproof glass sat a large irregular stone with chiseled words, a stone that looked like many others in the museum. Pointing at it, the guide explained, "The discovery of this seemingly ordinary stone was the key to unlocking our modern world to the world of Egyptian hieroglyphics and other ancient languages. It helped decipher the language of a culture that built the great pyramids some five thousand years ago."

Robin seconds Ashley's suggestion. "Rosetta Stone symbolizes genres of history, language, and culture just as books do. A unique suggestion. I love the name!"

Nicole's energy is in her ideas and opinions, which she shares unabashedly. She reads voraciously, often choosing books that have movie adaptations.

"Reading books is about imagination. I let my mind wander, finding life in the narration. Then I compare mine to the movie director's interpretation. One story then gives me two different experiences."

"Two birds with one stone," Robin jokes.

"Once in a while, my imagination aligns with the director's, and then I feel like I directed the movie myself. The book *Chocolat* and the movie by the same name is one such example. Set in a quaint French village, the alleys and the chocolate shop were exactly how I had envisioned them," Nicole explains.

Anita

Robin and Anita are appointed coordinators, with Robin selecting books and moderating, and Anita managing organizational issues. Book choices are alternated between fiction and nonfiction in broad categories: autobiographical, romance, historical fiction, memoirs, thrillers, and inspirational. Flexibility to read independently or join small self-scheduled groups for a read-aloud experience is a success.

The number remains static, but the composition alters. While some residents recover and return home, others deteriorate, requiring skilled nursing care, and a few unfortunately pass away, allowing new members to join in. Their tones and experiences mesh, conflict, and weave. Slow, soft voices and authoritatively loud voices clash, with softer voices prevailing and louder voices fading at the finish line.

Robin's "Elvis has left the building," her personal catchphrase to signal a meeting's adjournment, gets a few laughs. Elvis fans belt out his tunes, wisely skipping his iconic dance moves. One member earns applause for singing "Heartbreak Hotel" with conviction. "I could die..." he croons.

On cue, Lucy's ears perk, and with a quick flip of her furry tail, she springs to her feet to accompany Robin to their next adventure, which is pizza. Ashley's generously sponsored pizza and Pepsi are a nice touch.

"My favorite drink of all drinks," Anita says as she pours herself a glass of the icy-cold drink every month.

A fully engaged life suits Anita. Her hallowed cheeks fill. She gains weight. Her body tones. Her hair is manageable. And painting remains a constant, with an occasional day of melancholy, reverting her to her mindless habit of doodling.

Sunday dinners with Paul remain a consistent tradition too. He is running a successful business, with only two more semesters to complete his MBA.

Anita's everyday reflection in the mirror gives her the wrong impression that nothing about her has changed physically, but one look at Paul and she knows she is aging too.

"You keep me real," she tells him.

"Do I?" He raises an eyebrow. Like always, he doesn't ask for details.

Her parents are enjoying their downsizing and are even considering retirement. Ami is a full-fledged physician, planning her elaborate wedding. Cody is a happy bystander, eager to please everyone around him.

For years Anita carried guilt, which inhibited her from anything entertaining, subconsciously punishing herself for the misfortune she brought on her Papa, Maa, and Ami. For the pain she inflicted on them and for abandoning her daughter, she could not forgive herself.

Time is easing her guilt, permitting her company, association, and involvement. After ages of solitude, she looks forward to entertainment with anticipation. She has friends now. More than the one friend in Paul.

Elena is now a part-time receptionist at the front desk. "Writing is my major," she told Anita when she interviewed for a job in Anita's department. "And also sociology. I want to help."

"That sounds good, and we'd love for you to work here." Anita appreciated Elena's efficiency. "You can't be distracted though," she cautioned, making her a job offer. "Our residents need a lot of attention."

Elena was disappointed, as the morning shift Anita offered clashed with her summer classes. Later Anita recommended her for a receptionist position.

"And what about Dan? Tell him that the job in my department can be his if he wants it."

"Oh! He's already working at a restaurant, sniffing and sensing sauces like always. He calls himself a saucier these days and says he'll make his own line of them one day."

Pretty women and handsome men are aware of their attractiveness, much like a male peacock is in its impressive plumage. This is true of Elena. In her new job as a receptionist, not required to wear uniforms, her keen sense of dressing adds to her allure.

"You dress shabbily, they'll notice your dress. You dress impeccably, they'll notice you." Her mother quoting Coco Chanel, made an impact on Elena's impressionable teenage years.

In the book club, Elena finds an immediate comparison with her English literature classes. A few students eyeing a higher grade for participation take the discussion on a tangent, testing the ability of the professor to keep the discussion on point. Some are hesitant to share, for fear of ridicule. Most opinions are, however, guarded, carefully and tactfully worded, not to be labeled as radical in their thinking.

The group at St. Bona, a much older group, are all much too eager to contribute, with no care for grades. Decades of life experiences and perspectives make their opinions clear and direct. Stories are shared without concern for personal shame, ridicule, or judgment. If their words are sharp and ideas radical, they just are.

"If not now, when!" one interjects.

"We're too old to care even if judged," comments another. Happy to be there, their camaraderie is infectious, smiles genuine, and opinions real.

"When I was a little boy," starts a seventy-year-old gentleman, rambling, veering off point like a derailed train. Robin, a talented moderator, keeps the conversation on track, bringing context and color into discussions, pulling in comparisons between old masters and new writers. In her new role, her old job helps, closing in on her circle of life.

Robin's involvement is deep, like she is born for the role. She quotes authors and references texts with amazing accuracy. Quotations, idioms, similes, metaphors—she repeats some and comes up with many of her own. When Elena learns that Robin was an editor at a publishing company, she is not surprised.

As the book club evolves, one shares a poem and another a half-finished short story, seeking suggestions and editing help. Together they brainstorm ideas, and Robin, donning her editor's hat, helps refine, lending credibility and expertise to the collaborative process.

Elena wants to be a writer. Looking for inspiration and needing direction, she is seen loitering around the group during her breaks.

"Let's hear what this young lady has to say to our book club, to give us a millennial perspective." Robin initiates a conversation with Elena.

"What do you millennials think about the quote 'Better reign in hell than serve in heaven'?" comes the question.

"I was hoping to go to heaven one day, chief," Elena quips, without really answering the question.

For the next meeting, Elena brings a folder along, a paper carefully tucked inside.

53

ANTS

Elena
2002

When Elena was ten, she couldn't wait for her baby brother to be brought home. Eager to be a big sister, she competed with her mother for a motherly role. "Baby Bobby," she called him. She held his bottle and played with his tiny hands. She saw only one long line traveling across his palm and followed it with her finger. There were two long lines in her palm, in addition to numerous other smaller, lighter ones.

"Everyone is special in different ways," her mother explained.

Changing his soiled diaper only once wore out Elena's novelty. His incessant crying from colic did not help either. Multiple trips to the doctor's office, colic medicine, and a change of formula followed. She heard her parents talk about Mylicon and Bentylol for gas. Keeping up with the dosing and feeding him expensive formula was a constant stress for them.

As Bobby dictated her parents' schedules and moods, Elena felt out of place and slightly ignored. She adjusted and happily spent her summer days with her friend Tommy Gonzales, an eight-year-old neighbor. His mother became her de facto babysitter, and under her watchful eyes, Elena played with Tommy outdoors all day for an entire summer. Their day started on a creaky old swing set in Tommy's back-yard and then moved to hanging off the stainless-steel monkey bars, which were already hot. They rode bikes with their helmets on until the stifling heat drove them in for an afternoon of cartoons and ice cream.

Tommy's grandparents lived with his family. Originally from Guatemala, they talked to Elena in mostly Spanish, and by summer's end, Elena was replying in Spanish. Numerous aunts, uncles, cousins, and their flock of Guatemalan friends visited, gathering and finding a reason to celebrate around the year. Elena spent hours at Tommy's home, joining his large family gatherings, feasting on a variety of South American foods. To the ten-year-old Elena, Tommy's family's celebra-tions far surpassed her own small nuclear family's quiet dynamics.

Once they followed a trail of ants as the tiny creatures carried away cookie crumbs. The ants marched in unison, single file, like to the beat of a drum, along the pavement to the side of the house. The trail led to an anthill. They peered into the dark opening in the center, surrounded by a crescent mound of excavated soil. Hundreds of ants hurried in and out. Tommy and Elena wondered what arrangements the ants had for underground living.

The next day Elena rummaged through her mother's sewing box for a magnifying glass and followed the trail.

The tiny ants now looked large, and the crumbs they carried looked like massive boulders, almost three times their size. Their bulging eyes and narrow waists made them look like cute female anime characters. Closer to the anthill, she noticed three ants carrying in what seemed like a dead ant.

The site was comparable to a massive construction project. Over-powered by fascination, they spent hours watching. In one irresistible, unsuspecting moment, Tommy emptied a container of melted blue Icee onto the anthill.

Elena gasped. Tommy stood there with his impish grin. Hundreds of ants scattered, their systematic daily chores disturbed. The site trans-formed into something like the aftermath of a storm. For a long time, no further activity ensued.

Elena worried that the ants had all drowned.

The next day, as she approached the anthill, she noticed that Tommy was already there, like perpetrators who always return to the scene of the crime. Together they noticed that the rebuilding and repair activity had resumed. Elena wondered how the ants had escaped drowning.

She went to the local library and read *The Life and Times of the Ant* and *One Hundred Hungry Ants* but was most interested in their living habitats and social structures. She wanted more information. "How come the ants did not drown?" she asked her father. "And what happens when it rains?"

After much haggling, she was allowed to use her father's computer. The library was a great resource, but the magic of Google drawing instant information is what she wanted. In line with her interest in animals and their habitats, and her fascination with search engines, she explored the far reaches of the world on the World Wide Web.

When school reopened, her all-day outdoor rendezvous with Tommy slowly shifted to more time indoors.

By the end of summer, she called herself a myrmecologist, one who studied ants, and true to that, she took detailed notes on their habitats, habits, hostile conditions, and hostilities.

The following year, in middle school, Elena's nascent desire to write picked up momentum after she won the district-wide writing competition on the topic of "community." She'd revisited her writing journal and recollected her summer of Tommy and ants, and composed her paper.

54

___

HEROES OF THE WORLD

Elena

2002–2010

E lena opens a folder and extracts two sheets of paper frayed at the edges, stapled together. She looks up at Robin, clears her throat, and begins to read.

___

Ants first appeared on earth between 140 and 168 million years ago, many millions of years before human beings did, during the Jurassic period—a time when dinosaurs roamed the land and plant life consisted of mostly cone- and spore-bearing species. Despite their tiny size, ants have outlived dinosaurs and survived the Ice Age, with social behavior being one reason for their survival.

As social insects interacting in complex organized societies, they project one unified workforce, mostly working for the colony, not all of them reproducing. Building colonies with the purpose of creating a safe space for them to breed, to store food, and to protect themselves from predators, they are efficiently managed, ruled by hierarchies—one queen, a few winged males, and hundreds of workers.

The queen lays eggs, of which a majority turn into worker ants. They forage for food, clean the premises, provide defense, and feed the queen and the other young. One of the young grows to be a queen, and a few turn into males. The new young queen and a few winged males fly out of the anthill to establish their own new colony, to propagate.

Ant colonies have intelligent designs that prevent them from drowning when it rains. Channels are created underground during construction so water can flow away into those conduits, away from breeding grounds and living quarters. Some anthills are simple in their tunnels, which branch out from one central vertical tunnel, and others go several feet underground, consisting of a huge network of interlocking tunnels spreading for miles underground.

The mounds above the ground, some circular and some crescent-shaped, made of soil that has been dug out to make tunnels, help control the nest's internal temperature by the collection of solar radiation.

Ants are some of the strongest animals in the world, relative to their size, as they can carry ten to twenty times their weight because of their thick muscles. They use their bodies to form rafts and bridges. Under threat, each ant trips an alarm that releases a chemical signal. If the threat is imminent, thousands of ants trip their alarms as super-organisms, triggering a proportional protective response.

Ants have small brains but connect through pheromones, which they use to make quick collective decisions. A colony of ants acts like one single animal to accomplish tasks that are impossible for one individual ant. For some species, a solitary ant lives just six days, while a socially connected one lives for sixty days, a proof of how community living contributes to collective well-being.

Similarly, honeybees live in colonies with queens, males, and worker bees. They have larger brains than ants, and as such, they solve problems and memorize better—they can memorize which flowers have more pollen and which gardens have more flowers.

Human beings have brains that are the most evolved. Having segregated roles passed down generations, like in an ant or bee colony, to being able to choose what they do, hierarchies questioned and challenged, they have evolved. What they have fought for, and some are still fighting for, has been for independence to choose how they want to live. In that way they are different from the ant and the bee.

But it is the concept of community and cooperation that has allowed numerous living beings to survive for millions of years. And in varied roles, collectively, they as animals function better, propagating life on earth.

Everyone has a role to play in this world, whether they are assigned one or choose one for themselves. What matters is how diligently, efficiently, and fairly they carry them for the good of everyone and everything around them.

The lives of tiny ants to those of Homo sapiens are proof that communities flourish if they connect and support one another. So the ANTS, the BEES, the HOMO SAPIENS, and all animals in between who contribute to the idea of community living to continue life in the world, are "heroes of the world."

Elena finishes reading aloud, folds the paper in half, and returns it to the folder.

"Bravo. Well written for an eleven-year-old. I'm not surprised that this paper won the competition." Robin claps.

55

RETEST

Anita

2011

On test day Anita keeps her head down, paying no attention to her seating position. The specifications for the calculator have not changed, but there is no need for 2B pencils. Her pendant still hangs around her neck. Early that morning she takes a shortened version of a practice test to get into the rhythm, not to be intimidated by passages, equations, and numbers presented in test format. The first passage did not start with "Bird," and even if it did, she is ready to move forward, her confidence strong and her identity issues behind her.

On the assigned desktop, she clicks the answers. She moves through questions, occasionally looking at the clock, cruising at a comfortable speed. Only after the language arts section does she look around. Again she is seated in the middle of the room. No earthquake, no caving in this time. At thirty-five she is one of the oldest. She plows through trigonometry, calculus, and geometry—none of them remind her of doodling. Stuck on a problem, she recalls Ashley's advice: "Don't focus on how complicated the questions are—focus on how simple the answers tend to be," and then things fall in place. It works for science too. For government, US, and world history, she credits fifteen years of conversations with Paul.

She earns her high school diploma within twelve months of starting toward that goal, scoring 750, which translates to a GPA of 3.9. She calls Paul with the news, a rare call.

"Fantastic. Onto the next now," he says, more eager than Anita.

She won't call her parents until she reaches the next benchmark, which is registering for Guilford Technical Community College, Greensboro Campus.

"Papa, I'm enrolled in college now," she says, choking up. In person she will cry, so she has called them.

"Say that again, bitiya," he says, recently hard of hearing.

"Let me talk to her too." Rumi picks up the other extension.

"Maa, I'll be taking art and education for my diploma in college," Anita says.

This time her usually stoic mother chokes up.

Later, Anita says to Robin and Ashley, "To help you both is my sacred calling," she modifies the saying from the maternity ward, where she read it many years ago.

"Nah, that's not needed," Ashley says.

"You already do that," Robin says.

Stopping by on weekends, keeping Robin and Ashley company, and running errands for them are steps in that direction.

Her position as manager confirmed as permanent, the friends celebrate with cake and balloons.

For Ashley's birthday, Anita makes samosas in perfect triangles and pairs them with mango lassi. Harry bakes the cake. Rose arranges fresh flowers on the metal table outside, and they celebrate alfresco on Ashley's patio.

For Robin's birthday three days later, Anita roasts small pieces of boneless chicken marinated in yogurt reddy curry, and couples that with curried garbanzo beans cooked in tomato and cilantro. With steamed rice and naan as side dishes, Robin feasts on them Indian-style, eating with her hands and licking her fingers.

"Cumin and cloves! I haven't tasted them in ages!" she exclaims, savoring every bit of the spices.

"Moms and Pops, you should both try some too," she says to her parents, who are visiting.

"I agree. The best Indian food I've tasted," James exclaims.

"I'll try some chicken, but I'll need a fork and a knife, please," Lily says, nervous to see her daughter eating with her hands.

Change is sweeping through St. Bona. Merging and downsizing, new terms dominate meetings. Then rumors of a takeover by an out-of-state conglomerate come true.

The conglomerate, which owns a chain of assisted living facilities and nursing homes, prioritizes efficiency over care. Laundry services are contracted to a third-party service, and missed items of clothing go permanently missing. For economy of scale and cost savings, elderly care is taking a back seat. Redirection of the kitchen staff to other jobs introduces packaged frozen food delivered in trucks.

Robin's disappointment with the food at St. Bona has waned over time, but the smell and taste of plastic in the reheated, packaged meals is unbearable. Used to the rubbery overcooked meat and fish, the new chemical scent and flavor, and her heightened perception of them, are not helping.

For his part, the director is helpless, altered regulations and standards beyond his control.

Against all the changes that surround them, Robin and Ashley create new lives and new roles for themselves, along with an admirable standing in their own little community at St. Bona. To Anita, they are her teachers and mentors, but after her confession to them, they are her confidants too. She hopes their bond will grow into a beautiful, long-lasting friendship.

They are her inspiration too. Only time was to tell where that inspiration took Anita.

56

A PEANUT

Anita

St. Bona is short-staffed again, a perpetual problem that is worsening, as a fresh wave of layoffs is announced. Anita puts her administrative chores aside and volunteers to lend a hand to the crew. With her hands on her hips, she stares down the recalcitrant stains on the carpet and sighs. The scratched marble floor glares back at her. The facility is aging, and without repairs and updating, no matter how well the establishment is scrubbed, it has an unkempt look.

Ashley, perched in her wheelchair, and Robin in her favorite corner by the TV in the rec room, munch on trail mix, their midmorning snack. Laughing, they relax in each other's company, like a long-married couple.

Anita greets them.

The laugh is the only sound in the room until it abruptly ceases. A subdued cough follows. Then Anita hears the stridor.

From the corner of her eyes, she sees Ashley's panicked expression and widened eyes. Face ashen, Ashley clutches her throat. Anita identifies it as the universal sign of choking, pivots in that direction, and runs on the double toward Ashley.

Of all the *ER* shows and reruns Anita watched with her sister, the scene that comes to her is that of an attending physician talking to doe-eyed interns on their first day of ER rotation. "Recognizing an emergency is the most crucial aspect of emergency medical care."

Certain that she is witnessing one, in an authoritative voice she never knew she had, she summons an aide to help and instructs Elena to activate a code. She leans in on her BLS classes and follows the script she has seen so many times on the *ER* shows.

Ashley is slumping forward in her wheelchair. Anita positions herself behind Ashley and, with the heel of her hand, gives five firm, distinct back blows between the shoulder blades. When there is no response, she instructs an aide to help Ashley to an upright position, and then Anita encircles her arms around Ashley's narrow abdomen from behind. With both her fists placed above the navel, she gives five quick inward and upward thrusts as part of the Heimlich maneuver. Still there is no response. She repeats the Heimlich and then panics as she wonders what else George Clooney did on the show, as Dr. Ross, for a victim of choking.

Her mind relies on the TV show more than what she learned in her BLS classes, something about the power of the visual over the studied word.

Managing the ABCs of resuscitation, she checks Ashley's carotid pulse. If there is no pulse, she will start chest compressions. She is also trying to remember where the nearest defibrillator is. *One one thousand, two one thousand* rings in Anita's mind, when, as a sign of a successful Heimlich maneuver, a large peanut ejects from Ashley's mouth, followed by feeble coughing.

Ashley is laid on the floor, and Anita checks her pulse as Ashley attempts to sit up. Just then the nursing staff rushes in. Relieved that the emergency is resolved, they busy themselves checking Ashley's blood pressure and filling out many required incident reports.

"What's happened?" Ashley asks, as if waking from deep slumber.

"You choked on a peanut, but you're doing well now," Anita assures her.

"We should take you to the emergency room and get you checked out further," recommends the EMT. "Moses Cone Hospital is the closest. We'll take you there."

Anita stands up, staring at the EMT. She shudders. The name jolts through her body, shocking her every cell. Moses Cone Memorial Hospital, a level-one trauma center on North Elm Street in Greensboro, is a name strongly ingrained in her mind.

"I was talking while chewing," Ashley responds. "Look, I'm fine now. My doctor will check me out soon. I don't need to go to the hospital."

The lead EMT starts packing up. "Got it. Make sure you follow up with your physician."

Ashley nods.

Anita hurries away from the scene. In the bathroom she soaps her hands multiple times, as if to wash away her bitter memories. But she can't. Frames of scenes from her day of delivery sprout. The last frame that refuses to disappear is the time when she adjusts her daughter's cap before she is taken away from her. She slides down to the bathroom floor and sits there for a long time, longer than she ever sat in a bathroom without business to attend to.

Elena walks in. "Wow. I'm impressed with what you did today. You must have been a nurse in your previous life?" she gushes.

"Me? A nurse? I couldn't bear to work in a hospital. You know I'm just the lowly manager of housekeeping and dietary services."

"One day I want to be able to do what you did today. Save someone's life, you know, if there's a need." She looks down on Anita, their dark eyes locking. "I have to go back to my desk now. See you around." Elena tucks her hair behind her ear as Anita admires her tall, model-like figure and blemish-less olive skin.

Robin says at the next book club meeting, "When fat hit the fire, Anita came to the rescue. When I heard this wonder woman barking orders, I knew Ashley was in fine hands."

"Thank you for saving my life, Anita. I heard you were a real-life action hero. You'll make a great nurse. Have you ever considered that as a career?" Ashley asks.

"I'm not sure," Anita replies, not wanting to elaborate. "But one thing I am sure of is that you are never to eat a peanut again!"

Everyone agrees.

There is one other thing Anita is certain of. Changes were coming in her life and at St. Bona. While her plans were solidifying, those of St. Bona's were not.

57

DRIVEN

Elena

2012

I f Elena is particular about her appearance, her advance planning regiments her daily activities. For this habit, she was a role model in school. Every hour is clearly listed, and checking things off a list gives her a sense of accomplishment. "Driven" was how her teachers described her at parent-teacher conferences.

Lists on Post-its lay stuck to multiple surfaces.

"Ellie, you need lists to keep track of your other lists," her mother complained.

Elena is an organized, self-assured, self-reliant millennial, accepting of diversity and inclusive culture. However, less personal interaction and more electronic intrusion through social media describe her life. She is engaged but not wholly.

Keeping lists facilitates discipline, but they also make her impatient. She hurries to check them off, taking pride in her efficiency. Respectful, though with a certain human element amiss, she loves and values the people she cares for.

"Does she lack empathy at the cost of efficiency and her goals?" her parents wonder.

At St. Bona she answers phones and does what is expected of her. In between, she stays buried in her phone and her books, working on class assignments. In fact, she does not like the slow tempo around her. In that, the job at St. Bona is not an ideal fit for her.

"At a snail's pace! Slower than a glacier!" she fumes sometimes. Elena knows that most residents feel her impatience, but indifference to that sentiment is more convenient for her.

A year earlier she was admitted to Duke, but she declined the admission in favor of the scholarship offered at UNC at Chapel Hill. Her unbridled excitement and youthful exuberance dissipate, the disappointment of having to make that choice. But now with Dan at UNC, she's happy with the choice she made.

She has an overwhelming desire to excel in activities that interest her. Realization that the essence is in the detail helps her delve deep and wide, researching every means to learn and succeed. Fiercely competitive; hating to lose; grades, rank, and standing matter to her; the pressure self-inflicted.

In that, fear of failure lurks, like a mouse fearing an approaching cat. So she plans excessively for success.

Her fierce ambition is overwhelming and explains her need to pen work that resonates with others. "To be a world-class writer, to storm the literary world from the outset," she'd told her high school teachers.

Their attempts to infuse practicality were without success.

"That is a fine goal to work toward," said one counselor.

"A bit bombastic, isn't it?" her mother reacted.

As a teenager, Elena wrote her to-do lists by hand but later moved her journal-keeping to her laptop. She jotted down observations and anecdotes to use as writing prompts. Making numerous attempts to write stories based on these prompts, but eventually losing steam, some were left unfinished, a few were edited eventually, and many deleted if she didn't consider them worthy of saving when she revisited them.

As a rule, she never showed anyone her work unless it was an assignment for class, yet without writing, her day felt incomplete.

As a junior in high school, she had another minor success. A newly published romantic bestseller called *One Day*, written by English writer David Nicholls, was in line with her fascination with romance at the time. It followed the lives of two characters, Emma Worley and Dexter Mayhew, over a course of twenty years, and as a review characterized it, the book explored themes of love, friendship, regret, and missed opportunities, told every year on the same day where their relationship stood at that point in time.

Enamored by the premise of the book, for her final semester paper, she wrote an essay titled "One Day," chronicling one regular high school day as a part of the community she lived in. She highlighted her poignant observations as a snapshot at exactly one-hour intervals.

Starting with a thought of how invested her mother was in Elena's health and future that she toiled to get her breakfast together early in the morning, Elena moved to how her heartache from a lower-than-expected grade in math was tenderly alleviated by a friend who said the test was especially hard. In the following hour, it was about her disappointment for not being able to get the attention of a dimpled boy sitting next to her in class. Thereafter she wrote about how her science teacher's lisp was ignored by his students and how they respected him for being a dedicated teacher. She then elaborated the insecurity of a pretty classmate regarding her hair and how she compensated maybe by excelling in music. After lunch, in sociology class, when half the class was sleepy, how they helped one another stay awake. And what one student did to help another contain his loud hiccups.

So it went, balancing emotions of humor, attraction, and human vulnerabilities, reflecting life and community. A story of hope and disappointment, each instance like a block of a quilt, a piece of a puzzle, when pieced together covered the breadth of one's day, and by reflection, perhaps one's entire life.

"I like how you adopted a unique idea, making it your own," her teacher praised. "It resonates with the theme projected in *Ulysses*, by James Joyce. You should read it if you haven't already. The point made is how mundane everyday things become an integral part of our lives. Nice work."

Curious, Elena checked out *Ulysses* from the school library the same day.

"And could I use your paper as a prototype for future writing classes?" Her teacher's request was another endorsement that her writing career was on its way ... perhaps.

After many years of good grades, the award as the best student in language arts at her high school graduation was the final recognition of her ability.

The joy of storytelling remains, but how is she to know that writing will not become her chosen profession in life?

58

———

A LESSON

Elena
April 2012

"**B**idding farewell to my teenage years in a few hours!" Elena types this celebratory message on Facebook on the eve of her twentieth birthday.

While she juggles her cell phone and the land line, clicking Send on her cell phone, she answers the latter with a curt "How can I help you?"

She listens to the complaint for a moment. "I'll notify maintenance about your stuck bathroom faucet," she replies impatiently, disregarding other details.

Two hours later the maintenance crew arrives to find the resident nearly drowned.

As the tub was filling quickly, the resident managed to place the call from the emergency phone by the bathtub. Her lathered hands and soapy water made it impossible to get a grip, and soon realized she was in trouble. The harder she tried, the more she slid back in, unable to step out or reach the telephone.

Elena's inadequate response is marked in her file. An incident report is also entered. In response to the irate family's inquiries, out of shame, she apologizes to the manager and the resident.

For later that Friday night, Dan organizes a late-night party at a friend's terraced apartment to ring in her birthday. While at the party, the guilt comes after her second drink. The disgust comes right at the stroke of midnight, just as she blows out the twenty candles and cuts the strawberry sheet cake layered with heavy icing.

She can't drink anymore. All through her attempted laughs and dance moves, her mind is elsewhere, and her heart achy.

In the morning, her birthday, enveloped in guilt, she makes a journal entry. "Being selfless and self-centered are two different things. And I was neither, and thought that was good enough. I also assumed being goal-oriented and efficient was sufficient. But the important lesson is, if I'm to live and work among people, I must learn to live a centered, selfless life." Rereading the words, she is struck by how mature her self-reflection is. She ends it with "I AM NOT A TEENAGER ANYMORE."

She drafts a letter to her manager in longhand, projecting regret and outlining what she learned, explaining how she plans to rectify her inadequacy.

In Elena's transformation, Ashley sees a change in Elena's face, softer and radiant, like a happy-face emoji.

Anita senses gentleness, and in that, Elena looks even younger.

Robin hears a change in her voice. There is familiarity in it the whole time, but now it is laced with sweetness.

When Elena greets her with a "Hello, Chief," Robin likes it.

Elena calling Robin "Chief" is not without strategic intention. Elena needs her help. She needs a guide, a mentor, an editor. Robin, she finds, is one who encompasses all these roles.

She hopes to ask Robin for help one day.

59

WRITING

Elena

2010–2012

Elena's living arrangements in college are set to her specifications, conducive to her interests. She lives in a brand-new modern high-rise with good security, not too far from the college campus.

When she was five, she bargained with her parents for a brand-new bicycle. "I can wait for another year if that will allow you to buy me a new one."

Understanding her fetish for brand-new things and her excitement for retrieving items out of their original packaging, her parents indulged her, as she took good care of the things she owned.

But when it is time to buy her a car, this privilege is scaled back. In her immaturity, she tells her parents she will compromise on the overall quality of the car for its looks, if it were her choice.

"You can't really do that," they say, "and we'll buy the one you test drove that looks as good as new and has an odometer reading of six thousand five hundred and ten miles, to be precise."

Her studio apartment, sleek modern appliances, gray hardwood floors, and large windows are always in perfect order. By one of the large windows overlooking a pond is her desk, with neatly stacked books and writing supplies.

An alarm goes off at 4:30 a.m., except for Sundays. In the wee hours, she hopes not to be disturbed, as she needs quiet, complete quiet. "Even a falling feather disturbs," she jokes with Dan.

The barking of a distant pesky dog, creaking of floorboards from the floor above, and the dull voices of her neighbors carrying through the walls disturb her. At the crack of dawn, at 5:00 a.m., she works, hoping the world is asleep.

There is an additional benefit to waking up at this time of the day. She wakes up in the middle of REM sleep, her dream state. Remembering the dream sequence she is in the middle of, she falls back into light sleep. In this state of early morning semiconsciousness, the dream comes back to her in a more vivid form. In that instance her dream develops, gets modified, and is censored as needed. Just as the alarm goes off for the second time, she is fully awake and remembers it all.

Thus, when she rolls out of bed, a new idea is concocted, ready to be woven into her writing. Every day that she has a substantial new plot to develop on, she thanks Freud.

Occasionally she dreams of a missed test, unfinished project, or a forgotten essay and wakes up sweating profusely, worried about her grade and class rank, things that are crucial to her.

She types, spilling words page after page. Her thoughts, ideas, and dreams flow—poetry, plots, and people, metaphors and similes, invented and discovered, she does not revisit them until later that day. A routine, a plan, a schedule, a goal once made, she stays the course.

She types for exactly two hours and then climbs up six flights of stairs to the common lounge on the tenth floor, which is stocked with fruit, protein bars, and muffins. She sips her coffee meditatively, then munches on a protein bar, looking down at the world just as it is waking up. She picks up a fruit from an assortment as she heads out.

She types for thirty more minutes. At 8:00 a.m. she stretches on the couch and scrolls through her phone. Once caught up with messages and social media posts, she gets ready to attend classes.

There are stretches of days when nothing surfaces. "Freud on vacation." "My neurons are spent." "The well has dried." "Low on juice."

"Shelves are empty." She writes such comments on Post-its, sticks them next to her to-do lists on her computer screen, and shuts it down.

Then movies replace writing. A movie buff, she binges on all genres with equal intent, but rom-coms are her go-to style. Their easy storylines, engaging humor, and pleasing-to-the-eye-cast delivering promises of everlasting love relax her. She avoids the fast-moving thrillers, as she needs to understand every detail of how the mystery unravels, and often, it is not depicted in enough detail. There are too many loopholes, loose associations, and lost connections in the plot execution of thrillers to hold her interest.

If a movie catches her attention, she watches it on a loop, allowing her to rest her prefrontal thinking lobe while engaging her occipital and temporal lobes, so she pontificates to herself. If this ploy fails, she skips classes and heads home.

She watches Disney movies too, with Bobby, who, at the age of two, was diagnosed with autism, a constant source of worry for her parents. When Elena heard about it, the single palmar crease and her mother's reply of "Everyone is different" came to her mind as a telltale sign of it.

"His is not a bad case," his doctor had said. "He'll need help all along, in different measures. But he'll eventually learn to manage his affairs with some supervision."

Elena loves him, and every chance she gets, she watches him to give her parents a break. At home she snuggles with him on the couch and reads to him for hours. They eat Cheetos, her weakness, and Hershey's milk chocolates, his weakness, and call it their "vacation time." They work on numbers and sight words. He is making progress.

Driving him around and acting like a ten-year-old along with him helps her get back to writing.

Home relaxes her.

Since childhood, her love for writing has matched her determination to succeed. But her idea of writing a literary gem plays havoc on her and weakens her confidence. Everything she writes she considers amateurish, none of her writing matching the quality she dreams of. She does not share her writing, as her own quality grid, as she set it, is at a difficult-to-scale level.

After all the years of writing and rewriting, self-doubt about her natural talent and ability plagues her. Her bar is set too high, the grid too tight.

Through her sophomore year in college, she has been working on a story that is becoming a novel in length. She is creating a monster with too many characters and twists, the story drowning in lost plots and taking her down with it.

Unable to withstand the self-inflicted pressure of her own expectations, she considers dropping her writing project, along with her creative writing classes, and focusing on sociology alone as a major.

Writing is her passion, sociology is only an interest, thanks to her summer of ants. Writing is compared, critiqued, analyzed, and rated. Work in understanding social structure and relationships has no personal benchmark. To ease her performance stress, she is shifting in favor of interest over passion.

60

IDEAS

Elena

Two experiences in St. Bona bring her writing back to its original trajectory.

One is her observation of how the book club allows residents to venture out of their shells and come together. The books they read are not coveted as great works of literature, yet in their own simple way, the stories engage them, make them think, learn, connect, and if not, just enjoy a story. Simple writing is an art too, with its own appeal, she realizes.

"The more I share my writing, the more writing ideas sprout," Mary says, a septuagenarian member of the club. "It's like a well that refills with water the more you empty it, like a trimmed single stalk that sprouts more, and like a shaved head that grows hair back faster. Try sharing your work," she encourages.

It is the power of that suggestion that encourages Elena to share, regardless of how basic and incomplete she thinks her work is.

The second event that leads to her resolve to become a writer is her chance attendance of an impromptu session on writing at a bookstore.

A new book titled *A Writer's Dream* is being promoted. Just as she is flipping through the pages, a meeting with the author is announced.

She gets herself a vanilla milkshake, picks up a copy of the book, and settles down in the last row of seats. Clearly she is not the only wannabe writer in the audience. Toward the end of the presentation, the speaker asks the audience if there is interest in a writing exercise. Many nod.

The exercise is to elaborate on a prompt: "a thought."

A flurry of activity follows, with paper and pens being passed around. A few type on their phones. When asked for volunteers to share, Elena reads hers aloud.

"The thought of writing
Appeals, appeases, and attracts
Yet every word I write
I manage to redact
I wonder and ponder ideas
Then all of them I retract
My simple writing now
Is by my own contract
My act as a writer
Pray will have an impact."

She pauses, her heart pounding. "Am I expecting to be anointed a writer? Why am I so desperate to be validated?" She looks around for comments, realizes there are none, and sits down. Other participants are just as eager to share, in hopes of being applauded.

As the author signs her book, he reaches out to Elena and says, "We need young writers like you. If you find joy in writing, writing will find you."

The words "writing will find you" resonate with her, giving her hope.

The author's book sits on Elena's writing desk for weeks. She superstitiously believes it to be her focal point, her vortex of energy for her writing. She flips through its pages, not in the least bit interested in the content.

She wants no further instruction in writing. She knows good works of literature written by people who have no formal training in writing. She is keen on not having anyone else's writing style influence hers. The story and style have to be her own.

"The more you share, the more ideas will sprout" and "writing will find you" ring loud and clear, giving her hope. She considers the fortunate coincidence of meeting the book club member and the relatively unknown author whose encouraging words become her driving force, her serendipity.

61

THE TUTOR

Ashley

2012

"**M**ove the desks and chairs closer to the window," Ashley instructs as Karen and Harry slide them into place.

"How about this spot for the couch?" Harry suggests.

Ashley's living room is turned into a makeshift classroom with three sets of workbooks, supplies, and new laptops on the desks. Additional refurbished used laptops, Harry's contribution to the project, are placed on the breakfast table.

Following Anita's success with her GED, requests for help and guidance pour in from St Bona's staff. Those who did not have a diploma aspire to follow Anita's path, while those who already have one are now looking for guidance for future steps.

Never had Ashley imagined revisiting her role as a teacher, a role she inadvertently took on in college, for Jamila. Hesitant initially, concerned with constraints of her physical condition, she agrees to proceed, with reassurances from Harry and Robin, building on her experience tutoring Anita.

Her new moniker, "Ms. Ashley," excites her. She has committed four hours a week to her new role, taking on three students at a time.

Kainene, a twenty-year-old Nigerian immigrant, is the first to sign up. After enduring the humiliation of living in an immigration camp for five months, her family was finally granted asylum. She is grateful for the opportunity given to her family to live the American dream, while many of their compatriots are sent back, their application for asylum denied. Despite her heavy accent, she is proficient in English.

"Thank you, ma'am" is how she responds every time, adjusting her colorful hijab. Lacking the required paperwork to enroll in college, she needs guidance. Her goal is to get better in conversational English, earn her GED, and put herself through college.

Shawanda is perpetually late but also is the most diligent student. Social reasons beyond her control are to be blamed for her lack of education—taking care of her elderly father and navigating two bus transfers to reach St. Bona. As an apology, she arrives with a covered dish.

When she offers to drop out, Elena volunteers to give her a ride on her way to work.

It takes Shawanda twenty arduous months to get her GED, but she does.

"No one has ever taken as much interest in my education as you do, Ms. Ashley." She fidgets. "My teachers just passed me on to the next grade. They didn't bother to know if I was even learning anything."

Mary's goal is to teach her two young children how to read and to help them with school. "I was born with a shitty spoon." She bites her tongue and looks around. "Sorry, Ms. Ashley. I'm trying to lead by example. After dinner, we all sit together and do our homework. I want my children to be proud of me."

Majority had been in and out of foster homes, forced to fend for themselves as teenagers.

"We want better lives for ourselves and our children," say almost all of them.

Some stories are heart-wrenching yet believable, and others are unimaginable but true. One by one the students share their unique stories in hopes of unburdening the trauma that plagues them.

The most poignant conversations are centered around abuse—by foster parents, taunts by caretakers, deception by trusted family members, incest by an uncle, mistreatment by a babysitter, domestic violence, and so on.

When such stories are shared, Robin shudders. She could have easily been a victim of such abuse had she been placed in the wrong house. On such days a growing urgency to call her parents and thank them for making her a part of their lives takes root.

"Can't I tell you guys how much I love you both?" she says, sidestepping the sharing of stories that lead to the phone calls.

As for Ashley, stories of abuse trigger discomfort from recall, but lately guilt is playing heavier. She wonders if her parents' separation could have been avoided had she actively intervened, as talk of intimate-partner abuse, a newly introduced term discussed routinely in magazines and talk shows, recommends early intervention as a possible solution.

To the handful of employees who hold high school diplomas, Ashley and Robin become guidance counselors, advising them on courses to take and career paths to pursue, with St. Bona a temporary stop for them.

All is well until Ashley, getting ready for bed one night, turns to bid her Prickly Peter good night and notices movement on the windowsill. In the dim light, she blinks and then sees menacing eyes and a proboscis. They are there for a second, until they aren't. Ashley lies frozen all night, unsure if it is real or just her imagination. She doesn't dare scream, fearing it might reemerge.

At that instant the sad stories are more tolerable than the inhabitants of the crevice.

62

TWO DECADES

Anita
2013

"I can't believe it's been twenty years!" Anita exclaims when she is recognized for her two decades of service. Another plaque to adorn her office walls!

Coinciding, Elena is chosen as Employee of the Month, the award certifying her journey from an impatient teenager to a responsible, caring adult. She receives a framed certificate, which will be displayed in the lobby of St. Bona before she can own it.

Like at other assisted living communities, St. Bona is continually understaffed, but recently even more so. But for a few diligent long-term employees, it is a revolving door, spinning with temporary hires, the door well greased and oiled by staffing agencies.

Naivety compounded by the impatience of the newly hired staff works poorly. The staff is a fragile patchwork of newbies barely held together by a few sturdy veterans. So delicate is this fabric that it frays and nearly unravels multiple times.

"You're our permanent fixture," the residents say, relieved when a known face, like Anita's, comes to their aid.

Even in her previous supervisory role, Anita managed to stay attuned to the residents' needs, her help showing in the simple gestures of a gentle touch or a kind word. They carry as much power in healing as do medicines—this she knows firsthand from her experience at St. Bona.

But in her current managerial role, administrative tasks consume her days: tallying supplies, payroll management, scheduling, resolving conflicts, and writing evaluations, all from the confines of her office.

St. Bona's landscape is changing too. The aging facility needs upgrades, and tight budgets with Medicare and Medicaid cuts strain resources. In response to government scrutiny and reports of abuse, new administrative layers are added, prioritizing oversight over front-line care. Endless reports are now required to comply with state regulations. When Anita voices her opinions, decisions are made with no hope of them being heard.

She wishes the rumor that the director is resigning is just that, a rumor. But the disdain in his face at staff meetings when terms like *budget neutrality, streamlining, novel service models,* and *new mission statements* are discussed is consistent with the rumor. He is caught between residents' demands and the administration's budget woes, unable to pacify either.

The role of an administrator does not suit Anita anymore, her heart being in work that involves people. Francie Nolan in *A Tree Grows in Brooklyn,* the teacher in Nicole Frist, the pediatrician in Cody, and above all, Anita's draw to children are major directing forces. They coalesce, strengthening her appeal to be a teacher, an educator.

Enrolled in community college, she envisions furthering her academic journey. Inspired by her grandmother's emphasis on a professional career, she aims for a four-year college degree, a master's degree even, with a goal to build a fulfilling career in education. She dreams of herding children into the safety of her wings and helping students and parents understand each other—critical to the health of the family and the community.

It is a distant dream.

63

HAPPINESS HAPPENING DAY

Ashley

2013

"Let's run a 5K." Ashley pins a pink ribbon to her lapel and passes them around. "To honor Nicole's memory and raise funds for breast cancer research."

"Nicole would like that. I miss her energy in our meetings," a male member of the club says.

"I can't walk, let alone run," Ashley clarifies, overcoming personal reservation and embarrassment, given her physical challenges. "But a buddy system should work."

Nicole Frist's voice was noticeably raspy on that last day, but no one suspected it to be anything other than an ordinary upper respiratory infection. Tragically, she was found lifeless in her bed the next morning. Autopsy confirmed a pulmonary embolism, a blood clot that silently traveled to her lungs.

Ironically, Nicole, one of the original members, was one of the first that the book club lost. Her passing, the suddenness of it, highlights everyone's fragile existence at St. Bona.

By the time Achilles International, a nonprofit organization that pairs able-bodied runners with those with disabilities, is consulted, St. Bona's buddy system is already in the works.

The day before the race, Anita collects the team's essentials: name tags, T-shirts, water bottles, and bright-orange bib numbers. Robin, with her sunshades, is tethered to Anita, while Elena accompanies Ashley and her Hawking. Two additional members from the book club join their ranks.

The group merges with two hundred fifty other participants, while nearly eight hundred spectators line the streets to cheer them. With their bibs securely pinned, they set out to walk. Amid the mostly relaxed runners are a few serious ones. Many stroll with no pressure of speed, pacing, or time. The crowd includes the young and the old, a few tethered, many solo. Families push strollers, and fathers run with their young children. Girls trot with bobbing ponytails, while boys vie for their attention. They are all doing it in memory of a loved one or to simply support a good cause.

Ashley is unusually relaxed, a welcome change from her typical pre-race jitters. No need to obsess over the starting cue or a stretch. "Bohemian Rhapsody" is obsolete. She doesn't have to count from one to one hundred to focus or mind her distance. She will manage her Hawking's direction and speed.

Elena checks Ashley's posture and adjusts Ashley's hat against the scorching August sun. "Water, potty break, anything, please let me know," Elena says as the runners push off. "And remember, it is the journey, not the destination."

Ashley appreciates the reminder. She sits back. "Let the fun begin." She savors the scene around her and relaxes like she never has before. Unlike her previous runs, where she focused on her breathing, form, and foot strike, she now notices everything else around her—the people, the surroundings, and the atmosphere.

To Robin's large frame, her tethered buddy stands in contrast. As Anita struggles to keep pace with Robin's speed, it appears that Robin is, in fact, guiding Anita.

They are well ahead of Ashley and Elena. Ashley does not mind. She notes the speed Elena and her Hawking move at and calculates their journey to take seventy-five minutes. It is a far cry from her peak performance, where she had blazed through 5Ks in sixteen minutes.

It is a party. Music is blaring. At the halfway mark, the team stops at the drink stand and gulps down water handed out in paper cups. They approach the refreshment station not from hunger but from curiosity, and they take free protein bars for later use.

"Ninety calories each, ten grams of protein, and a whole lot of preservatives," announces Ashley, her old habit resurfacing.

Ashley turns to look at Elena. In the bright sun, her eyes crinkled, she looks like Harry in profile. Ashley takes a deep breath. "It's cheesy to say, but you're like a daughter to me, really. You could have easily been my daughter. See, our age group fits, and you've got a tall and slender frame, like me."

Elena's mouth falls open. "Did you have a daughter?" she asks, unusually curious and equally serious.

"No, never got the chance," Ashley replies ruefully.

At the finish line, Ashley remembers what running had given her. The memory of her father's outbursts and her attempts to escape agitation and agony is vivid. In a hurry she shakes off that memory and remembers the happiness running brought her.

While Elena gathers the rest of the team, Ashley turns back and says, "I'm happy today. Did you know that today, August eight, is Happiness Happening Day? We're making happiness, aren't we?"

"Yes, we are," Elena agrees. "Actually, not really for me." Her face shrinks. "Dan and I broke up last night," she says. "He's a nice man, very nice actually, but saucing and writing weren't going well together." She forces a smile. "You don't have to say anything. Forget I told you this."

"Okay then." Ashley puckers her mouth. A minute later she shifts her feet and looks down at her shoes. Of the hundreds of pairs she had, there was one elusive shoe, and that shoe she is wearing now. Her new golden shoes, shining bright, adorn her feet in pristine condition.

"Shoes on Amazon are not all that bad." She admires them.

"What are not bad?" Elena looks down before she lets out an expletive. "Shit, they're beautiful!"

"I had to have them for perhaps my last race." Ashley lets out a loud, hearty laugh.

For Ashley, in the final tally this walk with her friends is more satisfying than all the other races she participated in. This one has the purpose of supporting women and research. All that and honoring a friend's memory makes it meaningful.

In the early morning hours, Ashley dreams of her family. She is five and under the sunny blue sky. She lies in the hammock with her father. He is reading the story of the hare and tortoise while she squints at her mother, tanning by the poolside.

"Slow and steady wins the race." Her father closes the book.

She wakes up with a start, her heart racing. Confused for a second, she senses him sitting on her bed. She moves her hand in the darkness, feeling for him. He isn't there. As she looks toward the sliver of light streaking from under the door, she sees him leaving, saying, "Father of a girl is a lucky man."

Her father said that to her many times. She sits up, recalling her father telling her to slow down. "Dad, whether I like it or not, I am slower now," she says aloud, like she is talking to him.

Her father loves her. He would have let her have any number of golden shoes.

It is four hours later when the phone call comes. Her father died in his sleep, assumed to be from a heart attack. He was seventy-four and living alone. She loved him too, despite his despicable shortcomings. Yet she had selfishly longed for their family to stay intact. Whether her reluctance to confront the issue was selfishness, lack of maturity, or fear of standing up to her father, whichever it was, she feels utterly miserable now.

HARRY COMES TO CONSOLE HER. Rose visits too.

"He liked me," Harry says.

Ashley calls her mother. They reminisce between tears. Plans are made for his funeral in Charlotte at the church where Kelly is a board member. She is also the president of a nonprofit women's center that meets the needs of women below the poverty line. Ashley is particularly proud of her for that.

A handicap-accessible van is being arranged for Ashley's travel. Harry plans to ride with her.

"Do you want me to stay overnight?" Harry asks after a few hours, the first time for such an offer.

"I'm alright, Harry. No need for that," she says.

Harry gathers his keys and dishes. As he reaches the door, Ashley's piercing scream makes him drop everything. Stainless-steel dishes clatter on the floor, adding chaotic rattle to Ashley's screeching.

While Harry turns to stare at Ashley, she stares frozen at her armrest.

She is looking at large, round, menacing eyes and the sweeping motion of the antennae. It is the same creature she'd seen on her windowsill, only it is bigger, inches from her, its antennae extending, as if offering a grotesque handshake.

The asynchrony of the scream and the clattering sends the cockroach fleeing in one direction, while Ashley's Hawking speeds in the other. But when she turns, she is horrified to see half the creature's mangled, bloodied body stuck to the floor, while the other half is gruesomely attached to her wheelchair's right wheel.

Ashley lets out a second scream. Her instinct to abandon her Hawking and flee overwhelms her. In a momentary lapse, she forgets her disability and stands up. Harry swiftly jumps over the still rattling dishes and saves her wobbly body from collapsing onto the oozy cockroach mess on the floor.

After, Ashley can't bear to use her wheelchair. She begs for it to be sterilized, if there is such a thing for wheelchairs. Harry sets out to solve the conundrum, and after much debate and coaxing, Ashley is satisfied with a thorough cleaning at a car wash the next morning before their ride to Charlotte.

64

FOR RANI

Anita

2013

A nita, dressed in a long floral dress, chooses an intricate pattern.

"Is this the design you picked?" the lady asks, pointing to the picture in the book.

"Yes and no. Can you modify it like so?" Anita's instructions drown in the loud music that is playing.

She surrenders her palms for twenty-five minutes as the design is applied, following every line and dot as the green paste of henna flows out of the nozzle of a premixed cone. The lines of the initial grid laid on her palms remind her of her early doodling days. She is happy, but the memory of those times makes her reflective.

Her thoughts drift to her daughter. Is she dating, or even married? If so, what type of wedding was it? Did she have henna-adorned hands? She only has questions and no answers.

She shakes it off and joins a family dance for Sangeet, an evening of song and dance that doubles as a rehearsal dinner. She manages to fall in step with the others even as the long dress gets in the way. Ami's destination wedding along the Outer Banks, in the cooling temperatures of September, is a departure from tradition for the Kumar family.

Early next morning, Anita stands patiently for an hour as her mother's friend, an honorary auntie, drapes her in a saree. The five-yard-long material is wound around her body multiple times from waist down and is brought up to cover her bosom, over a fitted blouse. She walks nervously, fearful of tripping on the overhang.

The outdoor Hindu ceremony, set against a sunset backdrop and to be followed by a Western-style exchange of vows and rings, is a far cry from the usual ceremonial procedures of a three-day temple celebration.

The morning sunlight peeks through the fresh flowers that decorate a raised stage. As the priest reads Hindu rites in Sanskrit, the couple, draped in traditional clothes, red dots painted on their foreheads, exchange garlands. The evening unfolds with a ring exchange and "I dos," followed by a formal reception, where the couple once again dresses to impress, Ami in a long white gown and Cody in a tuxedo.

In her twenty years of service, apart from an occasional day off for a doctor's appointment and a week off to take care of Paul, Anita has been at work every weekday, her vacation days given away to colleagues for family emergencies.

"There are so many things to take care of. You have to take a week off for Ami's wedding," her parents said.

When she returns to Greensboro, she brings Indian desserts to share and gives Ashley and Robin pure wool shawls her parents brought from India as gifts. Both her hands are still adorned with deep-red stains.

She opens her palms to show them the design. No one notices a name etched. Drawn amid the intricately laid pattern on the palm of her right hand, camouflaged in the flowers and foliage of the pattern, reads "Rani," her secret ode to the memory of her daughter.

65

EDITOR

Robin
2013

"Thank you for sending me fantasy book recommendations in the genre for our book club," Robin says.

"You're welcome. I sent it in the Microsoft Word format as you requested," Elena replies.

"The voice synthesizer read the document to me, but I would have enjoyed it more if I heard it in your voice. But I should say, meticulous work, like you're submitting a paper for a grade. Detailed summaries, with reasons why you recommend a book, why you don't, including authors' bios. You certainly are an overachiever, dear."

"Hello, sweetheart." Elena approaches Lucy, unable to refrain from petting her. "Forget being an overachiever. I haven't achieved anything. I've been trying to write a book for two years and can't finish it."

Robin picks up on the disappointment. She can relate completely, remembering the time in high school when she desperately wanted to be a writer and couldn't be one. Her career choice as an editor fell into place only after her association with the drama club in college. She sees her own reflection in Elena—in Elena's penchant for books and interest in writing.

"You're too young to think that. Look, all I asked you for was a recommendation, and you wrote a whole thesis. Your summary opened a window into your writing ability. I'm sure you're on your way to becoming a good writer."

Elena blushes at the praise, hoping the prediction comes true. "Chief, I hear you were an editor once." Words tumble out before she can restrain herself. "Maybe then you can guide me with my work?"

Although this comes as a surprise, Robin is eager. "If you wish." She tries to sound nonchalant. "You see, as Stephen King once said, writers are human, editors are divine. So, I must be special. Anyway, find me after your shift ends."

"I'll send you my work like I did before," Elena says.

"Nah, I'd much rather have you read it to me," Robin says. "While I can adjust the voice settings on my screen reader to my preference, I crave real human interaction. The computer voice is stale."

An eager student, Elena arrives at Robin's apartment a minute before the appointed time, with her laptop in one hand and a copy of her printed manuscript in the other. Lucy greets her with her signature tail wag, and Elena scratches her back. She surveys the sparsely furnished studio. A walker is parked in one corner, and the white cane is leaning against the desk. No area rugs, to avoid tripping. A few cans of chilled Coke stand on a nearby wooden crate. Three books in braille lay on the coffee table.

They settle around a round white wooden table with four chairs. A single overhead light in a round shade shines a cone of white light onto the table, its circumference perfectly aligning with the rim of the table. Elena finds the detail amusing.

Anne of Green Gables and *Bridge to Terabithia*, dog-eared, sit on the nightstand. Elena wonders how much light Robin can see. Two bowls, one filled with nuts and the other with slices of green apple, lay in the middle of the table, like two museum pieces being displayed under focused light.

AFTER THE INITIAL pleasantries are exchanged, they go to work.

Upon inquiry about the genre, the intended age group of readers, and the inspiration behind her story, Elena explains, "I was told to write about what I knew best. When I was young, ants and their social structure attracted me. And in college the idea of cloning all but consumed me, and I considered biology as a minor. Lacing the two interests, I pieced together a story that lies heavily on the theme of community, but my drafts keep falling apart."

"There is a world of difference between the first draft and later versions," Robin says. "Writing the first draft is like stitching a dress from scratch—you're creating something new. The revisions are like altering the stitched dress, which doesn't fit well. It takes an inordinate amount of time and patience to redo the dress. And sometimes even then it doesn't fit so well. So writing is like stitching, and so is life. Making mistakes, mending them, learning from them. The hardest is mending the mistakes. With persistence, the stitching eventually comes together, life works out, and so does writing."

Given a stage, Elena delves into her childhood, incorporating Tommy Gonzalez, her phase as a myrmecologist, her *One Day* lead character Emma Worley, who also had lacked confidence as a writer, and her interest in sociology and cloning.

Robin hopes that Elena's good storytelling translates well to the written word.

They work like contemporaries, discussing scenes, sequences, structure, and story. Trying to find vocabulary and voice one day, then plot, purpose, and precedence on the next, they go through character development, chapter relocation, and draft modifications.

The experience transports Robin to her childhood and its accompanying nostalgia. She referred earlier to nostalgia as an evil twin, but now it doesn't seem so evil after all.

"Partake in repast of victuals and potables, lest starveling and thirst perish us," Robin says, using her Shakespearean English and pointing to the bowls on the table and soft drinks on the counter.

"What?" Elena says, with raised eyebrows and a sideways glance.

"I'd once memorized all the words in the *Oxford* dictionary. So many were archaic, superfluous. Remember, a good writer uses simple words strung together on sturdy threads so the sentence and the paragraph they form don't fall apart. Do not write like the Old English sentence I just said. All it means is, let's eat and drink so we don't starve and die. I mean to say, don't write in hard-to-understand vocabulary."

Robin's writer's itch is awakening, the process pulling her in. Her past anxiety of writing dispelled, she finds herself spending considerable time deciphering the project. Lying awake at night, she reimagines the plot, like it is her story and her writing. Fully cognizant that she can't do the writing for Elena, she reins in her excitement and separates her role from that of a writer to that of a mentor, a coach.

While the role of teacher-pupil, coach-writer is being established, the wish for a mother-daughter relationship descends on Robin out of the blue. She imagines Elena as her daughter. The thought makes her happy, but only temporarily, as reality gives her a sense of loss. Her feeling of detachment from attachment, which paralyzed her, has dissolved with time. Age, life, maturity, and self-awareness through Zen have changed all that. She longs for a daughter now, if it ever was possible to have one without being in a relationship.

"My son is making steady progress." Sachiko's voice reflected peace. Robin was happy that her good friend had an offspring.

Robin wants attachments now—Lucy, her parents, and her cousins are on one end, while Sachiko, Anita, her book club friends, knitting buddies, and Elena are on the other, Ashley being the most consistent presence among them all, stretching across the spectrum.

66

CHANGE

Elena
St. Bona
2014

As graduation approaches, Elena's book, her labor of love, needs months of refinement yet. Discussions with her parents and advisers fail to streamline options for a future career.

A flyer pinned to a bulletin board outside the administrative offices of undergraduate education attracts her attention. "Volunteer opportunity in Guatemala City," it reads. "To teach English to children who have little chance of learning it." She signs up through a grant offered by the university.

"Everyone needs to learn English," she tells her mother. "As the interconnected world is getting smaller, those who don't know English will be left out."

Perhaps it is her childhood kinship with Tommy Gonzales and his family, coupled with the familiarity with their culture, that draws her to the project in Guatemala. "I'll be fine," she reassures her father. "I understand the culture, you see, thanks to Tommy."

Once her plans for after college are set, she focuses on multiple deadlines. Lists are made and checked off. Submitting final semester papers and applying for a passport, scheduling hepatitis A and typhoid vaccinations, and preparing for the graduation ceremony make it to the primary list. Giving two weeks' notice to St. Bona and scheduling an exit interview are also added to this list. Selecting insect repellent, buying protein bars, packing a reusable water bottle and an umbrella, and shopping for linen pants and shirts make it to the supplementary list. Her long-term goals are saved for the tertiary list. Change surrounds her, and she is ready.

A rival conglomerate claims that its market research shows a need for a new assisted care facility in Greensboro, and it is moving ahead with its plans to build one. The director of St. Bona resigns amid rumors that he has been hired as a consultant for the new facility.

St. Bona, Anita's alma mater, has sadly been failing, but now the crumbling is hastening.

Recent stories of cockroach sightings hadn't prepared Ashley for her interaction with the insect, reality certainly more traumatic than the idea of it. Ashley's and Robin's friends are moving ahead with their plans to switch. Ashley's decision to move to the new facility becomes urgent, but Robin needs convincing first. Every direction and distance, curve and corner of St. Bona are committed to her memory. New place, new topography, new stress. Cost is a concern too.

Fortunately, Ashley's timely invitation to move in together at the new facility offers a choice. Ashley's financial adviser addresses Robin's worries, crunches numbers, and reassures her of the affordability.

Robin sees the world painted through Ashley's eyes and lends a helping hand when Ashley needs it. In this, Robin and Ashley believe that they made their own family, a family of retired sisters, more like Siamese twins, deeply connected, their physical attachment invisible. They read each other's minds and moods, as if their neurons trigger in rhythm.

Settled in at St. Bona still, contented, they look forward to everyday living, maintaining schedules, adjusting, and assisting each other. They engage with friends, participating in organized clubs and cultivating hobbies. They exercise, read books, laugh, and share. Together they have discovered the serenity of the outdoors.

As a pair, they are educators, writing coaches, and career counselors. Mentors to each other and to others, they are colleagues too, collaborating on simple editing assignments and tutoring. Challenging themselves with change, a move to a new facility for better services, they are brave.

They craft fulfilling lives within their constraints, mirroring the universal experience of individuals and families. Their loved ones hope this precarious harmony will endure.

It does, until Robin's accident.

67

CONCEALED

Anita
April 2014

Overcoming her reluctance to share her art, Anita designs and paints a card for Elena. Over the years she perfects the blending of doodling and painting, primarily focusing on faces in pairs, and later on eyes. Emotion, confined and hidden, is predominant. However for the card, she spends considerable time planning, and in an acute diversion from her routine, she omits faces and eyes altogether.

Elena is graduating; Anita is too. Anita has no desire to mark her own community college graduation, as she doesn't see it as an achievement worth celebrating in public, with others, yet. She has her eyes set on a bachelor's degree and further.

Anita seeks openness and clarity for her new project. She steps outside her condo, and under the bright-blue sky, and with nature as inspiration, she begins to create.

She falls back on their collective happy experiences at St. Bona for a theme—there are many to choose from. The garden comes to her as the first idea. Then she considers the 5K they accomplished together. Book club and their pizza parties appeal to her too. In the final inning, she doesn't choose any of them though.

Painted in a selected mosaic of vibrant colors, a young girl is flying off into the bright-blue sky, her wings spread wide, her long, straight hair trailing, while a group of women wave their goodbyes to her. Their backs sinuous and necks straight, no faces. The message inside is distinct, and the penmanship delicate. A rock garden, reminiscent of the garden at St. Bona, occupies one corner of the pale-pink envelope.

Elena studies the envelope. "Beautiful." She reads the message. "Your message is touching, and the painting is lovely. Is this your work? And if it is, I can't believe you kept it from us."

Elena's compliment is inviting, and unwittingly Anita is pulled into a conversation about her painting. She flushes. "It is a hobby, my happy space."

"I would love to be a part of that happy space—can I?"

The question, an inquisition into Anita's personal space, catches her off guard. "You're welcome to come and see my work." She surprises herself, her usual private stance melting away at the praise. Immediately she regrets the invitation.

For the first time, Anita openly acknowledges painting as a hobby. Her parents and Ami surely had glimpsed her easel, paints, and other supplies during their rare visits. If they were aware of her artistic pursuits in the aftermath of her pregnancy, such conversations were avoided. Their solo exposure to her art was the one painting that hung on her wall.

Anita hopes that Elena's interest is only in passing. Her call the following day and her visit two days later prove her interest as genuine.

Anita's regret turns to anxiety. Her apartment is orderly, but in preparation for the impending visit from her first-ever visitor, she paces, moving things around and then placing them back in their original spots. She retrieves a few canvases and dusts them. They haven't seen the light of day in years, though the paint and the markers have maintained their quality. She runs her hand over the faces and eyes, still remembering the emotion she carried when she created them.

"Please come in." Anita opens the door wider.

Elena pauses at the threshold, hesitating to step on the sparkling floor with her shoes on, unsure of Anita's preferences. Nevertheless, she proceeds.

The painting on the wall and a framed eight-by-ten-inch photograph that sits at an angle on an end table are the only decorative accents. Two lamps stand on either side of a black leather couch. Her old wooden table, at odds with the four plastic chairs, sits in the dining area. Entrances lead to two bedrooms. In the room to the right, an easel carrying an unfinished canvas, and in the other, lies a bed covered by a worn-out comforter.

They sit down at either end of the couch, Elena casually surveying the painting so as not to appear intrusive. Sitting on the same couch they are on is a tiny frame with exaggerated hair and eyebrows, and a cat in her lap. Numerous stars and circles are spread around them. Recognition spreads on Elena's face. Anita and a cat. Elena's eyes sweep for a cat when she hears a distant purr.

Anita senses an opening. "It is just me and my cat. Her age is catching up. She rests most of the day."

Elena's gaze settles on the photograph, its red frame nearly overshadowing the five adults dressed in Indian wedding finery, their clothes rivaling the frame's bold hue. Anita looks unrecognizable in the picture, with a red dot on her forehead, a wide gold choker around her neck, and dangling gold earrings. Her wrists are obscured by a dozen bangles. The newlyweds are in the center, wearing long garlands of roses. Their parents stand flanking them.

"At my sister's wedding," Anita explains. The presence of a visitor in her apartment makes her familiar space feel foreign, as if she is sharing her personal details and secrets with an intruder from another world.

Out of this awkwardness, Anita can only come up with light conversation. "We'll miss you at St. Bona. You made us fall in love with you," Anita says hesitatingly, having not talked about loving anyone in a long time. "Tell me more about your trip to Guatemala."

"Let's see where the experience takes me. Hopefully, it'll let me give back to society, and in return the place will give me the energy to complete my book."

Anita advances a tray filled with chocolate-covered strawberries and cookies toward Elena. "You may see my paintings as nothing more than random lines of color. None of them has ever seen the light of day. You'll be the first to see them," she says, preparing Elena for potential disappointment.

She retrieves a dozen or so of them, some from behind the couch and others from a coat closet. Neither of them says much through the demonstration of her canvases.

Elena reaches for a cookie and wonders what story of Anita's is concealed in the paintings. "I don't see random lines. This work is different from that on my card and from anything else I've ever seen. Doodling, painting. I've never seen them combined. I'm not an art connoisseur, but I think you have created something special." Elena bites into a cookie, as if celebrating Anita's art.

At the door when Elena turns to wave back to Anita, Anita has an eerie feeling that Elena will return one day.

68

VOLUNTEER

Elena

2014

Elena flies five hours on a flight from JFK to Guatemala City in early May, to board with the Garcias, her host family of four. Mr. and Mrs. Garcia, their six-year-old son, and their seven-year-old daughter live in a small, clean cement-block house with a tiled roof, a twenty-minute walk from the school. Mr. Garcia is the school's custodian, and Mrs. Garcia is a stay-at-home mother.

Mr. Garcia helps Elena carry her two large suitcases into a comfortably furnished room with a twin bed, a small dresser, an old plastic table, and a chair with a wobbly leg. A rickety fan with deep stains of dust rattles above. If the suitcases were to be in the room, there would be no moving space. Mr. Garcia volunteers to move them into a shed for storage once they are emptied.

Eager to show her appreciation, Elena opens one suitcase and motions the Garcia children to step in, as they stand peering from behind the entryway curtain. She gives the boy a new soccer ball and the girl a basketball. She places a baseball set and a few storybooks on the desk. "Los libros son para la escuela, pero ambos están invitados a tomarlos prestados." She smiles at them. "You can borrow them anytime you want."

"They understand English," Mr. Garcia says.

While the boy stands in place shyly, the girl steps forward to express gratitude in response to her father's prodding. She says "Thank you" when her father signals her to.

Elena's proficiency in Spanish, thanks to her association with the Gonzalez family, helps. Wanting to assimilate, she quickly learns cultural norms such as leaving shoes outside the home and avoiding touching anyone on the head, which is viewed as disrespectful.

A water tank perched on the tiled roof supplies running water for a limited time daily. She shares the single bathroom with the family, her three-minute shower with one bucketful of lukewarm water, consciously timed to accommodate others for their bathroom time.

Outside her bedroom window stand two tall papaya trees, their long, slender trunks topped with a canopy of leaves concealing large yellow papaya fruit under them. A mango tree fills the space between them. Along the front of the house, lining the road are plantain and coconut trees.

For her first meal with the family, she eats a thick rice stew with meat and vegetables, flavored with recado, chili peppers, cilantro, and garlic. "We call it 'pepián,'" Mr. Garcia says. "Do you like it? My wife is known for how she makes it."

Mrs. Garcia blushes. "We eat it with corn tortillas."

Elena masters crunching down on sugarcane stalks for their raw, sweet juice. She tastes papaya and mango for the first time and finds their flavors exotic, especially the mango. She watches Mrs. Garcia's skilled hands peel and slice a ripe mango, carving long slices around the pit. She demonstrates how to savor the remnants of the pulp and the juice off the pit, to taste the sweetest and softest part of the fruit.

"I love its color, taste, smell, and feel," Elena tells Mrs. Garcia after she slurps the juice trailing down to her elbow. "Only thing missing is the sound of the fruit—if only it could talk."

"Eat too many of them, and you will hear them too, their rumble loud and clear in your stomach," Mrs. Garcia cautions.

Elena heads to work armed with an umbrella, a stainless-steel lunch box, and bottled water. This routine is only part of her many adjustments. She perseveres, finding joy in connecting with the locals and inspiring them, helping them achieve possibilities beyond their local confines.

Assigned to work with eight-year-olds, she bonds with a boy with a sharp intellect and an impish grin. He shadows her throughout the day, reminiscent of her brother.

"You are an intelligent volunteer assistant to a volunteer!" she says to him.

Elena knows that when pressure to deliver mounts into high gear, the brain suffers. It refuses to cooperate. To counter that, she makes new Post-its and pastes them on the pillars of the Garcias' veranda.

"Relaxation stimulates." "Creativity is engulfed by the mundane." "Novelty and new locales recharge." "New experiences awaken ideas," the family reads as the notes flutter in the wind.

As a habit, after dinner Elena joins the Garcia children outside. Under the dim light of a single bulb while they work on their summer assignments, Elena types on her laptop, balancing it on a pillow in her lap. She rarely uses the desk in her room. The book that lay on her desk in her college apartment, once considered her focal point, is no longer required.

The reawakening starts with the scent of the first drops. As the monsoon rains lash outside, the sensory detail in her writing heightens, and her storytelling regains momentum. It begins as gentle trickles, merges into cohesive streams of thought, and finally folds into mighty rivers of plots and storylines. Her ideas transform into words that are as luminous as ocean pearls. She threads them into beautiful sentences, like strands of pearls on sturdy threads, as Robin suggested. As her sentences coalesce to form paragraphs, the strands gather to become pretty necklaces that embrace her pages.

There is now a proper flow to her chapters and her story. The book is within her grasp. A couple more revisions, a few modifications, polishing here and proofreading there, remained. She can't wait to share her work with Robin.

For Elena, the veranda and the Guatemalan monsoons prove to be just the spark she needs.

During her last evening with the Garcia family, Mr. and Mrs. Garcia toast her to cooled Gallo, Guatemalan beer. As she gulps down two bottles, she relaxes after months of feeling pressed for time. She cannot remember the last time she didn't have a deadline looming.

She playfully tickles the Garcia children and runs after them into the backyard, playing hide-and-seek. They run around large trees, including the papaya and the mango trees. The boy climbs up the mango tree with the smoothness of a gecko ascending a vertical wall. From his hiding spot, he playfully drops a ripe mango down at her. She catches it and bites into the skin, sucking the sweet yellow juice as it drips down her shirt. She slurps the soft pulp and lets out a loud, gurgling belch, mixing the sweet flavor with the bitterness of the beer.

"Yes, the mango is talking to me finally." She laughs. She hugs the tree and bids it goodbye. She looks up at the clouds and blows them a kiss for the monsoons. She walks onto the verandah and sits there quietly as the bulb swings gently from the beam.

Wrapping up her three months, she is grateful for the opportunity to contribute to the long process that educators and volunteers offer for the upward mobility of families. Her impact is minuscule, she knows, but would be amplified by volunteers who come after her.

As she leaves Guatemala on a bright morning in early August, waving goodbye to the Garcia family, content and happy to start her next chapter in life, she tucks the thank-you note handed to her by her eight-year-old assistant into her backpack. She boards her flight, gazes onto the tarmac, and notices an airport employee in an orange vest signaling his green flag as clearance for takeoff. She sees it as a beautiful metaphor for her own beginning. Discovering a little more of herself in this foreign country, she finds a path to her next adventure. She has, in fact, decided. She smiles contentedly.

Someday, if she is ever lost again, she knows she will return.

6 9

THE FALL

Robin
2014

"Quadrangle closed until further notice," reads the notice at the exit.

Unaware, Robin clicks past the sign, having missed the announcement the day before.

Fragrances from summer flowers fill the pleasant morning air of July. She adjusts her sunshades. On her usual early morning walk, part exercise, part reflective, she savors her quiet time in the garden, before company arrives.

In the stillness of that morning, she descends into the meditative mode she first experienced in Japan, Lucy ahead of her on a leash. Robin's morning telephone conversation is fresh in her mind. While she updated Sachiko about her possible move to another facility, Sachiko told her that Nobu, a senior in high school, was also preparing for change. "With a few accommodations, he's ready to take on the challenge of college." Her tone conveyed happiness and confidence in her son's readiness.

The garden reminds Robin of her father, her time with him at their garden at home being her happiest. While she read a book, her father's conversations with his plants filled the air. He'd conjure up recipes for breakfast and other meals, and how her mouth watered at the thought of the variety that would adorn their dining table later that day.

Startled to the present by at least four distinct voices that break the quiet, she turns in that direction. "Goddamit," she hears one swear. "The garden is supposed to be off limits today. Who let them in?"

Confused, Robin stalls when a high-pitched buzzing noise from an electric saw rings in her ears.

"God almighty" is what she hears before the words are drowned by the whooshing sound of a felled tree. Leaves graze her face. Branches crack and splinter until one lands on her. The leash pulls away, snapping her wrist, as a pitiful whimper is buried in a loud thud. Soon Robin hits the ground.

The slow motion and inactivity that Elena described as the norm of the facility are interrupted.

Hurried footsteps and panicked voices fill the air. "I saw a lady and her dog go down under the tree," bellows the man who seems to be in charge of the tree-felling project.

Frantically, twigs and leaves are cleared.

"Guys, I see shoes here. Hurry, pass me the saw so we can get to her," one elderly man in overalls directs.

Soon a segment of the branch lying across Robin is sawed off. "One, two, three, lift," is the last thing Robin hears before passing out.

Robin's body lies crumpled. Everyone is quiet for a moment.

"Oh, the poor soul," a new voice exclaims.

While blood drips steadily down her face, "Can you hear me?" yells a man hunched down by Robin's side.

There is no response. Applying pressure on a four-inch gash on her head, he checks her pulse.

"EMS should be here in five minutes," a St. Bona nurse updates as she inches closer to Robin. She places her index finger under Robin's nostrils, feeling for air movement.

"Let's do the same thing with this heavy trunk," commands the same voice as before.

The count starts, and Lucy comes into view.

"PLEASE MAKE WAY FOR US," the EMS team leader barks as he pushes through with his equipment. "Does she have a pulse? Is she breathing?" As he crunches the broken branches under his heavy boots, the ragged edge of one scrapes Robin's wrist.

To everyone's relief, she moans.

"Ma'am, we've got you," he assures. "Can you tell us your name?"

"Ahh, my head hurts." She groans. "What happened?"

"Her name is Robin," the nurse says.

Robin touches the latticework of scratched skin on her right cheek and winces. "It burns." She sniffs. "Am I bleeding?" Fragments of her crushed sunglasses are under her.

The EMS team introduces themselves.

"Robin, you're bleeding, but we have it under control. We think you have a concussion, and you need to be moved to an emergency room for a full exam."

Robin tries to sit up but is coaxed to lie back. She feels the ground around her. "Wait—where's Lucy? I don't hear her."

"A tree fell on you both. She's being taken care of by another team, and we're taking care of you."

"But why don't I hear her? I'm not going anywhere without her." Her voice cracks.

"You will soon. In the meantime we need to put this collar around your neck and move you onto a stretcher."

While the administrative office of St. Bona alerts Robin's parents about the accident, Anita sprints toward Robin. Coincidentally, it is Anita's last week of work at St. Bona, and she has days of personal time off still available to her. She'll use them. "Robin, I'm here to help you. I won't leave your side."

"Can I have my cane, please?"

Anita places it on the stretcher by Robin's right side, and she holds it tightly, with the urgency of a child afraid to let go of a parent's hand on the first day of school.

Anita grasps Robin's other hand, peering in the direction of Lucy.

"Ahhh . . . that hurts" comes the moan.

In the clearing Anita sees Lucy's hind legs twisted awkwardly. Her left hip is raw—an area the size of an orange is scraped off. The curl on her tail is soaked in blood. Anita looks away. "You don't worry about Lucy. I promise she'll be taken care of." Anita is near tears, but her voice doesn't give that away.

"Thank you for being here, Anita." Robin strokes Anita's tiny hand, the touch soothing her alarm.

"I'll drive my car right behind the ambulance."

"I want to hold Lucy. What's going on?" Robin slurs, like she is drugged.

"Just like you, Lucy is also being taken to a hospital."

But there is no response. Robin's head tilts, her body limp.

70

DEATHBED VISIONS

Anita

"I'll follow you to the hospital," Anita repeats, knowing Robin isn't listening. The name—Moses Cone Hospital—triggers heightened dread. A place she had vowed never to enter again. Stomach roiling, nauseous, she swallows the contents rising in her throat. She leans on her car door to steady herself.

Did she really have a choice now? She's compelled to help a dear friend who needs her. As the ambulance speeds away from St. Bona, Anita trails behind in her car, her heart seared by the red lights and her sanity drowning in the jarring honks.

She drives down NC 7 toward Interstate 40, unsure of herself. When the hospital comes into view, she doesn't recognize it. Two new wings stretch sideways from the main building. It has a revamped brick facade, a wider driveway, and a dedicated ER entrance under a spacious portico. Summer flowers bloom in beds along the driveways and frame the entrances.

An unpleasant aura descends on her, and she feels like she is losing control of the steering wheel, maybe even her life. She is uncertain if she can maneuver her way into a parking spot, but she manages. Resting her head against the steering wheel, she turns off the engine, breathes deeply for a few seconds, not knowing what else to do. She knows what the problem is. She has no one to lean on. Her imposed isolation is her own doing. Paul comes to mind. She hasn't shared her story with him, and maybe she could now. But could he possibly understand it this late in their relationship?

Could her parents and sister sympathize now? She is certain they have not returned here and have erased their memory of that part of their lives for more than two decades. Twenty-two years, to be exact. A different generation, but it isn't for her. Her wounds linger, her memory fresh.

She steadies herself and steps out. She follows signs to the ER and steps in, worried she will not make it past the entrance.

At the check-in desk, an ER liaison approaches Anita. "Robin is being prepared for emergency surgery to control bleeding in her brain."

Anita nods.

"I'll update you when I hear more. You're welcome to coffee." She motions toward a nook in the waiting area.

Anita is one among tens of people waiting for updates on their loved ones, their strained faces a silent acknowledgment of their shared vulnerability. As she waits, her mind wanders. Scenes from *ER* are rescinded temporarily and are replaced by the events of her delivery. She wonders if a baby is being born in the maternity unit that minute, and she hopes for happiness for the mother and child. She looks around for signs to the unit. It is beckoning, but she has no intention of exploring. She waits, restless, intimidated by her own thoughts. Before she realizes it, three hours pass.

A tired-looking neurosurgeon walks to her in the postsurgical waiting room. "Robin's condition is critical. It was touch-and-go there for some time. She had a lot of internal bleeding, but we have it under control. We're hopeful it'll stay controlled."

Anita turns faint. "Touch-and-go? Her parents don't live here, Doc. Hopefully, they can make it here soon."

"Let's hope so." He points to a nurse standing nearby. "She'll give you further updates."

Anita walks toward the ICU in a daze. Two Indian physicians walk past her, one of whom looks familiar, but she is not keen on acknowl-edging him.

Anita will be the only visitor for Robin until her parents arrive. Robin's pale body lies among crisscrossed tubes and cords. There is blood-tinged froth around a tube in her mouth. A machine breathes for her. Wrapped around her right upper arm is a blood-pressure cuff, and a pulse oximeter clings to the middle finger of her left hand. EKG leads read her heart. Sophisticated machines with numerous controls and sensors stand on either side of her bed, flickering red and green lights, and digital displays flash numeric readings. Alarms and beeping sounds are incessant in the entire unit. Anita's sense of déjà vu returns. For a fleeting moment, she feels like an actress being filmed on a set on *ER*, the chaos around her bedridden friend eerily resembling a scripted drama.

Medical personnel in green scrubs hurry past beds and machines. She can't tell a doctor from a nurse, as their doctor IDs hang in places as obscure as their notoriously illegible handwriting.

Anita's gaze settles on the hospital bed. Nothing about it has changed. The same metal side bars that she had clutched while pushing stand steadfast. She has no doubt that the mattress is as hard and uncomfortable as she remembers it to be.

Two intravenous lines placed in the big veins in Robin's elbow pit are running fluids, clear in one arm, blood in the other. Anita's hands turn cold when she sees blood in the bag. During labor, she had only one line. Too consumed by pains, she didn't feel the needle at all. A circular dark-red dot of dried blood on the dressing in the hollow of Robin's elbow triggers a cultural connection in Anita—a red dot her grandmother wore on her forehead, considered the third eye for spiri-tual enlightenment, was also a mark of marital status.

A nurse empties the bag collecting urine. Anita doesn't recall having one of those in labor. She tries to sit vigil all night but dozes off, waking up with a start when machines beep.

"We're monitoring the swelling in Robin's brain. It is increasing," Robin's physician updates in the morning. "We're doing everything we can to control it. By the way, when are her parents coming?"

"We're expecting them any minute." Anita's voice sounds tired.

Through all the medical drama and machinery around her, Robin looks peaceful, in a coma.

JAMES WALKS as if carrying the world's weight, like his father had before him, supporting Lily's frail frame. In a hurry, he lurches forward when he enters Robin's hospital room.

"My darling daughter, we're here to take care of you," he says, short of breath. The periodically inflating and deflating blood-pressure cuff drowns his voice. "We won't leave your side until you've completely recovered." His voice catches.

Robin, propped on a pillow, her face turned away from them, doesn't register.

When the surgeon enters the room, James and Lily stand to shake hands and introduce themselves.

"We are closely monitoring your daughter. The swelling in her brain is not improving as much as we'd hoped," the surgeon says. "For that, I'm doubling her dose of steroids." He hesitates. "She's critical, very critical. We're hoping she'll pull through."

Lily staggers and slides into a chair.

James blinks away tears. "Thank you, Doctor, for taking care of her," he manages, before grasping the IV pole for support.

James and Lily refuse to leave Robin's bedside. But when they get a call from the vet at St. Theresa's Animal Hospital the next day, they rush to see Lucy. Lucy's hind legs are in casts. "We debrided her skin wound." The vet adjusts the heavy bandage.

"Please take good care of our Lucy," James pleads with the veterinarian. "She's my daughter's lifeline. When my Robin gets better, she'll need her baby." His lips tremble.

"That we are. Her skin wound is infected, needing multiple dressing changes. She's getting antibiotics. When she'll be able to walk, we don't know yet, and we're making sure she is in no pain." The elderly vet looks at Lucy kindly.

"We love her." James swallows hard.

Each time an attempt is made to remove Robin's breathing tube, her oxygen levels drop. "She's not making enough urine, so we're giving her more fluids" is the assessment one day. "There's extra fluid buildup in her lungs," the next. "Her kidneys are failing—we may have to put her on dialysis soon" was the alert on the third day.

Through the seesawing of fluid, electrolyte, and oxygen levels, nurses prop Robin's head regularly and wipe the drool that collects around her mouth.

James leaves the room during sponge baths. On the fifth day, for nutrition, tube feeding is initiated. Her swollen left wrist is splinted for torn ligaments.

James and Lily are by Robin's bedside day after day, eager to monitor the latest developments. Anita's appeals to take breaks and rest at their nearby hotel go unheard.

Through false hopes and true setbacks, it is only after eight days that Robin's condition finally allows the removal of her breathing tube. It is replaced by an oxygen mask that covers half her shrunken face. As if to punish for the removal of one tube, a new tube, a thinner one thankfully, is inserted through her nose.

"We hope she wakes up soon. Coma and strokes are common after injuries like this. Memory and speech are also often affected, unfortunately," the neurologist cautions.

When James hears nurses talk about brain activity and permanent coma, he prays that his daughter doesn't end up in a vegetative state. "Please don't do this to our daughter. You gave her to us as a gift." James pleads with God daily.

After days of such prayers, Robin twitches her eyes and moves her fingers.

James perceives a gentle rhythm in her movements. "She's coming back. I know it. See how her fingers move like she's trying to read braille?" He won't stop saying this until the doctor announces that she is improving.

"Any deficit, physical or functional, will only surface with time. Let's hope there is none." The doctor gives them hope.

Happy with the progress, James and Lily retreat to their hotel for a break, their first in two weeks.

The next day, Anita drifts off to sleep in a recliner in Robin's room but is jolted awake by a sudden outburst.

Robin pulls off her mask, yanks out the tube from her nose, and looks straight ahead past Anita.

Robin pats the bed. "Pops, please sit with me." Her voice is hoarse, but she grins. In the next instant, she stretches her arm out, as if pointing to someone behind Anita. "Anita, I see your daughter there." Then she falls back on her pillow.

Anita sits up, stunned at the mention of her daughter. She turns to look. There is no one there.

She doesn't know what to do. "Are these the deathbed visions people talk about?" she says, asking no one in particular.

A gentleman and his two female colleagues huddle over a chart. The man, who carries the authority of a physician, turns around. "There is no such thing. She is not lucid, that is all, but this is improvement for sure." He approaches Robin's bed.

The mention of her daughter puts Anita in a trance. She knows it is impossible, but she wonders if her daughter is on the hospital premises, maybe in the maternity unit, where she left her. She rises and follows the signs, unable to ward off the unknown force directing her.

71

HALL OF INFANTS

Anita

Anita walks along the hospital corridors, following signs to a different wing. The interior has changed too. Spaces are bigger and modern. Recessed lighting highlights the pastel color on the walls, and plush carpeting gives the feeling of a modern hotel. Fancy chandeliers hang in some places too. Pictures of smiling patients and chubby babies are displayed strategically. But the look of anxiety on patients' and visitors' faces in the waiting areas makes it clear that it is a hospital, not a hotel.

At the entrance of the maternity unit, the sign that reads "Your health is our sacred calling" is nowhere to be seen. Anita feels like something personal has been taken away from her. In its place is a notification, posted on the left half of sliding double doors, informing patients that everyone has the right to medical care, whether they have insurance or not. Under it is another sign that lists more patient rights. On the right half of the double doors is a prominent sticker displaying a bold, red circle with a gun icon crossed out, accompanied by a clear warning: "No guns or other firearms permitted on the premises."

She stops at the front desk, knowing she can't proceed farther into the unit without having a family member or a friend as a patient.

She stands there, wondering if the sound waves of her daughter's newborn cries still hang in the air and if the image of her delivery is still imprinted on the walls. She doesn't know what she expects to find there. Taking an acute turn, she walks past the nursery. Seeing a nurse pushing a baby in a bassinet in the hallway, she cringes at her erupting emotion. She runs out quickly as a sob leaves her.

Keeping her tears in check now, she drives home. They turn into a deluge the minute she steps into her condo. Sprawled on her bed and sobbing, she lets her tears soak her pillow. It is as if the doctor's needle has pricked a hole in her heart, and the flood that she held back in a reservoir for twenty-two years is overflowing now, as her burden of love, the magic and mystery of motherhood on full display.

She wakes up in the middle of the night with matted hair, wet and salty from her tears.

"What was I thinking!" she says, and bawls again.

She has never cried for her daughter. Tears that defied containment. Tears of the heart, they were.

72

___

LETTING GO

Anita

"Where am I?" Robin asks softly. The question confirms that her speech is intact. "Where's my Lucy?" Her next question affirms that her memory is too. She moves every limb as instructed by the physician.

"You're lucky that you didn't have a stroke," the doctor declares.

"Hi there, darling." James approaches her.

"Pops? What are you doing here?" She's surprised to hear him. "Is Moms here too?" She sniffs. "Why does it smell like a hospital—am I in one?" Then, "Why don't I hear Lucy?"

Anita recounts the events that led to the hospitalization before Robin can ask any more questions.

"I went to see Lucy the other day. The doctor tells me she'll be discharged soon, darling." James kisses her forehead.

"So good to hear your voices. This accident Anita is talking about sounds like something minor. The last thing I remember is walking with Lucy. It looks like I'm doing well. So please don't worry at all." She reaches out a hand to touch her parents. "And when you visit Lucy again, hug her for me. My baby must be lost without me. I can't wait to see her." Robin squeezes her father's hands, his frayed bracelet still hanging on.

After more than two weeks at the hotel, James's and Lily's own supply of medicine is running low, and with Robin and Lucy improving steadily, they leave for Winston-Salem with a promise to return the following week.

The first time Robin stands up, she almost collapses, her sense of balance and orientation needing realignment, and her weak muscles needing strengthening. For physical and occupational therapy, Robin is to be transferred to an inpatient rehabilitation center.

"Lucy is allowed to join me there," she tells everyone she talks to. "I can't wait to hold her."

At the end of July, Anita's last day at St. Bona comes and goes. With Robin still hospitalized, and not one to seek attention, Anita declines a farewell celebration.

After days of introspection, making peace with her circumstances feels important. No longer anxious, she is determined to reconcile with her life's journey, with only a quiet acceptance of what had been and what lay ahead. There will be no tears this time.

ON THE LAST day of Robin's hospitalization, as her transfer to the rehabilitation center is underway, Anita heads back to the women's center at the hospital. It had been four years since Anita expected a knock on her door, the expectation that played heavily on her. She is still hopeful but doesn't see the point in waiting. Ready to move on, she, in turn, has knocked on a door, a door that promises to lead her to a garden full of children. That garden is now around the corner.

After two weeks of orientation, she will be a teacher's assistant at St. John's Elementary School, an inner-city school in Greensboro.

HOPING that someone else took good care of her daughter, she is ready to commit herself to making other children's lives better, working with one child at a time to make sure they do not go through what she went through in her childhood. Working with them will be the best way to give back to the world, where, in an ideal world, everyone feels that they belong.

She enters the waiting room and surveys. A large black TV broadcasting medical information lies muted against the backdrop of baby pictures displayed in large frames. Two families wait in opposite corners of the room, with backpacks and food wrappers strewn around them, like they are at a picnic. They look happy with anticipation. She wonders how long they have been waiting and for whom. Birth of a child, grandchild, niece, nephew?

The thoughts of her daughter's cries and images that agitated her the first time do not surround her this time. On her way to a new life, she has come to say her goodbyes.

She is happy. She clips on the visitor's pass when she hears a familiar voice.

"Anita, I didn't expect to see you here." The voice refers to the maternity unit.

Anita whips around to see Elena walking in. It has been three months. A surprise. She wears a white sundress, sandals, and a beaded anklet. A large jute satchel hangs over her shoulder. She looks different in a deep tan, her short permed hair reaching only to her collarbones.

"Neither did I expect to see you at all, let alone on this floor," Anita says, her voice soft.

"I just returned from Guatemala and had to see Robin. She looks tired, but I'm relieved she is doing well."

She notices Anita looking at her hair. "I couldn't take the heat in Guatemala, so I chopped my hair off. The hot, dry weather made straightening obsolete. So I let it be in its natural curls." She combs her curls with her long fingers.

She looks around, intrigued with the camped-out families on plush chairs. On the TV a doctor is extolling the benefits of breastfeeding.

"Did you know I was born here in this hospital? It's like coming home, I guess. I wanted to see the place, get to know the vibe. You know what I mean?" she says casually.

Anita cinches her eyebrows. Suddenly her airways clog, and air ceases to move in her lungs. Her blood flow stalls too. Her brain feels the lack of it. She is faint but steadies herself. Slowly, barely audible, she manages to say, "I delivered a baby girl here twenty-two years ago."

For only the second time in her life, she is able to share her dark secret. She waits for Elena to declare that she was given up for adoption. It has to be. Anita knows. The place and time are right; the vibrations are all there. Are their voices echoing the same frequency? Did their identities lie only in their voices, as they don't look anything like each other? Does she see Sebastian in the tall, pretty Elena? So many questions!

"You were born on April 12, 1992, then." She frames it as a question but pronounces it as a fact.

The thought that she is with her daughter, exactly where it all started, reverberates. She lowers herself onto a wide, pink-cushioned seat designed for pregnant women, not waiting for an answer.

Elena stiffens and lowers herself too. "What a coincidence. My family lives in Raleigh, and my brother was born in Raleigh" is all she says.

Anita closes her eyes and sits still, oblivious to the cheers of a family celebrating the arrival of a baby in their family.

"A baby boy. A big one at nine pounds," announces a middle-aged man who looks like the potential grandfather.

The windowless waiting room feels stuffed. Scenes from her delivery come alive. The searing pain returns, not just in the lower half of her body but in her entire being. She remembers Dr. Patel's attempts to ease her guilt. *"There is another adoption in progress too."*

Elena makes no reference to adoption. Anita stands up and hurries out, and Elena follows.

They take the elevator down, not having said anything to each other. Anita exits the elevator with crouched shoulders that shrink her frame further and a perplexed look that ages her. Elena shifts her satchel to the other shoulder and pauses, unsure which way to head. She merely glances at a map of the hospital layout and heads in the opposite direction.

At four in the morning, Anita is still awake when the telephone rings.

73

———

FURRY FRIEND

Robin

Startled by the ring, Robin feels for the phone.

"Hello. This is Dr. Rogers, from St. Theresa's Animal Hospital. I've called James Zymanski, who is listed as the first contact. But he isn't picking up the phone. Is this Robin Zymanski?"

"My baby. Is she alright? Please tell me she is." Robin's breathing turns shallow. She feels her watch.

"Is it possible for you to come and see her?"

Anita is still awake when the phone rings. She listens to Robin's hurried talk. "Don't you worry, Robin. No trouble at all. I'll take you there myself. I want to see her too."

At four in the morning, Anita maneuvers Robin's wheelchair through the narrow corridors of the animal hospital to get to Lucy's bed.

"We were treating her for a wound infection, but now it seems to have spread in her body." The assistant directs them to Lucy's room.

"We're not sure how much she can hear you," Dr. Rogers says when they get there. We've given her all the antibiotics we could, but she is not responding."

"Can I hold her?" Robin's voice quivers.

Lucy is gently lowered into her stretched hands. She lays her in her lap, enveloping her, stroking and caressing her.

"There is hope?" Anita asks timidly.

"I think the time to say your goodbyes is now." He hesitates. "I'm really sorry."

"My baby, my baby" is all Robin can utter between sobs, until the doctor says, "I think she's no more."

Anita is unsure how to tolerate two shocking events in less than twenty-four hours.

AT THE REHAB CENTER, Robin sits unresponsive.

"We need to make you stronger and independent again," the therapist says.

Lucy's ID hangs around Robin's neck. "Not today," she says, upon being prodded again.

"You've been here five days, and we haven't made progress."

Anita and James visit every day, but Ashley only rarely, her physical encumbrances interfering.

"Come back to us soon." She kisses Robin's hands.

"Anita dear, please give me updates," Ashley pleads. "Any time of day or night."

"Of course I will." Anita waves goodbye.

Robin listens to Lucy's recorded bark on her phone repeatedly. "My feet will never be warm again," she bemoans. "And I'll not be able to find my way again."

"Do you need warmer socks?" the therapist asks.

Robin doesn't explain.

"The day we brought Lucy home, it was like we brought a new baby home, remember that, Robin?" James tries to celebrate Lucy's life with his favorite memories of her, hoping that talking about her will ease his daughter's grief.

"How gentle she always was!" Anita remarks. "Her bushy tail and the curl were adorable."

Thinner already from two weeks in the hospital, Robin is more so now. Apathetic and listless, she sits in one place all day. Her meals are sent back untouched. The trash can is stuffed with hundreds of tissues soaked in tears.

"Darling, there is no harm in trying antidepressants again. They helped you last time, remember?" James suggests.

"There is a difference between grief and depression, Pops," she explains. "I'm not where I was many years ago."

Sachiko calls and talks to her for hours. "Life is a cycle. We all have an expiration date. Lucy did too. We come with a purpose, and to fulfill that purpose is our duty. Nothing beyond that is in our hands."

"But how will I live without her?" Robin asks.

"What about getting another dog?"

"No one can really replace Lucy." Robin resists every suggestion for intervention.

James makes another attempt to reach Robin. "I've been told that Medicare won't cover your stay here if no active treatment is being given. They're recommending that you see a psychiatrist, Robin. If you cannot walk independently and manage even simple tasks, we'll have to take you home. So tell us what to do, darling."

"You won't be able to take care of me, Pops. At your age?"

"Then you need to show us that you can manage on your own, like you did before, dear."

The suggestion of moving back home is all it takes. Soon she is training and strengthening. Once again, committing details to memory is what she relies on, her cane and ability to discern light from dark aiding.

When she is finally ready to be transferred back to St. Bona, she gathers a lock of Lucy's fur to model a tassel and fastens it at the top of her cane, where she feels her gentle reassuring presence.

74

ANCESTRY

Elena

Elena was homesick quite badly in the first few days in Guatemala, but the Garcia hospitality eased it. Eager to see her parents and brother after three long months, for more than one reason, she speeds down Interstate 40 to Raleigh. Reaching home just as her father returns from work, she surprises her mother with a big hug from behind as she stands facing the oven, cooking dinner.

"You, my dear, have been the most precious surprise of my life." Her mother pulls her into a proper hug.

"Me too." Bobby sandwiches himself between them.

"I belong to the same tribe too." Her father encircles them all in his long arms. They all stand huddled in the middle of the kitchen, encased in love and encircled by savor and spice from the oven.

"You have tanned badly." Her mother pours Elena a glass of wine.

Bobby bends and feels her ankle bracelet.

"Bobby, this is for you." Elena hands him an alpaca-wool sweater.

"So soft." He rubs it against his cheek.

She passes a sealed bag of Guatemalan coffee to her father.

"Mom, I hope you like these." Elena adjusts two ceramic pots on the mantelpiece as she tells them about mangoes. "Now I know why mango is called king of the fruit." She proceeds to show them the thank-you letter her student wrote.

After Bobby is tucked away for the night, her attitude turns solemn. She slides an envelope addressed to Elena Marks across the dining table toward her father.

The Ancestry website logo is prominently displayed on the top left corner.

"We don't often discuss it, but you guys have been transparent about my past. I know I'm adopted, like Bobby is too. I've felt secure knowing the truth. Today I went to Moses Cone Hospital to pay Robin a visit. You know, my de facto editor I've mentioned before? She's admitted there. While I was there, I strolled into the labor unit, just to check it. There I saw Anita, who I worked with at St. Bona. She said she'd delivered a baby girl there on the same day I was born, and she'd given the baby up for adoption. I was shocked. I don't look anything like her, so I didn't have the heart to tell her that I was adopted, without knowing all the facts. So I hurried to my apartment, grabbed the envelope, and drove straight here." Feeling parched, she drains a glass of cold water in one swift motion.

She pushes the envelope closer to her father. "And one more thing. You've been perfect parents to me. Never have I felt the need to find my biological parents. I only signed up for Ancestry.com on a whim but never intended to open the letter. Maybe I was interested in my genetic history, for a future day, when I signed up. By the way, Ancestry.com gives an idea of one's ethnicity based on genetic patterns but doesn't trace ones' biological parents. Maybe I wasn't going to open it, for Bobby's sake. You know how confusing it would be for him if a new set of parents and grandparents came into my life? Then he will have similar questions. As it is, it is hard for him to maneuver the regular day-to-day, so I didn't want him to get more confused."

She gestures toward the envelope. "Dad, can you tell me what the results say?"

Her voice is laced with a maturity that catches her parents off guard. In that moment her parents see their young daughter no more; she has become a confident adult.

Her father strokes her cheek. "Ellie, we've always wanted you to know this detail of your life. We wanted it to come from you. You're now mature enough to understand circumstances and accept them without judgment. It's, in fact, a special moment." He pauses and squeezes his wife's hand. "Truth is liberating for all of us."

He puts his reading glasses on, slides the letter opener under the glued flap, and extracts four pages in a trifold. The cover letter is addressed to Elena Marks. The three pages that follow have graphs, percentages, and predictions charted out with explanations of genetic origins, disease tendencies, and mutational possibilities.

He takes his glasses off, rubs his eyes, and looks at Elena.

The suspense lies heavy.

Elena looks at him. "So?"

75

BLESSINGS

Anita

2014

Having recently spent most of her time with Robin, whose discharge just about coincides with the start of Anita's orientation at St. John's, Anita doesn't have time to update her wardrobe. For her first day of orientation, she dons black pants and a pressed blue linen shirt, a gift from her parents. She hesitates before she puts on a scant layer of makeup and pink lip gloss.

As a teacher she will love her students, and more importantly, she will offer a sanctuary of acceptance. She will ensure they are seen and heard, things she desperately needed in her own school days. Though she can't relive the moments she missed with her daughter, working with children will give her a chance to reclaim a piece of that experience. Finding her daughter is no longer the sole driving force. Whether she comes back to her or not, surrounding herself with children and their innocent ways is a way to find closure—so she hopes.

When she steps into the school, she is more nervous than the new first graders. She remembers entering St. Bona for her first day of work as a teenager. She wasn't nervous then. No one had any expectations for a teen girl working in the housekeeping department.

But now she has her own expectations and commitment to implement her intentions.

There are three female and one male teachers' assistants in orientation, including her. The other two women are in their early twenties, and the man is a late bloomer, like Anita. The woman dressed in a silk blouse paired with capris and a stylish sideways French braid is Asian, once again reiterating the assimilation of immigrant families into mainstream American life, of children choosing careers of interest and parents allowing them to do so without the pressure of being physicians and engineers, like Anita's parents and their contemporaries did.

All three appear confident. The man is dressed in khakis and a T-shirt, and the other young lady wears a short summer dress and a matching ribbon that holds her ponytail. The women treat Anita and the male trainee like equals, devoid of age bias. That instant camaraderie eases Anita's anxiety.

Toward the end of her orientation, Anita is introduced to Ms. Karnes, under whose direction she is to work. A second-grade teacher with unbridled energy and a bright smile, she walks around effortlessly in her stilettos, in contrast to Anita's comfortable footwear.

A day before her official start as a teacher, Anita pays a visit to St. Bona. In the parking lot, she sees a familiar figure darting toward a car. "Mrs. Detris?" She approaches her high school counselor. She stands confidently, not looking for a pillar to hide behind this time.

"Hello, Anita. So good to see you." Mrs. Detris smiles.

"You remember my name!" Anita gleams. "What brings you here?"

"I'm visiting my mother. She needed extended care after surgery. She'll be discharged soon."

"Mrs. Detris, it is fitting that I see you here today. It is a sign. I am starting my new job as a teacher tomorrow, and I need your blessings."

"Congratulations, dear. You'll make a great teacher. I know it." Mrs. Detris extends her hand.

They shake hands and stand admiring each other for some time. Anita feels like an awkward teenager again, one who can't contain her excitement.

"I am proud of you. Good luck now. Keep in touch." Mrs. Detris reaches for her keys.

Anita walks into St. Bona with a spring in her step. Robin, back from rehab, is living with Ashley, her feet exposed, Lucy not resting on them. Lucy's St. Bona ID hangs around Robin's neck on a chain. Anita misses the yipping. Robin, face drawn, broad shoulders slouched, her body shrunken, has aged.

"Hello, my teachers. I came to offer you both my Guru Dakshina," Anita says. "My payback, my tribute, my gratitude. And also, I seek your blessings as I am now enrolled in North Carolina A and T State University for a bachelor's degree."

"Congratulations," Robin and Ashley wish in unison.

Anita reaches into a large bag.

"For your new place." She presents Ashley with a rolled canvas. Two faces reminiscent of Ashley and Robin are in a garden, surrounded by flowers, a pretty butterfly perched on Robin's shoulder.

"For you for dinner tonight." She hands Robin a serving dish filled with homemade chicken biryani, a specially flavored rice dish with marinated and slowly cooked pieces of chicken. She hugs Robin tenderly while Robin wipes her tears.

Ashley and Robin are moving, Robin reluctantly, for fear of having to memorize new configurations, distances, nooks, and crannies, all over again. The new facility promises better services with in-house physical therapy, an indoor swimming pool, and exercise classes. High ceilings, Wi-Fi, emergency alarms, flat-screen TVs, food that can be ordered off a menu are promised additional services. The facility offers three-bedroom condominiums for independent living, which Ashley signed up to rent.

Their sanctuary, the garden at St. Bona, will not be there. "We'll make do with a smaller one, Robin. I hear the greenhouse and the sunroom with skylights are ready," Ashley assures.

"And make no mistake," Anita says, "I'll be around from time to time to make sure that you, Ashley, don't get your hands on trail mix, and you, Robin, behave. And consider me on standby. I am serious—don't hesitate to reach out if you need anything."

"I don't doubt it at all that you will be back," Robin says in a frail voice. She gives Anita a brief hug so as not to get overly emotional. "Now if you guys will let me, I have my biryani to eat."

Ashley gives Anita a light kiss on her cheek, which lingers. "You will be sorely missed, dear. Now you get out of here before we change our minds about letting you go." She fidgets uncomfortably in her wheelchair and looks away.

They all try to maintain their composure.

Anita bids a swift goodbye and departs, watching the sun dip behind the tall trees at the western end of the campus's perimeter. St. Bona's days are numbered, its final farewell fast approaching.

76

WINDOWS TO THE SOUL

Anita

At St. Bona, Anita's office, however small it was, was her own. At St. John's she has no such sanctuary. She is to share the common break room and is back to having an assigned locker. These are minor inconveniences for bigger returns, she surmises. Reminding herself that having no expectations at St. Bona worked well for her at the start, she plans to focus on work and not worry about the outcome. Thanks to the orientation, she progressively gains confidence in her ability to perform her role.

Three weeks after her awkward encounter with Elena on the maternity floor, Anita's cell phone lights up with Elena's number. The unexpectedness of the call puts Anita on alert. She breaks into a sweat, and the phone almost slides out of her hand. The conversation they had rushes back. After Robin and Ashley, Elena is the only other person she has let in on her dark secret about her daughter. Considerably younger, how judgmental will Elena be of her?

"Can I visit you?" Elena asks.

Anita tosses all night—not knowing the reason for the visit is consuming her. Unusual for her, she thinks of her cat that night.

It is Sunday morning when Elena, without the hesitation of the first time, eases out of her shoes at Anita's door and steps in barefoot, Elena's habit of doing so in Guatemala coming to the fore.

Anita wonders how much about the visit she will share with Paul at dinner later that day.

Elena lays a box on the side table and approaches the painting on the wall, admiring it this time.

Anita studies Elena's profile, again probing her face for features of familiarity.

"I looked up the meaning of the stars and circles. I like what they represent."

Elena's comment jolts Anita from her reverie. "You do? Sadly, my cat passed on. She came into my life unannounced and left the same way too. It happened suddenly while she was at the vet's and I was at work. We didn't get to say our goodbyes, and I think she was being considerate of me."

Elena stiffens, then exhales. "I am sorry for your loss." She pauses.

"I brought mango-flavored muffins. I am probably the first one to concoct such a flavor. Ever since returning from Guatemala, I've craved mangoes. I hope you find them palatable." Elena tips her head toward the box.

Anita feels awkward, more than the first time, like her every move and every word is being analyzed in considerable measure. The usually reticent Anita continues to be herself, and the talkative Elena tries to find her footing with conversation.

They talk about Anita's training and new job. Sensing Anita's anxiety about dressing, Elena says, "You must dress the part of a cute teacher. You're still so young. I can help you shop if you want."

Anita has no doubt about Elena's capacity in this regard. She's seen her style for over two years.

They touch on the book club.

"I feel like I am betraying myself by changing jobs!" Anita says.

Anita is relaxing steadily, thankful that the topic of adoption is not broached. Between drinking coffee and eating homemade scones, their conversations meander from Robin to Ashley to Guatemala to Elena's writing.

Elena talks about her book excitedly, then understanding Anita's low-key temperament, calms herself and jokes self-deprecatingly about how her book has become an unending quest. "After so many years, it is coming together at a good pace. Thanks to Robin, our chief."

They finally settle on the more comfortable topic of Anita's painting, having talked about it once already during the previous visit.

"Let me see your latest work," Elena requests.

"Hmm. It's unfinished. But I can show you others." Anita's nervousness is evaporating, and she wants to believe that this is a casual visit with no agenda.

Anita brings out pieces of her art to display. There are more than a hundred paintings. It is as if she can't stop from extricating her art from their banishment. They are coming out from all directions, from closets, from under the bed, and from behind couches and armoires. Elena likens them to ants, like when they swarmed out of the ant colony in response to the Icee, in a chaotic but organized mass.

Anita never considered herself an artist, but twenty years of her work she lays bare, finally. She herself has never seen her work all at once in one place. Tens of faces and eyes, numerous expressions, hundreds of hues, thousands of strokes, some textured, some not, interspersed with doodling signs, were in the open.

One painting that gets Elena's attention is a solo one of a cat that eerily resembles a girl.

Not knowing what else to talk about, Anita goes to lengths to talk about her hobby, her ideas, and what they mean to her. She adds basic context and background to some of her works. True to her nature, she keeps the topic at a safe emotional distance, avoiding intimate details of her life and personal struggles.

Elena asks if she can take pictures of them. As if by plan, she has brought a real camera along this time.

"Which ones are your favorites?" Elena asks.

"All of them are." Anita believes it.

"Fair enough." Elena lines many of her own favorites along the long wall of the great room, tilts the blinds just enough for the right amount of light to filter in, and gets busy clicking.

Is this what she really came for? Anita asks herself as she bids Elena farewell.

77

———

TEACHER AT LAST

Anita

2014

The doors of St. John's Elementary School have been open for the new academic year for six weeks. They welcomed 225 returning students spread between second and fifth grades, fifty-four new first graders, and twelve new students into other grades. Six weeks was enough time for most children to fall in line with schedules and their teachers, but not for all. Teachers pay attention to the loud, naughty, and unruly. Anita seeks the quiet, timid ones who rarely speak. She knows what lurks in those types.

In Ms. Karnes's class, Anita helps with math, reading, and art projects, art being her favorite.

Art projects are beginning to be fall-themed, and some are aligned with the upcoming Halloween. As students trace leaves and color them in, do cut-and-paste projects, and make masks of monsters and lather them in drippy paints, the colors of fall and the excitement of Halloween are unmistakable.

As a teacher, Anita is more tired than she expected. Her hours of work are the same as before, but it is something about taking care of children and keeping up with their energy.

On one such evening of tired satisfaction, Elena calls, asking to meet yet again. "Is recess a good time?" She sounds eager.

It has been six weeks since they last met. Anita is too tired to question the intended reason for the meeting.

At recess the next day, they choose an outdoor picnic table on the school playground and sit facing children as they hop, skip, and jump.

"Ready or not, here I come," a second grader announces, peeking through half-closed eyes.

"The last one in is a rotten egg," another says as he races the others to the swings.

Once settled, Elena hands Anita a ten-by-twelve-inch gift-wrapped box.

"It isn't my birthday today." Anita weighs it in her hand. The box is heavy.

"Consider it an early Christmas present."

Anita peruses the geometric pattern of the wrapping paper for a future painting idea, as is her habit.

"I can't begin to guess what it is," Anita remarks, unsure if she should open it at work, but Elena prods her to.

She unwraps the box. Inside is a book, the cover adorned with a picture of Anita and the cat. In stunned silence she opens the book to find pictures of her paintings page after page. Some of her best works spread out in front of her on thick, glossy paper. In the perfect fall light, her paintings are alive on the page, their texture showing. She has never seen her paintings displayed as a collection, as a collage. The sadness that filled her while she painted some of them washes away in one moment.

"I printed the book for you. And I took the liberty of showing it to the owner of an art gallery I know. The owner is interested in showing two of your paintings in his gallery. And he said, and I quote, 'Maybe a whole show one day.'"

Anita contemplates, shakes her head, and smiles. "Interesting. Never mind my book that you printed—what about your book?"

Elena undermines her work. "The final draft has been ready for some time. It has been making its rounds through publishers. One publisher has shown a tad bit of interest in my book, but a whole lot of interest in printing yours as a coffee-table book. But the most interest came from the art gallery. And I am not surprised."

Anita is minding the time, cognizant of her break ending soon. Lost in thought she says, "Painting has been my savior. Like I told you, none of my paintings has seen the light of day. But if it can give joy to others, so be it."

"And I showed them the card you gave me, and they think it will make a perfect cover for my book, if it ever gets published. I am so excited."

"Cover for your book? What is your book about anyway? I've never asked."

"It is a futuristic story about a young girl Talame, who is born to save mankind. She is created as an amalgamation—you know, a clone, a superhuman made from genetic material of four mothers. She inherits the best of DNA from one mother, modified RNA from another, and advanced mitochondria and cytoplasm from the other two. See how your painting will be perfect for my cover? One heroine and a few mothers? Anyway, the story is about how when communities come together, everyone benefits. Community, sociology, it all started in middle school for me, when I wrote that paper on ants. I call that time my 'summer of Tommy and ants.' Only I didn't know then what it would mean to me. That story is for another day."

Before Anita can respond, Elena continues without pausing. Anita lets her.

"I've decided to enroll in the spring semester at UNC in their dual PhD program in sociology, to study ways of identifying the needs of nursing homes. Bringing resources and technology together to benefit residents. Ashley and Robin have shown me the way. I hold them in awe, how they are living independently, a lot on their own but with some help from others. I've always wanted to be a writer, but I don't need a job to write. I can do that anytime, anywhere."

"I agree," Anita says. "Robin and Ashley are special. I will be forever indebted to them. They helped me find myself, reach my goal. Looks like their lives have helped you decide your career and that Robin helped you reach your goal to write a book. Think about it—of all the possible moves in a game of chess, which is estimated to be more than the number of atoms in the universe, all four of us, like the pawns in a game of chess, converged in one place and collided with each other. Ashley, as my teacher, and Robin, as your editor, designed by destiny, I would say."

A minute passes. There is quiet between them, but children's voices are all around them as they are corralled back into the building.

They sit there, their shared experiences and interest in each other taking hold. The shedding leaves, in shades of red and gold, float around. The midmorning sun shines through the bright-red leaves of a scarlet oak, setting the tree aflame.

Elena gently advances two envelopes toward Anita. Both are addressed to Elena Marks. The return address for the first one is from Ancestry.com, and the second from the law offices of Harry, Reid, and Solomon.

"Remember what you told me at the hospital? Our talk about adoption and coincidence of birthdays was shocking. What I withheld from you that day is that I was given up for adoption too, on the same day. I was caught off guard and didn't know how to respond. I don't look anything like you, and I never really told my parents that I had signed up with Ancestry.com. I had to tell them that first. So I just left. And Ancestry.com does not confirm parentage, doesn't identify particular individuals—it just gives us an idea of ancestry. So I consulted a law firm for identification, for names, for confirmation."

Elena stops short of saying what the law offices of Harry, Reid, and Solomon found, and Anita does not ask.

Elena's words hang in the air. It takes a while before Anita registers what she said. When she does, she grasps the envelopes to open them, then stops.

She is rationalizing, preparing for the reveal. *Elena does not look like me. That is true. No amber eyes for sure. Do I see Sebastian in her then? Sebastian from twenty-two years ago! Do I remember his face?* She is not sure. Everything is unfolding quickly.

"Dr. Patel did say there was another adoption in progress on the maternity floor on the same day," she says aloud.

Does it really matter what the letter says? Maybe one day, but today I don't see a need for it. Elena, so put together, regal, driven, confident, and kind.

She is a queen, a Rani, in her own way, a special one, and she will continue to be one. As a teacher I am a mother to so many of them. Am I not? They are all around me.

Anita slides the envelopes into the gift box, along with the picture book, not sure when she will open them.

Elena looks quizzical.

"For another day," Anita says.

They linger side by side on a sunny fall day with a steady breeze, Anita with her gift box and Elena with a brochure from the University of North Carolina for the spring semester. A sudden gust of wind blows, flipping the brochure open. Peeking out from one of the pages is a sticky note with a scribbled heading: "My To-Do list." At the top, in bright-red marker, is the first item: "Find my father."

Anita contemplates this. She is happy. It will come together, she knows. After all these years, she is finally in a place of happiness.

Another gust of wind blows. Her long, wirelike hair in thick curls is pushed to one side, reaching Elena. Anita sees that her curls are entwined with Elena's, as if reiterating and reinforcing their bond, in whatever capacity destiny plans it to be.

"Hair like a bear." The dreaded chant echoes in Anita, like it is calling her from her past life. The saying that started it all. The same hair that played a cruel joke on her then is connecting her to a beautiful moment now.

The recess is ending. They stand up.

"I am small like a bird, but I can give big hugs like a bear," Anita says.

They hug, gentle and awkward to begin, tighter with intention a little later. Anita feels a chill. Winter is around the corner.

"This holiday will be different," Anita says to no one in particular.

She sees children filing into the school building. One child has been wearing the same frayed sweatshirt for two weeks. She makes a mental note of that. Another in her art class lacks her own set of coloring pencils—she has noted that too.

A tiny figure darts toward her; knee barely scraped. She sweeps the child into her arms and kisses her like she is her own. She sets her down, reassuring her that she will clean it and cover it with a Band-Aid.

The three of them then walk indoors holding hands, the child tightly grasping Anita's, while Anita secures Elena's in her other hand. They walk through the falling leaves, golden and crimson, colors of hope, holding a metaphor for things falling into place. Anita knows she belongs to this moment and the moment to her, in a happy place among children who need her. She has purpose. She finally belongs.

EPILOGUE

The *Good Morning America* interview is set up in the lobby, where Ashley is parked under the bright lights, with the interviewer seated by her.

"We are proud to introduce Ashley Spady this evening to our program 'Heroes Among Us,'" he announces to the camera. "Your donation of two million dollars is the single largest donation given in support of book clubs and running clubs in assisted living facilities in the state of North Carolina. And in addition, you are donating one million to a women's center in Charlotte. Please tell us about your inspiration to donate. Why now? And why these causes?"

Ashley has not faced a camera since her modeling days. Life has come full circle with her looks and mobility, but these issues ceased to trouble her a while ago. Today she is relaxed. She looks at the film crew. Her mom, dressed in a burgundy gown that reaches her ankles, the same gown she wore to Ashley's sixteenth birthday party, stands among them. "In this gown you look the prettiest," Ashley had said then. It fits her just as well after all these years.

Harry stands with Kelly, eyes locked on Ashley as he moves his hand onto his heart and pats it. Robin stands close to Harry.

"My parents are my inspiration. My father's generosity was a lesson in sharing early in life. The donation to the women's center is in honor of my mother's work." Beyond the lights, Kelly blinks away tears. Ashley starts with The Rosetta Stone Book Club and the story of Nicole and breast cancer, before she moves to share her life of running. "Running was a part of me, you see. It freed me, saved me."

Kelly nods.

"Given you have muscular dystrophy, how did you manage the 5K?" he asks.

Buddy system and the Achilles International, Ashley explains.

He turns to the viewers. "We are proud to recognize heroes among us. We wish great success for the initiative. Thank you, Ms. Spady, for your time on behalf of *Good Morning America*'s loyal audience. Good luck with your future endeavors," he says.

The camera is turned off.

Kelly approaches to hug Ashley. Harry blows a kiss her way.

They gather in the reception area, where drinks are being served. A cheeseboard, olives, fruits, and crackers are shared.

Robin recognizes James's voice. "Is that you, Pops? What are you doing here?" She turns in the direction of his voice.

"Come on, Bono. Let's go," she hears him say. There is a whimper. She turns in that direction.

"Robin, say hi to your new service boy." James hands her the leash.

"Pops, what are you saying?"

"We wrote to the company. They sent a trainer along with our little Bono as a trial. The trainer will be here for two weeks to help Bono acclimatize," he replies.

She picks up the pup and lays him across her lap. "Bono, did you say? Maybe we will call him Bona, for St. Bona." She laughs.

Anita and Paul are the last to arrive. Paul opens the door of his Cadillac for her. In his tailored suit, he looks the part of a successful businessman. He appears stronger, scoliosis resolved. Physical therapy is helping his gait. They walk through the lobby into the reception area. Cheers erupt. As the doors of the gallery open, Anita is the first to enter.

"Papa and Maa, come with me." She takes them in. They flank her. Scores of eyes surround them, some smiling, some peering. Set in pretty frames, her paintings are mounted under focused LED lights. Eyes, doors to the soul, small, large, dark, light, happy, sad, angry, irritated, teary, open, closed—all kinds of them, in stunning detail and perfectly three-dimensional.

The gallery is filling up. "Congratulations, Anita," many say.

"Great talent," add a few.

"It will be a sold-out show," someone predicts.

"All thanks to Elena," Anita replies. She grasps Elena's hand and walks around with her, greeting guests and being introduced to them.

The showstopper is displayed in the middle of the room, the gallery owner's pick. Large amber eyes stare at her. Anita gasps. The eyes that tricked her more than once. Only she knows the story of those eyes.

She likes that painting now. A "Not for sale" sign is attached to its frame, at her insistence.

Twice she had fallen, thanks to the painting, but managed to get up stronger. A reminder of the weakness she conquered, the failures she freed herself from.

"Say cheese," the photographer says.

Anita sits between her parents. Robin and Ashley are seated too. Elena, Paul, Kelly, Harry, James, Lily, Ami, and Codi gather around them. Freddie Mercury's "We Are the Champions" soars in the background. Anita is no longer confused about who the champions are, like when she was nine.

She knows the answer.

ACKNOWLEDGMENTS

I wish my father were alive today so he could read my book. He would have been the most proud, even if he thought my writing was basic and simple. See, I was never supposed to be a writer. It was too far-fetched a dream. But my father gave me the foundation and confidence that life needs to reach beyond dreams.

Writing happened by chance, with my husband's encouragement. During the lengthy process, his patience held, and his balance in life helped me.

Thank you to my two hardworking boys who bring me joy every day. They gently correct me when needed, teaching me the right way to live and perform.

My heartfelt gratitude to my mother and sister, who are integral to who I am.

Thank you to scores of friends, mentors, and colleagues who made this journey worthwhile. A special recognition of my book club friends who planted the idea of writing a book in me.

A shoutout to my cousin, Dr. Anand Marri, for his valuable feedback.

Much obliged to Dr. Suresh Reddy for his advice on publishing and marketing.

A special recognition and thank you to my beta readers for their time and interest in my work-they know who they are.

I am grateful to my editors, Liz Van Hooze, Julie Cantrell, and Dori Harrell, for their input, guidance, and encouragement.

Thank you to Janyre Tromp at Ember and Vine Press for streamlining the publishing process to meet every deadline.

ABOUT THE AUTHOR

SUNITA REDDY, M.D, is a practicing Obstetrician and Gynecologist. She has worked and lived with her husband and two sons in Dayton, Ohio. She currently works at Kettering Medical Center. This is her debut novel.

Her work as an OBGYN gives her the unique opportunity to counsel and guide patients through many complex issues they face every day. Her patients demonstrate tremendous resilience as they rise above tough challenges to better their lives through sisterhood, family support, and new medical technologies. In their tenacity and capacity for renewal, Reddy finds inspiration to tell their stories, offering a hopeful message about our human capacity for growth and redemption.

Issues such as infertility, adoption, domestic violence, and teenage

pregnancy are relevant current issues that need to be addressed. In
Before We Were Women, Reddy encourages women to empower themselves and others through kindness and to foster meaningful connections along the way.

www.beforewewerewomen.com

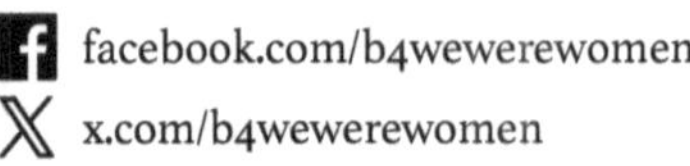 facebook.com/b4wewerewomen
x.com/b4wewerewomen